"**Come for the riotous D&D-style adventures and gently handled queer romance**, stay for the found family and the stories they weave together. I loved it."

—JAMIE PACTON, author of *The Life and (Medieval) Times of Kit Sweetly*

"**The perfect blend of romance, geekery, self-discovery, and creative storytelling**, *The No-Girlfriend Rule* affirms that even the bumpiest journeys can have joyful endings. Reading it feels like making new friends at a convention and immediately knowing you'll be BFFs for life."

—DAHLIA ADLER, author of *Cool for the Summer* and *Home Field Advantage*

"*The No-Girlfriend Rule* is a book about the most cherished of fat-positive traditions: taking up space. **I loved every part of this swoony, funny, heartfelt debut!**"

—ANGIE MANFREDI, librarian, and editor of *The (Other) F Word: A Celebration of the Fat & Fierce*

"Christen Randall's debut is a stunning story about finding love, friendship, and yourself. **This book is pure, brilliant joy!**"

—BETH REEKLES, bestselling author of *The Kissing Booth*

"Sometimes you have to pretend to be someone else to figure out who you really are. *The No-Girlfriend Rule* is **a smart, tender story about found family and unexpected romance**—both on the tabletop and off."

—KENDRA WELLS, creator of *Real Hero Shit* and *Tell No Tales*

CHRISTEN RANDALL

THE NO-GIRLFRIEND RULE

Atheneum

NEW YORK LONDON TORONTO SYDNEY NEW DELHI

An imprint of Simon & Schuster Children's Publishing Division

1230 Avenue of the Americas, New York, New York 10020

Text © 2024 by Christen Randall

Jacket illustration © 2024 by Simini Blocker

Jacket design by Rebecca Syracuse © 2024 by Simon & Schuster, LLC

Simon & Schuster: Celebrating 100 Years of Publishing in 2024

For information about special discounts for bulk purchases, please contact Simon & Schuster Special Sales at 1-866-506-1949 or business@simonandschuster.com.

The Simon & Schuster Speakers Bureau can bring authors to your live event. For more information or to book an event, contact the Simon & Schuster Speakers Bureau at 1-866-248-3049 or visit our website at www.simonspeakers.com.

Interior design by Rebecca Syracuse

The text for this book was set in Charter.

Manufactured in the United States of America

First Edition

2 4 6 8 10 9 7 5 3 1

Library of Congress Cataloging-in-Publication Data

Names: Randall, Christen, author.

Title: The no-girlfriend rule / by Christen Randall.

Description: First edition. | New York : Atheneum Books for Young Readers, 2024. | Audience: Ages 12 and Up. | Summary: When her boyfriend excludes her from participating in a role-playing game, high school senior Hollis joins an all-girls group where an in-game romance has the potential to be more than just pretend.

Identifiers: LCCN 2023016660 | ISBN 9781665939812 (hardcover) | ISBN 9781665939836 (ebook)

Subjects: CYAC: Role playing—Fiction. | Lesbians—Fiction. | Dating—Fiction. | High schools—Fiction. | Schools—Fiction. | LCGFT: Romance fiction. | Novels.

Classification: LCC PZ7.1.R366645 No 2024 | DDC [Fic]—dc23

LC record available at https://lccn.loc.gov/2023016660

TO YOU, IF YOU NEED HOLLIS
LIKE I HAVE NEEDED HOLLIS.
YOU ARE WORTH DOING
THE HARD THING.

THE NO-GIRLFRIEND RULE

1

THE WORST HALF SESSION OF SECRETS & SORCERY EVER PLAYED

HOLLIS BECKWITH WEIGHED the pewter miniature in the palm of her sweaty hand. It didn't look like high elf sorceress Alvena Ravenwood at all.

Beyond the lack of resemblance, Hollis wasn't sure what a character like this could really *do* in a high-fantasy setting like the Eight Realms, where adventurers wielded swords and sorcery on epic quests against evil. Her bikini top and thigh-high-split skirt weren't going to provide much protection on the battlefield, and her high heels weren't practical for traversing the continent's kingdoms. They didn't even allow her to stand up properly. The miniature leaned heavily forward, like the weight of every bad Secrets & Sorcery stereotype rested on her shoulders.

"She'll do, right?" the Secret Keeper asked.

"Uh," said Hollis.

She hadn't brought a miniature of her own, so she didn't have much choice. And if this was the first option the Secret Keeper—the game's head storyteller—had offered, Hollis was pretty sure there were no other girl miniatures in his bag.

She swallowed around the lump in her throat. "I mean, sure. Uh, thanks."

Leaning forward, the sides of her rickety folding chair protesting against her thighs, Hollis placed Bikini Alvena on the blank battle map.

All around the folding table, the other players did the same with their characters. A nervous college-aged boy across from Hollis had borrowed a miniature as well—a knightly, paint-chipped paladin wearing considerably more clothes than Bikini Alvena—which he slid beside hers. A woman in her early twenties had brought her own miniature, a hulking troll barbarian in a loincloth, which she pushed to the front of their haphazard line. A man with a weak chin and a silky wolf shirt had a figure in the same model as Alvena, but his had been painted with much more care, all the way down to her tiny, intricately shaded cleavage.

Both the miniatures and the players who placed them seemed much more at home in the cramped, dimly lit back room of Games-A-Lot—Hollis's local game store—than Hollis felt. For the past hour, she'd been trying to settle in among the sea of tables and the chatter of players gathered for tonight's open role-playing session. But it was no use. The room felt too small—or maybe Hollis just felt too big and too young. Most of the other players seemed to be at least college-aged. And they all seemed more prepared, too, with their own dice sets and game books and neatly filled-out character sheets (unlike Hollis's, which she'd scribbled in a rush earlier that same day). Moving as little as possible, Hollis cast a glance around her table for anyone else her age.

The only possibility was the boy sitting beside her, who was probably around her age—seventeen—or maybe a year younger. His bard miniature wielded an electric guitar that didn't match his doublet, tights, and foppish feathered hat. He placed the bard directly beside Alvena, its base crossing over the graph paper line and bumping up against hers.

"Hey," said the boy, leaning uncomfortably close to Hollis. "Maxx the Bard wants to know if your character is thicc like you."

What Hollis wanted to say was *Ew* and then *I don't know, is your character a creep like you?* but before she could find her voice, the Secret Keeper cleared his throat. He'd arranged a horde of goblin miniatures on the opposite side of the map, and now he began reading from the official *Realmsdelver Adventure Guide*.

"The party comes upon a group of goblins." His narration had the flat quality of someone put on the spot without time to prepare. "They stand with their crude short bows drawn but do not attack."

Finally, the moment they'd all been waiting for: combat. Since this was the first session of an open-to-the-public game, the group's role-playing had so far been stiff at best. Hollis had been silent the whole time, furtively flipping through her borrowed copy of the player's handbook as she tried to keep up. Maybe the framework of a battle would be just what the group needed to get them all on the same page.

Leaning in, Hollis opened her mouth to speak at last. She took a deep breath, and—

"'Newbs,'" the older girl cut in, pitching her voice down to a gravelly rumble to mimic her character's speech. "Axtar the Terrible's gonna run forward, his battle-axe raised high."

"Wait," said the boy playing the paladin. "We don't have to attack them. They haven't done anything yet."

"Oh, God." Maxx the Bard's player leaned in closer still. He dropped his voice, waggling an eyebrow at Hollis conspiratorially. *"Gay!"*

Hollis's folding chair creaked as she leaned away, but the table was so small that this meant leaning closer to the girl on the other side of her, and that wasn't an appealing idea either. Her muscles tensed, holding her uncomfortably in place.

"I know you're new," said Axtar's player in her regular voice, "but those are goblins. Goblins are *always* bad."

"I'm just saying," said the paladin boy, "could we at least try something other than hacking them up first? Maybe they'll let us pass through their village if we ask."

The man with the other Alvena miniature scoffed. "Yeah, right."

"While they're doing that," said the boy playing Maxx the Bard, somehow managing to loom even closer to Hollis, "can I roll to seduce Alvira? My persuasion modifier is plus 10."

Hollis froze. If she leaned any farther in her folding chair, she feared it would tip. The bland gray walls felt too close, pressing uncomfortably near to her skin.

"Come on, man," said the paladin boy. "You know S&S isn't just dice rolls and numbers! It's *collaborative storytelling*. We're supposed to be *creating* something together! Really exploring the world and playing our characters, and—"

"Ugh," said the other man. "Leave that soft-boy crap at the door."

"Okay, enough's enough," said Axtar's player. "Axtar is going to let out a guttural roar"—to demonstrate, she made a noise startling enough that several players at the more experienced tables turned their heads to look—"and then he'll chuck his axe at whatever goblin looks the meanest."

"All right." The Secret Keeper seemed thankful to finally have something concrete to do. "Make an attack roll against the goblin."

And with that, the game whirred back into motion. Players went back and forth rolling dice that Hollis wasn't sure she even *had* in the set her boyfriend had loaned her. It was as if every bit of last-minute knowledge he'd crammed into her brain was dribbling out her ears now that the time had come to use it. What Hollis wouldn't give now for it to be *him* seated next to her, instead of Maxx or Axtar, so that she could lean in and ask what she was supposed to be doing and where all this math was coming from. She wished, not for the first time, that she was playing her first S&S game with him instead.

But his group had a rule that came before any in the player's handbook: the No-Girlfriend Rule. It barred Hollis specifically—and any other future girlfriend hypothetically—from playing in the boys' weekly S&S game.

The No-Girlfriend Rule was the only thing that had kept Hollis desperate enough to stay seated at a table full of strangers in a windowless dungeon of a room for two hours (and counting). Her eyes wandered toward the store's front door.

"Hello, earth to Elvira," came the voice of Axtar's player from beside her.

Hollis's attention swam back to the table. For an instant, she wanted to protest that her character's name was *Alvena*, but she only said, "Huh?"

"It's your turn! What did you roll?"

Hollis picked up one of her dice—the largest, with twenty sides, which her boyfriend had said was the one used for most rolls. Unsure what she was even rolling for, she shook it clumsily in her palm and let it drop to the table in front of her.

The die landed with a 1 face up—the lowest number she could have possibly rolled. Alvena would be last in the battle order. Hollis settled into her folding chair, leaning as far away from Maxx the Bard's player as possible, and waited.

As soon as the table was sent on their fifteen-minute break, Hollis texted her boyfriend:

can you please come pick me up??

Her plan was to exit Games-A-Lot as casually as possible and wait for Chris on the bench in front of the vitamin shop next door. But as she approached the front door, cold can of Dr Pepper (purchased from Karl behind the shop counter) in hand, she stopped. The woman who played Axtar the Terrible was on the other side of the smudgy glass, smoking a cigarette and laughing with some of the other players.

Hollis was trapped in the vestibule, stuck in the stale smell of cigarette smoke, her Dr Pepper gradually warming in her hand as a nervous sweat gradually warmed her brow.

She willed her phone to buzz.

Games-A-Lot was the kind of place where Hollis had hoped she'd fit in. The shop was a shining beacon of geekdom that even its cramped, dusty shelves, poor fluorescent lighting, and run-down-strip-mall location couldn't dim. That the local game store was on this side of the river—in Hollis's hometown of Covington, Kentucky, and not the infinitely more hip and happening Cincinnati, Ohio—made it feel even more accessible. She couldn't see herself reflected in the store's hand-painted sign (which depicted a knight on horseback in front of a castle tower, a busty, freshly rescued princess riding behind him), but she had convinced herself that she *could* see herself in the back room, playing Secrets & Sorcery.

She had been wrong.

It would've been nice to say she was surprised, but in truth, what had happened tonight was exactly what Hollis had feared. Even though she'd spent a solid three weeks searching for a game, even though she'd read every comment on this group's Meetup page to vet their friendliness and general safety, even though she'd given herself a mental pep talk in her mom's car on the way here earlier, it had still ended up a disaster.

Hollis shook her head at herself and backed into the vestibule corner, trying to stay out of sight of Axtar the Terrible's player. Her back pocket buzzed and she almost dropped her Dr Pepper in her rush to retrieve her phone.

christopher: couldn't hack it huh

Fingers hovering over her screen, Hollis thought about what to type back. In a way, it was Chris's fault that all this had gone so poorly—and that Hollis was here at all. Secrets & Sorcery had been *his* game, something he'd played with the boys since the summer before ninth grade, when Hollis was as good as one of the boys herself.

But Hollis had never *really* been one of the boys. Every Monday, she'd stood on the outskirts of the group as they rehashed their Friday game blow by epic blow, good enough to listen but not to be truly included. Her status became all the more apparent halfway through freshman year, when she and Chris—tired of always being accused of it anyway—started dating. Suddenly, Secrets & Sorcery came with a No-Girlfriend Rule. And to be fair, Hollis had never cared much. Beyond stealing Chris's *Monstarium* (the S&S book that held all the lore and stats for the monsters of the Eight Realms) for art inspiration and following other artists who liked the game on social media, she was a casual fan at best.

But now senior year loomed on the horizon, and Hollis knew things were going to change, even if she didn't yet know how. Her crew (or, really, Chris's crew, which Hollis had inherited through proximity and convenience) would scatter to the corners of the country—or at least the greater Tri-State area—in just a few short months. For so many years, the boys had been all Hollis knew. And if she couldn't predict what happened next, she wanted to be part of what happened *now*.

For Chris and crew, that was Secrets & Sorcery. So Hollis had set out on her own to prove she could indeed hack it. Maybe, if she could prove herself in a game of her own, she could show Chris that she was worthy of a spot in his.

If nothing else, it would give her something to talk about on Mondays. Hollis couldn't be one of the boys, but she could at least be part of the conversation.

And that started now, with a clever reply to Chris's text. With the back of her hand, Hollis wiped her reddening cheeks, brushing away pearls of sweat. But before she could type that there had been plenty of hacking, actually, another message appeared.

christopher: omw

Well. At least her rescue was impending—and none too soon. Inside the store, the boy who played Maxx the Bard crept closer. Though he was pretending to look at the dice display on the other side of the glass (a bright spot in the dim store, featuring small, sparkling boxes of dice in every color of the rainbow), it was clear the treasure he was *really* searching out was Hollis. He grinned at her, his waggling eyebrows working overtime.

With a sudden, pressing need to look occupied and unapproachable, Hollis busied herself with the only feature in the vestibule—a community corkboard. Pushpinned on it were at least five layers of advertisements for everything from monster truck rallies to FPS-style recruitment flyers for the Army. A page of watercolor paper caught Hollis's eye. It was washed in a pleasing mix of lilac, tangerine, and buttercup. In round, not entirely neat handwriting, it read:

> Looking for a roleplay-heavy, story-driven game of Secrets & Sorcery?
>
> I'm looking for you.
> I'm starting a new girl-friendly,
> LGBTQIA+-friendly campaign and need a few
> more daring adventurers to join the party.
> Want to roam the Realms with us?
> Send me an email by August 21.

Carefully cut fringe at the bottom of the paper read *TAKE ME!* *gloriawith12os@gmail.com*. Only three were missing. Five were vandalized in red pen to say *1-800-BITCH.COM* instead.

Hollis read the flyer again, then once more for good measure. A strange sort of fluttering built in her chest. She wasn't sure what kind of game she was looking for, but Gloria-with-12-Os's sounded much better than the one she was in the middle of walking out on. Maybe she could give it a try.

But today was the twenty-second. She'd missed the application deadline by one day.

Maybe this was a sign. Maybe she just wasn't destined to play Secrets & Sorcery. She'd always been more of a non-player character than a high-stakes adventurer, anyway.

"Hey, Alvena," said Axtar the Terrible's player as she shoved the door open and pushed past. "You coming back in, or did we scare you off?"

Her barbarian laugh told Hollis that she suspected the truth.

"No, no." Hollis's fingers tightened around her Dr Pepper can. Her chest tightened with anxiety. She blinked, suddenly acutely aware that her eyes were a little too big, and shook her head. Her hair stuck to her sweat-sheened skin where the frizz bobbled against the back of her neck. "I'll be right in, just finishing my drink."

"Yeah. Sure thing, kid."

Hollis watched human Axtar disappear into the store and hoped she never saw her again. Her back pocket vibrated.

christopher: here

christopher: where u at

Hollis typed back one-handed.

coming.

She spared one last look for the dingy game store and the adventuring party she was leaving behind. But it wasn't Maxx the Bard's player, still lurking by the glass, that caught Hollis's eye. It was the sunset-washed flyer.

Hollis reached out, fingers closing around one of the fringed tabs. She wasn't entirely sure why she did it, but she did it all the same. The weight of the paper was pleasantly thick between her thumb and index finger.

With a decisive motion, she tore it off. It ripped unevenly, leaving the *.com* behind.

Hollis tucked the slip of paper into her back pocket with her phone, and then she pushed open the door and walked away.

"And then, after she was done hacking up this goblin with her battle-axe, do you know what she did?"

Hollis leaned forward from the back seat and accepted the vanilla cone Chris handed her. This was one of the perks of dating the person who had been her best friend since middle school: he was able to tell when something was Threat Level: Vanilla Cone. Chris raised a blond eyebrow before leaning back out the window of the Sentra to get his own ice cream.

"She goes, 'And then Axtar leans in and cuts his ear off and spears it on the spike-chain necklace he wears.'" Hollis took a lick of her ice cream, which was already beginning to melt in the heat of the summer night. "Who in their right mind would do something like that?"

"Axtar, it sounds like." This came from Landon—Chris's *other* best friend and his group's Secret Keeper since freshman year—who sat in the front seat. Landon's lips rippled with a poorly suppressed smile as Chris pulled out of the McDonald's drive-through.

"I mean, can you *imagine*?" Hollis shook her head. "That ear is going to start stinking in, like, a day. Who even knows what kind of creatures they'll have following the stench."

"They?"

"Huh?"

"You said *they*," Chris said through a mouthful of soft serve. "Don't you mean *we*?"

"Oh." Hollis frowned at her cone. Here in Chris's car, with the familiar squeal of an unreplaced belt and the crackle of his nu metal through blown-out speakers, she'd expected the events at Games-A-Lot to feel less bad. But instead, they somehow felt worse. Landon, lanky and looming in the front seat, reminded her too much of what she was supposed to prove by going to this game—and of what she hadn't.

Hollis shook her head. "No, I don't think I'll be going back again."

"Come on, Hollis," Chris chided. "Don't quit so soon. You looked for that game for weeks! You've just got a meathead barbarian. Every table has a meathead barbarian."

"Yeah." Landon looked at her through the rearview mirror. "Quitting is for quitters, Hollis."

Hollis wanted to remind them that she wouldn't have had to look for a different group at all if Chris's S&S group didn't have the No-Girlfriend Rule—and if Landon didn't gleefully enforce it. But the car, usually comfortable, felt too small from the back seat. There wasn't enough space for all of Landon's judgment—or Chris's disappointment. She swallowed a mouthful of ice cream instead.

"I mean, it wasn't just that player, though. There was this guy, around our age, who was playing this bard—"

"Oh, bards." Landon gave a short, knowing laugh.

"I swear if Axtar hadn't sliced the goblin's head open so fast, he was going to try to seduce it."

"Gay," said Chris, not unlike Maxx the Bard's player at the table.

The word had been startling enough coming from Maxx in the back of Games-A-Lot. From Chris, it was even worse. It sank like a stone in Hollis's gut.

She swallowed, trying to make it sit comfortably. But no matter what she did, it wouldn't, and so she tried to explain around it.

"Come on, Chris, he was *the worst*. He kept asking if Alvena was thicc. With two *C*s."

"Well, is she?"

"Chris." Hollis raised an eyebrow at him.

She wasn't mad, not really. This was how their relationship had always worked: Hollis found herself overwrought, and Chris said goofy things to distract her until she calmed down. It happened so often that there was a worn spot on the side of the passenger-seat upholstery where Hollis's fingers had worried the fibers thin. She couldn't feel it now—how the edge of the seat closest to the window grew threadbare at hip level—not with Landon in the front. But just knowing it was there was a kind of comfort anyway. It stilled her, softened her to Chris. He still had a chance to walk them back, especially since he had just rescued her and bought her ice cream.

"I'm kidding." Chris turned onto Hollis's street. "But that's how bards are, you know?"

"Surely not every bard is a total douchebag."

"That's literally what bards are for, as a class," Landon piped in, a bit of his own ice cream dripping down the patchy scruff on his chin. "It's basically Rules as Written."

Hollis wanted to say *Ew*, but Landon was so confident that he didn't even bother to turn around and look at her while he made his proclamation. Instead, he just glared at her through the rearview mirror, his gray eyes daring her to contradict him.

Hollis sighed and looked away. She finished the last bit of her ice cream.

"What he means is some of this comes with the territory, unfortunately." Chris pulled up in front of Hollis's house, parallel parking behind her mom's car. In the glow of the streetlight, his frizzy blond hair haloed as he shook his head. "The game's just like that."

Hollis wanted to believe he was wrong. She wanted to believe that the game her boyfriend loved enough to spend every Friday night standing her up for wasn't just *like that*. She didn't want to think that in order to share this interest—to make the most of their senior year together, to finally, really fit with the boys in a lasting way—she would have to be *like that* herself. Like Maxx, with his anachronistic bass guitar and dubious understanding of consent. Or like Axtar, with her bad attitude and knowing glances.

If the game really was just *like that*, Hollis didn't want to think about what that said about Chris. About her. Her soft serve sat uneasy in her stomach, and she suddenly felt much colder than ice cream should have made her.

"Yeah," she said, gritting her teeth against the chill. "Maybe you're right."

"I usually am," Landon said.

"Here, let me let you out," Chris said, unbuckling and opening the door. He folded his seat forward, and Hollis scrambled out.

In the hot night air, they stood eye to eye, looking at each other like they were waiting for something. The welcome sign for their neighborhood glinted over Chris's shoulder, the *E* of its mosaic-tile EASTSIDE changed by time or vandalism to an *L* so that it felt like all of Last Side was waiting for something too.

Chris was the first to move, leaning forward and pulling Hollis into a lopsided hug. From the front seat of the car, Landon hollered a long *"Woooooooo."*

Hollis rolled her eyes, but she wrapped her arms around Chris's waist. Like the rest of him, it was neither thin nor stocky but somewhere in between. For a moment, she stayed there, her head hovering just over Chris's shoulder, her nose twitching when his wispy blond hair tickled it, trying to muster up the courage to ask.

It was a long shot, and she knew it. Still, she asked it in a whisper so Landon couldn't hear—and so Chris *could*—how much she wanted it.

"Are you sure I can't play S&S with you on Friday?" The words were small on her tongue. "I know the rules now, and I promise I won't mess up."

The effect was immediate. Chris pulled away, cocking his head so the frizz of his blond hair poufed to one side. Around them, the cramped car-lined streets pressed in, watching as closely as Landon was from the front seat.

"You know I can't make that happen, Hol," he said. "The rules are the rules."

"I know, I know." And she did. Her heart still sank as she looked down at her feet. "It would just make it so much easier to play."

"Yeah," Chris said, "but maybe if you give the Games-A-Lot group another try, it won't be so bad. You just have to find your people."

Chris was her person; he had been since sixth grade. It would be so much easier for him to stay her person forever if he just let her play in his game.

But for Chris, the guys always came first.

Hollis looked up and tried to give him a smile anyway. Chris grinned in response, then turned back to the car. Over his shoulder, he said, "See you Monday at school, okay?"

"Oh, yeah," said Hollis. She tried to match the enthusiasm in Chris's voice when she added, "Wouldn't miss it."

Everything in Hollis's room was secondhand. The blue upholstered armchair in the corner, buried beneath a pile of clothes in various stages of needing to be washed, she'd inherited when her grand-mother moved in with her aunt. The faded quilt on her bed once belonged to her mother, and the heavy wooden bed frame had been her father's, before her parents divorced and he moved out. Even the knickknacks were mostly scavenged—interesting props left over from school plays, a jar of buttons of unknown origin, a green glass wine bottle left over from Christmas and stuffed full of twinkle lights from the thrift shop.

The only thing entirely her own was her desk. It wasn't particularly impressive—as the daughter of a teacher in a single-parent house-hold, nothing Hollis had was—but she had put it together entirely on her own after she'd picked it out from Target at the beginning of freshman year, and it felt like *hers*. It was made of white particle board and covered in nicks and paint drips and stray pencil marks, because it was also where her art lived. And for that reason it was her most cherished possession. Hollis spent the majority of her time at home bent over it, perched in a repurposed chair from the kitchen dining set, her hand wandering over the page as her mind wandered to other worlds.

It was where she found herself soon after she'd watched Chris pull away.

Once she'd gotten home, she'd tried to draw them out—all the characters from her half session of S&S. But even Alvena Ravenwood, whose intricate robe and long, wavy hair she had imagined in careful detail for weeks, eluded her. Each time Hollis touched her pencil to a blank page in her notebook, the characters came out all wrong.

By the time she had not-finished three attempts, Hollis gave up. Pushing her notebook away, she leaned back in her chair and frowned when her phone poked her backside. Shifting, she pulled it out of her back pocket and stared.

Stuck in the cracked corner of her case was the slip of paper—the one she'd taken from the Games-A-Lot community board. In the light of her desk lamp, it seemed even nicer than it had in the vestibule. Hollis ran her fingers over the rough grain of the paper, along the line where lilac faded to buttercup. It was so much more artful than anything she'd produced in her notebook all night.

Hadn't Chris said she needed to find her people?

If he didn't believe that she could be his person, she had to *show* him she could be. The boys always seemed to be at their closest when they talked about their S&S game—as if it were *them*, not their imaginary stand-ins, adventuring together every Friday night. Hollis was sure that their ability to survive untold peril every week as a party in the game meant that they'd be able to survive whatever came after senior year, too. For her and Chris, though, there was no such certainty. Not *yet*, at least. Finding the right S&S group meant finding a way to prove herself to the person she least wanted to leave behind.

Hollis unlocked her phone and pulled up her email app. Before she could second-guess the impulse, her thumbs started to fly.

to: gloriawith12os@gmail.com
from: justhollisb@gmail.com
subject: s&s game

----

gloria with 12 o's,

as of right now, i'm 21 hours and 32 minutes late for the deadline to do this, but here goes:

i saw your flyer at games-a-lot, and i think i'm the kind of player you're looking for. or i could be, if you let me try.

i'll play whatever character you need me to play. i just really don't want to have to play with the creeps at games-a-lot anymore.

hollis b.

The moment after she finished typing, she thought about deleting the email. It was a long shot at best. And it was almost certainly too late, anyway. Whoever Gloria was, she'd probably already found enough of her own friends to fill her game by now.

Hollis's eyes drifted back to her notebook and the failed sketches of her failed S&S character. In her head, Landon's voice repeated the noise of the night in an endless loop: *She couldn't hack it; this was just how the game was; the rules were the rules and there was no room in them for Hollis.*

She took a deep breath, held it in her chest, and hit send. Then, for three full breaths, Hollis just blinked down at her phone, unsure if she was mortified or impressed by what she'd just done.

Her Secrets & Sorcery future now rested in the hands—or, more accurately, the inbox—of Gloria-with-12-Os.

2

SECRETS AND SERVERS

HOLLIS CHECKED HER inbox for the third time since pouring herself a bowl of cereal four minutes ago. It stayed stubbornly the same: just an advertisement for the plus-size store at the mall (*Back 2 School Babes: 100% Fashion, 50% Off!*) and Julie Murphy's most recent *Just Peachy* newsletter.

There was still no message from Gloria or her 12 *O*s.

A hollowness yawned open in Hollis's chest. She should have known. Sending that email was foolish. The lack of response was a sign that what Chris said in his text was true: she couldn't hack it. Cold dread descended on her, closing like fingers around her lungs.

Hollis shook her head and tried to keep the anxiety at bay. It was much too early in the morning for this. And maybe Gloria-with-12-*O*s hadn't even seen her message yet.

Still, she thought she'd better check her spam box. Just in case.

There it was, at the top of her screen. Hollis exhaled. The hand constricting around her rib cage released as she read *re: s&s game*.

to: justhollisb@gmail.com
from: gloriawith12os@gmail.com
subject: re: s&s game

Girl, chill.

21 hours and 32 minutes is not the end of the world. We still have a place for you at our table. We were going to do a chat on the group Discord server around 2PM today. Can you make it? Follow the link below. If not, let me know and I can email you the minutes.

Welcome to the party, Hollis B.

—G.

Hollis gave a squeal so awkward-sounding that under any other circumstance she would have been embarrassed hearing it come out of her mouth. It filled the small kitchen, bouncing off the green-painted walls and echoing down the hall.

"You okay in there, Hollis?" her mom called from the living room.

Hollis cleared her throat and reminded herself to breathe.

"Yeah, Mom. Totally fine."

Once she calmed down, Hollis typed back *yeah, sounds great, see you then* and hit send. She was so excited that she didn't even feel embarrassed for saying *see* when she wouldn't be seeing anyone or anything but text on a screen.

Was it silly to get nervous about a Discord chat?

Probably.

Was Hollis Beckwith still nervous about a Discord chat?

Absolutely.

She locked herself in her bedroom, telling her mom she had last-minute summer reading to churn out before school started tomorrow. It was believable enough; the senior English class had been assigned a "modern" retelling of Shakespeare's *Macbeth* that had probably last been modern in maybe 1997. She'd complained about it so much over the past few weeks that her mom didn't pry now.

And so Hollis had thirty minutes alone before the online meetup with her new Secrets & Sorcery group. She set up her laptop—which was almost as outdated as the *Macbeth* retelling—at her desk. She'd tried setting up in bed, where she'd be more physically comfortable for a chat of unknown duration, but it just didn't feel like the right place to be. The hard press of her thinly cushioned wooden chair was a price worth paying for the right headspace, she justified.

When she'd finished setting up—making sure she had a notebook, a good pen, and her small collection of Prismacolor markers handy, just in case—Hollis still had fifteen minutes to wait.

As she read over Gloria's email again, her stomach roiled. She didn't want to click the "join server" link too early and look as desperate as she felt. She didn't want to click it too late and look like a jerk, either. No, Hollis wanted to join the server just the right amount of time before the chat started to convey that she was taking this seriously but not too seriously and that maybe she had a life outside of an S&S group chat on a Sunday afternoon.

That time was 1:52 p.m.

When it arrived, Hollis tabbed over to the email and clicked.

----------**beckwhat** *hopped into the server.*----------

Aini 1:52 PM
Oh! Is this her?

Gloooooooooooooria 1:52 PM
Yes, this is Hollis.

Welcome!

uwuFRANuwu 1:53 PM
KDJAJFHJFAJFAF

HELLOOO HOLLIS IM FRAN

iffy.elliston 1:53 PM
hey hollis

beckwhat 1:54 PM
hey everyone!!

Glooooooooooooria 1:55 PM
Aini, I know Maggie can't make it today. Can you make sure she gets up to speed when you see her next?

Aini 1:56 PM
Yeah, totally.

Glooooooooooooria 1:56 PM
Are we good to get started, then?

uwuFRANuwu 1:57 PM
YEE

beckwhat 1:57 PM
yes please!

iffy.elliston 1:58 PM
i'm a little in and out finishing up this whack summer reading but i'm here

Aini 1:58 PM
Yeah, let's do this!

Glooooooooooooria 1:59 PM
Okay, okay.

I don't need you all long today, I promise.

Let's start with a quick roll call. I'll go first.

I'm Gloria (she/her) and I'm your Secret Keeper, obviously. I've been playing Secrets & Sorcery for five years, but don't get to do a lot of actual playing because I usually Keep instead. If you have any new player questions (or old player questions), I'm your girl.

Next!

uwuFRANuwu 2:03 PM
I"M FRAN. THIS IS MY FIRST GAME!!! gloria is letting me play finallyyyyy.

oh also gloria is my sister

and a loser :/

luckily it doesnt run in teh family uwu

Aini 2:03 PM
I'm Aini (she/her). I played in Gloria's last game. Shout-out to my mom for having no chill and talking about my nerdy hobbies to exactly the right coworker . . . and to Gloria for taking me in even when her mom was like, "this woman I work with has a gay daughter who wants to play S&S with other girls."

Gloria's totally underrepresenting how awesome she is, by the way. She's the best.

uwuFRANuwu 2:04 PM
NEXT

Aini 2:04 PM
NEXT!

uwuFRANuwu 2:05 PM
lololol jinx aini

u owe me a soda

oh also i use she her pronouns uwu

Aini 2:06 PM
Rude!

I'll get you a Coke, though. 😂😂😂

Oh, we have Maggie (she/her), also. She's my school friend and she's new to the game.

Okay, NOW next.

beckwhat 2:16 PM
hey, i'm hollis (she/her). i'm new to the game too but have been a fan from afar for a while ♡♡. really excited to play!!! (edited)

next!!

iffy.elliston 2:22 PM
ugh sorry y'all macbeth is going to be the death of me i s2g

i'm iffy elliston (she/her) i've played a couple games before but they never ran very long so i'm glad to find a dedicated group

bless that game store flyer

beckwhat 2:23 PM
@iffy.elliston do you go to holmes, iffy??

iffy.elliston 2:23 PM
i do

beckwhat 2:23 PM
sweet, me too!!

iffy.elliston 2:23 PM
nice

you get your macbeth done already?

beckwhat 2:24 PM
"done" is a subjective term . . . . . .

Glooooooooooooria 2:24 PM
Take it to the DMs girls. We're talking S&S tonight!

Next on the agenda: expectations and rules.

uwuFRANuwu 2:24 PM
BORINGGGG

dont u look at me like that gloria marie

shes looking at me irl like
(ʊ̄‸ʊ̄)

Glooooooooooooria 2:25 PM
https://bit.ly/TableGuidelines

I've made a Google Doc with my expectations for table etiquette. Please read it. I trust it will be fine with everyone, because it's just basic human stuff like respect each other, don't be a transphobe or homophobe, etc. There's a place for you to "sign" once you've read so I know you agree.

Aini 2:26 PM
I told you she was the coolest, didn't I?

Glooooooooooooria 2:27 PM
And yes, I know this is a little extra, but I'm on a gap year before college. You can take the girl out of school but you can't take the school out of the girl.

Instead of writing papers, I'm writing S&S guides.

Oh, and I'll add some information on adaptations I've made for the Eight Realms setting to make it a little more inclusive, and some character creation guidelines to keep in mind while you start brainstorming characters.

uwuFRANuwu 2:28 PM
IM GOING TO PLAY A BARBERAIN

BRABEREEIAN

THE ONE WHO SMASHES STUFF!!!!!!!

Aini 2:29 PM
I'd be disappointed by anything less, honestly, Fran.

Glooooooooooooria 2:30 PM
Actually, I'd like to get everyone together soon so we can create characters and roll stats in person, especially since a few of you are new to the game. I figure we could find a standing day and time that works for everyone and start then.

How would Friday evenings at 6PM work?

Aini 2:31 PM
I can make that work.

uwuFRANuwu 2:32 PM
YEE

duh

Aini 2:33 PM
I'll text Maggie to ask, too.

iffy.elliston 2:33 PM
i can't promise every single friday

i have gsa stuff then sometimes

but i can do most of them

beckwhat 2:35 PM
here for fridays for sure! (edited)

Glooooooooooooria 2:36 PM
Okay, okay. How's everyone's transportation situation? We'll play at my mom's house, starting this Friday. We're on the west side of Cincy, in Price Hill.

Aini 2:36 PM
I drive so I'm good.

So does Maggie.

iffy.elliston 2:36 PM
i drive too

beckwhat 2:38 PM
i don't.

ugh, i'm sorry.

i'm in covington across the river, too.

uwuFRANuwu 2:38 PM
RIP @*beckwhat*

beckwhat 2:39 PM
i can get an uber.

iffy.elliston 2:39 PM
that is nonsense

i'll come pick you up

beckwhat 2:40 PM
are you sure you don't mind?? (edited)

iffy.elliston 2:40 PM
i don't mind at all

Aini 2:41 PM
Just bring good snacks, Hollis!

As your payment.

beckwhat 2:41 PM
i'll throw in some gas money, actually.

iffy.elliston 2:42 PM
even better

Glooooooooooooria 2:43 PM
Aini brings up an important point.

uwuFRANuwu 2:43 PM
CUPCAKES

Glooooooooooooria 2:44 PM
We rotate who brings the snacks every week.

uwuFRANuwu 2:44 PM
CUPCAKES CUPCAKES

Glooooooooooooria 2:44 PM
Do you want to volunteer for the first session, Hollis?

No pressure.

beckwhat 2:45 PM
yeah sure i can bring snacks!

uwuFRANuwu 2:45 PM
CUP!!! CAKES!!!!!!

beckwhat 2:45 PM
i can even bring cupcakes.

uwuFRANuwu 2:46 PM
ur my new fave

move over aini

aini who????

Glooooooooooooria 2:46 PM
First, does anyone have food allergies/restrictions?

uwuFRANuwu 2:47 PM
i only eat cupcake U-U

Aini 2:47 PM
Maggie's vegan but she always brings her own stuff, so you're go for cupcakes as far as I'm concerned.

Glooooooooooooria 2:47 PM
Okay, okay.

That's everything then. You are a very efficient group. I think we're going to make a great team.

The only one I'm worried about is Francesca, honestly.

Aini 2:48 PM
Ahhhahahahaha!

uwuFRANuwu 2:48 PM
safjasjfkjkLJSLKJALFKJFJOIJI

how dare u

Glooooooooooooria 2:49 PM
Feel free to chat here whenever you want.

And @ me if you need me.

uwuFRANuwu 2:49 PM
ヽ(@^▽^@)ﾉ

Aini 2:50 PM
Bye, Gloria!

Bye, everyone!

iffy.elliston 2:51 PM
see y'all

beckwhat 2:51 PM
thank you gloria! ♡♡♡

Hollis spent the next thirty minutes rereading the entire chat log. Even when she reached the end again, she couldn't be sure what, exactly, had just happened. All the other girls seemed to be friends (or sisters) already, which made Hollis an outsider, which didn't feel fantastic; she was already an outsider in Chris's game. Still—no one, not once, had asked her if she was thick, with or without the two Cs, and so the group at least had that going for them.

Maybe another read would help her decide.

The wheel of her hand-me-down mouse clacked a weak protest as she scrolled back to the top of the chat log.

3

IS IT FRIDAY YET?

"WE START, UH, Friday," Hollis said.

She and her group, which was Chris and Landon and their friend Marius, stood outside Holmes High School, their backs pressed against the brick wall. It, like everything else about her high school, was old and in disrepair. Most students in Covington attended Catholic schools, and Holmes's neglect showed just like the holes in its public-school budget. About a dozen or so students milled around nearby, all fellow geeks gathering in their morning hangout spot.

"Seems like forever away, I bet," said Marius.

Hollis nodded and crossed her arms over her chest. She wasn't used to being at the center of a group conversation. For the last three years, Monday-morning catch-up had always been about the boys' S&S game. It was nice, if strange, to have something to contribute for once. Maybe her plan was working already.

"That sounds pretty cool, Hollis," said Chris, giving her a blue-eyed wink. He took a sip of his energy drink and then passed it to Marius—their before-school ritual. "It'll keep you away from that bard dude, too."

"There's literally always a bard, though." Landon, looking especially pale and scrawny in the morning light, snorted a laugh.

"Oh, was the Games-A-Lot game no good?" Marius raised an eyebrow and took a swig of Monster.

"Wasn't really my scene," Hollis said with a shrug. Sweat beaded on her brow. Even in the shade, even at the early hour before school started, it was already hot. Though Covington was only divided from the Midwest by a river's width, it was still technically in the South, where August meant summer was over only in spirit.

"You're really going to play with a bunch of girls." Landon crossed his arms over his chest, his voice flat, like her group wasn't even worth an actual question.

"Yeah." Hollis had just said that, pretty clearly.

"Huh."

Huh was a code word for Landon. It meant there was something else he wanted to say—and not once had it ever been something good. Hollis tried to ignore him, hoping that if she didn't ask, he wouldn't say.

But Hollis never had much luck when it came to Landon.

"I just think it's funny," he said. Hollis drew in a breath. "I mean, a bunch of girls playing Secrets & Sorcery? No thanks."

"Hmm." Hollis hummed out her exhale slowly. She hoped it sounded as noncommittal as she felt about this line of conversation.

Usually, Chris stepped in around this time and told Landon to shut up. It was why they started dating in the first place; when Landon joined the group in freshman year, Chris's interjections happened so often that everyone assumed he and Hollis already *were* together. And because Hollis and Chris had been best friends since both of their parents divorced in sixth grade, they thought they might as well let everyone be right. It meant neither of them had to be alone or try to find someone else, and they already knew all the important things about each other. But now, in this moment, Chris was distracted trying to tame the blond flyaways of his hair, a task as useless as Hollis trying to shut Landon up herself.

Hollis stared at Chris, her eyes boring into the side of his head as if it were a red-alert button she was trying to push telepathically.

"It's a guys' kind of game, isn't it? All the hacking and slashing and stuff." Landon sucked on one of his chapped lips, considering. "It's probably a bunch of butches playing," he concluded, and then, like it was a true concern of his, "Just don't turn into a lesbian, okay?"

Annoyance flared hot across Hollis's cheeks. *You don't just* turn into *a lesbian; it's not like being a werewolf or something*, she wanted to say. Landon's glare practically dared her to. But anxiety tightened around her rib cage, deepening the red of her face. Hollis shook her head instead.

"Yeah, okay," she said. "I'll do my best."

Her mood darkened significantly (Landon's specialty), Hollis turned to head into the halls for her first day. This movement was enough to pull Chris back into what was happening.

"Landon's just jealous you'll be spending time with real human girls," he said, soothing. "I think it's cool you found a game. But you know what's cooler?"

"These fresh braids," said Marius, almost but not quite running his hands over his hair.

"Yes, *and*," said Chris, looking toward the brick walls of their high school, "we're about to walk into the first day of our senior year. The first day of the last hurrah for our epic real-life adventuring party."

Hollis waited for the *huh* from Landon.

"Too right, my dude," he said instead.

Chris slung an arm over Marius's shoulders, then did the same over Landon's slumped ones.

Hollis knew he was being theatrical. It was one of the reasons dating him was so comfortable; it was easier for her to blend into the background when Chris was in the foreground, always demanding attention. Still, there was something genuine to the misty look in his eyes. Senior year *meant* something to him, the same way it meant something to Landon, to Marius—to their *real-life adventuring party*—and not to Hollis.

She swallowed the lump that was suddenly in her throat.

"May we roll high and never split the party," said Marius.

"That's taking the S&S metaphor too far," said Landon. "I'm out." And then, shoving Chris hard in the direction of Marius, causing them to knock hips, he started toward the side door of Holmes High School on his own. The door groaned when he opened it.

"Huh," said Hollis, but it didn't have the same effect as when Landon said it.

A step and a half behind the rest of the group, Hollis walked into the first day of her senior year, already wishing it were Friday.

The week always moved slowly for Hollis when she was in school.

It moved especially slowly when it was her First Week of Senior Year. People said it like that—as if it were a proper noun. All her teachers talked about it during their First Day speeches, before they made everyone play the same get-to-know-you games, even though roughly the same group of kids—with some regrettable inserts, like Landon— had known each other since elementary school. They talked about it at the Welcome Seniors assembly, with all the staff lined up on stage. They even talked about it in the teacher's lounge after school, where Hollis waited for her mom to finish hosting the Creative Writing Club or for Chris to finish band practice, whichever came first, so one of them could take her home.

These, her teachers said, were some of the best days of their lives. The seniors needed to cherish them while they lasted, because they *wouldn't* last forever. Before they knew it, senior year would be over, and they would all be off to college.

It didn't matter, not really, that most of the students at Holmes would end up at Northern Kentucky University, only a ten-minute drive from where they all sat now, with maybe a lucky few ending up at the University of Cincinnati across the river—and some, like Hollis, probably struggling to get into any college at all. The End of Senior Year, like the First Week of Senior Year, sounded dramatic when they said it. Final. Isolating.

Every time it came up, Hollis couldn't help thinking about the Secrets & Sorcery game looming at the end of the week. How important it was. How much was at stake for her and Chris. The closer it came, the less sure Hollis was that she wanted to go at all. If the boys were right—if the game really was just *like that*—she couldn't imagine it being much fun, even with Maxx the Bard taken out of the equation.

But with the End of Senior Year also looming, getting closer with every step she took through the halls of Holmes—hand in awkward, sweaty hand with Chris—Hollis told herself she was making the right choice.

If she could make it through enough games to show Chris that she could do this thing, that was one less wedge the end of the year could drive between them. Before they'd ever been Hollis and Chris, boyfriend and girlfriend—before they were even Hollis and Chris, lopsided middle school best friends—they had been *Beckwith, Hollis* and *Bradley, Chris*, class roll-call neighbors since kindergarten. Chris was her constant. The idea that something like graduation could force space between them (a space that was admittedly also sometimes filled by *Bowen, Madison*, depending how the classes were split) was frightening.

Secrets & Sorcery was the perfect solution. She just hadn't anticipated how much extra worry it would add to her week.

Hollis was well aware of how much worry she could fit into seven days. It was practically her extracurricular activity. But *this* week, it was as if she'd found a way to squeeze in even more worry than the usual amount.

Some of it was the stuff she always worried about. Would she be on time? Would she remember her good pens? Would she have everything she needed in her tote bag?

Some of it was the stuff she had gotten used to worrying about in the weeks leading up to the half session at Games-A-Lot. Would she remember which dice did what? Had she read the handbook enough times to remember all the rules? If she rolled a Natural 1 and failed miserably at something important, would the rest of the group forgive her, or would they laugh her out into the street?

But this week brought all new worries, and it was because the group she'd be playing with on Friday was way, way cooler than she was.

She knew this because she had Instagram-stalked the girls she would be playing with. It was a bad habit, but she did it anyway.

Gloria Castañeda was a year older than Hollis, as evidenced by a deep dive all the way back to a cap-and-gown graduation picture from the prior school year. Since her profile text was just a Colombian flag and a Pride flag, Hollis had had to keep digging to find out more. Most of Gloria's pictures were at exciting places, like a park or a street market or some hip café. There were lots at Cincinnati Children's Hospital, too, where she either worked or volunteered.

Gloria was also horribly, tragically beautiful.

She was a fat girl, like Hollis, but where Hollis had a round belly and thighs that Landon had called "cottage cheese–y" in gym freshman year, Gloria had curves and softness in all the same places plus-size models did. What was more, she had the sort of confidence Hollis dreamed of. It hung on her red-lipped smiles, clung tight to her hips, peeked out above the waistline of her jeans like her belly button beneath black-and-white-striped crop tops.

She was the kind of girl Hollis only drew about.

In some of Gloria's pictures was a younger girl—like Gloria in miniature, only sharper, thinner, and dressed exclusively in bright colors. Though Hollis couldn't confirm it, there was something about the look on the girl's face (enthusiasm bordering on franticness) that matched her sense of Fran's energy.

Then there was Aini.

From what Hollis could see—which was a lot, because Aini posted *everything*—Aini Amin-Shaw was cool in a way Hollis had only ever encountered in books or movies. Her short-cropped hair was black—or rather, the shaved sides of her hair were black and the top, a mess of thick curls, was a different color every couple of grid rows: neon pink, spring green, banana yellow. She wore the sort of effortless-looking clothing people spend hours putting together, only the way she wore them made her look like she'd just rolled out of bed looking perfectly disheveled.

What was more, Aini always seemed to be around someone cool, doing something cool. It was hard to tell where she went to school, but wherever it was looked much nicer than Holmes High. It was also impossible to tell which crowd she hung out with because *all* of them—jocks and geeks and e-girls alike—showed up in her pictures. There was even a photograph of both her parents (a South Asian man and woman with smiles as wide their daughter's) clearly having the time of their lives at a private meet and greet with the Cincinnati Zoo penguins for Aini's seventeenth birthday.

The only way Hollis could describe Aini was that she seemed to be *A Lot*. Staring at a photo of Aini leaning toward the camera and laughing open-mouthed, her vibrant curls tossed by a wind the photograph couldn't catch, Hollis wasn't sure whether she wanted to be part of that *A Lot* or have nothing to do with it.

From Aini's page she found Maggie's, a white girl who went to the same school. Maggie's account was blue-check verified with over ten thousand followers. Why, Hollis wasn't exactly sure. Her photos were an even split between vegan food, outfits of the day best described as witchy grunge, aesthetic-heavy bedroom pictures, and selfies. Of all the girls, waifish, blond Maggie Harper was perhaps the most impressive—or verifiably the most impressive. At least, no one else in the group could boast Reels with over fifty thousand views.

Hollis didn't have to Instagram-stalk Iffy Elliston, since she also went to Holmes High. Though her name hadn't been immediately familiar to Hollis on Discord, she'd seen the tall, slender Black girl around the halls since the First Week of Senior Year began. Iffy was the president of the Gay-Straight Alliance club, secretary of National Honor Society, and their school's first trans delegate to the Governor's Youth Advisory Board. There were plenty of busy students at Hollis's school, but Iffy was next-level busy: she was everywhere all at once, a true force to be reckoned with. Hollis didn't have to wonder how cool Iffy was, because it was completely obvious to anyone who passed her in the hall.

And then there was Hollis, whose secret Instagram was exclusively pictures of her own drawings, each with less than ten likes, and who was president of exactly nothing.

Well. President of worrying, maybe. Her stomach flopped as she stared at her phone.

Even if these girls were way cooler than Hollis, she reminded herself that they were still a better bet than the group at Games-A-Lot. Besides, *she* didn't even really need to fit in with them. That was what her character was for. Now she just needed to create one interesting enough to take up space among such an interesting group of people.

To save herself the stress, Hollis decided—then undecided, then redecided, in a loop about six times a day—to recycle Alvena Ravenwood for this game. The sorceress hadn't even gotten a fair shot at the table, for one. And for another, it saved Hollis from having to remember a completely new spell list for another character class.

As Friday grew closer, Hollis was increasingly glad for this decision.

She still worried about it.

Before she had time to register how it'd happened so quickly, Hollis found herself in the kitchen on Friday afternoon putting the finishing touches on one of two different kinds of cupcakes: strawberry with lemon icing. Their counterparts, chocolate with chocolate icing (always a winner), were already iced and ready in a plastic carrier.

The half pan of vegan cupcakes she'd attempted from a boxed mix she'd found at Kroger was in the trash. The way they'd turned out, it was the kindest place for them.

Hollis's tongue peeked out from between her lips as she concentrated on piping. She loved how the icing sugar sparkled in the late-afternoon light, which shone in through two wide kitchen windows: one of the perks of living in an old, skinny townhome built long before it was standard for every house to have electricity. Straightening up and rolling her shoulders, she glanced across the countertop again, eyeing the clock on the stove. 5:07 p.m.

Iffy was planning to pick her up at five thirty, early enough to make sure they had time to get through traffic, locate Gloria's mom's apartment, and find a parking space on the street by six. She had twenty-three minutes to finish the cupcakes and double-check her tote bag for the third time, just in case.

When she was about halfway done decorating the pink cupcakes with light yellow icing, the kitchen door swung open and Hollis's mom walked in, her salt-and-pepper hair in an unraveling bun and half a banana browning in one hand. She looked tired in a way she only ever did at the start of the school year, when she was adjusting back to being Ms. Merritt, Creative Writing and Theater Teacher at Holmes High School, instead of Donna or Mom. At first, when she and Hollis's dad were newly divorced, Hollis had worried that her mom's exhaustion meant she, Hollis, had done something wrong. But now, nearly six years later, she knew it would just last a few weeks and then everything would even out, regardless of anything Hollis did or didn't do.

With a heavy thud, Donna dropped her bag on the kitchen table and ditched the banana beside it.

"Smells good in here, Hols." Her mom waltzed over—that was how she moved, like a dreamy old lady, dancing wherever she went—and leaned her head on Hollis's shoulder. Her cheek was warm enough that Hollis could feel it against her neck.

"Thanks," said Hollis. "Just baking some cupcakes. Don't worry, I saved you two of each." She nodded in the direction of the other counter, where four of her less-pretty cupcakes were stashed in an open Tupperware. "I need to take the rest tonight."

"Oh?" Her mother leaned a hip against the edge of the counter. "What's tonight?"

Hollis hesitated, debating whether or not to tell her. She decided that here, in their familiar kitchen with its dated wood cabinets and rattly fridge (covered from top to bottom in years of Hollis's art from school), she felt safe enough to voice the truth. At least some of it.

"I've got a thing," she said.

"Yeah? What kind of thing?" This was how her mother pried. There was nothing nagging in her tone; she was genuinely interested.

Hollis sighed.

"I'm going to go play a game with some girls," she said. "That Secrets & Sorcery game. I found a new group without—I mean, at least it *seems* like it doesn't have—any creeps. I think it's going to be a better fit."

"Hey, that's good. That's good."

There was something else in her mom's voice.

Hollis tried to pin it down as she scooped up a fresh spoonful of frosting. *"What?"*

"Hmm?"

"Hmmmmm?" Hollis stopped and looked over at her mom. It had been just the two of them for so long that Hollis could always tell when she wanted to say more but was holding back. "What else?"

"Oh, nothing." Her mom waved her hands dismissively.

Hollis pursed her lips. *"Mom."*

"No, no," her mom said, but then continued, her voice teasing and light, "I just think it's a little dorky, Hols, is all."

Hollis blinked. Part of her wanted to protest. The rest of her wanted to agree.

Instead of responding, she sighed and went back to her frosting. Her eyes slid sideways to the clock again. 5:23 p.m. Seven minutes.

"I have to finish this," she said, a little shorter than she probably should have. "My ride is on her way."

"Hollis." The sound of her mom's footsteps came closer.

Hollis's eyes remained stubbornly on her work. "What."

"Hollis."

She looked up, embarrassed for a reason she couldn't entirely place. "What?"

"Very seriously, if you're into it, I'm into it." Her mom squeezed her shoulder, lingering close just long enough for Hollis to catch the shift of her features from playful to earnest. The kitchen brought this out in her sometimes, and she transformed into not Ms. Merritt or even Mom but Single-Mother-Trying-Her-Best-with-a-Child-Her-Ex-Husband-Often-Called-*Challenging*. Hollis was sure it had something to do with all the memories baked into the place. "And I'm proud of you for putting yourself out there. I know how hard it is."

Hollis went quiet, covering her relief by finishing the icing on her last cupcake. *She* wasn't even sure if she was into it, but she was pretty sure she wanted to be. For now, that was enough.

"Thanks," she said, and slid over the emptied bowl of icing. Her mom always liked to lick the spoon. "It's tart. The icing, I mean. It's lemon."

"But you're sweet enough to make up for it." Her mom bumped her hip against Hollis's.

Hollis snorted a laugh. "Wow, and you think Secrets & Sorcery is dorky."

Her mom winked and picked up the bowl. "Let me know how it goes, okay? Break a leg, kiddo."

"So."

Iffy Elliston side-eyed Hollis from the driver's seat of a copper-colored Honda Accord that was at least two years older than either of them. There were rust spots over the tires. Hollis had been afraid bits of the car would fall off when she slammed the door.

"Are you excited?"

"What?" responded Hollis, and then, immediately after, "Oh. Yeah." She *was* listening, but she was also thinking about at least three other things (how the cupcakes would fare as they went over the upcoming pothole; whether she'd remembered her copy of the *Player Handbook*; whether Iffy being three minutes late would ruin their chances of finding a street parking spot that wasn't several blocks away), and so it took her a moment to sort out which thing she was meant to be talking about out loud. "Really excited. And also nervous."

"Girl." Iffy looked over at her fully, her natural curls tossed in the breeze from her open window (the Accord's air-conditioning didn't work). "Why on earth."

Hollis never needed a reason to be nervous. But she had one

today, at least. She looked away, stomach churning. "I'm new. I don't want to mess it up."

"You can't *mess up* Secrets & Sorcery," Iffy said, a grin ghosting across her lips as she shook her head. "We're making it all up."

She had a point. Hollis shrugged, fiddling with the hem of her shirt.

"I mean, I know. Rationally." Rationality hardly ever stopped Hollis's worrying.

"Unless you think you've got a bum imagination or something?"

"No." Well. "Well, I mean—"

"I'm kidding, Hollis." This was the first time Iffy had said her name out loud. The sound of it smoothed away part of the edginess Hollis felt. Iffy's laugh filled the front seats as she flipped on her turn signal. "I think you're good."

Hollis looked over at Iffy. Though her eyes were back on the road as they crossed the bridge over the river, out of Kentucky and into Ohio, she was smiling. It was the sort of smile that made Hollis smile too, involuntarily.

Maybe she *was* good—or, at least, she could be—with Iffy.

4
SESSION ZERO

WHATEVER AMOUNT OF comfort Hollis had started to feel in Iffy's car vanished as soon as they parked it (a block and a half away from Gloria's place).

Iffy carried in one of the two flimsy cupcake trays. Hollis's bag was crammed so full with dice and pencils and paper and her copy of the handbook that it kept slipping down her shoulder and threatening to knock the other tray out of her hands.

When they made it up the stairs to the door of the apartment, they found a note.

Adventuring Party—Come in, thanks, G.

Iffy pushed the door open and went inside, which left Hollis on the landing alone for a moment. Like the apartments in Covington, this unit was one of perhaps four subdivided from an old Victorian house. And like many in Covington, this Victorian was in a state of regretful decay, obviously well cared for but old enough that even attentive stewardship couldn't keep the sag on the side porch from showing or the brick walls from needing a fresh coat of hunter-green paint. But despite the similarities, something about the apartment being in Cincinnati made it feel different.

Hollis gave one last look over her shoulder into the hot Ohio night.

It was the last view of relative calm she had. Taking a deep breath, Hollis stepped over the threshold into the apartment and pulled the door closed behind her.

"Gloria! *Gloria!* They're here! The other two girls!"

A head of messy dark hair popped out around a corner farther into the apartment, down a short hallway. Just as quickly, it disappeared, then reappeared all at once in a rush of limbs running right toward them. The younger girl from Gloria's Instagram rocketed into the living room, moving faster than should be allowed. She screeched to a halt a little too close to Hollis.

"I'm Fran!" said Fran, almost as loudly as all her caps-locking and key-smashing made her read when she typed. "Which one of you is Iffy and which one of you is Hollis?"

"Uh," said Hollis.

"Iffy," said Iffy, raising one hand from the cupcake tray she carried.

"So *you're* Hollis," Fran said, pointing.

A beat passed before Hollis replied, with a grimace, "Yep."

"Great, well." Fran turned on her bare heel, heading off again, back to where she'd appeared from. "Come on, we've been waiting for you."

Iffy shot Hollis a glance that said she wasn't sure what to make of the personified caps-lock key smash that was Fran. The look Hollis returned made Iffy laugh into the collar of her shirt as they followed the younger girl through the living room, past the kitchen, and down a short hallway. On the left, through an open doorway, was the dining room, where the rest of the group had gathered. Hollis's heart and head raced too fast at the sudden sight of so many strangers to register much more about the room than the round table they were all milling around.

"See," shouted Fran. "They're here!"

"At last," said a girl with dark blond hair. She sat near the far wall, her arms crossed over her chest.

"Welcome, gals," said another girl—Gloria, Hollis noted in a daze, recognizing her from Instagram. She was even more stunning in person.

"That one is Iffy—"

"Hey, Ai, get in here," shouted the blond one.

"—and the other is Hollis, obviously—"

Hollis swallowed.

"What did I miss?" a voice called back from where the hallway continued farther on.

"It's good to meet you," said Gloria, smiling.

"—and *those*—"

"Are they here? Tell them not to take my seat," shouted the voice from the other room.

"—are my CUPCAKES!" Fran finished her introduction and rounded on Hollis with a frenzied grin.

The blond girl was standing up. "Here, Ai, I'll take—"

"Which flavors did you bring?"

Hollis blinked down at the demanding middle schooler who had a hand on one hip and an accusatory look in her eyes.

Across the table, Gloria sighed wearily. "Francesca, *calm down*, they're not just for you."

"—this seat here and you can take—"

"Yeah, Hollis, what flavor am I holding? I know one is—"

Hollis's eyes snapped to Iffy, who was shifting her hold on the cupcake box, and—

"I mean, they're *basically* for me; it was *my* idea to have them."

"—*your* seat, Your Highness."

"Chocolate, but Hollis must have those, because these look—"

Fran screeched in delight. *"What did you say?"*

Hollis's heart was racing, she noted dimly, to the rapid-fire pace of the conversation.

"Chocolate and what?!"

"I think she said strawberry something."

"Fran, *sit*." Gloria's voice cut through the din. "They're not going anywhere. They're cupcakes. They don't have legs."

Hollis's legs itched beneath her, urging her to run.

"But *I* do, and I want at least five!"

"Thank *God*." A person appeared from the other end of the hallway. Hollis recognized Aini from the shock of color on top of her head—bright teal today, a change from the red in her last Instagram post. Aini sank down into the seat the blond girl had just vacated. "I'm so ready to get started."

"*That* is the most sensible thing anyone has said in the last five minutes. Everyone, come sit." Gloria spoke with such a calm authority that everyone—even Hollis, who had been hovering frozen in the doorway—listened and went quiet. Hollis put her tray of cupcakes down on the table and eased into an armless wooden chair between Iffy and the girl with the dirty-blond hair, whom she recognized as Maggie now that the pounding in her chest was beginning to subside.

To calm it further, she unpacked her things: her notebook, a good pen, and her favorite pencil, in case she needed to draw. Everyone else had unpacked, too, and the surface of the table was scattered with gaming gear: the core rulebooks; notebooks and pens in various shades of ink (Fran's side of the table was particularly colorful); bags and boxes of dice; phones with their faces turned down or, in Maggie's case, upturned and flashing with Instagram notifications; a trifold screen on Gloria's end, behind which she sorted unseen notes and who-knew-what-else.

The round oak (or oak-finish) table didn't *look* like the sort of place where something extraordinary was about to happen. It just looked like a crowded, cozy, middle-class dining room. Hollis wasn't sure whether that made her feel better or worse. She swallowed, which did nothing to help her decide, and looked tentatively across the table.

"The cupcakes are, uh," she said quietly as she put her tote bag on the floor beside her chair. "Strawberry with lemon icing, by the way."

Fran, who sat directly across from her, answered by squealing and taking five.

"Okay, okay, I'll take one too," said Gloria. There wasn't really a head of the table, as it was round, but the way Gloria drew attention made it clear that if there *were* a head of the table, it would be exactly where she was sitting. Hollis couldn't be sure whether it was the calming cream paint of the walls or Gloria's gentle, close-lipped smile that made her shoulders start to relax as she settled in. "Should we do a roll call so we can put faces to screen names?"

"Yeah," said Iffy, shrugging out of her jacket. "Though I'm going to guess this one"—she pointed across the table—"is Fran."

"How'd you know?" Fran asked through a mouthful of cupcake.

Beside Hollis, Maggie snorted.

"So, yes," said Gloria. She gestured to her left. "This creature is my little sister, Fran. No, Francesca, *please* do not talk with that much food in your mouth, I just wiped down the table. And I'm Gloria, your Secret Keeper." She turned to her right, nodding for the next person.

"I'm Iffy," said Iffy, giving a short wave.

Hollis hesitated two full breaths before she said, "Uh, Hollis."

"Maggie," said Maggie. In person, her petite frame and moony blue eyes were as perfect as they were in her Instagram pictures. Her outfit and makeup were put together in a way Hollis had never seen outside of social media. Out of all the girls, Maggie looked the least like someone who would want to spend her Friday night playing a pretend fantasy game with a bunch of other nerds. In fact, she didn't look nerdy at all. Somehow Maggie's presence at the table felt a little like a prank. Hollis resisted the sudden urge to squirm, wishing she were sitting next to anyone else.

"And, *obviously*, I'm Aini." Aini finished the round of introductions with a mock bow, and the way she said her name made Hollis believe it *should* be obvious to anyone, even someone who hadn't stalked her Instagram.

"Right, well," said Gloria, "let's get started."

"Please," said Aini.

"Mmmpfh," sprayed Fran.

Hollis only blinked. From what she remembered of the start of the boys' game back in freshman year, first sessions were nothing but pure disorganized disasters as the players fumbled through the rules of the game. She steeled herself. There was already such a chaos of noise and newness around her; she wasn't sure she could take much more.

But when Gloria spoke, it was calmly, like she had a plan.

"So what I like to do whenever I start a new game, especially with first-time players, is to get everyone in the group together to run character ideas," said Gloria. She glanced in turn around the table. "I'm sure you hear a lot on the internet and stuff about party balance and filling roles, but I don't think that's super important. What I *do* think is important is for us all to be on the same page in terms of inter-party vibes."

"Oh, smart," said Iffy. "So we don't wind up with, you know, five moody bards from the South Coast."

Hollis's lips pressed into a line at the mention of bards.

"Exactly," said Gloria. "Though, honestly, I've always wanted to play an all-bard campaign, like they're a boy band on tour or something. Anyway, yes, that, and to make sure we don't have any weird lone-wolf characters and we all play nicely."

"Or nice-*ish*." Fran grinned devilishly, her teeth as iced as the cupcake she clutched.

"I told you she'd be trouble," Gloria said to them all. Hollis could also tell it was a warning; it held the same weight as her mom's teacher voice. "So. What is everyone thinking about playing?"

"I'm going to play a barbarian," Fran volunteered first, crumpling two empty cupcake wrappers together in her fist with gusto. "Her name is Mercy Grace, which is ironic, you know, because she's trollkin and like eight-foot-five-hundred. Oh, and she likes to *smash stuff*."

Fran gave a satisfied smile, dropped the cupcake wrappers on the table like a mic, and leaned back again. Hollis and the rest of the girls waited for more detail, but after a few quiet breaths, it appeared that was all there was to Mercy Grace.

"I'll be playing a bard," Aini chimed in next. "A boy, because I can't resist the lesbian urge to gender-bend, okay? He's half fae and half human—and Brown, of course. He plays a lute, but I think that's less for his magic and more for fun."

Beneath the table, Hollis wiggled her big toe inside her right shoe. She had been hoping to avoid bards altogether.

"I'm going to play Tanwyn Silva," Maggie said next, but her voice changed as she spoke—it went both deeper and softer, with a round whisper to her *S*'s. In a heartbeat, it was like Maggie was someone else, from another place entirely. "An albino faun rogue from the Fernglen in the Third Realm, Lott's Valley. She's a sneak and a thief, but she's got her heart in the right place. She's a folk hero among her fold—the whole steal-from-the-rich, give-to-the-poor thing."

Hollis considered Maggie as she spoke. The perfect shine of her lip gloss didn't seem to belong to someone who would talk about their S&S character in such detail. She'd certainly done more research than Hollis. Behind pursed lips, Hollis's teeth clenched.

"Oh, I like it," said Aini, apparently not surprised at all. "So she's already had a little adventuring experience?"

"Yeah. Or, well—" Maggie looked to Gloria.

"Yes, that's fine," said the Secret Keeper. "I was going to start everyone at Level 3 anyway, so we're not so squishy as a whole."

"Good," said Iffy, "because I was thinking I'd play a river elf sorceress, but I haven't figured out much of a background yet. I wanted to see how I could hook her into the world."

"Well," Gloria said thoughtfully, "we're going to be starting the adventure in Fallon's Landing, which is a delta valley by the Cerulean Sea. The city has a guard, the Cerulean Guard—I know, real original—which relies heavily on magic users."

"That could work." Iffy began to make neatly lined notes in the small notebook she'd brought with her.

Hollis, on the other hand, didn't think that could work.

She was supposed to play a sorceress.

Iffy must have caught the gentle panic settling across Hollis's features as she glanced up. She raised an eyebrow at her.

"You okay, Hollis?"

"What? Oh, uh, yeah. Fine. You know, I'm not sure what I want to play, actually."

This was nicer than saying *I was going to play a sorceress from the Cerulean Coast, too, but I can't now that you are.* Already, Iffy had been too nice for Hollis to say something like that. But this had the unfortunate side effect of making Hollis look like she hadn't given any thought to the game they were about to play. Like she didn't care as much as they did.

Her heartbeat ratcheted up. She looked down at the table, willing her cheeks not to turn red. With the nail of her thumb, she began worrying a divot in the wood.

"I think I just want to fill in what, uh. What we might need. For the group."

"Hollis, you don't have to fill any gaps." Gloria's voice was reassuring but firm. "What do you *want* to play?"

"I'm really . . ." She should dump the cupcakes out of their tins and run now. Hollis swallowed, then finished a beat too late, "Open. To anything."

"Really, girl," she heard Iffy say from beside her. "You can play whatever you want."

But Hollis didn't want reassurance. Her fingers closed hard around her pencil. It slipped where she held it, slick with sudden sweat. Despite her best efforts, color rose in her cheeks, and she was pretty sure if she didn't keep her eyes on this one exact spot on the page of her unlined notebook, she might start babbling about Alvena. Or crying. Or both.

What she wanted was an out.

There was an excruciating beat of silence, and then: "We need a healer." It took a moment for Hollis to realize Aini was speaking to her. She chanced a glance up from her notebook, flicking her gaze toward Aini. She caught Hollis's eye and held it. Something wobbled in Hollis's chest. "What about a paladin?"

"*Oh.*" Hollis hadn't thought about that before.

"That's a cool idea," said Iffy. "Like a knight. They have high magic and high strength, usually, so they're good for healing *and* for kicking ass."

"Yeah!" yelled Fran. Her hoard of strawberry cupcakes finished, she had switched to chocolate. Dark icing lined the corners of her lips.

Hollis's only frame of reference for paladins was the boy from Games-A-Lot who had tried (and failed) to spare the goblins, and the time Chris had considered playing one but had ultimately gone with a rogue because paladins were not, in his words, "murder-y enough" to keep up in a game run by Landon. But from what the other girls were saying, a paladin sounded like it might actually be the right fit for her.

"Maybe she could also be in the Cerulean Guard?" Her question was tentative, aimed in equal parts at Iffy and Gloria.

Iffy nodded. "We could be in the same regiment," she offered. "Instant connection. Backstory gold."

"Yeah." Hollis's racing heart slowed slightly. "Yeah, I could probably play a paladin."

"It sounds like you already are." Aini looked smug.

"She could be an elf, too," Iffy suggested.

"I don't know," said Hollis. "What about a human?"

"You could be anything in the Eight Realms, and you want to be a human?" Aini glanced at her sidelong, a certain sparkle in her eyes. "Bold choice."

Hollis hadn't thought of it like that—but now that Aini had said it, she wanted it to be true. "Uh. I guess?"

"That deserves a cupcake," said Fran, shoving a strawberry one in her direction.

Hollis laughed and accepted it, taking a bite. Unlike Fran, she chewed it completely before replying, "Thanks."

"Look at you, already working as a team," hummed Gloria. "I'm so proud." She began passing out copies of printed character sheets from the pile beside her. "Okay, okay. What I like to do next, usually, is—"

Before she could finish, Fran grabbed the canvas drawstring pouch in front of her with icing-sticky fingers, opened it, and turned it upside down. About twenty dice in different sizes, shapes, and colors clattered across the table, rolling out like a resin tidal wave.

"Oof, kid, you're going to wake up Miss Virginia again," said Gloria, exasperation coloring her words. She looked to the other girls. "She's the woman in 1B. I'm her carer while I'm on a gap year. She's very sweet, but she gets cranky when Franny wakes her up after six p.m." Her lips pulled into a tired smile as she looked back to her sister. "Which is *always*.

"Franny's right, though. Let's get out our dice and start rolling some stats. Record them in the appropriate boxes on the character sheets I just gave you. Fran, can you work with Hollis and Maggie, since they're both new?"

"You know, I'm new too," Fran complained. "Technically."

"Yes, but I also know you've read the handbook cover to cover at least ten times." Gloria arched an authoritative eyebrow. "Help the new ones."

"Yes, *Mom*," she sighed, and then shoved Aini beside her. "Switch seats with me."

"No way," said Aini. "This is my spot. From now unto forever."

"Rude," Fran said, then started half dragging, half scooting her chair around the table. Hollis scooted away from Maggie to make space. How she'd gotten paired up with the two most intimidating members of the group, she couldn't say.

"All right, kids," Fran said when she came to rest between Maggie and Hollis. "Please tell me you have dice."

"I—yes," said Hollis, fishing in her tote bag. Somehow—stupidly, she tutted inside her head—she had forgotten to get her set out. It was still in the small, rectangular plastic box they were sold in. A set of seven dice: one each with twenty, twelve, eight, six, and four sides, and two with ten sides, for rolls that required a percentage. She had borrowed them last weekend from Chris for the Games-A-Lot game. These particular dice were neon green with white swirls and numbers painted in red, like a nineties Christmas.

Maggie's pearly, purple-numbered dice were still in their box too. She rattled them for Fran.

"Okay, good." Fran took a swig of her Coke (it seemed Aini had made good on her Discord promise), wiped her mouth with the back of her hand, and nodded. There was a grim edge to it. Gloria's easy, leading charm was clearly not something her younger sister had inherited. "So what we need to do now is roll for all your stats. Please tell me you know what stats are."

Maggie and Hollis exchanged a look, neither sure whether the question was rhetorical or not.

"Well?" pressed Fran.

"Stats are statistics," said Maggie. "The numbers that represent your character's abilities."

"Yes." Fran clapped, once and sharp. "At least you know that. Bonus points if you know what the six main stats are."

"Uh, yes," said Hollis, with a tentative look at Maggie for confirmation. "Fortitude, which is, like, your ability to withstand physical demands. Strength, which is obvious. Dexterity—how nimble or sneaky you are. Then Intellect, which is your intelligence, and Intuition, for stuff like common sense and being able to read people, and Charisma, how influential or charming you can be."

"Give the girl a cupcake," Fran said approvingly. She took one for herself instead. "So, we need to roll six scores, one for each ability. We're going to do that by taking your d6—that's how people who know what's up talk about their dice, by the way, *dee-six*, so *please* don't let me hear you say 'six-sided dice' or 'six-sider'—and rolling it three times. If the total is below six, you can reroll. Let's do that now."

"Here," interjected Aini from the other side of Maggie. Hollis hadn't realized she'd been listening as she did her own rolls. "You two can borrow some of my d6's. It makes it more fun if you roll them all at once."

Aini slid several mismatched d6's across the table. Hollis took the two Maggie handed her: one glittery navy and one striped through with rainbow colors, like an LGBTQIA+ Pride flag.

"Should we do it together?" Maggie asked.

That a girl like Maggie would be rolling dice at all still seemed outlandish to Hollis. But she needed this game—and these girls. If she was going to prove to Chris that she could fit into *his* game, she had to fit into *this* one first.

The thought of actually doing so opened up something in her

chest—something expansive, exciting, *terrifying*. Her face flushed with it.

"Yeah, sure," she replied. "Why not?"

Hollis's stomach flopped as she rattled the dice between her palms. In not-quite-unison, Maggie rolled and Hollis followed. Three dice clattered to the table in front of her.

"Ooh, bad luck." Maggie shook her head, adding up her dice. "That's an 8."

Hollis's luck was better, with a total of 14. She grinned at her borrowed dice.

"Nice," said Maggie, nodding. "Let's go again?"

The clattering of their dice joined the clattering of Aini's and Iffy's from opposite sides of the table. Maggie had a run of bad rolls to start off, but she ended by rolling an 18—the highest possible roll, Fran said, a hint of envy in her voice.

"Soooo," she drawled, taking the wrapper off yet another cupcake. "Now you match the numbers with the ability levels you think they would have—you know, what they'd be good or bad at in character."

Hollis wasn't sure what her yet-unnamed paladin might be good or bad at, but putting her scores into place would at least help figure out those aspects of her character. She did know to put her highest score in Charisma; it was supposed to fuel her spell-casting ability, since her magic would work on the strength of her conviction. Playing a high-Charisma character would be a challenge, but Hollis tried not to worry about it now. She worked down from there, her scores descending from Strength, to Dexterity, to Fortitude, to Intellect, which left her very lowest score for Intuition.

That, at least, felt like it wouldn't be much of a stretch. Hollis Beckwith didn't think of herself as the most intuitive of girls.

Fran talked both her and Maggie through the rest of the numbers part, all their ability score improvements and extra perks. The hardest part was figuring out the modifiers each stat gave them, but Fran impressed on them that it was also the most essential. The ability modifier was what they'd add to their rolls during the game to determine the success or failure of their actions.

As a paladin—a holy warrior—Hollis's character would need a god to follow, too. Without overthinking too much, Hollis flipped to a table of the gods and goddesses in the handbook and found a cool name: the Just and Terrible Mistress. She was the goddess of the sea, which made sense for the seaside Cerulean Guard, and her holy symbol was pretty (a stylized symmetrical pair of waves crashing in on themselves), and so Hollis wrote it onto her character sheet.

When it came time to pick out her equipment, she waved to catch Gloria's attention. The Secret Keeper stood and approached, leaning over the back of Hollis's seat.

"Hmm?" Gloria hummed.

Hollis took a deep breath. "I was looking at the starting equipment here, and I was wondering, uh. I don't see it on here, but I was wondering if maybe I could have plate armor for my paladin?"

She wasn't sure where the idea had come from, but it had stuck in her mind as soon as Aini suggested playing a paladin. Though Hollis still knew very little about her character, she was absolutely sure she wore plate armor. Maybe it was the contrast with Alvena, who only wore a fancy robe. Maybe she just wanted to draw it. Either way, it was important. Hollis could feel it in her bones.

Gloria tapped a finger against her red lips, considering. "Full plate?"

"Um, yes. Please."

"That's a little high-level to start, I think," Gloria said. "It wouldn't scale well with the rest of the party."

"Ah, that's fine." Hollis frowned at her character sheet. "I understand."

"No, no, wait," said Gloria. She leaned down closer to Hollis. It gave the impression that their conversation was just as close, just as private. "Maybe we can compromise. What if . . ." She was quiet for a moment, her head tilting to the side. "I know you're not sure about your character's backstory yet, but what if we gave them a really nice breastplate—which is like baby full plate? It will scale better with a bunch of Level 3s, and it can be a nice way to explore some of their history. What do you think?"

Hollis bit her lip, mulling it over. "Can I have time to think about it?"

"Yes, Hollis, of course." Her voice and smile were warm. "You can always message me on Discord if you have other questions about it."

"Yeah, okay," said Hollis, her spirits lifting.

"Okay, okay," said Gloria, standing. She raised her voice to address the whole group. "Aside from spells—casters, please pick those before next Friday—is everyone done with their character sheets?"

"Aye, aye, captain!" cried Fran, who had somehow rolled her character stats and filled in all her information in a third of the time it had taken Hollis.

"Yeah, I think I got it," said Aini. "You good, Iffy?"

"Yep, all set here."

"And Fran got us set up, too," said Maggie, gesturing between herself and Hollis.

"Nice work, everyone." Gloria took her seat at the head of the table—or rather, made her empty seat the head of the table again by filling it. She clapped her hands once. "I'd like to pull from your backstories for the campaign, so check in with me sometime soon about what I can use or if anything is off-limits. Otherwise, that's everything I needed from you tonight."

"Oh, *dang*," grumbled Fran. "That's it? No teaser for next week?"

"Fran, we're not using a prewritten module." Gloria frowned. "I still have to write the adventure."

"You can make it up on the fly!" she protested.

"No." Gloria shook her head. "Plus, these girls still have to drive home. Not everyone lives here like you do."

Fran, visibly deflated, let out a "Fiiine" in response.

"This was really cool, though, Gloria." Iffy stood from the table and stretched out her long limbs. "I've never played a game with a starting session like this."

"Yeah," said Hollis. "This was great."

She tried again to compare tonight with the half session she'd played at Games-A-Lot, but the sessions had so little in common. She already knew more about all these characters than she'd known about any of the ones she'd played with then—even Maxx the Bard, whose sole character trait seemed to be Hit On Things. She knew even more about them than she knew about Herbie Derbie, Chris's first S&S character, who'd been something of a legend at their lunch table for the last four years. That same expansive feeling grew in her chest again, swelling warmly. For the first time that night, Hollis felt sure she was on the right path. She couldn't wait to tell Chris about her paladin. Maybe they could even brainstorm about her breastplate together.

"Really great," she echoed.

"Thanks in no small part to me, of course," added Fran, jumping up from her seat with a broad grin.

Gloria started to pack away her things, which signaled everyone else to do the same. The room filled with shuffling as Gloria asked, "So we'll start with session one next week?"

"Yes."

"Yeah."

"Sure."

"YEE."

"Um, yeah."

"Wonderful." Gloria smiled warmly at them all. "I'll see you all then."

"Thanks, Gloria," said Hollis. She tried to make sure she sounded as grateful as she felt.

"No problem, Hollis." She beamed. "I'm happy you made it to us."

"Same," said Aini, nodding fervently.

"I mean, you brought cupcakes, at least," added Fran with a shrug.

By the time Hollis followed Iffy out of the apartment, she couldn't wait for it to be Friday again.

"Is it just me or was that really cool?"

Beside Iffy, Hollis grinned. "It wasn't just you."

"Good." In the empty street, Iffy's voice sounded pleasantly loud, nice and round and a little bit Southern. "Because that was the coolest game of Secrets & Sorcery I've ever played, and we haven't even played yet."

"Right?" In the dark of the night, Hollis floated a tentative grin at Iffy. "And I'm glad our characters will know each other."

Iffy made it to the driver's-side car door, unlocking it manually; the Accord wasn't the kind of car that had an automatic key fob. Hollis waited on the passenger side for Iffy to unlock the door from within.

All of a sudden, the slap of running feet sounded against the sidewalk behind her, then came to a stop as quickly as they'd begun.

"Hey, Hollis." Hollis glanced over her shoulder to see a blur of brown skin and a white T-shirt take shape in the darkness. *Aini.* "You forgot this."

Aini held out a small plastic box of dice, balanced in the center of her palm.

"Oh, uh." Hollis reached out one hand to accept them, the other still on the handle of Iffy's passenger door, waiting for the click of the lock. As her fingers closed around the box, they brushed against Aini's palm. Involuntarily, Hollis smiled. "Thanks."

"Oh, uh," said Aini back, grinning. "You're welcome. You can't leave your dice behind. You'll need those every game, you know. Rookie mistake."

"Yeah, well," Hollis said. She was glad, at least, that it was Aini and not Fran, whose insistence on eating another round of cupcakes when Hollis divided them out at the end of the night made her seriously concerned about the current state of the younger girl's sugar high. "Now I know. And they're not really my dice, anyway."

"Oh yeah? I definitely saw you rolling them all night."

"Loaners," she said. "From my boyfriend."

"*Ah.*" Aini's hand rose to her chest as if she were wounded. She ran her other hand through her teal hair, curls falling back into perfect not-place as she moved. Her hair looked even cooler up close. Hollis wanted to draw it. She had the exact right shade of pencil for the teal. "Must have been why you were rolling so crap all night."

"*Excuse* me." Hollis laughed. "I rolled perfectly average. Above average, in fact."

"Average is cute, but I rolled two 18s."

"Oh yeah?"

Aini quirked a confident eyebrow. "Yeah. So you better watch out, Hollis Beckwhat."

"It's Beckwith."

"It's Amin-Shaw." Her smile was bright white in the night. "I'll see you next Friday, Hollis."

And as quickly as she'd come, Aini Amin-Shaw was off again, jogging back toward the old Victorian and dodging around the late-blooming rosebush in front of Miss Virginia's apartment.

Iffy's passenger-side door creaked and then opened into Hollis's thick thigh. Iffy's voice drifted out from inside. "Are you getting in or what?"

"Yeah, sorry." Hollis watched as Aini disappeared into the rectangle of light in the Castañedas' doorway. "I forgot my dice."

5

CHARACTER CHOICES

BY THE TIME Sunday rolled around, lazy and never long enough, as Sundays always were, Hollis still hadn't stopped thinking about session zero with Gloria and the girls.

She was supposed to be doing her homework for Ecology, the class seniors took when they were too tired to take any other science. But instead of drawing out a diagram of the water cycle when she sat down at her desk, Hollis drew characters in her notebook.

That was the most productive thing she'd settled over the weekend—her character. Her name was Honoria Steadmore. She was twenty-one, young for a captain in the Cerulean Guard. She came from a family that was the fantasy version of upper middle class. Hollis had briefly considered making her poor, but Hollis was already poor in real life. It seemed only fair to give Honoria spending money if she could, even if all of it was imaginary.

In the short biography she'd typed up for her, Hollis had kept details about Honoria's life brief. For one, she remembered Maxx the Bard's player spending the first fifteen minutes of that dreadful Games-A-Lot session talking about Maxx's tragic and isolating backstory, and she didn't want to do that herself. For another, keeping the backstory open would give Gloria more to pull from; she'd given the Secret Keeper free rein to use whatever she wanted to for the game's plot, however big or small a part it might be.

But mostly, Hollis kept the biography short because she wasn't a writer. She was an artist, and so she'd spent her weekend drawing a portrait to include with her biography when she posted it into the Google Doc Gloria had shared on the Discord server.

Like Hollis, Honoria was white and had curly brown hair, but Honoria wore hers in a short bob with blunt bangs across her forehead. She had blue eyes (which were more exciting to draw than Hollis's own brown ones) and fat, freckled cheeks that always had a little flush to them, just like the tip of her nose. Both girls were round, but Honoria was round in the softer, gentler way Gloria was—the exact way Hollis wasn't.

Because Honoria was part of the Cerulean Guard, Hollis made that her primary palette color. She wore it in a sash around her waist and on the tunic under her armor. Because it contrasted nicely, Hollis had also given Honoria's palette a deep, rich red, which showed up in leggings and in the cloth she wore around her neck like a bandana. Chris had advised her on what sort of sword she should carry (talking her out of a war hammer), but in the portrait, she left it sheathed at Honoria's side, hilt just peeking out from behind her wide hips.

The crowning piece of Honoria's design, though, was her breastplate armor. Hollis had gotten it approved specially in a direct message with Gloria. It was a family heirloom, made of a special metal—cobaltril—that the Steadmores had mined many generations ago. Over the years, they had tucked away small bits of the precious metal—prized throughout the Realms for its strength and striking blue coloration—and combined it with copper to forge a piece of armor. Since the fine art of cobaltril mining and crafting had been long forgotten, the armor was priceless.

Hollis had spent a solid five hours working out the intricate inlay of the two different metals. She'd even broken out her metallic watercolors—a Christmas gift from last year that had been too pretty, and too costly, for her to touch since—to color the half-length portrait she had drawn. On the stark white page, the shimmering blue and copper shone especially nicely.

Honoria was Hollis but better. She loved that about making art. While *Hollis* could never be as cool as Gloria and the girls, *Honoria* was definitely as cool as everyone else in their adventuring party.

Now, as Hollis sat doodling at her desk, the Honoria she sketched was much less meticulously drafted—more cartoony, less exact, except for the key details of her breastplate. She penciled in Iffy's river elf sorceress, whom Iffy had named Nereida. Though the thought of approaching Iffy at school still made Hollis's belly ache, the pair of them had been DMing on Discord since Friday night. They weren't friends, probably, not yet—but Hollis thought they could be one day. She already knew more about Nereida—and Iffy—than she did about anyone else in the group.

Hollis drew Nereida the way she imagined her from Iffy's excited messages, making her tall and lean like Iffy herself but distant in a way Iffy wasn't. Carefully selecting a pencil, she shaded a light touch of cerulean into both women's clothing.

The pair of them looked natural together. She was glad Honoria had Nereida. She was also glad she had Iffy—even if it was mostly on the internet.

Though she ached to flesh them out further by adding details and shading, Hollis shook herself. She had homework to finish, and it was getting dark outside. The dinette chair groaned beneath her as she shifted, tucking her notebook and the S&S adventure away for another night.

Luckily for her, Honoria and Nereida weren't going anywhere. Their adventure was just beginning.

"I mean, paladins are cool and all," Landon said over his school lunch (peanut butter sandwich, Tater Tots, two ketchup packets, and white milk).

There was a *but* coming. Landon chewed it along with a mouthful of sandwich.

"*But* the rest sounds pretty dorky."

Hollis rolled her eyes.

"I mean, you're not playing, so," she started without thinking. She wanted to add *So you can take your "dorky" and shove it*. But Landon raised an eyebrow at her, and so she shrugged and ate another tot, letting her protest die on her tongue.

"Come on, Landon." Chris threw a pepperoni from his pizza—a luxury delivered each day by LaRosa's—at his face. It missed, flopping limply onto the chipped round table—one of several dozen crammed into the austere, not-entirely-clean cafeteria of Holmes High. Chris picked up the pepperoni and popped it into his mouth, leaving a circular grease stain on the tabletop. "Not everyone likes hack-and-slash all the time."

"Yeah, that's true," said Landon. "But the funny thing is, *you* do."

"I'm flattered, really, but I'm not everyone, I promise."

"Igor the Terrible has killed many men," said Landon, slipping into an accent worthy of Igor, Chris's barbarian character in the boys' current game. Usually, Hollis enjoyed Landon's game talk, albeit begrudgingly. Yes, he was kind of a tool, but when it came to Secrets & Sorcery, he had an eye for detail and a clear love for the game. Though she'd never admit it out loud, the obvious appreciation in Landon's voice whenever he talked about the boys' characters was one of the reasons she wanted to join their game. No matter what changed after graduation, she was confident Landon would make sure their game stayed the same. There was no way he'd let go of something he loved so much. And Hollis wanted in on that.

As if he could hear her thinking about him, Landon rounded his gaze on her, his smile wicked. "And one or two of them might have even deserved it."

"You should watch it, Landon," said Chris, "or Igor the Terrible will come for you next."

The conversation quickly branched into whether or not Igor, the Secrets & Sorcery character, could take Landon, the seventeen-year-old boy, in real life. Despite the obvious answer, Landon insisted he would triumph. Hollis's mind and eyes wandered.

On the other side of the cafeteria, sitting with a large group of people who looked like they were having a lot more fun than Hollis, was Iffy Elliston, mid-laugh, her slender hand covering her very white teeth. She swatted playfully at the arm of the person sitting beside her—a hulking jock with a winsome smile almost as bright as Iffy's. Whatever joke they had just shared was, apparently, hilarious. The table, so full it was clear the others sitting there had needed to pull up extra chairs to fit, overflowed with so much joy that even the dingy white of the concrete-brick walls behind it seemed brighter and more inviting.

The vibe at Hollis's table was so entirely different, it hung in the air like someone had cast a Thorn Cloud spell.

Maybe Iffy could somehow feel the way Hollis sank into her chair just thinking about the difference, because at the exact moment, she looked up. Her smile was still radiant and toothy. It was exactly the smile Hollis had imagined on the other side of all those Discord messages over the weekend. Iffy waved at Hollis across the room.

Hollis, without thinking, waved back.

"Yikes," said Landon.

Apparently the debate of Landon versus Igor had been either resolved or dropped, and now three additional pairs of eyes stared back at Iffy.

"Why's that weirdo waving over here?" asked Landon.

Hollis's head snapped in his direction, her eyes narrowed. *"Landon."*

"What? I'm not a transphobe, but—"

"Literally no one who says that *isn't* a transphobe." Iffy's friendly smile still shone bright in Hollis's mind as she blinked across the table at Landon.

"Whatever." Landon rolled his eyes. "But seriously, why's she looking over here?"

Chris was conspicuously quiet. Hollis glared at the side of his face before responding, "She's in my S&S game."

"Ooh, damn," said Marius.

"Chris, I'm telling you, dude," said Landon. "You better watch out or Hollis is going to turn into one of those weirdos too."

Hollis's face flushed hot, and she took a deep breath.

"Guys," said Chris, finally, after seeing the look on Hollis's face. "Axe it, for real."

But it had already happened. Even at this distance, these two worlds colliding left Hollis feeling uncomfortable and guilty. With the eyes of two tables on her, she couldn't escape it.

"You know what," said Hollis, "I have to go, actually." She stood, shoving her chair back with a screech. "I'll see you after school, Chris."

But Hollis didn't see Chris after school.

She didn't see Marius or Landon, either.

Instead of riding home with Chris in the Sentra, Hollis waited until the end of her mother's after-school theater program, drawing pictures of Honoria defending Nereida in battle and feeling horribly guilty about not doing a better job for Iffy in real life.

Because it was the second Friday she'd spent doing it, waiting for Iffy Elliston to text her those three little words (*hey i'm here*) from the driveway should have been easier.

It wasn't.

Last week, Hollis had cupcakes to keep her hands and mind busy in the time between school getting out and Iffy getting to her house.

Now she had no such distraction, so both her hands and her mind ran unchecked. Sitting at the kitchen dinette, in a chair the exact same as the one at her desk but somehow also entirely wrong, Hollis Beckwith was a blur of anxious motion.

With a frenetic energy she only got when she was both very excited and terribly nervous, Hollis drew in her notebook. She filled the page with the characters everyone had discussed last Friday, working off the biographies they'd pasted into the Google Doc during the week.

First was Maggie's albino faun, Tanwyn, a hooved half-human, half-goat woman. Hollis drew her draped in several layers of black shirts and cloaks, all in different states of fading from sun and use, like Maggie had described in her biography. When there were enough folds to hide anything a rogue might need to conceal, Hollis colored Tanwyn's eyes ruby red, just a shade darker than the flames of the campfire she sat beside.

Hollis had to Google what a half fae looked like (an especially handsome man, more or less) and what exactly a lute was (a small bent-up guitar) when she started on Aini's bard, his mouth hanging open mid-song as he played. Like Aini in real life, Hollis made the bard—Umber Dawnfast—the shortest member of the group. She borrowed a shade of brown close to Aini's own for Umber's skin, since she'd said he was Brown too, but at the highest parts of his features— the tip of his angular nose, the ridges of his pointed ears—she added a faint bluish glow, like a dramatic highlight, in a nod to the fae side of his ancestry. It peeked out through the V-neck of his navy-and-gold doublet, shining on the gentle curve of his collarbones.

Beside the bard, she drew Fran's hulking barbarian—Mercy Grace—clapping along to Umber's song. Fran's biography was the barest of them all (and mostly in caps lock, as Hollis had expected), so she took some liberties in her features, making sure to leave battle scars on her cheeks and muscular arms. One thing Fran did mention specifically was Mercy's love of collecting loot, which Hollis represented in the barbarian's clothes: nice trousers and a fancy tunic about a size and a half too small (on permanent, unwitting loan from a noble's wardrobe), as well as two intricate, bejeweled sandalwood hair combs tucked into Mercy's hair on either side of her tightly shaved undercut. Because she was part troll, her skin had a greenish cast and she towered a good foot and a half over Nereida, whom Hollis added sitting nearby in her understated but finely crafted Cerulean Guard sorceress's robe. The silver thread woven into the silk echoed the shine of the circlet Nereida wore around her brow. Her coily hair haloed out from beneath it. Nereida was Black, and as a river elf she bore hints of aquatic heritage: the slightest webbing between the bases of her thin fingers and a navy cast to the tips of her pointed fin-shaped ears.

Even with her elaborate cobaltril breastplate, Honoria, sitting with Nereida, looked quite plain beside them all.

Hollis's hand swept out, uselessly smoothing the page.

Twenty-six minutes until five thirty.

Twenty-six minutes was way too long.

While her hands worked, so did Hollis's mind. It wandered back to lunchtime, to what Landon had said. Rationally, she knew it was all ridiculous. But that didn't make the thoughts go quiet. As she started coloring finer details, the constant tapping of her big toe inside her shoe making the lines erratic at their edges, the words circled.

Hollis is going to turn into one of those weirdos too.

Hollis is going to turn into one of those weirdos too.

Hollis—

This was a step in the wrong direction. Not toward the boys' group, but firmly toward the weirdos. And there was *already* so much about Hollis that made her a weirdo. Her body. Her need to beg rides. Her anxious, arty brain.

Did she really need more?

And wouldn't it be easy enough to send Iffy a DM telling her she couldn't make it? She was already silent in the group server, too nervous to venture back into the fray after that first chat. The girls probably wouldn't even notice if she left. And she'd only been to one session anyway. It hadn't even been a *real* session, only planning. Hollis planned original characters on her own all the time, so if she ditched, it wasn't even like she had wasted her time. And it wasn't like they needed her to stay.

Maybe Chris and Landon had been right all along. Maybe she *couldn't* hack it in the world of S&S—in *their* world.

Hollis put down her colored pencil, a shade of linen white for the highlights in Tanwyn's fur. Her hand hovered toward her phone.

But then she remembered her conversation with Gloria about the cobaltril breastplate, and Iffy's excessive use of smiley-face emojis when they'd planned Nereida and Honoria's backstory together, and Aini going out of her way to make sure Hollis didn't leave her dice behind.

Hollis sighed. She couldn't choose to let them go. Not yet, when she still had so much to prove. She left her phone where it rested.

Digging in her tote bag for the right shade of blue to touch up Umber's half-fae highlights, Hollis's hand touched the bottle of her anxiety medicine. She took it out of her bag, uncapped it, and shook one of the pills out into her palm. Better to take it now than later, at her own kitchen table and not Gloria's.

She checked her lock screen.

Twenty-five minutes.

6

GATHER YOUR PARTY

THE CHAOS, AT least, she expected this time.

"Hollis! Iffy!"

Of course it was Fran's voice Hollis heard first, coming from behind the heavy wood door before it was even opened. Surprisingly, it was an older woman in blue medical scrubs who answered the door.

"Hello, girls," said the woman. "Please, come in, and take Francesca wherever you're going."

Before either Hollis or Iffy could step over the threshold, Fran was on them, throwing her arms around their midsections and dragging them into the apartment with her like some overly affectionate creature from the *Monstarium*.

"Maggie brought a veggie tray for snacks," she informed them, her voice long-suffering. "I think our only option is to shun her."

"Hello to you, too, Fran," snorted Iffy, but she followed the younger girl down the hallway toward the dining room all the same.

"She's enthusiastic," said the woman, coming to stand beside Hollis after shutting the door. "You'll have to forgive her for it."

"Oh, you're her mom," said Hollis, and immediately made a face at herself for how stupid she sounded.

Fran and Gloria's mom laughed.

"Yes, I am," she said. "Call me Johanna, please. I'm thankful for

71

you girls letting Franny play with you. She's been having such a hard time, and I can already tell it's helping."

This was the first Hollis had heard about this, but she tried not to let it show on her face when she asked, "Oh?"

"With her diagnosis and the new meds and all." Johanna's gaze lingered on the hallway, where Fran and Iffy had disappeared. "You throw in ADHD with the dyslexia and that gifted brain of hers, and, well, you know how middle schoolers can get. But having a place at the big girls' table has made such a difference."

"Oh," repeated Hollis, looking down the hallway after Fran too. Hollis had once been a middle schooler with a diagnosis and new meds herself. "I, uh. Know how it is," she said, looking back at Johanna but not quite meeting her eyes. "So I'm glad it's helping."

"Me too. Well, I'm on my way out to work. You can follow the noise." Johanna smiled, then added, "And there are pizza rolls in the freezer if you end up needing a little more than a veggie tray."

Hollis smiled back. She left Johanna in the living room and followed her ears to the dining room.

The noise from the table washed over her like a wave, but this time it wasn't overwhelming. Instead, the chatter of voices and the clatter of dice were welcoming. Somehow the small dining room felt less intimidating than the last time she'd been there. Without the crush of anxiety tunneling her vision, it even looked comfortable. The cream of the walls softened all the chaos, calming her, calling her in.

Hollis took the same seat she had last week, so the seating arrangements went from Gloria at the head-that-wasn't-a-head of the table clockwise to Fran, then Aini, then Maggie beside Hollis, then Iffy on her other side. She started to empty her tote bag of all the things she'd need: her character sheet, now complete with spell lists and inventory; her same set of loaner dice from Chris; her art notebook. The dice she lined up neatly on her character sheet, nudging her d4 back into place when Fran's poorly stacked dice tower toppled, scattering half a dozen d12's over the table. The notebook she left closed but nearby, just in case something happened that was important to draw.

She was about to turn and show Iffy the paladin spells she'd picked for Honoria when she heard a plucking of strings. In the madness of getting settled, Hollis had somehow missed noticing that *Aini Amin-Shaw had a ukulele.*

"You play ukulele?" she asked Aini without thinking.

"I do now." Aini strummed a pleasing chord. "I thought this was the closest I could get to a lute, and our fearless leader agreed to let me use it as musical accompaniment."

"That's cool," said Iffy, rolling her d20 and frowning at the result—a 6—before rolling it again.

"What are you doing?" asked Maggie.

"Warming up my dice."

"Don't waste all your good rolls before we start!" said Fran.

Iffy raised an eyebrow at her. "I'm trying to waste all the *bad* ones."

Fran huffed, but Maggie, clearly inspired, started to warm up her d20, too.

"Do bards typically play an instrument at the table?" asked Hollis, entranced by the twinkling melody Aini plucked out.

"*Aini* typically plays an instrument at the table," Gloria replied from the other side of the Secret Keeper's screen, a cardboard quadrafold barrier that hid her notes from the table as she set them up for the session.

"Yeah, she played a penny whistle in the last game, when she played a ranger," said Fran.

"You play penny whistle, too?" Hollis asked Aini.

"No," said Gloria. "That was the problem. We compromised this time on something she can at least make music with and not just screech and wake up Miss Virginia."

"I'll save the metal covers for another night." Aini stopped playing to draw a cross over her heart with one hand. "Cross my heart."

Gloria shook her head in mock exasperation. "Okay, girls. If everyone is here and ready, why don't we play some Secrets & Sorcery?"

"YES!" shouted Fran.

The rest of the table fell silent as they all turned to Gloria and waited expectantly for the start of the game.

Gloria went still, illuminated from overhead by the warm yellow glow of the stained-glass chandelier. In contrast, Hollis's heart raced in her chest. It pounded and hammered furiously, as if the feet of every adventurer from every game of Secrets & Sorcery were setting out on an adventure through the gate of her rib cage. After what felt to Hollis like an eternity, the corner of the Secret Keeper's lips twitched into a smile. She drew in a breath (Hollis's caught in her lungs).

And the game began.

"With bustling streets and a citizenry striving for the finer things in life, Fallon's Landing—the capital city of the Second Realm—lives up to its cosmopolitan reputation. Today is Blessing Day, a local holiday for thanking and affirming the governing families of the city." Now and then, Gloria's eyes flicked downward as she spoke, probably to the notes she'd prepared for tonight's adventure. Hollis listened closely, her breath still shallow in her chest, her gaze going soft as she focused. "Every corner and balcony are hung in cerulean and bright green, deep purple and periwinkle, amber and pine—the colors of the governing families.

"The movement of feet and the scent of cool ale in the air—"

"Ale!" shouted Fran.

"*Shhh,*" Aini hushed her.

"—and the riot of color seems to condense in the city's center.

Everyone is packed into a wide central square, from which all the roads in Fallon's Landing spoke out. At the very center, a stage of shining wood has been erected.

"This is where the five of you find yourselves. You've been hired on as security for the event." Gloria paused, taking a moment to look at each of the girls at the table. When her brown eyes met Hollis's, Hollis flushed with excitement. "Why don't you each tell us—briefly—what brought you into the employ of the city for the day and where you are in the square."

She nodded a silent *You start* to Fran.

"Hi," said Fran. "I'm Mercy Grace. I'm here to smash stuff if this event goes south, and also for coin. I'm standing by an ale cart—to guard it, of course."

Gloria raised a perfectly sculpted eyebrow but didn't interject. She looked to Aini next.

"Umber Dawnfast, at your service." Aini launched into a British accent that even Hollis could tell was posh, like someone from the fancy parts of London might have. She strummed a four-note chord on her ukulele. "You'll notice me because I'm the best-looking guy in the square. I've got no reason to be here other than being at the center of things. And that's exactly where I am—to the left of the stage."

"I'm Tanwyn, and you probably don't see me, actually," said Maggie, who was next around the table. She spoke with the same strange, beautiful accent as she had last Friday. Hollis bit the inside of her cheek. Of course Maggie would be flawless at S&S, too. "I'm in the shadows near an alley, obviously, here to lighten a few heavy pockets."

The table went quiet for a solid fifteen seconds, which was how long it took Hollis to realize all eyes were on her.

"Oh, God, it's my turn, isn't it?"

Gloria nodded encouragingly.

Hollis tried very hard to feel encouraged, but she hadn't prepared an accent, and suddenly the prospect of talking as Honoria in first person seemed absolutely mortifying. When Chris talked about his characters, it was always in third person, and any voice he had ever done was to make people laugh with him, like the voice was a joke. If she tried to use one now, Hollis feared it would just make the girls at the table laugh *at* her, like *she* was the joke.

"Uh, I'm going to play Honoria Steadmore," said Hollis in her regular voice. "She's here because she's a guard and she has to be here, probably. And she'll be standing near the stage too, maybe on the opposite side—next to your character, right?"

Hollis threw Iffy a desperate look.

"Of course, Honoria," said Iffy. "Nereida is standing next to Honoria, looking stern. As a captain of the Cerulean Guard, she's on the job too."

"Ah. Then you two and Umber, who are all by the stage, will have a nice view of Wick Culpepper when he steps onto it," said Gloria.

Something uncomfortable flopped in Hollis's chest. She—or, well, *she* being Honoria—knew Wick Culpepper. He was one of the few solid details Hollis had put into her character's biography, a social safety net in case Honoria didn't fit into the group and needed a non-player character to lean on. Wick was the second son of the High Alderwoman of Fallon's Landing, a commander of the Cerulean Guard, and Honoria's boyfriend. Having a boyfriend in real life made things easier for *Hollis*—or, at least, it guaranteed she always had someone to hang out with—so she thought it was fair to give Honoria the same safeguard. Wick was also, other than Iffy's character, the only real tie she had to the story at all. Hollis swallowed hard.

Gloria, it seemed, was pulling Honoria's backstory into the game first.

"'Good morning, people of Fallon's Landing!' cries Wick," said Gloria, and Hollis was relieved to hear it wasn't in a perfect, beautiful accent like Aini's or Maggie's but just her own voice, if a little lower and a little louder. "'And welcome to the commencement of the Blessing Day celebrations. This year, you've truly—'

"But Wick stops abruptly as a flash of lightning splits the sky. After the shock of it, you realize . . . that's not natural lightning. It flashes again, a red so deep, it's almost black."

A collective shiver ran around the table as Gloria grinned at all of them. Fran bounced in her seat, her lips pressed tightly together, trying to suppress a squeal. Aini leaned harder over her ukulele, fingers tensing on its neck.

Hollis closed her eyes for no longer than half a second, imagining the deep red flash of lightning illuminating them so she would remember exactly how she wanted to draw it later.

"Out of the ozone," Gloria continued, "creatures emerge, as if they've erupted from the light itself. At first, you might think they're birds. They're about the same size. But their wings aren't feathered. They're held aloft by the thinly stretched skin of bats' wings.

"As your eyes start to adjust, you realize that these creatures have the bodies and heads of cats. With a chorus of strange meow-like screeches, they *attack*."

Screeching, Fran leapt to her feet, nearly upending her wooden chair. Hollis had been so invested in Gloria's narration that the sudden movement was enough to make her jump.

Gloria simply said, "I'm going to need you all to roll initiative."

This was it—the first roll of the night. Hollis picked up Chris's loaner d20. It felt like the weight of her future in her palm.

"Should we all do it together?" asked Aini.

Suddenly that felt important to Hollis—the five of them rolling together, handing their characters over to fate at the same time. Excitement surged through her.

"Aini, you're such a cheeseball," said Maggie, but she waited to roll.

"On three, then?" asked Aini.

"On three," Iffy confirmed.

Hollis swallowed, then nodded.

"One—"

She moved her wrist, shaking her d20.

"Two—"

It rolled, cool but steadily warming, across her palm.

"Three!"

And all at once, the fates of five S&S characters went skittering over the oak-finish tabletop.

It felt like Hollis's die would roll forever, until—

Well.

It came to a stop, landing on a 9. One corner of Hollis's mouth pulled down into a frown.

Hers wasn't the only frown, either. Aini shook her head disapprovingly.

But Fran squealed, "YES!" and Iffy said, "Not bad, not bad," and Maggie clapped her hands together, sending her collection of silver bracelets twinkling.

"18!" yelled Fran, swatting at Gloria beside her.

"Hold *on*, Francesca. We take turns at this table. I have to write all this down." Gloria's pencil scratched invisibly behind her screen. "That's 18 for Mercy, okay. Umber?"

They took turns reporting their rolls, but no one's roll beat an 18. Fran beamed.

"That means Miss Mercy Grace is going to go first," said Gloria. "But maybe we should get out our map."

Leaning against the rail of Gloria's chair was a roll of graph paper, an orange hair tie around its middle keeping its tube shape. Gloria slid the hair tie off first, then rolled the paper out onto the table.

The map Gloria had made was as impressive as the map at

Games-A-Lot had been disappointing. Drawn by hand in colored pencil, it showed the square of Fallon's Landing. The lines weren't as crisp as they might have been if Hollis had drawn it, but what the scene lacked in technical execution, it made up for in attention to detail. Everything, down to the ale carts and the balconies hung in the house colors, was represented in a one-inch-by-one-inch grid.

Hollis looked up from the map, her face glowing. "Gloria, this is *amazing*."

"Thank you, Hollis." Gloria spared her a special smile. "Okay, now would be a good time to place miniatures if you have them. If not, you can use a die to hold your place. D12's work well because the only class that ever uses them are barbarians, and I know Fran has—"

By way of finishing Gloria's sentence, Fran pulled out a miniature she had clearly made herself. It was about three inches tall, Christmas-tree green, and constructed of nondrying modeling clay. The prominent features of the blobby shape were a pair of huge fangs and two raised arms holding an oversize and rather lopsided battle hammer.

"—that monstrosity," finished Gloria.

Hollis was thankful for not having to use something like Bikini Alvena again. She slid her d12 onto the gridded map, next to the central brown-shaded square that represented the stage.

A flutter of nervousness rippled inside her rib cage as she looked sideways to Iffy.

"About here, do you think?" she asked.

"Looks good to me." Iffy slid her own d12 in beside Hollis's.

Gloria placed small squares of paper, an inch by an inch in size, around the map. Cats with bat wings were drawn on each one in a very cartoony style.

"Nimyr!" said Fran.

"No, Fran, her name's Nereida," said Iffy.

"No, the monsters, they're—"

"A mystery, Francesca." Gloria cut in, her eyebrows stern. "Because your character would need to make a roll to know what they are, hmm? This is a metagame-free table."

"Yes, *Mom*," grumbled Fran, clearly annoyed.

"Okay, okay," said Gloria. "Don't pout so much, Franny. Mercy is up first. What would you like to do?"

That simple question—*what would you like to do*—sent a shiver through Hollis's body again.

"Well, I've been in the ale," said Fran, "obviously, and so I'm a little confused about what is happening. But when the nim—uh, the *creatures* start showing up, I'm ready to smash them! I'm going to saunter—"

"Does Mercy Grace, trollkin barbarian, really saunter?" asked Aini with a cheeky grin.

"Yes, she does. She's a lady and she's been in the suds, Aini!" With a hand, Fran made a shooing motion in Aini's direction. "I'm going to *saunter* over to"—Fran moved her modeling clay homunculus a few squares across the map—"this guy, and I'm going to try to smash him!"

"Sure," said Gloria. "Roll to attack for me, please."

Fran's d20 clacked over the table. She grinned at whatever she rolled—Hollis couldn't see over the not-so-miniature—and then counted her attack bonus on her fingers.

"Does a 14 hit?" she asked, smiling so wide her jaw strained.

"Yes, it does. Roll damage for me, please."

Fran rolled the same kind of die Hollis and Iffy were using as their miniatures: a d12.

"Oh! Nice! 12, pluuuus 2! *14 damage!*"

"Nice one, Mercy," said Gloria, making a note on her page. "So, Mercy, you swing your hammer high over your head and bring it down through the air to the spot where this strange creature floats on leathery wings. *CLANG*, it sings against the cobblestone streets. There's a bit of broken-up stone where you hit, and when you lift your hammer again, all you see is cat-bat splat on the ground."

With long, perfectly polished red nails, Gloria plucked up the paper Mercy had targeted and removed it from the map.

"And with that," said Gloria, "you've vanquished your first foe."

"YEAH!"

"Hell yes!"

"Woo!"

Hollis turned to her left and high-fived Iffy in celebration, then shot Fran a thumbs-up. With one foe down, she could already see why Chris and the boys always talked about the fights in their game so much. The excitement was electric.

"You can call me Queen Mercy Grace, thank you," said Fran, giving a series of little bows.

And so it went around the table. Maggie went next with Tanwyn, who stuck to the shadows and shot at one of the bat-cats with her short bow but didn't manage to take it out. Iffy took aim with Nereida, sending a clever blast of water magic at one of the three creatures on their side of the stage. Aini's bard, Umber, followed suit, aiming for the same creature Nereida had targeted. With the combined psychic damage from his Sticks and Stones spell ("Hey, you, ugly," Aini said in Umber's flawless English accent, shrugging when Maggie side-eyed her), the creature fell out of the air with what Gloria said was an insulted expression on its frozen face.

Before Hollis could take her turn, the monsters had their round. Typical—she *would* roll so low that even the weird cat monsters were quicker than Honoria.

What followed was a flurry of movement and rolling dice as Gloria masterfully commanded the monsters across the map.

"'AHH! *AHH!*'" shouted Mercy when one of them attacked her for a single point of damage.

"'Not so fast, fiends,'" said Tanwyn, dodging the two that targeted her.

"Oh, thank God," said Iffy when her mage armor protected Nereida from an attack.

Prang, prang, said Umber's lute (and Aini's ukulele) as he took two points of damage from another.

"So I just . . . erase the 24 and change it to 14?" Hollis asked when the two bat-cat creatures attacking Honoria landed attacks, one of which was a "double-damaging Natural 20"—something those in the know seemed both in awe and in fear of, which Hollis didn't really understand.

"Yes, correct," said Gloria, finishing up moving all the cutouts around. "And that's the end of the creatures' turns. Honoria, you're up next. Take your revenge."

"Yes, okay." Hollis took a deep breath, trying to shake off the chaos of the attack round. Earlier, after school, Chris had given her some insight into how a turn in battle was supposed to go—the best strategy for attacking enemies, when and how to heal—but in the heat of the moment, she couldn't remember a word he'd said. "Honoria is concerned about Wick up there in all this mess. So, uh. She'll keep half an eye on him, and then she's going to reach up to grab at the bat-cat tangled in her hair, and cast . . ."

Hollis trailed off, looking over the list of spells she'd spent three hours copying from the handbook onto lined notebook paper. She was quiet for what felt like much longer than any of the other girls at the table. In her chest, her heart quickened. She was holding things up.

"Let's do a Searing Shock, Level 0, and try and get him out of there," she finished.

"That's an offensive spell roll for you," said Gloria. "Go ahead, please."

Hollis rolled, watched, and tried not to recoil when a collective groan rose around the table.

"Oh *noooo*," trilled Fran. "A Natural 1!"

"The opposite of a Natural 20," Maggie remarked helpfully (and grimly). Hollis didn't understand that, either.

"Unfortunately, Honoria, when you reach up to try to fill the creature on your head with a spark of righteous energy, something catches your eye," Gloria narrated. "In another flash of deep, dark red lightning, you see movement on the stage.

"You can just make out the shape as the red light engulfs it. Honoria, a breath catches in your chest as you watch—the light so bright it's blinding at first, then darkening and condensing on itself until the figure disappears into the ether.

"Wick Culpepper has vanished."

This, Hollis could understand.

"No," she breathed, and in that moment, Honoria felt very much like *Hollis*, watching the boy she cared about disappear right before her eyes.

"To the rest of you, this all transpires in a flash of a second. But to you, Honoria . . ."

Gloria trailed off, but she didn't need to finish. Hollis nodded solemnly. To Honoria, it was an eternal, impossible moment.

"And," said the Secret Keeper, with the same pleased grin at the effect she was having on the other girls, "that will bring us back to the top of the round. Mercy, swing away!"

The next few rounds passed both very quickly and very slowly for Hollis. A nervousness fell over her—one that was excited but perhaps not in the best way. Though she knew it was just words, that no one was in real danger, and that she, Hollis, had *not* just watched her boyfriend get taken away in a flash of red light, it *felt* real. As the tension escalated, so did Hollis's anxiety. She tried to calm herself by counting the rectangles in the room—a trick she'd learned from her therapist a long time ago, when she'd first started seeing him—but aside from the bland abstract painting in its frame and the bases of the two decorative sconces hung on either side of a round mirror, the dining room had few to offer.

The hits kept coming. By the time the creatures' turns came around again, Hollis had erased and rewritten Honoria's hit points until they read a smudgy gray 3.

"And this nim— I mean, creature," said Gloria, indicating the bat-cat to Honoria's right flank, "will try to attack you. Does a 17 hit?"

Hollis nodded, breathless.

"Okay, okay. So this creature wheels down toward you, its little cat teeth sinking into the skin of your throat for 3 damage."

Oh no.

Hollis erased her hit points again.

Oh no.

And replaced them with a 0, striking a line through its center.

"Honoria is down," she said, her voice small.

"Oh *no,*" said Aini, leaning hard over her ukulele.

"Ah." Gloria's voice was different than before, softer. "Those of you with a clear line of sight to Honoria—Nereida and Umber, certainly— see the paladin in the shining blue breastplate fall, her back slumping down the stage slowly."

"What!" shouted Fran.

"Is she *dead*?!" screeched Maggie from beside her. Hollis shook her head. *She* had taken the time to read the rules. Maggie should have done the same so Hollis wouldn't have to hear the Secret Keeper confirm what she already knew but didn't want to hear.

"No, no," said Gloria. "But she will need to start making Fate Rolls. A 10 or higher will be a pass; anything below is a fail. Three either way will determine Honoria's Fate. And, since it's your turn, Honoria, please make your first Fate Roll now."

Hollis's hand shook as she picked up her d20. Once again, it felt heavier than it should—this time as heavy as a shining blue breastplate on Honoria's unconscious shoulders. It rolled solidly in her palm, then clunked onto the table.

Swallowing, Hollis shook her head.

It was a 9. A failure.

On her character sheet, she marked off one skull-shaped box under *Fate*.

A hush went around the table as Gloria reminded Fran it was Mercy's turn again.

"Shit," said Fran.

"Francesca," said Gloria, frowning.

"Shoot," Fran corrected deliberately. "Shoot, shoot, shoot." She pursed her lips, twitching them rapidly from one side to another, thinking. "I know ale always makes Mercy feel better. I'm going to—I'm going to grab a mug of ale off the ale cart, and I'm going to hurl it in Honoria's direction and hope she can get it!"

A beat of silence. "What?" asked Aini.

"I don't know!" Fran wheeled from side to side, rolling her dice. "It's a 12, what do I add, what am I even doing?!"

"Let's, uh," said Gloria. She cocked an eyebrow at her sister. "Let's call that a ranged attack?"

"But I'm not attacking her!"

"It's a similar mechanic to trying to aim an arrow, though."

"But," said Fran, but whatever was on the other side of the word died in the girl's throat from the look her sister gave her. "My Dexterity is minus 2, so it's a 10."

"Okay," said Gloria, nodding. "A mug of ale explodes against the stage next to Honoria's head, splattering her with ale."

"Does it heal her?" cried Fran.

"No, Fran, it's ale."

"Sh*oot*," said Fran, scowling.

"I'm next, right?" Maggie cleared her throat. She scanned her character sheet, but if there was a healing potion there, she didn't offer it. Hollis frowned down at the table. "I'll aim my short bow at the cat-bat who did this and use my Thief's Keen Eye skill."

"Roll the attack with advantage, then."

"Finally," hissed Maggie, looking at her dice. "Natural 20."

It made a bit more sense to Hollis now, suddenly, why such a thing might be good.

"Nice. Roll with double-dice damage."

"That's—that's 13!" Maggie crowed, triumphant.

"And like that," said Gloria, "the creature at Honoria's throat falls out of the air. It doesn't look quite dead yet, but it's on death's door, for sure."

"I'm going to—" Iffy stood up from her chair beside Hollis, hovering over the table to get a better view of the map. "Sorceresses don't have healing magic. I can't— Okay, what I'm going to do is sidestep this way, here." She pointed and mimed Nereida's movement with her body. "So I'm angled like so, facing these two ass-clowns." She indicated two of the cat-bats to the right.

"Heh," said Fran.

"And I'm going to use a Level 2 Thunderclap, if that's cool," finished Iffy.

"Yes, that's very cool," said Gloria. "That's a defensive roll for those two cat-bats, which—what is your spell strength?"

"It's 14," said Iffy.

"They both fail. With a thunderous clap that accents the flashes of red lightning, these two creatures are knocked back fifteen feet—or they would be if they didn't fall out of the sky halfway across that distance."

"About time," said Iffy. She rubbed a reassuring circle on Hollis's shoulder. "We got this, Honoria."

But Honoria was not sure that they had this. She was unconscious. And Hollis was equally skeptical, because the monsters' turn was coming. She had read enough to know what that could spell for her Fate. One hit to an unconscious character from a monster counted as two failed Fate Rolls.

That would be the end for Honoria Steadmore.

What was more, it would be the end of Hollis's venture into the world of Secrets & Sorcery. Already she dreaded telling Chris that she'd failed out of the game *twice* in a row. Last time had been bad enough, and that situation wasn't even her fault. Hollis could only imagine what Chris would say when she told him she'd gotten her character killed during the first hour of gameplay.

Her only chance now rested on the foppish shoulders of Umber Dawnfast. Hollis didn't dare look across the table at Aini. From two seats down, the girl in question took a deep breath.

"All right, here's my turn," she said, and then went into that posh English accent. "I see the beautiful girl who has fallen, and I see how she looks like she might just be resting, and how the blue in her armor brings out the blue in her eyes, which are—open, staring?"

Without looking up, Hollis nodded. It would be a beautiful death to draw, at least, the way Aini talked about it.

"And I think to myself, *Not today*," said Aini as Umber. "I step away from the creature attacking me—"

"That will provoke a retaliation attack," said Gloria. "For a 13 to hit."

"That'll hit," Aini said in her own voice.

"Yikes," hissed Maggie. "What even is your armor rating?"

"It's a 12. I'm a soft boy."

"That's 2 points of damage," said Gloria.

Aini slipped back into Umber's voice. "I turn to this girl, and I stoop, and grab her by both shoulders, and I close my hands maybe a little too hard on them. And I say, 'Not today,' out loud this time. 'It's not time.' And I cast Level 1 Healing Hold on Honoria."

"Roll the healing for me," said Gloria.

"It'll heal her for 4 points," said Aini.

"Which is more than enough to bring Honoria back to the Waking World."

Finally, Hollis looked up. She was just in time to catch Aini smiling gently at her.

"Welcome back," said Aini and Umber.

Hollis hadn't realized they were there, but suddenly she became aware there were tears on her cheeks. She wiped them away furiously with the back of her hand. Blinking hard against all the wet, she said, her voice hushed, "Thank you."

Hollis could barely focus on the rest of the battle. By the end, she knew only that they were victorious.

"I'm going to, hmm," said Maggie, when the fray was over and the townspeople were being safely ushered away by other Cerulean Guards, their healers tending to the wounded. "I'm going to go check on the bat-cat that almost killed Honoria. I want to see if it's still alive."

Gloria paused for a second, and then nodded, seemingly to herself.

"Roll an Animal check for me, please," she said.

"It's a 15," said Maggie in Tanwyn's voice. "I've always been good with animals."

"Well," said Gloria, "it's clearly alive. Just very badly battered. It would take some healing spells for it to recover. With that roll, you also recognize it is indeed a nimyr. But you've never encountered any nimyr that look like this. Typically, they're docile creatures. These seem to have been twisted somehow—by magic or nature, you're not sure."

Maggie was quiet for a moment, then nodded.

"I scoop up the injured nimyr in my cloak and fashion a sling to hold it to my chest," she said. "I'm going to take it with me."

Hollis's eyes widened, incredulous.

"What?" said Aini, but it was in Umber's voice, so it sounded more like *Wot?* instead.

"No way. That thing almost killed Honoria," said Iffy. Hollis wasn't sure whether it was actual Iffy or Nereida. It was in character for them both.

"So the rest of you are gathering up to hear this, right?" asked Gloria.

"Yeah," said Fran. "I'm going to saunter over."

"Again with the sauntering," Aini said, and elbowed Fran in the arm.

"'I can tell these nimyr have been tainted,'" said Maggie as Tanwyn. "'I believe it's worth keeping one to see what we might learn from it.'"

"'I don't know,'" said Aini as Umber. "'What do you think, fair paladin?'"

Hollis was quiet. At first, she'd thought it was a pretty tasteless move, caring for a creature that had almost killed a party member. Now she could see the wisdom behind Tanwyn's decision, but she still thought it was inconsiderate. She just couldn't figure out a way to say so that didn't sound rude to Maggie.

Hollis, as Honoria, shook her head. "Honoria's going to look up at the stage and then back at everyone gathered around her. And she says, 'We have bigger problems right now. Wi—Wick Culpepper was taken.'"

"And that," said Gloria, clapping her hands excitedly, "is where we're going to take our mid-session break!"

And all around the table, the girls erupted in cheers.

While the rest of the girls spilled out of the side door that branched off from the kitchen and onto the porch, for fresh air, Hollis wanted nothing more than to open her notebook and start drawing the scene that had unfolded at the table. Already, the glint of Honoria's armor in the flashing red lightning sparkled in her mind's eye, begging to be put down on paper. After a quick trip to the bathroom down the hall, she headed back to the table and her notebook.

But someone else had beaten her to it.

Aini Amin-Shaw looked up from the open page. "Did you draw all this?"

"Uh," said Hollis. Panic rose in her like bile, burning hot in her throat. It took Hollis *much* longer than a week to trust someone enough to share her art. And Aini had just taken it. "Yes."

"Even this?"

Aini held open the page with the drawing of the group gathered around the campfire. Hollis cocked her head to the side, unable to help noticing even through her panic that she hadn't made Mercy quite large enough.

"Even that, yes." She nodded stiffly.

"*How*, though?" Aini asked. "*I* didn't even know Umber looked like that, but seeing him now, that's exactly how Umber Dawnfast looks." She touched one gentle finger to Umber's lute where Hollis had put extra care into the wood inlay on its neck, her eyes wide with appreciation.

"Hey, thanks." Hollis's fear subsided somewhat; at least Aini wasn't being critical. Her cheeks did the annoying thing they always did when people complimented her art: betrayed the composure of her words entirely by burning a warm red. "I read everyone's biographies and stuff."

Aini looked up at her with a fond smirk. "Wow, Hollis. Who knew you were such a dork."

When Landon—or even Chris—said the same thing, it earned him a glare. But Aini said it more like a compliment. Hollis smiled. "I'm glad you don't think it's weird."

"What? No, it's awesome," Aini said. "I already have fan art. I'm famous."

"Well, technically, Umber is," said Hollis. "I didn't draw *you*."

"Not *yet*," said Aini, flashing a smile. "Anyway, can I show the others?"

"Please don't, no," said Hollis. "I—uh." She shrugged, as if it wasn't a big deal. "You know, I don't show people my art so fast."

Embarrassed realization flooded Aini's expression. "Oh shit, Hollis. I should have asked."

Hollis couldn't quite meet her eyes. "Yeah, probably."

"Yikes, I'm sorry. Will you ever forgive me?"

"Yeah, probably." Hollis was quiet for a beat. "I mean, you did just kind of save my life."

"Yeah," said Aini. Her expression shifted, softened. "About that—"

"What do you *mean* I can't know that?" Fran burst into the kitchen with a bang. The side door swung hard in her wake, its blinds flinging out like a dramatic plastic cape behind her.

On the table, Aini casually shut Hollis's notebook. Hollis threw her a thankful look.

"That's metagaming, Francesca," said Gloria. "Just because *you've* spent hours on end reading my *Monstarium* doesn't mean Mercy Grace has. There's no way in all of the Eight Realms she would know what the hit points of a nimyr are because nimyr *don't have hit points* in the Eight Realms."

"Sure they do," argued Fran. "How else did we kill them?"

"It's a mechanic we apply to the game from the outside," Iffy interjected as she followed them inside—which was a good thing, since Gloria appeared to be reaching her limit. "They don't exist within the game world itself."

"Well, I think that's booty," said Fran, "and so does Mercy Grace."

"Well, tell Mercy Grace I said sorry next time you talk to her, Fran." Gloria sat back into her chair. Instantly, it became the head of the table again, and the rest of the girls filled in around her. "But until then, she still doesn't know the hit points of a nimyr."

"If there was any place Wick would have gone willingly," Hollis said, "it would be this."

Gloria had just finished describing the small, cramped sea cave where Honoria and Wick snuck off to sometimes, when their duty got to be too much and they needed to hide away for a while. After Hollis filled the others in about Honoria's in-character boyfriend, they all agreed looking for him in a familiar place was the best course of action. If he'd needed a safe space to hide, Hollis was sure this would be it.

"Can I . . ." Iffy looked down at her character sheet. She swallowed a mouthful of celery from the veggie tray, which the table had become snacky enough to break into. "Can I have Nereida do a Magic check? I'd like to see if there's any, you know, teleportation or anything magical that feels similar to the way that red lightning felt back in the square."

Iffy's die clattered to the table. Hollis lifted her elbow to make space for it to roll.

"Not great. That's a 12."

"Okay, okay," said Gloria, and she nodded. "With that roll, unfortunately, Nereida, when you reach out with your arcane sense to try to see if there's been any magic used within the space, you can't be sure. But, oh—wait, wait . . ." Gloria trailed off, cocked her head to the side. She blinked slowly a few times.

Then, sudden enough to make Fran shriek, Gloria pushed her arms out from her chest, her hands sweeping in a large arc as she made a whistling, whooshing sound.

"All of you feel a rush through your body. It has a crackling, electric feel, putting Tanwyn's wool on end. It grows stronger and stronger until it starts to steal the breath from your lungs—a powerful surge of magic, the likes of which not even Nereida has ever felt before."

Hollis cast a look at Iffy, who was looking right back, her brown eyes wide.

"When it's almost too much to bear, the feeling collapses and condenses into an itchy sensation in your brain. And there, in the very back corner where you hide all your deepest fears and worries, you hear it."

"WhatdoIhearwhatdoIhear," whispered Fran, pulling her legs tight to her chest as she leaned forward, eyes wide.

"Ahh ha haaa," laughed Gloria, her voice deeper and darker than Hollis had ever heard it. *"Ahhh ha ha ha haaaaaa,"* she laughed again. "Sinister laughter shakes you to your very core, sending chills down your spine.

"Aaaaand that's where we're going to end for the night." Gloria looked around the table at the girls' shocked faces, her grin wicked and triumphant.

"What!" yelled Fran, her arms exploding into the air.

"Whaaaaat," intoned Iffy.

"You're brilliant, Gloria Marie Castañeda," said Aini, head shaking slowly with impressed disbelief. *"Brilliant."*

Hollis clapped at least five times before she caught herself and stopped.

"No, there has to be more," said Maggie. Her eyes were tired but sparkling with excitement—a reaction Hollis still didn't expect from her. "Right? We can keep playing."

"It's eleven at night, Maggie," said Gloria, gathering up her papers behind the Secret Keeper's screen.

"I can stay longer," Hollis offered.

Iffy raised an eyebrow at her. "Girl, I have a volunteer thing early tomorrow morning," she said. "Are you going to walk back to Covington?"

"I don't have to drive home! I can keep going!" Fran bounced eagerly in her seat.

"I have to write what happens next, Franny," said Gloria. "We'll play again next Friday, okay?"

A chorus of yeses echoed around the table. Hollis's came a little too fast, a little too loud.

"Keep an eye on the server, too," Gloria said. "It'll be like our home base when we're not at the table."

"Well," said Iffy, standing, "we have to get going."

"Yes, okay," said Hollis, packing up her things quickly. "Thank you, Gloria. This was great."

Gloria grinned at Hollis, and then looked around appreciatively at the rest of the group. She gave a shrug like it was no big deal, but her voice was earnest, warm. "It's only as great as you all make it."

"Thanks, everyone," Hollis amended, and followed Iffy toward the door.

"Girl," Iffy said, ducking under Hollis's arm as she held the door open. "I'm so glad you didn't die tonight."

Hollis laughed. It was such a strange thing to hear. It was also deeply felt, a bright glowing thing in her chest.

"Yeah," she said. "So am I."

7

HIGH ALDERWOMAN MERISH

"HUH?"

Hollis glanced up from the page in her notebook where she was shading in the hollows of Honoria's eyes. After two tries, she'd finally gotten the color right, lit harshly from overhead as the paladin stood in the shadow of the central stage. Since getting home on Friday night, Hollis had drawn the Blessing Day battle at least twenty-three times—two of those this morning during class.

Somehow it still wasn't enough.

"I *said*," Chris repeated, swatting at her pencil, "tell the gang how it went. On Friday, with the—"

"Lesbians," supplied Landon.

"With the *girls*," corrected Hollis.

She'd already told the story to Chris once, while they took turns losing to each other at Mario Kart in his mom's living room on Saturday. He had been supportive. Excited for her, even, though he'd still stomped her on Rainbow Road. But earning Chris's approval when they were alone was an entirely different experience than trying to recount the story to Landon with the whole lunch table watching. She shrugged. "It was a good game, that's all."

"Oh, come on, Hollis," said Landon. "Don't be like that. You know

I'm kidding. I've been wanting to hear an S&S story from you for forever."

If that was true, he could have invited her to the boys' game ages ago. She briefly thought to remind him of this, but instead just rolled her eyes and stayed quiet.

"I want to know too," said Marius. "First games always have the goofiest shit. Remember when we first started, Chris, and we had no idea how the mechanics worked at all, and so you tried to have your character—"

Chris laughed and threw his voice up a few octaves in a bad Chipmunk impersonation. "Herbie Derbie, gnome rogue."

It echoed around the cafeteria, causing more than a few faces at adjacent tables to turn his way. Hollis, beside Chris, shrank away into her notebook.

"Oh, God, Herbie Derbie," laughed Landon.

"—you had Herbie fire his crossbow at that goblin." Marius was already dissolving into laughter at the memory. Amusement curled the corners of his words. "But you rolled a Natural 1, and so Landon had you fall into that dead horse instead, and then next turn you were like, 'Oh shit, I need to stand up!' and Landon made you roll for it and you rolled a Natural 20, and so he was all, 'Somehow, this—' *Pffffft.* 'Somehow this little gnome thief falls into a dead horse, gets covered in'—HA *HA!*—'gets covered in horse goop, and then springs up like the smoothest dude anyone has ever seen, cleaner than when he fell in!'"

By the time Marius finished, the other two boys were laughing so uproariously, Hollis could hardly hear the end of the story. But she didn't need to; although she hadn't been Chris's girlfriend yet, she remembered the boys talking about it when it'd happened. She laughed too—a small, reserved laugh, especially in comparison to the raucous noise of the boys.

"Well, we didn't have anything like *that*," she said.

"I would hope not!" With a thumb, Chris wiped away the tears from the corners of his eyes. He shook his head, his halo of blond hair ruffling like his lingering laughter. "We were such dweebs back then."

"Well, thankfully everyone—even this girl Maggie, who is also new—pretty much understood the rules." Hollis left out the part about how she still couldn't understand why someone like Maggie would *want* to know the rules of S&S in the first place. "And even if she didn't, the Secret Keeper's little sister, Fran, who plays with us—"

"Aw, she lets her *widdle sistewr* play?" Landon cooed.

Even though Fran was only twelve, Hollis was fairly sure she could kick Landon's ass. She was small but merciless. Hollis thought about informing him of this, but instead she just said, "Ugh."

"Come on, now," said Marius. "You were going to tell us about the game, not just your cool new friend."

Hollis's voice retreated as the silence stretched out. It was Chris who spoke up instead.

"So, they started out in Fallon's Landing—"

"Typical." Landon rolled his eyes.

Chris ignored him and went on, telling the story of the nimyr fight. It didn't do the battle justice, but hearing it from Chris instead of Hollis helped keep Landon's mouth shut. And she had to hand it to her little band of adventurers: even with Chris missing some of the more interesting parts, it sounded pretty epic. Hollis smiled down at her sketch as she listened.

"Aren't nimyr those sky cats that girly sorceresses like to have as pets?" asked Landon.

"Well, these ones were different, right?" Chris looked to Hollis for confirmation. She nodded. "They looked more like bats or something. They took Hol's paladin down."

"Your paladin was taken down by a *goth cat*?" Landon laughed.

"There were a lot of them," Hollis protested, color rising in her cheeks.

"Ah, the lower levels," said Marius, wistful. "They're so squishy."

Landon rolled his eyes. "But did she die, though?"

"No." Chris swiped a Tater Tot from Landon's tray and ate it. "She got saved by the bard; his name is Umber—"

"I thought it was all girls," said Landon.

"This girl Aini plays him," said Hollis with a shrug.

Landon made a face that wouldn't have looked out of place on Maxx the Bard.

"Watch out for that," said Marius. "You know how bards are."

"Yeah," said Landon. "Wick or Wicket or Whatshisnuts better watch out for Mrs. Steal-Your-Girl."

"Like you'd know anything about *that*, Landon. You've never had a girl to steal," Chris said, and threw a pepperoni at Landon's face. It splatted greasily against his cheek.

"Dude," Landon whined.

And just like that, the discussion of Hollis's game was over.

It should have felt good for the discussion to occur in the first place. This was what she'd wanted: for the boys to take her and her game seriously. For them to realize that she could be an important part of *theirs*, too. But as the conversation moved on to Landon's careful skin-care routine and Chris's pepperoni throwing off a week's worth of work, the focus on her game didn't feel like a win. Her cheeks still burning red, Hollis wished it had never even happened.

By the time she got home, it was two and a half hours after school had let out—all because Chris had marching band practice. Sometimes she wished she could just ride the bus. Technically, she could; she had in middle school, before she started at Holmes and could ride with her mom, which she did until Chris got the Sentra and she could ride with him. But just the thought of those brown plastic seats—and the sweaty, smelly, sneering bodies crammed two or three to each—made her stomach roil. Between the tight quarters, the loud noise, and the inescapable taunting, the school bus was far from an ideal place for a fat girl with anxiety.

Hollis plopped into the peeling seat of her desk chair and opened her laptop as fast as she could, as if doing so could make up for lost time. Slowly (and with a great rattling sound that always made her worry), the ancient computer whirred to life. While she waited what felt like much longer than usual, Hollis fiddled with her box of borrowed green dice, trying to turn it over in her hand without making its contents rattle.

She was about to turn on some lo-fi when her start-up apps finally launched. Instantly, dozens of frantic pings sounded from her speakers. The group Discord was active. Messages flashed in the top right corner of her screen faster than Hollis could read them.

As quickly as she could, Hollis skimmed over the conversation she missed. (Fran's tendency to steer the conversation in strange directions didn't make it any easier to decipher.) When she'd caught up, Hollis took a deep breath, tried to settle the awkward fluttering that had taken up residence somewhere between her rib cage and her belly, and told herself *she could do this*. She could wade in. Even Maggie, also newly added to the chat, was holding her own. Surely Hollis could, too. After all, she and Iffy already chatted daily in DMs. And now that they'd played a real session together, Hollis thought maybe they were all practically friends.

It still took her a moment, and another deep breath, before she finally typed:

beckwhat 5:46 PM
looks like i missed a party! (edited)

iffy.elliston 5:46 PM
bitch, where have you been?

beckwhat 5:47 PM
uh, at school.

with you.

Aini 5:47 PM
Holliiiiiiiiis.

beckwhat 5:48 PM
hey aini!!

uwuFRANuwu 5:48 PM
ONG HOLLIS YOU MISSED ALL TEH FUN

magnitude10 5:49 PM
You missed a lot of nonsense.

iffy.elliston 5:50 PM
girl, get the app

that way you can take all of fran's quizzes right when she spams them

which is always

uwuFRANuwu 5:51 PM
YES it is very important I know what color Honorias aura is U-U

I do not make the rules I only enforce thme

with an iron fist :/

Aini 5:52 PM
Yes, come to the dark side.

beckwhat 5:52 PM
okay.

you got me.

i'll do it.

Hollis picked up her phone, which was about as old and battered as her laptop. Once the app finished downloading, the first message that popped up on her lock screen was:

Aini 5:54 PM
Hey.

Do you still have that picture you drew?

Hollis slid her finger across her screen. She had expected Discord to open to the group chat, but Fran's last message (*DO IT IFFY!!!!! DO IT NOW!!!!!!!!!*) was missing. So were all the rest.

Aini had sent her a private message.

beckwhat 5:55 PM
hey.

yes, i still have the picture.

Aini 5:55 PM
Perfect.

Send it to me.

Please, I mean.

beckwhat 5:56 PM
which one?

Aini 5:56 PM
There's more than one?

beckwhat 5:56 PM
there are now.

do you mean the one you stole a look at? (edited)

Aini 5:56 PM
Yes, Buckwho, that's the one.

You make Umber look cooler than he really is.

beckwhat 5:57 PM
i don't know.

umber is pretty cool.

Aini 5:57 PM
Please don't tell him that, he's got enough of an ego already.

beckwhat 5:57 PM
too late! hold on a sec!! (edited)

From her tote bag, she dragged out her notebook. Ignoring the steady stream of group messages sending her phone buzzing, she cobbled together her usual setup for photographing her art (a DIY light box leaned up in the corner where her bed met her art-plastered wall), then opened her notebook to the same page Aini had opened last Friday. Steadying her hands as best she could, Hollis snapped a picture. She sent it on to Aini.

beckwhat 6:05 PM
here you go ma'am.

Aini 6:05 PM
Thanks, Hollis.

You're the coolest.

beckwhat 6:05 PM
i thought that was umber?

Aini 6:06 PM
Ah, yes. Sorry. I forgot.

I think you could give him a run for his coin, though.

Something flopped, awkward but not unwelcome, in Hollis's chest. Not sure how to reply, she quickly typed:

beckwhat 6:06 PM
no you.

i have to do homework.

talk later!

bye.

And then she closed the app as quickly as she could.

Her fast exit didn't stop her from seeing one last message from Aini: a screenshot of her lock screen. She had zoomed in on the image Hollis sent and centered Umber and Honoria.

She had to admit, Aini *did* make her feel kind of cool. Her fan art had a fan.

With her phone still buzzing against her desk, she flipped her notebook to a new page and started drawing, homework forgotten.

"Hey, girl."

The voice was familiar, but Hollis couldn't place it. She blinked once, then twice. It was a beat too long before she turned around.

Iffy stood beside her, leaning up against the wall like she had been there all along. "Oh, Iffy." Of course it was Iffy. Hollis shook her head.

"You all right?"

"Yes, sorry—" The truth was that Hollis wasn't used to talking to Iffy here, at school. Whenever they talked, they were either in the battered bucket seats of Iffy's Accord, sitting next to each other at the Castañedas' oak-finish table, or on Discord. There was something incongruous about Iffy and the spartan walls of Holmes High School, like the latter were somehow too plain a backdrop for a person as interesting as her. Still, Hollis knew this wasn't polite to say out loud, and so instead she said, "Still waking up, is all."

"Midweek slump, girl, I get you," Iffy replied, gracious as ever. "Hey, I was wondering, do you want to come home with me tomorrow before the game? So we can put together snacks before we go, without having to rush."

"Huh?"

"For S&S, Hollis." Iffy perched a hand on her hip. "You really *are* still asleep. I got snack duty tomorrow, and I want more of a cupcake situation than a celery situation."

"Fran might riot if we had celery two games in a row," Hollis agreed.

"That's what I'm saying! I was thinking of maybe making some mini pizza bites to keep Miss Francesca at bay." Iffy gave Hollis a knowing grin. "I've got a couple odds and ends to work on for National Honor Society before we leave, but I figure sticking together would mean less rushing around."

"That sounds fun, actually." And it did—with Iffy. Hollis smiled back warmly. "I'll bring my dice and stuff to school with me, and we can leave from here?"

Iffy laughed, a sound rich enough to fill the whole hallway. "She's awake at last."

Iffy's house was a lot like Hollis's house, which was a lot like most houses in the Eastside neighborhood: a pre–World War II town house not yet flipped by the developers from Mainstrasse; on the wrong side of Covington to be considered safe by the rich white people who lived close to the river; and with no good off-street parking.

The two girls were in the kitchen, which was smaller than Hollis's but much nicer. It had a newer fridge and bursts of turquoise and orange all over: in decorative plates, in potted silk flowers, in pot holders Iffy told Hollis she'd made at camp when she was eight that her mom wouldn't let go of. They stood side by side at the counter closest to the oven, a two-girl snack assembly line.

"So what I'm thinking," said Iffy, who was on mini-bagel-splitting duty, "is that the spooky laughter we heard at the end? Was the Big Bad."

"Oh, absolutely." Hollis nodded agreement. Her job was to put a spoonful of pizza sauce on each half of the mini bagels, then set them on an ancient baking sheet. "You don't get maniacal, disembodied laughter like that from anyone *but* the be-all, end-all bad guy."

Iffy accidentally broke one of the bagels she was splitting and gave Hollis one half before popping the other into her mouth. "I fink anyone who can put foughts in your head like that ith Big Bad matherial," she said through her mouthful.

"Iffy, gross," Hollis giggled, but bit into her bagel half all the same. "Buf you're righ'," she said, then swallowed. "But then there's the nimyr that were . . . What was the word Gloria used?"

"*Corrupted*, I think." Finished splitting bagels, Iffy joined Hollis at the baking sheet, topping the sauced halves with shredded cheese.

"Yes, that. I think that's important to look into. Especially with the smell in the air after the battle—Gloria said it was like ozone, which makes sense with all the lightning, but also like something sweet we couldn't place."

Iffy's lips rippled with a badly suppressed grin. "Corruption smells sweet?"

"No, no," said Hollis. "*No*, come on, don't look at me like that. I mean, we should all look for something that turns regular creatures all weird and that has those two smells."

"Roll you a Smell check, then, Hollis, go on," said Iffy.

Both girls laughed. Their banter and bagel-making carried on so easily that it was a while before Hollis realized she didn't feel nervous in Iffy's kitchen at all.

Later, in the bathroom off Iffy's hallway, Hollis rifled through her tote bag for her pills. Drinking from the tap with her cupped hands, she took her evening medication, then turned off her alarm so it wouldn't sound on the ride over to Gloria and Fran's apartment.

Session two was nerve-racking for two reasons.

One: because despite protestations from Fran (who had just finished her social studies homework, and who was especially grumpy because of it), the group decided as soon as they sat down that they would be the ones to break it to High Alderwoman Merish that her son was missing. They almost *hadn't* decided this: Early on, Maggie had echoed Fran's objections, pointing out that Tanwyn wouldn't care where Wick had gone. And it looked like Iffy might agree too. She pushed for checking in with the Cerulean Guard instead, because she was sure that was where Nereida would want to go first.

But as the three girls started planning how to approach the barracks, Hollis saw something shift in Gloria's expression. The Secret Keeper was sorting through the notes behind her screen, but a gentle sort of panic had added edges to the corners of her smile. It was slight, and Hollis only recognized it because it was something that happened to her—the feeling she got when she was at her most anxious but was least able to do anything about it.

Resolve settling in her chest, Hollis made a split-second decision.

"Actually," she spoke up—and then immediately wished she

hadn't, as five pairs of eyes turned on her at once. Hollis looked around the table, searching for someone to get on her side. "I think it's really important we go see the High Alderwoman."

Aini quickly caught her gaze. And when Hollis glanced back to Gloria, Aini's eyes followed. She gave Hollis a nod. "Yeah, I agree." She turned to Iffy. "I'm sure the Guard would send us to see her anyway."

For a moment, Iffy considered this, then said, "You're right. Okay, I vote for the High Alderwoman too."

Maggie shrugged. "I'm sure she's got a few trinkets that could use redistribution," she conceded.

"*Ughhhh*, fine," groaned Fran—and with that, they'd made their first truly collective decision as a party. Hollis was fairly certain there was a hint of relief mixed into the otherwise-confident twist of Gloria's grin as she steered the party toward the city's heart.

But this led to the second reason the session was so nerve-racking: because Hollis had been the one to speak up (and because of Honoria's high Charisma score), she had been nominated one of the representatives to speak for the whole party, along with Umber.

What had seemed like a good character choice two weeks ago now seemed to Hollis like a very big, very pressing mistake.

The two trays of mini bagel pizzas Hollis and Iffy had brought quickly dwindled down to one, thanks in large part to Fran—whose appetite was as ferocious as Mercy Grace's—and to Hollis herself, who had stress-eaten at least four in the past ten minutes. Since Aini was clearly much more comfortable being in charge, Hollis let her take the lead, trying to fade into the background as Gloria talked them through the next step in their adventure.

"Okay, okay." Gloria nodded. "You reach the front of the chamber, where four ornately carved chairs stand empty. On a platform above those, a fifth chair is occupied. The woman who sits there seems to take up the whole platform, simply because the personality she projects is so strong. She's tall, muscular, and a lot younger than you'd think for someone who'd been made High Alderwoman of Fallon's Landing, with gray curls and dark eyes. She's wearing robes of a similar cerulean as in Honoria's and Nereida's garments, as well as a rich green. She looks down at you as you approach.

"This, you all know, is High Alderwoman Merish."

"Dang," whispered Fran under her breath.

"*Shhh.*" Maggie hushed her.

"All right," said Aini. "I'm going to step up to the edge of the platform." She paused and looked across the table toward Hollis.

"Honoria is also going to do that," Hollis said, her words stilted.

"And I'm going to say," said Aini, before switching into Umber's flawless accent, "'Good High Alderwoman, we come to wish you a happy Blessing Day. I'm afraid, though, we also come bearing bad news. You might have noticed that the revelry outside has died down. Surely you hear there are no cheers in the streets. No merriment.'"

"'Do not tell me what I am sure about.'"

Hollis watched Gloria in disbelief. Everything about her, from the look in her eyes to the set of her lips, had shifted as she embodied the High Alderwoman. Gloria herself was so kind, and yet in that moment, Hollis was scared half to death of her.

"'That's, well.' I stand as straight as I can and give the High Alderwoman a really winning smile," said Umber through Aini. "'There's been a slight *incident*, Alderwoman. It seems some magical force—'"

"'You allowed a magical disruption to mar the city's celebration? Were you not hired as guards to prevent this very thing from happening?'" Gloria turned the Alderwoman's sharp gaze on Hollis and Iffy. "'Nereida, Honoria, you are captains of the city guard. Is this the sort of work you deem acceptable?'"

Hollis went very still.

So far, she had been able to coast in their game—to blend into the background the same way she always did with the boys. But between Aini's earlier cues and now Gloria's, it looked like she was about to be dragged out of the shadows—whether she liked it or not.

Cold fear clawed at her insides. Slowly, she looked up from her character sheet. The full power of High Alderwoman Merish looked back at her through Gloria's eyes.

"In a word," said Hollis, only as Hollis. "Uh. No."

Her eyes darted to Aini's. She didn't like to be put on the spot like this, especially not when Aini had been doing so well on her own. For a panicked second, she held the other girl's gaze.

It was Aini who broke eye contact first, turning to Gloria and leaning in.

"'I think what Honoria means,'" she said as Umber, "'is—'"

Hollis was still watching Aini. Her confident grin, the name of Hollis's character on her lips—how easily she shouldered her spot as leader of the party. It looked good on her.

Something about Aini drew Hollis in, made her want to be part of the scene in the same way. Hollis still couldn't be the center of attention. But maybe *Honoria* could.

Borrowed bravery filled her chest.

"'They took Wick,' Honoria says," cut in Hollis. "'I don't know who did it, or why, or how, but there was a magical storm, and once it cleared, Wick was gone. I don't pretend to know anything more.'" The words spilled out of her. She felt a little wild, a little out of control—like it wasn't *her* saying them but someone else talking out of her mouth. "'But I can promise you, if you let us—if you let *me*—I will find him.'"

"Oh, that's good! That's good," Fran whispered.

Aini, across the table, gave Hollis a small smile.

Hollis's hands shook in her lap. She wasn't sure why.

"Roll me . . ." Gloria cocked her head to the side, considering. "A Persuasion check."

Hollis nodded, looking down at her sheet. Persuasion was a skill associated with Charisma. The die she rattled in her palm felt electric.

She let it fall from her hand. It bounced once, then rolled, then teetered to a stop.

The flat face of the die read *20*.

"That's . . ." Hollis smiled at the green-and-white die, then up at Gloria. "That's a Natural 20." She absolutely understood the appeal of the highest roll now.

Hisses of excitement sounded around the table.

"All right." In an instant, Gloria assumed the countenance of High Alderwoman Merish again. "The High Alderwoman looks at you for a moment, and you feel exposed to the very core of yourself. But, Honoria, you know this woman. What's more, she knows *you*. She's the High Alderwoman, yes, but she's also the mother of the boy you grew up beside. And though she's never let the overlap of your personal lives influence your professional ones, it's Wick's mom you see staring back at you now with shadowed eyes. In the silence that follows your promise, you realize her eyes look . . . *tired*. A moment of empathy passes between you.

"'Your words are stirring, Honoria,' she says. 'I will grant you this quest. And the rest of you—will you join my guard's captain in the search for my son?'"

"I will," said Umber, as fervently as Honoria had.

"I will," said Nereida, close beside Honoria as always.

"I will," said Tanwyn, her strange, sultry voice doing kind things to the words.

"I will," Mercy said, and then added in a growl, "for coin."

"Fran," hissed Aini.

"Roll a Persuasion check," said Gloria, eyeing her sister.

"Damn it, Fran," said Iffy.

Fran's hands were a flurry of movement as she grabbed and rolled her die. "Well, that's a 10."

"*Really?*" groaned Maggie.

"And with my bonus of minus 2 . . ."

"You've got to be joking," said Aini.

Fran made a sour face, like the next three words tasted terrible in her mouth. "That's an 8?"

"So, okay." Gloria made a strange face to herself, eyebrows pinching together in brief confusion. "You watch as each of your companions, in turn, agrees to join this quest as a charge of the High Alderwoman of Fallon's Landing . . . and then as your trollkin companion tries to shake her down for coin. The Alderwoman goes quiet, then heaves a *very* heavy sigh, saying, 'You will receive your agreed-upon daily compensation for the duration of the search.'"

"AND," said Fran.

"'Thank you, High Alderwoman,'" Aini broke in, Umber's voice panicked on her lips. "'We won't disappoint you. Your son will be safely returned soon.'"

Gloria arched an eyebrow. "The High Alderwoman fixes Honoria with a knowing stare, then says, 'I should hope so.' She gives the rest of you a solemn nod, then a wave of her hand—and it's final enough to understand you're being dismissed.

"I think that's a good place to take a break, don't you?" Gloria grinned around at the table.

"God, yes," said Iffy. "That was intense!"

"That was *awesome*!" shrieked Fran, her arms flailing with excitement.

"*What?*" Maggie gaped at her. "You almost blew it for all of us!"

"But I *didn't*, did I?" Fran beamed. "And I got us paid!"

The table dissolved into break-time chaos, and Hollis sat quietly for a moment just watching it. It would be nice to tell Chris about this—that Honoria had been a source of something good for the group, instead of something stressful, like last week.

She was pretty sure her Secret Keeper had a hand in that. As

Gloria stood (chiding, "If you had rolled *any* lower, Francesca, I swear . . ."), grabbing several mini pizzas to take onto the porch with her, she caught Hollis's eye. Wordlessly, she flashed a thumbs-up. The motion was small enough that Hollis was sure no one else had seen it. *She* would have doubted she'd seen it, if it weren't for Gloria's wink that followed.

Red rose in Hollis's cheeks as she simply nodded back and smiled.

8

YOUR FUN IS WRONG

"**WHO EVEN USES** a farmer as an NPC?"

Without much aim, Landon flung a Frisbee toward the next target on the course. He didn't play disc golf (*not* Frisbee golf, as he'd corrected her earlier), but he'd dragged Chris, Marius, and Hollis out to play nonetheless. Apparently, a YouTuber he watched said it was a good way to pick up girls. As his disc sailed past the chain-link goal and on toward the restroom, with no girls but Hollis around to watch, she had her doubts.

A beat passed before she realized his question hadn't been rhetorical.

"Uh," said Hollis. "Gloria, I guess?"

Hollis had just filled the group in on the end of her game's second session and the non-player character Gloria had introduced: a farmer named Cletus whose cows had been corrupted, like the nimyr in the city. They'd followed the trail of one such corrupted cow north, until Cletus heard a strange sound coming from a nearby cave. This had been enough to start them on the first leg of their journey, and Gloria's horrible farmer accent (which was more bootleg Mario Brother than country bumpkin) had been a highlight of the night.

Hollis left that last detail out. Somehow she didn't think it would help Landon take her game any more seriously.

Marius stepped up next. He set his shot and let his disc fly, with much better results. After they'd all gone (except Hollis, who wasn't interested enough to invest in an expensive Frisbee), the group marched off to chase down Landon's disc.

"I'm just saying." Landon had been *just saying* things like this for the last half hour they'd spent at Devou Park, the hilly green space on Covington's west side. "I'd never use a farmer. What do they even know? It's supposed to be like peasant England. They weren't *smart*. An NPC should be a cult leader or something."

"Oh yeah," Marius snorted, toeing the thick grass. "Because *peasant England* was full of cult leaders."

Hollis shot Marius a grateful smile, but he was busy paying attention to Landon and didn't notice.

"Okay, fine, whatever," Landon went on, undeterred. "But that's the S&S standard. The way things are. There's *always* a cult or a goblin king or a dragon or something. Clearly this Secret Keeper of yours doesn't know her lore."

Breathing into the incline of the disc golf course, Hollis shook her head. It had been clear to her right away that Gloria knew at least as much about Secrets & Sorcery as Landon did. She'd never once asked her Secret Keeper a question she didn't have an answer for.

"Actually," she started, but Chris cut her off.

"Maybe she's just trying something new," he said, spinning his Frisbee on his finger. "Changing it up."

Yes, that was it. Hollis nodded at Chris's back where he walked ahead of her. But as she was about to speak up again, Chris broke into laughter, and Landon and Marius both joined in.

"Yeah," Landon agreed. "Sorry, Hollis, but I don't even think you're playing real Secrets & Sorcery if it's like that. It sounds pretty gay."

Landon turned, looking back over his shoulder at Hollis. She stopped in her tracks, eyes squinting into a glare. Something small but fierce kindled hot in her chest. What she wanted to say was that

Landon clearly didn't know what he was talking about. That he didn't know all the headcanons she and Iffy had already built into their backstory. That Hollis's art had been more inspired these past few weeks than it had in *months* of fandom drawing, and that her newest sketchbook was already more than half full with images of her adventuring party. That as soon as the last session had ended, goofy Farmer Cletus and all, Hollis was already waiting for it to be Friday again, just to see what happened next.

Why was any of that less real than how the boys felt about Landon's brutal campaign?

But her mind was already cycling his insult over and over, the words coiling and twisting in her head. The sweat on her brow went cold.

What she managed to say instead, her stomach twisting, was, "Whatever, Landon."

This only made Landon laugh harder. He picked up his Frisbee, shaking his head at her.

"Oh, come on, Hollis," Chris said, taking a few steps back to stand beside her. "Don't get mad. He's joking. It's kind of part of it all, talking shit on other people's games."

Hollis frowned. Not once had anyone from *her* group said anything bad about anyone else's, even though they all knew other people who played the game. Maybe that was just another way they were playing the game wrong. She swallowed around the sudden lump in her throat.

"Do *you* think it's not even S&S?" she asked, her voice dropping low so only Chris could hear. She slowed her steps, wanting to put space, even if just a little, between herself and Landon's opinions. "The way we play?"

It felt important for her to know. That was the whole point of this adventure in the first place.

"What I think," Chris said, sighing but smiling, "is that my girlfriend plays S&S, and that's pretty cool. Landon can't say that, can he?"

Encouraged, Hollis smiled back. "Landon can't say anything about a girlfriend."

"That's right," said Chris, louder this time. "Because *Landon doesn't have a girlfriend*."

"Not when I have to play with dudes who suck at disc golf as much as you," Landon said, then headed toward the next hole.

Chris gave Hollis a look, one she struggled to read but thought must mean *Landon is an idiot, am I right?* That's what she settled on, at least, as she and Chris and Marius all trudged after him.

But as she followed in Landon's footsteps, his words still whispered in her mind. *There was something wrong with the way she played S&S.* Somehow, even when she *tried* to play their game, she still couldn't quite find her way into their group. She was still always a few steps out of sync, the same way she was now as she huffed up the verdant hill behind them.

Somehow the promise of Friday now seemed a little less exciting.

The battle, like the journey to it, was long.

"This is just . . . ," Iffy started, then trailed off, shaking her head.

Beside her, Hollis nodded in agreement.

When Hollis sat down at the gaming table a few hours ago, she hadn't been sure what to expect. Landon's words still lingered in the back of her mind, murmuring that whatever they did, it wasn't going to be *real* S&S. And when Iffy, running behind from an afterschool student council event, was later than usual picking Hollis up, her worry had only compounded. Hollis had wanted to believe the promises she hissed at Iffy under her breath as they rushed in late at 6:05—that things were okay—but Landon's words echoed in her brain on a loop. *They were playing the game wrong.*

When the girls had finally started playing, Hollis became even more afraid he was right. Fran monopolized the first half hour or so with breakthrough chatter about the vocabulary quiz she'd failed ("Who even *cares* how to spell *reproachfully*? Literally no one will ever use that booty word," she screeched between rolls), fueled no doubt by the dozens of homemade samosas Aini had brought for her turn at snack duty. And Maggie had been overly concerned that they not leave any tracks in-game, which Hollis didn't understand and was (if she was honest) more than a little annoyed by.

But eventually they'd made it to the cave Farmer Cletus sent them to investigate, their exploration of which became the group's first dungeon crawl. The natural cavern slowly gave way to a purposefully constructed (and mysteriously abandoned) outpost, each room more elaborate than the last. It was, without a doubt, the most difficult challenge they'd faced together since the start of their quest. And emerging from an underground river in the final chamber was a river elf, perhaps an original inhabitant of the space, who had fallen to the same corruption they'd seen before. With mottled skin and a craggy maw ("I've been waiting for her to say *maw*," whispered Aini, beaming at Gloria), it had attacked the party single-mindedly.

The initial fight had been hard, but what was worse was the body, tattered from the scuffle and whatever horrible fate had befallen it before that, reanimating itself when the party finally paused to collect themselves and heal after the battle.

At present, Tanwyn's dagger was sunk into the creature's chest. Removing it, they had learned quickly, put it right back on its feet.

"We need to find a way to put it down," said Umber. "Permanently."

"She was one of my people," said Nereida, looking at the body so hard she seemed to look through it, to what it might have been when it was alive. "Whatever we do, we're going to do it with respect."

"I think I can be of some service here." Honoria stepped forward. "I'd like to perform the last rites for this being."

The only problem was, Hollis didn't know what last rites were like in the Eight Realms.

"Uh," she said, blinking and looking over at Gloria. "I assume Honoria would know what the last rites should be?"

"Yes," said Gloria. "She would."

Aini, on the other side of the table, grinned. "What are the last rites, then?" she asked.

Gloria let out a short sigh through smiling lips.

"Okay, so," she started. "The Last Rite of the temple you're from, Honoria, is actually oddly fitting for the situation. As someone who follows the Just and Terrible Mistress, the Goddess facet of the sea, those of your order administer water burials." Her hands wove through the air as she spoke, as if trying to meld the comforting creams and oaks of the dining room together with her words, transforming the space into something ancient and holy. "So what you'll do is you'll take a shroud and you'll wrap the body in it, making sure to include personal belongings that will weigh the body down and help it sink. Then, you'll bless the body with holy water and send it to sea. The idea is that from the water we all come, and to the water we shall all return."

An appreciative hush fell over the group.

"Wow." Aini perched her chin on her fist, propped up on an elbow. "You're making this all up as you go, aren't you?"

Gloria didn't say anything, but her smile curled harder into the corner of her lips.

"God," said Aini, a very Umber-like twinkle in her eyes, "that's so hot."

Hollis pursed her lips and looked away. The beat of her heart quickened and something unattractive flushed across her cheeks at Aini calling Gloria *hot*. Maybe she was more of a bard than Hollis realized.

"All right," she said, trying to shift back into her Honoria headspace.

Iffy made the game so special for Hollis, and this was her chance to return the favor. She wanted to do this moment justice. "I'm going to look around in these wardrobes. Is there anything I can use in there?"

"Roll an Investigation check," said the Secret Keeper.

"That's a 15."

She was able to find a cloak, deep blue green in color. In a chest, lock expertly picked by the party's rogue, she found some fine cups that Mercy and Tanwyn immediately began to bicker over ("Is this really the time, ladies?" asked Umber), but also a battered iron shield from ages past.

Hollis took great care describing Honoria's actions—how she gently fashioned the cloak into a shroud, folding the shield safely against the elf's chest inside of it. As she wove the words, she felt the story come to life around them, enclosing them comfortably within the walls of the Castañedas' dining room.

"So I don't think it's pretty," she said at last, hands miming the finishing touches on the burial shroud. She looked to Iffy, searching her friend's face. She hoped her care showed on her own. "Maybe it's not even right."

"Nah." Aini's voice sounded in between her own and Umber's. She wore the same look as before, the one that might have easily belonged to the bard, but this time it was focused solely on Hollis. She smiled, a small gesture that set Hollis's insides fluttering. "I think it's just right."

Hollis smiled, squared her shoulders, and imagined the weight of Honoria's breastplate armor resting on them. "It's right for us, at least. Would you like to say a few words, Nereida?"

"No," Nereida said, shaking her head. "Words aren't my strong suit. I'll just—"

Moving her hands in quick, precise motions, she cast a simple Light spell on a copper coin from her purse and tucked it into the front of the shroud.

"May the light guide you," she whispered.

Honoria nodded and took out her flask of holy water. With a few sweeping arcs of her arm ("Is this how you do it?" Hollis asked Gloria. "It's how *you're* doing it," said Gloria to Hollis), she blessed the body before them.

"Let me help," said Umber, walking up to stand beside her.

And together, with Nereida watching beside them, Umber and Honoria carried the body to the riverbank and eased it into the water. As far as any of them could tell, the body stayed still—finally at peace.

"And that," said Gloria, her voice quiet, "is where we will end it for the night."

As the other girls packed up and chatted on their slow ways to the door, Hollis hung back, her fingers trailing over and over down the curved wooden back of her usual chair. For a moment, she hesitated, Landon's words holding her back, but then she spoke up.

"Hey, Gloria?"

Gloria, rolling up tonight's hand-drawn map (this one mostly in shades of gray and blue, for the river elf encounter), paused to look up at Hollis. "Hmm?"

"I just wanted to say I really like the way you run Secrets & Sorcery." She gave her Secret Keeper a small, private smile.

"Thank you, Hollis," Gloria said, fingers lighting briefly on her heart. "I really like the way you play Secrets & Sorcery."

Hearing those words meant more to Hollis than she'd anticipated. With Chris's opinion of her game always ghosting in the back corners of her mind, she spent so much time worrying she was doing it wrong. Something like pride swirled in her chest. "It feels like this is the right way to play, you know?"

Gloria shrugged. "I think as long as everyone is having fun and feels included, every way can be the right way." She smiled, soft and genuine. "But I'm very glad you found your place in our group."

"Now maybe you can find your place in my car," Iffy called to Hollis from the front door, where she stood waiting with Maggie and Aini.

"Yeah," said Aini. "The party can't go home without you."

"Hey," protested Fran from the sofa. "I am also in the party, you know."

"We'll take you in our hearts, Franny," Maggie said as she opened the door.

"I'm coming!" said Hollis. And, with the rest of the group, she stepped out into the night.

9
ANYWHERE, ANYWHERE

"I MEAN, NOW I *really* want to get whoever did this," Iffy said on the drive home.

Hollis sat in the passenger seat of the Accord, all four windows rolled down. At this time of night, with the summer finally fading away and fall creeping in, the air was almost pleasant and smelled like changing leaves. Hollis anchored her right palm on the frame of the window, fingers moving up and down, riding the wind.

"After all that?" Iffy said. "That bastard—he's going *down*."

"Oh, yeah." Squinting one eye to watch the motion of her hand, Hollis searched for the right words. "Tonight's session was really intense."

"Truly, girl. Also—damn, where did you pull all that from?"

"Huh?"

"All the stuff with the burial rites and shit."

Hollis blinked. "I mean, that was mostly Gloria, wasn't it? She made it all up."

"I mean, yeah, I was there." Iffy flipped her blinker on, turned onto another road. Back on their side of the river, the scenery was more familiar: tightly packed row houses with short, black Stewart Iron Works fencing in states of repair that varied depending on the block. Here, on Russell Street, most of them shone neat and point-tipped in the streetlamps. "But the way Honoria did it all, finding the shroud and all the stuff to tuck into it, like—it was just so cool, Hollis."

For her part, Hollis thought it was pretty cool too. Most of the cool part belonged to Gloria, though; she had just acted it out. Like a playwright giving good lines to a bad actor—the lines would still be good regardless.

Still, there was something special about watching Iffy's face as she told Hollis's part of the story—the story they'd all told together, the two of them and Aini. Even with the chill of the air rushing through the open window, Hollis felt warm with it. She hoped that was what Iffy felt, too.

"I don't know." Her hand moved up and down, up and down. "That was more Honoria than me. She has a mind of her own sometimes."

"Oh, thank God I'm not the only one. I've felt like Nereida does her own thing too," said Iffy. "I thought I was weird."

Hollis was about to say, *Well, maybe it's not that you're not weird, but that we're both the same kind of weird.* She only got so far as opening her mouth when the back pocket of her jeans (the hip pockets on this pair were sewn together, like they were on so many plus-size pants for whatever reason) buzzed.

Iffy raised an eyebrow. "Someone is blowing you up."

"It's probably my mom," said Hollis, pulling her phone out.

But it wasn't her mom.

On her screen, flashing in rapid succession, were three Discord messages. She read the notifications in order.

Aini 10:48 PM
This is probably going to sound creepy and weird.

Aini 10:48 PM
Saying it will probably sound creepy and weird makes it sound creepy and weird.

Aini 10:48 PM
This is the worst.

"What's she saying?" Iffy asked.

"Nothing." Hollis shrugged. Something in her chest quickened as she tucked her phone away again, like she was hiding a secret. But that was silly. She just couldn't chat with Aini now, not while Iffy was driving her home. It would be rude. "But I do get what you mean."

"About what?"

"About it feeling like the characters play themselves. A couple weeks ago, I felt super awkward for talking as someone else in first person. Now it's like—"

"—a second language, right?"

Hollis smiled and nodded.

"See," said Iffy, "you get it."

"I think we just get *each other*, Iffy."

"You know, I think you're right, Hollis." Pulling to a stop in front of Hollis's house, Iffy turned toward Hollis with a broad grin. "I'm glad I started giving you a ride."

Hollis returned the smile. "Me too."

"And *that*," said Iffy, "is enough sentimental bullshit. It's a Friday night, and it's late. Let's get you home. Fridays are for samosas and sleeping!"

"Ah, yes," said Hollis. "The lesser-known S&S."

"Girl, you are such a dork," said Iffy, shaking her head fondly. "I love you."

It slipped out so easily from Hollis's lips that she didn't realize how important it was to her until after she'd clambered out of the front seat and slung her heavy tote bag over her shoulder: "Love you, too, Iffy. See you on the server."

Hollis didn't bother changing into pajamas. Instead, she just kicked off her shoes—black flats from the same store she got most of her clothes—and tugged off her bra. Before she took off her jeans, she retrieved her phone from the back pocket, then flung the pants (and their useless sewn-up side pockets) toward the clothes pile in the corner of her room before slipping between her bedsheets.

And only then did she allow herself to open the Discord app.

Aini 10:49 PM
Hollis?

You there?

Aini 10:50 PM
I know you're not driving.

Aini 10:54 PM
Clearly, I've terrified you.

I hope you can find it in your heart to love a weird creep like me again, someday.

Until then, I'll be here, staring into the middle distance.

Hollis smiled, small and closed-lipped, and shook her head. In these messages, Aini sounded more like Hollis than Hollis did. Her fingers flit across the screen, nails clacking against the glass.

beckwhat 11:12 PM
aini amin-shaw, please calm down.

Aini 11:12 PM
Oh, thank god.

I thought you were breaking up with me.

There was a quickening in Hollis's chest.

beckwhat 11:13 PM
what.

Aini 11:14 PM
Unfriending me forever for being a weirdo who messages you like sixteen times on the way home from a S&S game.

beckwhat 11:14 PM
it was, like, six messages.

Aini 11:15 PM
Nine individual messages.

Not that I counted.

beckwhat 11:15 PM
are you trying to get me to break up with you? (edited)

Aini 11:16 PM
Wow, called out, Buckwheat.

beckwhat 11:17 PM
will you just tell me what you desperately needed to tell me, please?

Aini 11:18 PM
Oh, yes.

There was a reason for all this, wasn't there?

So anyway, as I was saying.

I hope this doesn't sound weird and creepy, but I've really enjoyed the interactions between Honoria and Umber in the games we've played.

Hollis smiled at her screen. Pulling her quilt tighter around her, she snuggled into the warmth that this message flooded her with. Hollis had felt the same ever since that first session, when Umber had saved Honoria from certain doom. It was nice to know Aini did, too.

She suddenly felt very much a part of something, sharing this feeling with Aini. Like they were on the same team. Her short nails clacked against her phone as she replied.

beckwhat 11:20 PM
if that is weird and creepy, then i'm also a weird creep. :/

Aini 11:21 PM
You've got to let me get to the weird and creepy part.

beckwhat 11:22 PM
okay, aini, weird and creep me out.

Aini 11:22 PM
So, I have . . .

Made a playlist for them?

beckwhat 11:23 PM
. . .

Aini 11:24 PM
You can break up with me now.

beckwhat 11:25 PM
what, no!

aini, that's so cool

Aini 11:26 PM
Oh, phew.

https://bit.ly/AnywhereAnywhere

Call me a weird creep, but I just kind of think they have a thing going on?

A full minute passed in which Hollis did nothing but blink at the glow of her screen. She had felt that too—the subtle pull toward Aini at the table, the attention to her storytelling and her words, the way she always looked forward to drawing Umber most when she doodled the party in the margins of her notes. For another thirty seconds, she thought about what to say. At first she banged her fingers on the keyboard in an attempt to borrow one of Fran's all-caps key smashes, but then she backspaced, took a breath, and tried something different.

beckwhat 11:28 PM
oh, yeah, they're like, totally in love.

i'm glad i'm not the only one shipping them.

Aini 11:29 PM
RIGHT?

beckwhat 11:31 PM
yeah, i kind of realized last session that they have some chemistry. (edited)

i mean obviously we should let it play out, i don't want to force it. it wouldn't be fair to them. or wick.

Aini 11:32 PM
No, that would be irresponsible.

Very not-Honoria of us.

beckwhat 11:34 PM
but we should give them a ship name.

Aini 11:35 PM
Are they going to be sailors now?

beckwhat 11:36 PM
no, but i'm so here for that au.

Aini 11:37 PM
Hollis, I didn't know you were bilingual.

beckwhat 11:38 PM
oh my god aini.
and here i thought you were cool.

Aini 11:38 PM
Not as cool as you, apparently.

beckwhat 11:39 PM
actually i think this is the opposite of cool.

it's fandom speak.

au = alternative universe, like, something other than the main canon.

Aini 11:40 PM
So, like, a different Eight Realms where Honoria and Umber are pirates.

beckwhat 11:41 PM
HA.

that's actually a really common au.

i thought you didn't know this stuff?

Aini 11:42 PM
I'm a quick study.

beckwhat 11:43 PM
then a ship name is like a cutesy name for your pairing. relation*ship*.

usually a combination of the character names.

Aini 11:45 PM
Like Rules, from Euphoria.

beckwhat 11:45 PM
WHAT.
you know all of this, don't you.

Aini 11:45 PM
I do.

beckwhat 11:46 PM
and you've been letting me ramble on.

Aini 11:46 PM
I have.

beckwhat 11:47 PM
oh my god.

Aini 11:47 PM
I just like it when you talk about things you're into, okay?

Hollis hummed a sigh.

beckwhat 11:48 PM
you're such a weird creep. :/

Aini 11:49 PM
That's what all the girls tell me.

So.

What's the ship name?

beckwhat 11:50 PM
i was trying to think.

umber and honoria don't combine well at all.

umboria.

humber?

humber maybe.

Aini 11:51 PM
Hollis.

Humber sounds like a cucumber with a bad cold.

We can't do that to our children.

beckwhat 11:52 PM
well!!!

what else you got, aini.

Aini 11:54 PM
What about . . .

Her surname is Steadmore.

beckwhat 11:54 PM
correct.

Aini 11:55 PM
I know. It wasn't a question.

And his is Dawnfast.

beckwhat 11:55 PM
!!!

Aini 11:56 PM
What if we do ...

STEADFAST.

beckwhat 11:56 PM
STEADFAST.

there is literally nothing else we can do.

Aini 11:57 PM
Steadfast it is.

I'll update the playlist title.

I'm also making it collaborative, so you can add songs if
you want.

beckwhat 11:59 PM
i know how a playlist works.

i won't pretend i don't.

like someone else i know.

Aini 12:00 AM
And she's cute when she's sassing, too, dang.

Okay, Beckwhy.

It's actual midnight.

We just had a really intense session.

Let's get some sleep.

You can tell me how much you love my musical taste in the morning.

beckwhat 12:01 AM
yeah, sleep sounds good.

Aini 12:01 AM
I'll talk to you soon.

Sweet dreams.

And before Hollis could find the right emojis to send, Aini's green online bubble changed to the empty black bubble of having just signed off.

Hollis, in a sudden rush she couldn't quite explain, scrolled back up through their conversation until she found the link Aini had sent. Clicking it launched her Spotify app and pulled up *anywhere, anywhere | a steadfast playlist.*

Her eyes flashed down to the songs. The first one had been added last week.

Hollis smiled. A whole week of a hidden playlist. It felt like discovering a secret, like Aini had given her a gift she hadn't even meant to.

Hollis pulled her patchwork quilt up to her chin, hit play, watched the thirty-second ad to get thirty minutes of free music, and listened to the first song.

It was instrumental, and fittingly titled "Intro," by a band called the xx. It started off sparse, just a few simple, repetitive notes on guitar over drums and (Hollis strained to listen, keeping the volume low for the late hour) maybe synth. As the song progressed, it became dense, with moody, non-lyrical vocals laid over the top of the track. It sounded like the start of something—a little unsure, a little exciting, smooth and the smallest bit dark with promise of things to come.

If she'd has to pick a first song for a playlist about her S&S character's budding crush, she couldn't have done better herself.

But like Aini had said, it was late, and like she had said back, sleep really did sound nice. Hollis pressed pause and put her phone on her nightstand. With "Intro" looping in her mind, she did her best to drift off to sleep.

It didn't take nearly as long as usual.

10

A BRAND-NEW RIDE

HOLLIS DIDN'T MESSAGE Aini on Saturday to tell her how great her musical taste was.

She didn't message her on Sunday, either, or even on Monday morning. Doing so would take a bravery Hollis didn't have on a normal day, when the bold nighttime and the strange otherworld of life after a hard S&S session felt far away.

Still, she listened to the playlist on the way to school, in her mom's car. She'd listened all weekend, too.

It turned out Aini Amin-Shaw was even cooler than Hollis had originally suspected. Almost every song on the playlist was a deep cut, and many of them were from years ago, when Hollis herself still listened to Q102, the pop radio station from Cincinnati, and hadn't even discovered independent music. Most of the songs were from queer artists, too: favorites of Aini's like Tegan and Sara ("the grandmothers of sad gay girl tunes," Aini had DMed her after adding a new song into the mix) and girl in red and dodie. It felt a little strange, listening to them and knowing they were from Aini. But when she imagined Honoria into the *she* in the lyrics and Umber's lilting accent into the voices over the chords, Hollis could see how well each song fit the ship.

Aini was very good at this.

So good, in fact, that Hollis briefly considered sharing the playlist with Chris that morning when he and the boys met her at the wall outside school. At the very least, their music selection in the Sentra could use some variety; they always listened to Chris's nu metal when he drove her anywhere. There were a few bands on the playlist Hollis knew Chris would like—like M83, whose epic "Outro" begged to be a S&S game soundtrack.

But as Chris came up and swooped her into an uncomfortable spinning hug, and Landon made obnoxious kissy noises, and Marius cracked open a Monster energy drink the same way he did every Monday morning, Hollis slid her phone (and its Spotify app) back into the pocket of her jeans.

Her friendship with Aini was still so new and, if Hollis was honest with herself, so confusing; the more she got to know Aini, the more she questioned why someone so genuinely cool would want to be her friend in the first place. And somehow their friendship still existed, thrilling and a little bit terrifying and something else she couldn't quite pin down, weighing lightly on her like the weight of a playlist in her back pocket.

In front of her, Marius passed the Monster can to Chris, who spit a stream of the energy drink at Landon like an immature fountain statue.

Maybe the Monday-morning recap wasn't the right time for these two worlds to collide.

And maybe she didn't even want them to. Not yet, at least. Like that first secret week of the playlist that existed before Hollis knew it did, this felt like a special secret she wanted to keep all for herself.

But what Hollis was realizing now, sitting in first-hour math class, was that she'd spent so much time over the weekend listening to the playlist and debating whether to add a few songs of her own (she hadn't yet) that she hadn't studied *at all* for the test she was now taking. The numbers on the page swam into the letters, all the x's and the y's. But all Hollis could solve for was the xx.

She finished her test early. Finishing early always made her suspicious that she was missing something vital everyone else knew, which was what took them so much longer. She shifted in her plastic desk chair, looking around like she could track down that missing something if she only cast a furtive glance in the right direction.

To pass the time, Hollis drew in the bottom half of the page, left empty for three bonus problems. She wouldn't be solving those—she wouldn't get the points anyway—but she was thankful for the extra blank space.

With "Intro" still playing in her mind, Hollis tried to capture the feeling of the song. In rougher lines than she usually used, she penciled in two figures—one quite tall with round, powerful thighs and strong arms beneath breastplate armor, the other on the shorter side, with lanky limbs and a lute slung over his back. She placed them on opposite sides of the page's center, their backs to the viewer and their heads looking over their shoulders, not quite at each other. On their faces, she tried to place the same feelings the song gave her: excitement, uncertainty, cautious optimism. The possibility of being on the brink of something epic.

Beneath them both, she wrote *Anywhere, Anywhere* in a looping, slanted script.

She was halfway through cleaning up the second word when the bell rang and Mrs. Grimes said, in her scratchy Southern drawl, "All right, y'all, pencils down and papers in."

On her way out the door, Hollis turned in her first Steadfast drawing without having time to take a picture.

"Hey, girl."

This time, Hollis didn't have to look to know it was Iffy. Just the sound of her voice lit up the hall so much brighter than the fluorescent bulbs overhead.

"Hey," she said, turning toward that light with a smile.

"Don't go smiling at me like that yet. I have bad news for you."

Hollis's smile faltered.

"Okay, ouch, but more suitable, I guess." Iffy shrugged, unfazed. "GSA is doing a last-minute thing on Friday, and I can't miss it since I'm the president, so I'm going to have to miss the game."

"Oh."

"So I can't give you a *ride*," she said, making a sympathetic face.

"*Oh.*"

Iffy nodded. "I know."

"That's fine," said Hollis, though she knew her face said something else entirely. "I'll let Gloria know I have to miss, too."

"What?"

"I don't have another ride on Friday. Mom's here until late with the Dead Playwrights Society, and Chris's S&S group meets that night too. It'll be fine." It wasn't. Hollis's stomach sank like a stone. "We can get the girls to fill us in on Discord."

"Hollis, you are full of such nonsense." Iffy pulled her phone out of her hip pocket. Her thumbs flew over the screen for a second, and then Hollis felt a buzz in her back pocket.

iffy.elliston 9:10 AM

hey girls

i had a thing come up friday so hollis needs a ride

who's got her?

"Iffy," said Hollis, the same way so many of them found themselves saying Fran's name around the table on Fridays: a little admonishing, but also appreciative.

"You're not going to miss just because we're doing a sit-in at that shitty bakery in Florence," said Iffy. "I bet—"

Iffy's words were cut off by the buzz of their phones in their hands, half a second apart.

Aini 9:11 AM
I got her, don't worry.

Just give me your address before Friday so I can GPS it, Beckwhere.

"Aini coming in clutch," said Iffy, giving Hollis a high five. "That bitch is quality, I tell you what."

"Yeah." Hollis smiled—ostensibly at Iffy but mostly to herself. Her cheeks warmed, pink and pleasant-feeling. "She's pretty cool, I guess."

On a normal Friday, Hollis would be waiting for Iffy and sketching calmly at the kitchen dinette, the nervous feeling she'd had that first evening having melted away. When her mom came home from school (usually ten minutes or so before Iffy showed up), she would tell her she was going to Gloria's, and her mom would say, "I know, honey, that's where you went last week."

But *this* Friday, Hollis was waiting for Aini, not Iffy, and so instead the waiting went like this:

"Shit, shit, shit," said Hollis in the bathroom mirror.

She'd spilled sweet tea all down her front. And despite her best efforts to blot it away with a wet washcloth, a watery stain stretched all the way up to her collar.

It had taken her fifteen minutes to pick this blouse.

The waiting also went like this:

Hollis, refilling her spilled tea, had a moment of gut-dropping panic in which she thought she was supposed to be bringing snacks again this week. She only recovered her (admittedly tenuous) calm after checking the Discord chat and remembering it was Fran and Gloria's turn this week.

And it went like this, too:

Hollis peeked through the closed blinds for the ninth time, watching the street corner, before she realized she didn't even know what Aini's car looked like.

Hollis was used to worrying, but this was a *lot*, even for her. Usually, she wouldn't be so nervous about her outfit or about being at the door at exactly the right time; Iffy was always a few minutes early or late, and other than Maggie, all the girls were pretty laid-back when it came to how they dressed.

But this week, with Aini's playlist having confirmed that she was, in fact, the coolest girl in town, everything felt different. More high-stakes. Like Hollis needed to be cool too—to be more like Aini. She wanted to appear smooth and put-together and *not* like she'd been waiting by the door for Aini to arrive, double-checking that her sneakers were tied so she didn't trip on the laces.

Or where she was when the doorbell rang and Aini actually arrived: mid-hand-wash in the bathroom.

"You've got to be—" Hollis muttered in protest, rushing out of the bathroom. Darting into the kitchen, she grabbed her tote bag from the table and headed down the short hallway to the front door, framed photographs of herself at various ages staring down at her from the walls as she went.

"Sorry," she said when she opened the door. "I was peeing."

"Always such a charmer, Buckwhere," said Aini, shaking her head. She had changed her hair color again, from faded teal to an orange so deep yet so bright it was almost neon. Neon autumn oak leaf. It was a color only someone as confident as Aini could pull off.

And she had just told this girl she'd been peeing. Hollis's face flushed.

"Yes, well." A sloppy save at best. "Are you ready to go?"

"Yep." Aini twirled her keys on her index finger. "Let's hit the road."

Hollis followed Aini down the front path toward the car.

"Here," said Aini. "The door's a little tricky; you've got to open it just so."

She opened the door, which didn't look tricky at all, then trotted around to her side of the car. Trying not to feel mortified, Hollis sank into the passenger seat.

It was the nicest car Hollis Beckwith had ever been inside. She didn't know enough about cars to know what sort it was, but it was a respectable hunter green, with four doors and brown leather interiors, unlike the stained tan upholstery of Iffy's Accord or the gray-and-random-rainbow-party-print of Chris's Sentra. As she settled into the supple seat, Hollis suspected it was heated. It felt pleasantly warm under her bottom.

It also felt like she should be embarrassed about her house, with its tiny, messy front yard (which was mostly unruly beds of zinnias that needed to be pulled out for the coming winter) and its painted brick, the red faded from years of sun and rain. Aini's car probably cost more than her mom's mortgage.

"Would it be really corny if we listened to the Steadfast playlist on the way?" Aini slid into place behind the steering wheel.

What Hollis might have said if they had been chatting on Discord was *I don't know, Aini, when has being corny ever stopped you before?* Even thinking it pulled a smile across Hollis's lips, sent a fluttering of jittery wings beating inside her rib cage. But chatting on Discord with Aini from the comfort of her room was, it turned out, very different from chatting with Aini while sitting in the front seat of her car, which smelled like all that brown leather and also like something she guessed was just Aini: dark and woodsy, with a hint of something green and floral. Saying those words out loud here felt impossible.

So Hollis just said, "I think it's fine."

And so they rode to Gloria's apartment listening to *Anywhere, Anywhere* on Spotify (which played via Bluetooth straight through the sound system, without ads). Aini missed all the shortcuts Iffy usually took, so when they finally found a parking spot a street over, they were almost late.

"Ah." Aini tapped the clock face of her console. "A literal minute to spare."

The clock clicked over to six p.m.

"Or, well, al—"

REHN, REHN, REHN, REHN.

Oh no.

In a motion she desperately wanted to be smooth, Hollis tried to yank her buzzing phone from her back pocket to silence it. But Hollis Beckwith wasn't smooth. She banged her elbow on the boxwood panel of the door beside her ("*Damn it,*" she huffed), and her phone slipped from her hand and onto the impeccably clean floorboard below. Because she was round and cars were hard to navigate with a belly, it took a heavy rock forward for her to be able to bend to retrieve it. Her phone helpfully kept blaring that earsplitting noise the entire time. Finally, her finger jabbed at the screen to cut it off.

"I . . ." Hollis wanted to say sorry, or maybe just melt into the leather beneath her and let Aini leave for the S&S game without her. Instead, she just said, "Should probably take my meds."

After all *that*, she definitely needed them.

"Yeah, no problem." Aini, like always, didn't seem bothered. "Here." She turned and ducked around to the back seat. "I keep water handy for this reason."

"For girls freaking out in your front seat before they take their anxiety meds?"

"Yeah, it happens a lot," said Aini, smooth in the way Hollis had failed to be just a moment ago. She handed Hollis a mostly full glass water bottle. "No, Hollis, because I usually take my meds on the way home on Friday nights."

Fishing in her tote bag for her medicine bottle, Hollis snorted. Aini and her sweet, silly jokes.

"If we run late, especially," Aini said, her voice still light but also serious. Her hands worked through the air as she explained. "I take them later because my antidepressants make me really sleepy, even after, like, two years. Not to overshare or anything, but that's kind of why I'm here. I got really bad last year, you know, with isolating, even with the meds. But playing S&S with Gloria every week helped pull me out of it. Even on game nights when I didn't want to show up as Aini, I knew I needed to show up as my character, for the party. It's part of the magic of gaming, I guess." She waved her fingers and grinned, but her expression was earnest. "Sometimes it's easier to be yourself when you can pretend to be someone else for a while."

Popping her pill into her mouth, Hollis looked at Aini. She didn't look like the kind of girl who would need antidepressants. She certainly didn't act like she did. But, Hollis reminded herself, mental illness didn't *look* like anything. Maybe this Aini, the one sitting beside her speaking frankly about medication and her mental illness, was the Aini she got because her meds were working.

Hollis swallowed hers.

"Mine make me feel a little checked out for, like, fifteen minutes," she shared, shrugging. "But I've been on them since sixth grade, so I'm used to it now, mostly."

"Oh," said Aini, her head cocking to the side again.

"Sorry, yeah, I shouldn't talk about it," Hollis corrected. Chris and the school gang never liked to be reminded of Hollis's mental health issues.

"What? No, that's fine, duh." Aini waved her hand like it was nothing at all. "I had just noticed that when you first get here, you're always a little more quiet than usual, but then you come right back to regular Hollis."

"Oh, yeah." It was Hollis's turn to cock her head, considering. "That might be why. Or, you know. The anxiety thing."

Aini laughed. In the enclosed space of the car, it rolled pleasantly around them. Even before it stopped, Hollis already wanted more of it.

"Yeah, you know, or that." She smiled. "You good?"

As if she were at a medicine counter at a hospital, Hollis opened her mouth to show she'd taken her pill.

"There's a good girl," Aini said, then laughed again and added, "Oh my God, please pretend I never said that, okay?"

Hollis grinned wide. "As long as you forget I told you I was peeing when you got to my house, it's a deal."

"Oh, that?" Aini shook her head. "Oh, no. I'm going to cherish that memory forever."

Hollis flushed. She wasn't sure whether she was more embarrassed about the peeing part or the forever part.

"I'm getting out of your car now, Aini," Hollis said. And she did.

With the sudden absence of the heated seat, her butt felt especially unwarmed in the chilly night. She headed toward Gloria's door, Aini following with short, brisk steps behind her.

"Sooooo," said Aini, her voice dragging out the *O*, intentionally awkward.

"Sooooo," said Hollis, doing the same.

And then, at the exact same time, they both burst into fits of laughter.

"Oh my *God*," said Hollis, between rib-aching draws on her diaphragm. She didn't remember the last time she'd laughed so much in one four-hour stretch. Then again, she couldn't remember the last time an S&S plan had gone so spectacularly sideways. She could still see in the theater of her mind the way Mercy Grace had suddenly popped back into existence when the invisibility spell Hollis and Aini (who were piloting Nereida for the night in Iffy's absence) had read wrong tuned out to work nothing like they'd thought, could still hear Fran's shrieking screams as she mimicked running from the town guard.

"For real," said Aini—or rather, mouthed Aini, mostly, because she was laughing so hard. Hollis could just barely hear the breathy, wheezy words underneath the sound. In the golden glow of the streetlamps overhead, with one hand on the steering wheel to guide them home, Aini was beautiful, like a still life in motion Hollis was suddenly itching to draw.

Aini shook her head and turned smoothly, crossing back over the Ohio River. For the whole length of the Clay Wade Bailey Bridge, their laughter smoldered in the air between the front seats.

"But seriously," said Aini when they both finally calmed down. "Which of us is going to tell Iffy we got Nereida arrested the first time we ever tried to play her?"

"Don't say it like *that*!" Hollis dissolved into laughter again. "That makes it sound so much worse!"

"Oh, as if *hey, Ifs, darling, we got Nereida arrested, but don't worry, the rest of the party got arrested, too* sounds any better!"

Hollis scrunched her nose playfully. "Well, when you put it like that, I guess it really doesn't."

"Yeah, I didn't think so." Aini shook her head. "So much for Gloria trying to give us a nice, easy session after last week. Leave it to Mercy to get us all thrown in jail."

"We'll never know who would have won the drinking contest now," said Hollis, her chest still aching from laughter.

"Oh, Umber. Hands down."

"What?!" Hollis shook her head. "Honoria is a captain of the Cerulean Guard. You better believe she can drink ale with the best of them."

"Oh, I'm sure she's entirely capable," said Aini, and Hollis could tell she meant it. "But Umber is a bard. Drinking is kind of his thing."

Right. To be honest, Hollis sometimes forgot Umber was a bard. It wasn't because Aini was bad at playing him. She played an excellent bard, and her ukulele was a great touch. It was more that when Hollis sat at the table with Aini—and when Honoria adventured with Umber—she felt so far removed from the invasive, icky feeling she'd had during the dreadful Games-A-Lot half session that the word *bard* didn't seem like something she could apply to either Aini *or* her character. Even when Umber flirted with Honoria—which he did, blatantly, in ways that made *Hollis's* cheeks flush and her heart flutter at the table—it was always flattering and never creepy.

Landon would probably say Aini was playing a bard wrong. Hollis, though, felt pretty sure Aini was doing it exactly *right*. It was impossible not to be drawn in.

.She rested her elbow on the central console, just to get closer, and said, "Eh, maybe you're right," like it was a concession.

"Nah," said Aini. "That's usually you." And Hollis could tell Aini meant that, too.

As they approached Fourth Street, Hollis almost pointed out the shortcut Iffy usually took when she drove her home. It would shave a good few minutes off their trip. But an extra few minutes with Aini felt like a better way to pass the time. She didn't want to leave the blue glow of the car's sleek speedometer (or the radiant warmth of Aini's smile) just yet.

Shaking her head to herself, Hollis leaned forward, reaching toward the dashboard.

"I'm turning this one up," she said, and cranked up the volume on an Ezra Furman song from the Steadfast playlist—but not loud enough to drown out the musical sound of Aini's lingering laughter.

The following Monday morning, Hollis got last week's math test back.

C−, said the letter grade at the top, which was better than she was expecting. The number beside it said she'd just barely made the cutoff, only a point away from a D+.

Taking this as a Monday-morning miracle, Hollis flipped to the back page. Her illustration of Umber and Honoria was still there, their eyes not quite meeting over their respective shoulders. With her finger, Hollis traced the line of Umber's gaze.

But it wasn't only the look in Umber's eyes that caught her own. In the same red pen Mrs. Grimes used for grading, there was a note scribbled in the once-elegant, now-aging cursive of her math teacher.

I don't think this is how you apply the formula, the note said, *but these two are cute. +1.*

Hollis snorted a laugh.

"Are you quite all right, Miss Beckwith?" asked Mrs. Grimes, now making her way down the row an aisle over as she continued handing back the tests.

"Yes, ma'am," Hollis said.

When Mrs. Grimes turned to the next aisle, Hollis eased her phone out of her back pocket and snapped a picture.

Opening up Discord, she pulled up her messages with Aini and attached the image, then hit send.

beckwhat 8:34 AM
steadfast just saved me from a d+ on this math test.

11

LACIE WITH AN *I-E*

ON WEDNESDAY, HOLLIS went to Chris's house to hang out and to play video games—or, more accurately, to sketch in her notebook while Chris played video games.

"Oh, damn it," he shouted from the other side of the sofa, throwing a hand up in the air. The motion jostled Hollis's cushion and her hand slipped on her paper. If this had been out of the ordinary, she might have huffed at having to dig for her eraser in the space between her thigh and the arm of the sofa. But she was used to it. She had been erasing Damn It marks from her line work since sixth grade, back when they were only Darn It marks.

Hollis smiled to herself mildly. It was times like these when she felt most in sync with Chris—just the two of them, alone but together, doing their own thing. It reminded her of middle school, back when they first became friends. Because *Bradley, Chris* usually came after *Beckwith, Hollis*, they'd often ended up next to each other on assigned seating charts. Sometimes Hollis wondered if it was all those years sitting together at trapezoid tables that made their relationship work. The convenience of this closeness had certainly made it much easier to be his friend originally.

Chris often said that what he liked about having Hollis as his girlfriend was that he didn't have to try so hard. On Wednesdays, Hollis thought she understood what he meant (even though her mom had frowned when Hollis once tried to explain it to her). It was enough for both of them to just exist, quietly and without effort, in the same space together.

Hollis erased the Damn It mark, sweeping the leftover grit away with the side of her hand. She asked, "Did you get ganked again?"

"Yes. There are two twelve-year-olds camped in the alien base, sniping people. Dickholes." He added into the headset that bobbled by his lips, "Yeah, that's right, I'm talking about you two. Uh-huh. Yeah. Well, I'll make sure to tell her." His hand covered the microphone. "They said my mom didn't mind their dickholes last night."

Hollis snorted. Twelve-year-olds.

She returned to her sketch of Honoria and Umber from last session, when the party had been thrown into jail together. She was sketching the place where Umber's head rested on Honoria's shoulder as they sat beside each other on the cell floor when Chris's front door banged open, then closed again.

"'Sup, bitch," said Landon.

Again, if this had been unusual, Hollis would have looked up from her artwork, but she had been hearing Landon call Chris a bitch ever since the two became friends freshman year. She moved just enough to angle her page away from Landon's prying eyes and began shading in Umber's curls where they cascaded onto Honoria's shoulder.

"Oh my God," said a voice that definitely wasn't Landon's. It was high and sweet and long on the vowels. At *this*, Hollis looked up.

There was a girl in Chris's living room.

She was small, though not quite as small as Aini. Compared to Hollis, she was petite in every way. She was beautiful, too, with long blond hair and bright blue eyes. And she had the unfortunate quality of being practically glued to Landon's side, holding his hand so hard that her knuckles were white where her fingers laced with his.

Hollis shot Chris a look that said, very plainly, *What the hell*. But he was busy getting killed by the twelve-year-olds again, and so he missed it.

"You gotta help me, bro," he huffed. "These MOTHERFU—"

"Hollis, slide me a controller," Landon said, plopping into the armchair by the sofa.

The girl slid into the seat with Landon, somehow fitting into a space clearly only meant for one. One of her hands disappeared between the upholstery and Landon's hip. Hollis was glad she couldn't see where, exactly, it had gone.

"You're Hollis," said the girl.

"Um," said Hollis. "Yes."

"I'm Lacie," said Lacie. "With an *I-E*."

"Hey . . . Lacie."

"Yeah, *that's right*, dickholes," said Chris. "My boy just spawned in!"

"I'm about to check you," said Landon, "*and* wreck you."

Lacie-with-an-*I-E* giggled.

"He's so hot." By some miracle of space, Lacie managed to wiggle closer to Landon, reaching up to run her fingers through his flat hair. On the far side of the sofa, Hollis frowned. Everything about Lacie—from her already knowing who Hollis was to her thinking Landon was attractive in any way, shape, or form—was off.

"I didn't know Landon was bringing a friend," she said to the room.

If she'd known it was all right to bring friends to their Wednesday hangouts, Hollis would have invited Iffy or Aini. At least then she would've had someone to talk to while the boys blasted aliens.

"Girlfriend," grunted Landon, mashing on the controller.

"For a whole week!" said Lacie proudly, like this was a feat. "Landon finally saw me looking at him in band, but I'm sure you've heard all about it."

Hollis had never heard anything about Lacie, whether over the last week or before. Or maybe she had? She couldn't be sure. Last week she'd been much more worried about Aini—Aini's playlist, Aini as her ride, Aini as her sudden, impossible friend. It was possible Lacie had been around, but Hollis's attention had been elsewhere.

"Wow," said Hollis. "Congrats."

"And this is our first double date!" Lacie reached up to pinch Landon's cheek. Instead of jerking away, which is what Hollis would have expected him to do, Landon leaned into her touch, then turned his head to the side, making a kissy face and trying to catch her fingers with his lips.

"Landon, *no!*" she squealed, but allowed her fingers to be caught anyway.

No, thought Hollis, she probably would have remembered if Lacie had been around last week. There was no way she and Landon could have been missed, being this . . . *Cute* wasn't the right word, because Landon was involved. But even Hollis couldn't deny that the pair of them had something sticky-sweet going on with all that PDA. It looked natural, the way Landon pretended to gobble up Lacie's fingers, covering them with what were probably very dry, chapped-lipped kisses. He was so distracted by her that he died in-game, respawned, and didn't even stop to swear at the twelve-year-old who'd done it.

Landon was attentive with Lacie, the same way he always was with the boys' S&S game. And as with the boys' S&S game, it was hard for Hollis to see this in action and not feel horribly on the outside of it.

"Oh, you're asking for it now!" cried Chris, and he swore colorfully.

Hollis looked over at him, across the two empty couch cushions that lay between them. Though Landon and Marius sometimes razzed them for it, she had never really minded the lack of clingy contact between her and Chris. They kissed sometimes, when Chris wanted to, and it wasn't the worst. And they hung out practically always—or at least when neither of them was playing S&S with other people—even if they weren't ever hanging *on* each other.

Sometimes, when she was anxious, Hollis worried maybe there was something wrong with her for not wanting all of that with Chris. But on most days, she simply chalked it up to them being different. They had been friends for so long before they started dating, for one. For another, they just weren't that kind of couple. And, at least on most days, that was okay.

But with the stark contrast of Lacie and Landon right there, it was harder for Hollis to ignore the distance between her and Chris. In fact, Lacie and Landon, tangled up in their chair, looked a lot like Umber and Honoria did in her drawing—like they fit together, wherever they were.

Hollis frowned down at her sketch, at the natural way she'd drawn them together, and wondered where she'd pulled that inspiration from. It certainly wasn't from her and Chris. The way Honoria leaned into Umber so naturally reminded Hollis of being in Aini's car, reaching forward to turn up a song Aini had picked out for her—for Honoria.

Hollis never had trouble being close to *Aini*.

She closed her sketchbook abruptly.

"Oh, shoot," she said, looking at her phone. "When did it get to be eight? I have to head home."

"Do you need a ride, Hol?" Chris asked, but aside from mashing the right trigger on his controller, he didn't move an inch.

Hollis really did need a ride. Her house was a few too many blocks away for her to walk in the dark. Covington never felt unsafe in the daylight, but on this side of Madison Street at this time of night, it transformed into a different place, all retreating taillights and suggestive shouts from around the corners. Hollis wasn't keen to encounter anything that lurked around the corners at this hour. But when she imagined sitting in Chris's front seat, all she could think about was sitting in *Aini's* front seat. Her chest fluttered as if she were hearing the contagious, twinkling sound of Aini's laughter all over again.

"Nope," she said, popping the *P* sound. "I got this."

She stood. Before she crossed in front of the screen, she waited for Chris to nod—their system so she didn't cut off his line of sight at an important moment.

"See you tomorrow," he said.

"Yeah," she said. "See you."

"Bye, Hollis," called Lacie. She bumped her shoulder playfully into Landon. "Lan, say bye to Hollis!"

"Yeah, Lan," said Hollis. Literally no one, ever, called Landon "Lan"—except Landon himself, when he introduced himself to girls. Apparently this time it had stuck.

"Bye," he said. Hollis could hear the eye roll in the word.

"He's so *cute*," said Lacie.

And before she was forced to process *cute* and *Landon* in the same thought again, Hollis stepped out into the night alone.

Uncommon Grounds Coffeehouse was a little too cool for Hollis.

It was only a few blocks closer to the river than Hollis's neighborhood, but those few blocks made a world of difference. Here, the turn-of-the-century townhomes had been renovated and flipped, their roofs subdivided and their rents raised. Many of the arty young people who'd made the neighborhood so interesting in the first place had been pushed out, replaced by middle-aged couples with children or dogs.

Uncommon Grounds had been around before all that—was so cool, it was perhaps one of the reasons the area got developed to start with, Hollis sometimes thought—and even the dark, original hardwood floors held a shine of something special, like the boards themselves knew how rare the place was.

If it was too cool for her, it was certainly too cool for Chris. But both of them sat at one of its mismatched tables regardless, each clutching a cup of black coffee.

It didn't taste terribly good, but then Hollis hadn't yet gotten a taste for the stuff, so even good coffee—this was supposed to be good coffee—didn't do much for her. But ever since she'd left last night's video game session, Hollis hadn't been able to shake the feeling in her stomach that she had done something wrong. Maybe it was all that PDA from Lacie and Landon, or that she'd left when she really could have stayed a little longer, but something felt off. In an effort to settle the feeling, she'd suggested that she and Chris stop for coffee after school so they could spend some time together, just the two of them.

"Mmm," she said, nodding at Chris. "Good, right?"

Chris had started drinking coffee in middle school and was proud to say so, loudly, to anyone who would listen.

He shrugged. "It's all right, I guess."

"Come on," Hollis said with a grin. "I know this place is your favorite. Don't play it cool for— Oh."

Hollis's phone buzzed where it rested on the table between them. Picking it up, she saw a handful of notifications from the Discord server. Though she didn't read all the messages, she could tell the conversation was about the party's prison stay. She caught one in particular from Aini (*Honoria is literally our only hope! She's always the one carrying our party's two collective brain cells*) that made her laugh as she slid her phone into her tote bag.

"What's so funny?" Chris asked, taking another sip of coffee.

"Oh, just some game stuff." When Chris raised an eyebrow, Hollis waved a dismissive hand. "Stupid stuff about us getting thrown in jail, you know, little inside jokes."

But Chris wasn't laughing. He scowled down at his cup.

Hollis looked on, bemused. "If it's bad coffee, Chris, we can get them to make something else."

"It's not that," said Chris. "I just think it's . . ."

He trailed off, which he didn't do often. Hollis had known Chris long enough—six years long enough—to understand it meant something was bothering him.

"Hey. What's up?"

"It's nothing."

"Come on." Hollis dipped her head to the side. "You can pull that stuff on the boys, but I know better."

"No, it's—" He started and stopped, then shook his head once. "I just think it's shitty of you to read your S&S Discord while we're hanging out, especially if you're not going to tell me about what they're saying."

Whatever she had been expecting, it wasn't that.

"What?" Hollis shook her head, taken aback. "I didn't."

"How did you know it was a bunch of jokes, then?"

Hollis cocked her head to the side. "It was just the notifications, Chris. I just saw one, like, in passing."

"It's still not cool to leave me out like that."

Hollis snorted a laugh.

Across from her, Chris crossed his arms.

Hollis blinked at him incredulously, her smile falling away. "Hold on. Are you—you're serious?"

He shrugged again.

There were many things Hollis thought to say about this. That it was ridiculous, first and foremost, because it was. That she literally hadn't done what he said she had, for another, because there was no way reading *one message*—unintentionally!—counted. And that if anyone should know about leaving someone out of their S&S game, it was him, because the No-Girlfriend Rule still barred her from joining his in perpetuity, regardless of whether *she* shared *her* inside jokes and Discord chats or not.

There were so many things to say, but Hollis was too surprised and upset to get any of them out. She felt her cheeks start to flush. "Oh my *God*," she said instead.

"Come on, Hol." Chris's eyes pleaded with her. "You know what I mean. Don't be like that."

Be like what? she wanted to say. *You?*

"You know, this coffee sucks," she said instead. "I think I'll go home."

"Hollis," sighed Chris. He ran his hand through his hair in frustration.

She pushed up out of her armchair, taking her almost-full coffee mug to the bussing cart near the trash can.

Chris trailed behind her, hands in his pockets. "Can I at least give you a ride?"

Hollis shrugged. She had forgotten about that piece of this equation.

It was going to be a very quiet ride back to her house.

It wasn't a fight, not yet, but Hollis's anxiety warned that it would be soon.

"Is this going to be a big deal?" Maggie asked, crossing her arms over her chest the same way Gloria would soon be crossing a storyline out of their S&S game.

Gloria had just introduced the next path of their journey: after their release from jail, the party's continued trek north would take them through the Fernglen. As soon as the Secret Keeper said that name, Maggie immediately withdrew.

Tanwyn hailed from the Fernglen, apparently, and Maggie was *not* interested in going back home.

"It doesn't have to be a big deal, if you don't want it to be," Gloria, ever the diplomat, said in her best Secret Keeper voice.

But to Hollis, sitting not-quite-across from Maggie, it certainly felt like a big deal. For one, she had never seen the influencer lose her composure like this; Maggie seemed genuinely uncomfortable, which put Hollis on edge too. And she wasn't the only one, either. Beside her, Iffy sat unnaturally still, and Fran, unable to keep a straight face under even the best circumstances, was doing an impression of the grimacing emoji, looking back and forth between Maggie and Gloria.

Hollis's mind swam with yesterday's Uncommon Grounds incident. That same energy rippled around the table this Friday night. Given how quiet Chris had been at school all day—given how comfortable she felt in her renewed silence with him—Hollis wasn't sure she could handle the same sort of schism at this table, too.

Hollis's chest tightened as she waited for the same shutdown to happen between Gloria and Maggie. Her mind raced with anxiety.

"I just—" Maggie stopped. Closing her eyes, she took a deep breath, then started again. "I just really like that I can fade into the background with Tan." As she spoke, her finger ruffled the same corner of her character sheet over and over, turning it soft. "In real life, I'm kind of always *on*, you know? I kind of always have to be *Maggie Harper*, so it's really nice to just be the weird goat girl with the bat-cat here in the Eight Realms. That's part of what I like the most about playing with all of you. It's sort of like a vacation. In a good way."

"Hmm," hummed Gloria thoughtfully. She took a moment to give Maggie's words space, then said, "I would love to find a way to both honor those feelings and also give your wonderful, weird goat girl a place in our story together, but we can put that on hold for now if you want."

Maggie considered for a moment, while the rest of the table waited quietly. Finally, she said, "We can go forward now, but maybe after the game you and I can talk about backstory stuff for the future."

Gloria nodded. "That sounds like a great plan to me."

And then the game moved on. Gloria went back to her narration; Iffy relaxed, her pencil poised to resume take notes; Aini patted Maggie on the shoulder, then strummed a ukulele chord; and Fran went back to stacking her dice into a tower, her face the blank slate of trying to pay attention.

It was only Hollis who needed a moment to process what had happened. There had been no *huh* to challenge Maggie's feelings, no accusation that she was being shitty or uncool, no suspicious silence to shut anyone down. And Maggie wasn't even an experienced player, like Aini; she'd known Gloria exactly as long as Hollis had, which was certainly less than the six years Hollis had been friends with Chris.

In her back pocket, Hollis's phone, with an unanswered text from Chris left on read hours ago, felt heavy.

Beside her, Aini nudged her with her elbow. The small movement was enough to bring Hollis back into the game, setting her thoughts aside to worry over later.

In the coming days, Hollis would read about the vanished Fernglen in her notes (and note the arrow she'd drawn—which Iffy had highlighted bright orange—connecting it to a question mark that represented whatever had taken Wick), but what stuck with her as she packed up her notebook and her borrowed dice was less about the game and more about the girls. If a disagreement like tonight's had taken place at her lunch table, it would have become a full-on fight. Her argument with Chris, for that matter, only fell short of a fight because that wasn't the sort of thing they did. Hollis didn't have much in the way of examples—not from Chris and especially not from her parents, who had fought easily and about anything until they divorced and Hollis's dad vanished from both of their lives—but she suspected that something special had happened tonight. She thought it probably had a lot to do with Gloria and the sort of friendships she worked hard to foster around her table.

The sort of friendships Hollis was increasingly unsure she had with her *real* friends—or even with Chris.

Guilt surged, hot and fast, through her chest. It was only now, after the unexpected events of the session, that Hollis stopped to think maybe Chris hadn't been upset about her messages—maybe he'd been upset about *her*. The whole reason she'd suggested they get coffee in the first place was to give them some one-on-one time, a bit of space to remember themselves and their friendship.

If she was being honest, Hollis didn't think she had done anything wrong. Glancing at her messages hadn't taken anything away from their time together. *Chris's* reaction had been what ruined their time together. But, like she had last night, she now found herself sitting with a strange feeling of having done something wrong.

Hollis understood what it was like to feel left out of an S&S game. *She* had felt that way for years. The last thing she wanted Chris to feel now was as left out as she did. Even if by accident, she had made him feel exactly that at Uncommon Grounds.

So when Hollis got home, she flopped onto her bed, picked up her phone, opened her text thread with her boyfriend, and typed.

you know, i was kind of a jerk yesterday.

it was supposed to be a time for us, not the girls.

i'm sorry.

ice cream this weekend?

Three little dots appeared right away, and then:

christopher: yeah sounds good

christopher: pick you up after church?

Though she still couldn't shake the feeling of wrongness, Hollis nodded to herself.

it's a date.

12
SLEEPOVERS & SORCERY

HOLLIS'S PHONE BUZZED on her nightstand. She opened one eye and saw:

Gloooooooooooooria 6:23 AM
@everyone

Gloooooooooooooria 6:23 AM
Who's up?

Gloooooooooooooria 6:23 AM
I've got a last-ish minute proposition.

Even for a school day, it was too early for this. Hollis sat up in bed anyway, yanking her faded quilt up with her as she went. Wiping the goop from her eyes with the back of her hand, she reached for her phone and read through the rapid-fire conversation.

Gloooooooooooooria 6:24 AM
So here's the deal.

Mom's in Columbus for the weekend for some nurses' seminar, so Franny and I have the place to ourselves.

So what I'm asking is . . . sleepover session tomorrow?

uwuFRANuwu 6:24 AM
YEEEEEE

Aini 6:25AM
OH HECK YES.

Sorry.

Got possessed by Fran there for a second.

Oh, heck yes.

iffy.elliston 6:26 AM
i have a volunteer thing saturday afternoon and a big birthday extravaganza for a friend all day sunday and i still need to shop for that and also finish this bitch of a paper for AP english but my friday night is still free

but if i get less than an a on this paper i hope you know im coming for yall

thats a yes of course in case yall couldn't tell

maggnitude10 6:27 AM
I'll order pizza for us all!

This place on the east side does a good vegan pizza.

In the bleary light of the too-early morning, Hollis Beckwith smiled so hard her cheeks hurt.

beckwhat 6:28 AM
regular pizza for me, please.

but otherwise i'm so down for this.

The bottom of her screen read *several people typing*: a new favorite sight of hers, because it meant all her friends were excited about the same thing she was, at the same time. Still, Hollis closed the app and turned the notifications off. Just for the next few minutes, she told herself. Surely the first-ever Secrets & Sorcery sleepover warranted a few more minutes to rest her eyes. Shifting, she settled back into her sheets, her soft quilt still fragrant with sleep.

"So what do girls even do at sleepovers?" asked Chris, who sat beside Hollis at the lunch table on Friday.

Lately, their table had gotten cramped. Lacie-with-an-*I-E* had started sitting with them, the chair she wedged between Hollis and Landon becoming permanent. She brought two auxiliary friends with her: Tabitha, a girl goth enough to do her name justice, and Wendy, who explained that she spelled her name *Wyndee* so her cosplay accounts had more of a brand.

"*Those* girls?" Landon cocked a daring eyebrow at Hollis. "Probably have pillow fights and make out."

"I'm listening, I'm listening," said Marius, leaning in.

"Get out, Marius," snapped Hollis, the pit of her stomach dropping.

"Or LARP as whatever slutty characters they're playing." Landon paused, considering. "Are any of the girls even hot, Hollis? Or are they all, you know—"

Landon looked her up and down, his expression unimpressed.

Hollis's stomach plummeted further. She shrank back, retreating behind arms crossed over her chest.

"You know I'm just kidding, Hollis." Landon shot her a greasy grin. "You're pretty hot for a fat girl."

"Seriously, though." Chris cut in, brow furrowed. "What are you all doing?"

"I don't know." Hollis shrugged, her eyes darting away. "Playing S&S, I assume, since it's our usual game day. And eating snacks. And, you know, sleeping."

"Wow," said Marius. "That's a lot less exciting."

"You're right." Landon draped his arm over Lacie's shoulder, a smug sneer fitting over his chapped lips. "You'll let us know if any hot lesbian shit goes down, right, Hol?"

Slowly, Hollis let out a long breath. Some deep-seated instinct inside her warned her to keep quiet. Hollis never liked attention from Landon, but when he got on kicks like this, she liked it even less.

She frowned down at her square-shaped pizza. A moment ago, she had been so excited for the sleepover—she had taken Fran's latest quiz earlier without protest ("What's Your Sleepover Girl Persona?"; Hollis was the Girl Who Secretly Wants Her Hair Braided; *LMFAO DONE!!!* said Fran)—but now she was embarrassed. The last time she'd gone to a sleepover was in elementary school, where her main goal had been trying (and failing) not to be the first girl to call her mom to come pick her up. She hadn't needed to worry about her sleepover-mates' sexualities then—or about what the sleepover might make others think of her. But now Landon's voice swelled in her mind, using *lesbians* like a dirty word. Hollis's thoughts filled with Aini, with her Pride dice and cool hair.

Landon was wrong. There was nothing swear-worthy about Aini Amin-Shaw.

"Hey," said Chris, shaking Hollis's attention back to the table. Like Landon had done to Lacie, he draped his arm over Hollis's shoulders. It was probably meant to be reassuring, but she found it jarring instead. Chris's arm never fit well around her shoulders; she had to lean down uncomfortably to accommodate him. Chris smiled at her. "I think it'll be fine. It sounds like fun. Really."

Hollis swallowed. Landon's words still repeated in her head.

There were only six short hours between her and finding out.

The Factotum, an arcane collective in the north of the Third Realm, was a place of great knowledge—but that knowledge came with a price. The party had decided that the extensive libraries housed within the alabaster building were the most likely place to find information about what might be causing all the corruption and vanishing in the Realms. As the de facto leader of the group, Honoria had been attempting to use her Diplomacy skill to persuade a Lorekeeper to allow them immediate library access because of the dire nature of their quest.

It wasn't going well.

"Oh my *God*," breathed Hollis, clapping her hand to her eyes.

"You've got to be kidding me," said Maggie from the other side of Aini.

But Hollis wasn't kidding—she had rolled a Natural 1, *again*. Her fourth one of the evening.

Instead of gathering around the table, tonight the girls were strewn around the Castañedas' cozy living room, relaxing on the overstuffed couch or piled two-deep into matching beige armchairs or, like Hollis, sitting cross-legged on the plush cream-colored rug. Their comfortable sprawl gave a more casual feel to the game. But still, so many critical failures stung.

"'Ahhhh,' says Bern," said Gloria. Bern was an NPC she had only just introduced to the party. They'd all instantly loved the nervous gnome, with his receding hairline and his mid-level-management desk job. Gloria, as Bern, wrung her hands. "'See, here's the thing. I'd *really* love to sneak you wonderful folks through. You've been nothing but kind.'"

"'But,'" said Hollis for Honoria, her voice heavy with both their failures.

"'*But*,' says Bern, 'the thing about that is there's a whole hierarchy of policy and procedure we have to follow, and the guys upstairs are *real* sticklers for P&P. You and your party will have to go on a quest to prove your usefulness to the Factotum.'"

Around the living room, the girls groaned. This was exactly what they had been trying to avoid. It would save them a week's time in-game.

"I'm sorry, girls," said Gloria, as herself again. "The rolls just weren't there."

"Hollis," intoned Aini bleakly, "I think Maggie was right. Your dice are cursed."

"They're not even *her* dice," said Iffy, flopping back in her chair, exasperated. "She borrowed them from her boyfriend."

"I told you, that's what's wrong!" Maggie sipped a Sanpellegrino. "They're not attuned to your energy."

"Oh, lord," said Aini, flicking a piece of popcorn across the coffee table at Maggie. "Here we go."

"I'm serious," said Maggie, dodging out of the way.

"I don't know about that crap," said Fran through a mouthful of Pringles, "but I do always have bad rolls when I use Gloria's dice."

"Ay, Francesca." Gloria wrestled the can of Pringles away from her sister. "What did I tell you about getting into my dice?"

"I'm blanking on that one," Fran said. "If I had more Pringles, I might remember." She stuck out her tongue.

"I'm serious." Gloria's voice dipped low, more like Hollis's mom's teacher voice than her own Secret Keeper voice. She bit a Pringle in half like it was a threat. "Those are *mine*."

"Maybe we should get Hollis to touch them, then." Fran's fingers darted forward in a flash and captured the other half of the chip from her sister's hand. "She can curse them, too, and make all your monster rolls booty!"

"Okay, y'all are goofy," said Iffy, rolling her eyes with a smile. "But every girl needs her own set of dice."

"Yeah," said Aini. "It's Geek Feminism 101."

"Wellll . . ." Gloria gave Fran one last stern look, her eyebrow cocking high up her forehead, before turning back to the party at large. "You're all already too distracted to keep going for the night, and, Hollis, darling, you really *are* rolling terribly. My vote is we car-pool to the game store and get this girl some good dice."

"YES!" shouted Fran, bouncing where she sat on the floor. "Field trip!"

"We don't have to stop playing for me," protested Hollis.

"Have you seen what you're rolling?" asked Maggie. "We sort of do."

Hollis's expression soured, but Maggie was smiling. Maybe, she realized, it was actually a joke. She tried joking back.

"One, rude," said Hollis. "But two, yeah, you're right. We can at least go look."

"I'll drive." Maggie grinned and swept past Hollis, Fran already following after her. "I think we can fit everyone in the Suburban."

More than once in the weeks since she'd been there last, Hollis had thought about what it would be like to go back to Games-A-Lot.

Sometimes she'd thought that she would take Chris and the gang with her, and that maybe Landon's loud lectures about lore and what "fake fans" got wrong would make her stand out less. Sometimes she'd thought about going in with her mom, because surely no one would bother her with a parent around, geek street cred be damned.

She had never thought about going with the girls, but that was how she arrived: rolling up six deep in the Suburban with loud pop music blaring through the speakers.

Hollis hung off Iffy's arm as they pushed through the double glass doors. The foyer still stank of ancient cigarette smoke, but it now competed with the floral, woodsy smell of Aini behind her and the vanilla-sugar-and-Pringles scent of Fran on her other side. When they made it into the store proper, they were all laughing loudly enough that Karl at the counter looked up disapprovingly.

"I'll be in miniatures," said Maggie. "Reaper just put out a new faun that looks perfect for Tan."

"I've got to check in with a friend about party stuff," Iffy said, hanging back by the door and taking her phone out of her pocket, "but I'll be right back."

Fran and Gloria headed off toward the counter, but Aini stayed at Hollis's side, following her over to the dice display on the far side of the counter.

With Aini beside her—and with her friends dispersed through the store, separate but still very clearly together—Hollis could finally see the appeal of Games-A-Lot. The dusty old shelves no longer looked sad and cobbled together. Now they shone with possibility: new games to play together, ideas for Christmas gifts she knew the girls would love. The chatter floating from every corner of the space was less intimidating; now it sounded like Fran's squawking and Maggie's laughter and Gloria's smooth, even voice in conversation with shop owner Karl's nasally one. Even the dim lighting felt less oppressive and dungeon-like than she remembered—or maybe "dungeon-like" had simply become a quality she associated less with dark, dank, unsafe spaces and more with the comfort of the girls around her, their shared adventure ahead of them.

Hollis's lips pulled into a pleased smile when they reached the dice display. In one fluid motion, Aini drummed her fingers across the shelf top.

"So what are you thinking? Staying on theme for Honoria with bronze or blue? Maybe orange, like your favorite color? Something wild like, oh, I don't know . . ." She picked up a small, rectangular box of dice. "Vomit-colored speckles?"

"Those are truly vile," Hollis replied. But she smiled even as she said it; she couldn't remember telling Aini her favorite color was orange, but she was right. It was. It had been showing up more and more in her art lately—ever since it had shown up in Aini's curls.

Aini blinked at her innocently. "Vomit not your thing? Huh. Weird."

Hollis shoved Aini's bony shoulder. The motion sent a thrill of excitement through her core. "Get out of here, Aini Amin-Shaw."

"Oh, first *and* last names," Aini said with a wide grin. "She's mad now! Fine, no vomit dice, got it. How do you feel about glitter?"

Hollis was about to say *Really good, actually*, but the words froze in her throat as a flash of movement caught her eye, drawing her attention through the open double doors into the back room.

There, sitting at the same table where she too had sat all those weeks ago, was the boy who played Maxx the Bard. He looked up in time to see Hollis looking at him. And winked.

"Oh God." Hollis snapped her gaze downward.

"Hey," said Aini. In an instant, she shifted closer to Hollis, standing straighter, stiffer, and more alert. "What's up?"

Hollis's heart rate, for one. She could feel it surging behind her rib cage the same way she could feel the boy's eyes on her skin. She tried to swallow the pounding sensation down, but there was a sudden, impassable lump in her throat. Hollis was surprised the words she said next could make their way out around it. "Remember that guy I told you about? The real, just, like, *creep*?"

"Maxx the Bard, yeah." Aini's dark brown eyes swept the space. "Oh, gross. That's him, isn't it?"

Hollis screwed her eyes tightly shut for a second, trying to breathe. "That'll be him."

"What a creep," said Aini. "Want to give him a show, if he's going to be a weirdo and watch?"

Hollis's eyes snapped back open. "I don't ever want to go near him again, Aini."

"Ew, of course not. Don't worry. I got you." Aini half raised her arm and arched an eyebrow. "May I?"

Swallowing hard, Hollis nodded.

Without another word, Aini trilled a rolling laugh that earned another glare from Karl and slipped her arm around Hollis's waist.

"You're so right, babe," she said, a little louder than she really needed to.

It took a second for Hollis to realize this was her line. She tried to think of something clever to say, but she was distracted by Aini's sudden move—and by how, even though she was so much shorter than Hollis, her arm still slotted perfectly into place around Hollis's hips. Her skin prickled beneath her shirt where Aini's arm rested. The pounding in her chest intensified, suddenly taking on a different rhythm entirely.

Instead of something cool, she said, "Oh my God," and put her arm around Aini's shoulders. It felt comfortable and correct there. It felt impossible, too: the same way Hollis felt as Honoria when Umber was being particularly flirty.

"Come on." Aini nodded back to the dice. "Which are you thinking?"

Hollis strained to regain her focus, trying to pull it away from the spaces where Aini's skin was separated from hers only by her own navy striped shirt. It took some effort to train her eyes back on the dice display.

She had ten dollars in her pocket—gifted to her by her mother to use as "fun money." With rows of colorful dice sparkling in front of her like treasure, and Aini's closeness making her chest warm, this certainly counted as fun. One box caught her eye: an orange set, swirled through with streaks in several shades and opacities of the same color. Among all the others, they were unique.

Hollis picked it up. "What about these?" she asked, holding the box in the space in front of them.

"Ah." Aini bumped her hip against Hollis's and ran her free hand through her hair dramatically. This stirred the Aini Smell in the air, something Hollis found pleasantly overwhelming standing this close to her. "I see where you get your inspiration."

She hadn't noticed before, but now that she looked, the colors *did* mimic the fading shades of Aini's orange curls.

"You know it," Hollis said, and then added, a beat too late and a little awkwardly, "babe."

Aini beamed. "Those are the winners. Let's find the other girls and see what they say."

And though she didn't really have to—Gloria was still at the counter, casually chatting with Karl, and the other three girls were all within earshot—Aini turned and walked with Hollis past the open doorway to the back room.

As they passed the boy who played Maxx the Bard, she waved.

"*Aini,*" Hollis hissed under her breath.

"Come on," she hissed back. "Let me have fun with it."

Hollis looked over her shoulder—over *Aini's* shoulder—and toward the back room. She caught the back of the boy's head as he turned away, his shoulders a bit too stiff to be casual.

"Okay," she said, turning back and bending close to Aini so her voice didn't carry. "That was pretty badass."

"Oh, I know I am." She hip-bumped Hollis again. "You don't have to tell me."

And in that moment, Hollis felt kind of like a badass, too.

Aini's arm stayed around her waist until Hollis got to the register, and then, with a last, thrilling squeeze, she wriggled loose. Cold flooded the spaces where Aini's arm had been; Hollis frowned against the sudden lack of warmth. Doing her best to act unbothered, she checked out anyway, Maggie directly behind her in line. Both of them left with a brown bag—Hollis with her dice, and Maggie with more miniatures than Hollis, who was good at painting, could have painted in a week.

Maggie turned the music back on as they all started to pack back into the Suburban.

"Oh, hell yes!" cried Iffy as soon as the song started. "Turn this up!"

Maggie obliged, the premium speakers of her SUV bumping the music through the entire parking lot.

And then something happened that only ever happened in teen dramas on television: Iffy jumped out of the SUV and started to dance right there in the parking lot, her moves smooth and rhythmic and effortless. She reached out a hand to Fran, who was closest, wordlessly inviting her to join in. And so Fran—with an excited screech as she jumped out of the car—started to dance too. What she lacked in Iffy's effortlessness, she made up for in enthusiasm and moves per minute.

"You think *you're* slick, Francesca?" laughed Gloria, and then she, too, spun onto the impromptu dance floor they'd created in the empty parking space beside the Suburban. Gloria's moves were hip-heavy and inviting, and so Hollis, despite not knowing the song—something by Dua Lipa, maybe?—joined in as well. Her movements started off stiff and self-conscious but smoothed out in the unplanned moment to something almost fluid. Hollis was struck by the sudden urge to laugh, with the thought that if she didn't, something good and glowing might bubble up inside of her to bursting, and so she did. The sound spilled out of her, its own kind of music, perfectly at home with the chords that surrounded her from the speakers.

Hollis turned back toward Aini, who still stood half in the SUV with Maggie. With one hand still clutching the brown paper bag that held her new dice, Hollis made two finger guns. She aimed both at Aini, then aimed both at the ground beside her, then aimed back at Aini again. It probably looked stupid—but Hollis, repeating the motion again, didn't care. She just wanted to dance.

No. She wanted to dance *with Aini*.

And her stupid finger guns worked. With a smile and a shake of her head, Aini jumped down from the back driver's-side door of the SUV and came to dance beside Hollis. Her body moved as if the rhythm came from her very soul, every part of her—from her toes to her shoulders—dipping and rising with the beat. With a shake of her head (but also a grin), Maggie joined in at last, her long, lithe limbs flailing in time with the bass line.

And in the flickering light of the streetlamp overhead, Hollis knew that this was what going to Games-A-Lot was supposed to be like. With Gloria and Iffy singing along loudly to the song; with all their hips and feet and hands moving together, mostly to the beat; with Aini in motion beside her, and in front of her, and behind her, electric—the dingy little parking lot transformed entirely. It was no longer a place of shame and discomfort.

It was a place for friends.

So Hollis danced with hers, carefree and laughing.

Apparently, Fran snored.

As the last girl awake, Hollis was the only one to discover this. The noise ripped out from the tiny girl at even intervals, rumbling over the newest season of *Never Have I Ever* playing softly in the background.

All six of the girls had decided to sleep in the living room. They crammed together, some of them on makeshift pallets on the floor, cobbled together from comforters and pillows from the unused bedrooms. Iffy had barely managed to put her pallet together before she fell asleep, exhausted from the evening or her busy week or both. Hollis had been prepared to sleep on the floor too, but Aini had campaigned for her to have the sofa. She must have rolled a high Charisma check, because that was where Hollis stretched out now.

Against the soundtrack of the TV and the sound of Fran's snores, Hollis reflected on the evening. It sounded dramatic even in her head, but she was pretty sure it had truly been the best night of her life. Not in a perfect-prom-night way, or even a perfect-day way. She had still gone to school, and she had still been around Landon, and if it had been a *truly* perfect day, neither of those things would have happened.

But this—trying (and failing) to fall asleep in an apartment full of girls who she was lucky to call her friends—was as close to perfect as Hollis could get. The room around her, once such a source of anxiety, was a comfortable safe haven, all cream colors and caramelly wood and vanilla candles and deep-seated-armchair coziness. For the first time Hollis could remember, she felt like she belonged. Really, truly belonged.

It was also—and this felt cheesy, too, but she thought it anyway—the first time she'd experienced firsthand what it meant to be lifted up by a bunch of girls she liked very much. Or actually, she realized, probably *loved*.

She did. She loved them. Even Fran—who carried on snoring, blissfully unaware of Hollis's late-night sentimentality.

Hollis matched her breathing to that slow rhythm, and in doing so, even Fran's snoring became a kind of comfort. She was a good kid, Fran. And Iffy—God, Iffy was great. Even Maggie had grown on her from that first session, when she seemed so untouchable. Gloria had something to do with that; she was the bright red string that bound them all, bringing them together in so much the same way as she did the story around the oak-finish table.

And then there was Aini, who slept on the floor below her, a foot and a half away at most. Just visible over the edge of the sofa, her orange curls had grown even wilder from tossing and turning. Aini had been Hollis's champion tonight, putting Maxx the Bard in his place and dancing with her under the flickering streetlamp in the parking lot. Hollis's heart thudded fondest of all for her.

Maybe it was the early hour, but Hollis was reminded of the Fernglen—how it had brought them all closer together as a party, even when everything around them was falling apart. Her tired mind connected it to Games-A-Lot, her own personal Fernglen of sorts, and how tonight the girls had come together as a real-life party around it. Around *her*.

But there was another *her*, one Hollis couldn't get out of her head. In the glow of the TV, she swirled in shades of marigold and ocher: Aini Amin-Shaw, with her arm around Hollis's waist, with her feet dancing against the cracked asphalt, with the toothy smile always ready on her lips, glowing bright in the whirl of Hollis's thoughts. Maybe it was just the night—not perfect-perfect, but as close to it as Hollis Beckwith felt she could come—but it felt important to do, and so Hollis did it: She reached down toward Aini with one hand. She held her hand there, close, her palm opened and upturned. Waiting.

Hardly a breath passed before Aini's hand slipped into hers, their palms pressed tight together. As their fingers tangled together, Hollis exhaled, warm and deep.

In the dark of the night, and to herself only, she smiled.

"Good night, Hollis," Aini whispered up from her pallet on the floor.

"Good night, Aini," Hollis whispered down from the sofa.

13
CH-CH-CHANGES

"I'LL HAVE THE fried pickles, please," said Hollis. "And, like, a bucket of ranch on the side, if you don't mind."

Chris gave Hollis an unreadable look. He swiped his card for their order nonetheless, and they walked from the counter to their usual booth. It was a late lunch, but Hollis had had so many pancakes for breakfast at Gloria's that she'd only just gotten hungry.

"You're chipper," Chris said as they sat.

"You know me. I love fried pickles."

"Well, yeah," he said, and smiled. Sort of. A gloominess hung around him. "Seriously, though. Have they changed your meds or something?"

"*Chris.*" Hollis didn't mind talking about her medicine with Chris; he had been around since before she was even put on it. Usually, though, *he* minded talking about it with *her*. "What? And no, for your information. But what are you even talking about?"

"I don't know." He shrugged. "You've just been so . . . buzzy lately."

Hollis frowned. "Buzzy?"

"I mean, I don't know." Chris stopped, chewing the words and the inside of his cheek. "Normal Hollis wouldn't order a, what did you say? *Bucket of ranch.*"

He had a point, maybe. "A bucket of" was the phrase Aini had used for her syrup preferences this morning, when she'd smiled and passed the pancake platter to Hollis as if nothing out of the ordinary had passed between them the night before. Involuntarily, Hollis closed her hand beneath the table. If she moved her fingers just right, she could imagine the feel of Aini's tangled up with hers. There in the booth, her cheeks burned even thinking of it.

"What?" She tried to chase both the color and Chris's gloom away with a grin. "But you know I love my ranch, Christopher."

"It's not just that. It's—it's, like . . ."

"Hold on," said Hollis. She looked at him then—really looked at him. His eyebrows pinched together, worrying a wrinkle between them. His gaze didn't quite make it to her eyes. "This is really bothering you, isn't it?"

He shrugged. "Yeah, I guess."

Hollis pursed her lips. "Come on. Tell me what's going on."

"I don't want to make you mad."

"You won't. I promise."

Chris shook his head. "Don't, Hollis."

"Come on, Christopher Bradley. Out with it, or I'll pull it out of you with my own hands."

"That's just it, though, isn't it?" Chris waved his hands toward her as if to say *All of that*. "That's not something Hollis says. You're just so extra lately."

Hollis blinked. "I'm what?"

"Just." Chris huffed a short sigh. "Regular Hollis wouldn't act like this."

"*Regular Hollis?* Who is she?"

"She's my girlfriend," he said. "You should meet her. Nice girl. Doesn't act crazy extra at lunch when I'm buying her fried pickles."

Hollis leaned back in her seat, crossing her arms. "So now I'm crazy *and* extra."

"Order number thirty-two," said the cashier over the loudspeaker.

Chris threw up his hands. "You've just been really different since you started hanging out with your S&S group."

Hollis went very still, except for the smallest lean of her head to the left. "Are you being serious right now?"

Chris let out a short, angry breath. "I told you you'd get mad."

"No, what you said is you didn't want to *make* me mad, which," she said, shaking her head, "I don't know how you could think you wouldn't, saying something like that."

"See? You're doing it right now."

"Order number thirty-two?" repeated the cashier on the loudspeaker.

Hollis's cheeks were hot. "Is saying it's unfair to call a girl out for having friends *extra*?"

"No, it's just—"

"Because maybe I am extra, then."

"No! Just." Chris floundered. "Like, the Hollis I know isn't like this. You aren't like other girls."

Hollis blinked, then narrowed her eyes. "Funny thing about that one, Chris—"

He looked at her pleadingly. "Hollis, please."

"Order number thirty-two?"

She leaned forward. "—is I'm *exactly* like other girls."

And as soon as she said it, she knew it was true. She, Hollis, *was* exactly like other girls, and that was a powerful thing. Who *wouldn't* want to be patient and strong like Gloria, or funny and brilliant like Iffy, or warm and charming and maddening and beautiful like Aini?

"Hollis—" Chris started.

"No, you can't *Hollis* me on this one," she snapped. She wouldn't allow it. Fresh off their sleepover, Hollis felt a little strong, too. A little unstoppable. She closed her hand beside her on the bench and imagined Aini's cupped close inside it. Hollis squared her shoulders.

The loudspeaker crackled. "Double order of fried pickles, extra ranch?"

"And also, I think you're getting *extra* confused with *happy*," said Hollis. "Why else would you think it was my meds?"

"Hollis," Chris pleaded.

"Order thirty-two, last call?"

"*What?*" Hollis snapped.

Chris lowered his voice. "Are you going to go get your fried pickles?"

"Yeah, I am," she said. "With *extra* ranch."

And when Hollis pushed up from the table, it felt *good*—to push away from Chris. Usually, she associated these kinds of comments with Landon, who put no limits on the number of stupid, horrible things that came out of his mouth. But Landon was nowhere in sight; this was entirely on Chris. It wasn't a comparison that sat well with Hollis. Hips swishing in a way that would have made Gloria proud, she walked away.

It was only when she got to the counter that she remembered she'd have to sit back down with Chris to eat the pickles, since there were too many for her to eat on her own. She remembered, too, that she'd have to get a ride home with him after. And she remembered— belatedly—that the whole reason she'd started playing S&S and met the girls in the first place was as a way to get closer to Chris, not to cause a fight with him over fried pickles on a Saturday afternoon.

She'd been so afraid she wouldn't be able to prove herself good enough for him. Now it seemed like she was proving to be too *much* for him. How had that happened?

All the fight went out of her by the time she plopped back down into the bench opposite her boyfriend.

"I'm sorry," she said, at the same time Chris said, "I'm sorry."

For a long, silent beat, they just looked at each other. Maybe she would have laughed—maybe she should have—but there was still some truth to the words she'd said, and something inside her chest wouldn't allow her to take them back. She shrugged. "I don't want to fight, Chris. We've been friends too long for this."

"Yeah," he said. He couldn't quite look at her. His gaze held steady on a place just over her shoulder. "You're right. Just, like, so much is about to change after this year. I don't want one of those things to be you, Hollis."

And what she might have said, if it were Aini sitting across from her, was that having friends like the girls didn't change her. They made her more like herself, like who she was *already*. But then again, if it were Aini sitting across from her, she wouldn't even have to say that; Aini already knew. She knew, and she liked that version of Hollis enough to hold her hand as she fell asleep.

Hollis didn't have to prove anything to Aini. She was good enough for her as she was, extra and all.

At this thought, a flash of guilt surged through Hollis's chest. Taking a deep breath around it, she said, "Okay. Then I'll try not to."

They ate their fried pickles in silence, dipping them in extra ranch.

Over the next couple weeks, Hollis did her best to *not change*. But everything else carried on changing anyway, like Chris's words had been some kind of challenge.

School changed, for one. The first few weeks of senior year were what Hollis's mom called "bird weeks," because they absolutely flew by. With the arrival of October, crisp and flavored of pumpkin spice, the quick but casual pace ended and suddenly everything was serious. Hollis felt betrayed. Even her art teacher, Mr. Stackhouse, put her nose to the proverbial grindstone, requiring the class to complete a reproduction of a famous illustration with a personal twist. Not even painting Honoria as Albert Lynch's *Jeanne d'Arc* could detract from the difficulty of the assignment.

Her homework hours swelled. Her drawing hours dwindled. She predicted her grades would stay more or less the same. And always looming in the distance was the threat of college, with its application deadlines and standardized test scores that made Hollis feel permanently three steps behind.

The dynamic of her lunch group shifted, too. At first, Hollis thought it was because of Lacie-with-an-*I-E* and her friends, but she had grown to mostly like Tabitha and at least tune out Wyndee. She tried to tell herself that it wasn't because of her fight with Chris. But whatever the cause, the tension had still grown. It sat with them all at the lunch table now, taking up silent space between them—a new kind of *extra* all its own, one that fit as poorly into the group as Hollis feared she herself did.

Looking for a way to spend her lunches free of Lacie-with-an-*I-E* prompted the first of two good changes for Hollis: she started spending a few lunch periods each week studying with Iffy. It wasn't *her* choice, strictly speaking; her history teacher had suggested (firmly and with no other options) that she get a tutor as midterms approached, to give her a chance of passing. Hollis had been resentful about this, until Iffy mentioned she needed a warm body to tutor because it would look good on her application to Howard. Since then, Hollis was happy to spend her lunch periods on Tuesdays and Thursdays in 1800s America with Iffy.

But the most dramatic—or at least the most important—change was how she got to her S&S game on Friday nights.

After their seventh Friday session (which they spent fetching potion ingredients for the Factotum, thanks to Hollis's abysmal rolls the week prior), Aini offered to give Hollis a ride home, since an unusually frazzled Iffy had to rush back to put the finishing touches on her presentation to the Governor's Board. And somehow, the following Friday evening—as Hollis sat sketching and brainstorming what to research now that the party had access to the Factotum's arcane library—it was Aini she waited for.

As she squinted through the darkness, picking her way down the front path to Aini's car instead of Iffy's, Hollis wondered how, exactly, things had come to be like this.

Like the rest of it, she decided it simply had.

Aini opened the passenger-side door for Hollis. The sound of the newest Steadfast song, "Die Young" by Sylvan Esso, spilled out into the night.

"So," Aini said as she walked around the front of the car to the driver's side. "I wanted to pregame our plans for tonight. I was thinking . . ."

But what exactly she was thinking was lost to the music as Hollis sank into the heated seat. She smiled to herself.

If this was changing her, even a little, she decided she wouldn't mind.

14
FANTASY GOOGLE

"OH MY GODDDDD," groaned Fran—only her mouth was still half full of pretzels, so it sounded more like *of my gothhhh*. She swatted away the crumbs that had sprayed from her mouth onto her character sheet, then swallowed. (If she noticed Gloria's epic side-eye at this display, she didn't let on.) "Isn't there like a fantasy Google or something?"

"Yeah, Fran, there is," said Iffy, dice in hand. "Her name is Nereida."

Over the past hour, Iffy had completed a complicated series of rolls. Unlike Fran, who kept huffing impatiently into fistfuls of snacks, Iffy was in her element.

Still, even her best work was yielding few results.

Iffy pursed her lips. "This time," she said after a pause, "I'm going to look for anything that mentions vanishings and the transmogrification branch of magic."

But her fifth Research roll of the night was too low—*again*. Even Gloria, who always kept a good game face, was starting to look worn.

"As you start reshelving tomes," she narrated, "Bern steps back up to the group, and he says, 'Ah, yes, um, hello. It's me. Ah—Bern. It's getting quite late, and clearing one mission for the Factotum only grants nonmembers so much time within the library, you see.'"

"You're saying we have to leave?" Mercy Grace sounded hopeful for the first time in hours.

Gloria blinked her eyes wide, in character. "'Miss Mercy, ah. You see . . . Yes. Unfortunately. It's strictly a matter of policy and procedure, of course.'"

Hollis, as Honoria, was pretty sure this also had at least something to do with the fact that Mercy, bored, had started to pick splinters off the fine mahogany table around which the five adventurers sat in-game. A pile of toothpick-size wood chips had grown beside her chair.

"We can start the paperwork for a new mission," said Tanwyn. With a clopping of her hooves, she stood from her seat. "It's really no problem."

"Maybe not for *you*," Nereida cut in, her eyes flashing in a way Honoria hadn't seen since their days in the Academy. "But *you're* not the one who's been doing all this research work."

"I—" started Tan, but Umber cleared his throat, silencing her.

Nereida's lips tightened. "Give me one more chance, Bern." It wasn't a question. It was hardly even a request. Nereida was already standing from her place at the table, her cerulean robes swirling around her as she turned sharply on her heel and headed back toward the stacks.

"Wait." Honoria stood too.

Far away, at the round table where six girls sat playing S&S, Hollis turned to her left.

"Hey," she said, placing her hand on top of Iffy's where it fisted around her d20. Beneath her palm, Iffy's sharp knucklebones flexed hard. "Is everything okay?"

"*What?*" Iffy snapped back, sounding neither like her character nor herself.

Hollis blinked but didn't turn away. Instead, she dropped her voice lower and squeezed Iffy's hand in her own. "I just want to make sure you're okay, Ifs. These rolls have been rough."

Again, Hollis felt Iffy's hand flex beneath hers, and for a moment she was afraid she had overstepped a line in their friendship. But then Iffy's fist unclenched under hers, the dice she'd been clutching clattering to the table.

"Yeah. Sorry." Iffy sighed. "I'm trying to think of the right thing to look up, y'all, but I just . . . I have this personal essay to write for Howard that's killing me, and GSA is starting its winter fundraising and I have all these postcards to address to local businesses by tomorrow, and my friend Peter's going through it with his boyfriend and needs some extra love right now, and I'm trying to deal with all *that* and also get *this* right with Nereida." She blinked down at her dice intently. "I don't want to let her or the party down, but I kind of have a lot of dice rolls going on in real life right now, too, if you know what I mean."

"For sure. That's a lot," Hollis agreed.

"Yes," said Gloria. "Thank you for sharing all that with us."

"And Nereida isn't on her own, either," said Maggie, her keen blue eyes flicking over her character sheet. "Come on. Let's help her out." She slipped back into her lilting Tanwyn voice. "I'm going to chat up Bern and try to make him feel more favorable about our search here."

"I'm just going to go to sleep," said Fran as Mercy Grace, laying her head down on the table. "It's really the best thing I can do for any of us."

Aini picked up Umber's lute and, without a word, started picking out a twinkling, gentle tune. In the calm that followed, Hollis held Iffy's gaze.

"I know you've been shouldering a lot of work here—"

Iffy exhaled hard. "Mm-hmm."

"And we owe you. *I* owe you. Don't let the time crunch get to you, Nereida. You can do this. We've got your back."

In the Factotum Library, Honoria gave Nereida's arm a squeeze.

"As I close my hand around her arm," Hollis said, doing the same at the table in the Castañedas' dining room, "I'm going to say a little prayer to the Just and Terrible Mistress, and I'm going to cast Sea God's Blessing on Nereida at Level 5."

"That will be a +5 to whatever roll you make this time," Gloria informed Iffy. "Now, tell me. What would you like Nereida to look for this last time?"

Iffy sucked in a deep breath, her nostrils flaring. Hollis could tell by the look in her eyes that she was running over every bit of information the party had gathered—every late-night Discord chat the girls had spent dissecting the game, every bit of lore research she had likely done on her own—because Iffy, like Nereida, was the scholar of the group.

Slowly, Iffy exhaled. "I want to look for children's rhymes."

Gloria's eyebrows rose high up her forehead. "Can you clarify?" she asked.

"I want to see if there are any books of children's rhymes that might have to do with local folklore," Iffy said. "Particularly anything that's ever fallen out of favor or been banned. *Especially* if it has to do with vanishing landmarks or twisted-looking creatures or warnings about either."

In the Factotum Library, Nereida turned and disappeared down the rows and rows of shelves.

The group didn't hear back from her for what felt like hours. Mercy followed through on her threat to fall asleep, a puddle of drool pooling around the pile of splinters she'd picked off the table. Bern tapped his foot nervously as he listened to Tanwyn's chatter, his eyes darting around from time to time. Umber pulled off a corner from a page of forgotten notes, wadded it up, flicked it at Honoria—which earned him a shake of her head—and winked, which earned him a smile.

Finally, Tanwyn stood. "I think—"

"I think I've found it," cried Nereida triumphantly, popping around the side of a shelf. Tan startled back into her chair. Mercy startled awake with a small poot.

("What?" demanded Fran as Gloria rolled her eyes. "She *is* a troll!")

Nereida walked slowly as she returned to her seat, as if the book she held might startle, too, without the utmost care. She opened it gingerly to a page already marked with one of her hair ribbons. And from it, she read aloud:

> *"When the flowers go missing*
> *And you can't find the trees*
> *You won't see, but you'll know:*
> *They're with the Vacuity.*
>
> *When the children are vanished*
> *And the beasts cursèd be,*
> *They've met the Unmaker:*
> *They're with the Vacuity.*
>
> *When the day turns to darkness*
> *And backward waves the sea,*
> *It's not long for the rest:*
> *We'll be with the Vacuity."*

A hush fell over the table, both in the Factotum Library and in the Castañedas' apartment.

"Wow," breathed Fran.

"I know," said Iffy. "Eerie, right?"

"No," said Fran. "I mean *wow, Gloria is a terrible poet.*"

Dice clattered threateningly behind Gloria's Secret Keeper screen. Fran blanched. "I mean—she's a great poet! What a rhyme!"

"What *this* means," said Aini, refocusing the conversation, "is we have a name now."

"Is it a name, or a place?" Maggie mused out loud.

"I was wondering the same thing," said Iffy. "It seems like it could be both."

"I don't know," said Hollis, eyes darkening, "but that line about *the rest* has me worried."

"Let's puzzle *the rest* out after a break," said Gloria, sitting up straight with a red-lipped grin, "because I've got to use the bathroom."

"Me first!" shouted Fran, and she took off.

Hollis pushed up from the table slowly, waiting for Maggie and Aini to head toward the side door before she addressed Iffy again.

"Do you mind if I catch a ride home with you tonight?" she asked. "I'd really like to help you out with your postcards."

"You don't have to do that," Iffy said, waving her hand dismissively. Still, there was a fond sparkle in her eyes. "I can handle it. I just get stressed out sometimes."

"I mean, *I* stress out so much it's basically my non-S&S hobby." That made Iffy laugh, and so Hollis laughed too. "But really. I want to help. And anyway, what kind of ally would I be if I didn't support the cause?"

Iffy rolled her eyes like this was a funny joke too, but then she gave in. "Okay, girl. Persuasion check passed. But I warn you: if we stay up too late, you're going to have to spend the night."

Hollis smiled. The idea of sleeping over with Iffy made her heart feel light, giddy, *good.* "Oh no, if you insist." Then, jerking her head toward the side door: "Come on. Let's get some fresh air. I feel like *I've* been sitting in the library for hours."

And so they headed out to join the rest of the girls on the porch, but not before Hollis made one last note in her notebook: *The Vacuity — Big Bad.*

15

HALLOWEEK

"**WHAT ABOUT THIS** one?" Maggie held a wig up to her head, stark white against her dirty-blond hair.

"If you want your Tanwyn costume to look like drag Andy Warhol, then maybe," said Aini. "Otherwise? Give it a skip."

Hollis, down the aisle from the girls, had to agree. After they'd all decided via Discord chat to come to Friday's session dressed as their characters in honor of Halloween, the three girls had arranged to shop for items for their costumes after school on Wednesday. At least, Aini and Maggie were shopping for items for their costumes. Hollis was eyeing price tags and resigning herself to getting creative with things she already had at home.

With only four days left until the holiday, the costume shop was extremely busy. But even still, Maggie was unstoppable. Her outfit (which had garnered an impressive twelve thousand likes on her Instagram, Hollis saw earlier) already looked like a more expensive version of the witch costumes in the store. She was right at home in a crowd, navigating the packed aisles like she owned them. In contrast, Hollis turned the corner to the next aisle and almost bumped into a mom with a toddler. Aini snuck past her, dodging the mom's cart and holding a pirate shirt up to her chest.

"White is boring as hell, I know," she said, "but with a little dye, what do you think for Umber?"

Hollis eyed the puffy-sleeved polyester shirt, making a face but saying nothing.

This, apparently, spoke volumes to Aini. She nodded resolutely. "Thank you for this helpful information, Hollis. I'll keep looking." And she was off down the aisle again.

Hollis was left alone. The thought of dressing up as Honoria was exciting, but daunting. Honoria was so strong and sure, and Hollis was so . . . not. There was also the fact that Honoria didn't have to worry about finding clothes to fit her plus-size body in the fantasy world of the Eight Realms. Whereas Hollis, across the river in Cincinnati, Ohio, did.

The few costume items she'd found that *did* have a plus-size option were the one-size-fits-all kind of plus-size that let Hollis know, in no uncertain terms, that she was not part of the *all*. They certainly weren't designed with bellies or hips like Hollis's in mind.

After a long search—interrupted periodically by Aini's or Maggie's miniature fashion shows—Hollis found one item to try: a men's faux-chain-mail shirt, made out of some truly horrible plasti-fabric. It wasn't perfect, but if it fit, she might be able to turn it into Honoria's cobaltril breastplate.

Unlike the other two girls, Hollis didn't wait in the dressing room line to try her costume piece on. The idea of standing around with a bunch of straight-size girls and their armfuls of cute straight-size costumes made her skin feel uncomfortably tight. Instead, she found a quiet corner of the shop and tried to shimmy into the scratchy shirt.

It wouldn't even go over her shoulders.

"Excuse me," said a worker in a bright orange vest, coming around the corner. "Can I help you?"

Hollis's face flushed hot and red, her shoulders not even halfway in the shirt. "No, no. I'm fine. Uh, thanks."

"Costume try-ons are for fitting rooms only," said the girl in the vest, her shoulders slumped in a way that told Hollis this was probably not the first—or second, or third—time she'd had to say it today.

"Okay," said Hollis. "Noted."

And the girl walked away, leaving Hollis alone once again. She tugged the shirt back over her head at last and tried very hard to pretend she hadn't heard the seams popping when she'd stretched out of it. As neatly as she could, she folded it again and tucked it back into its plastic bag. After hanging it back on its peg, she went to find Aini and Maggie.

"Not a bad haul." Maggie held up an armful of bags and blister packs, mostly in shades of albino-faun white and sneaky-rogue black. "I'll find a wig online. I'm sure they could overnight it."

"What did you find, Hollis?" asked Aini, looking up over her own armful of items.

Hollis's cheeks were still flushed and warm. She tried to look normal, but inside she felt like lumpy garbage—a familiar feeling, one she encountered anytime she tried to shop at straight-size stores. "I'm just going to DIY it."

"What?" Maggie shook her head. "No way. Let's find you something cute, my treat. I saw this crusader costume—"

"No, it's okay," Hollis assured her. "I'll find a thrift shop or something."

"Oh, perfect!" Maggie lit up. "I couldn't find any pants I like. We can find those and something for Honoria there."

Hollis could recognize that Maggie was trying to be nice. But this was something thin people—especially frustratingly beautiful and clearly wealthy thin people like Maggie—didn't understand about shopping while fat. Though she was sure *Maggie* would find a dozen suitable options for Tanwyn's pants at a thrift shop, Hollis knew *she* would be hard-pressed to find anything for herself at all. Plus-size sections were notoriously limited, even without factoring in how a size 22 from the nineties was entirely different from a size 22 from now, or that a size 22 at one store was completely different from the same size at another. Then there was the current oversize fashion trend to take into account, which meant straight-size girls pulling the larger sizes off the shelves for themselves. Add in the inevitable grumpy old lady talking trash about fatter bodies from the 1X section, and thrift shopping (like most shopping, for Hollis) was an endeavor best taken on alone.

Hollis looked at Aini. Aini looked back. Her expression was casual, but Hollis could tell she was considering something.

"Do you want to go now, Hollis?" Aini asked lightly. "Or later?"

"I was thinking later, actually," said Hollis, latching on to Aini's suggestion gratefully. She swallowed deeply, breathing into the electric, staticky nerves that had threatened to close around her chest. Hollis wasn't able to stop the anxiety entirely, but with Aini's eyes on her, warm and brown and glittering, she could at least calm it until it was just a quiet drone of bees needling inside her head.

"Come on," said Maggie with a grin, oblivious. "Let's knock it out now; we're all together."

"Actually"—Aini yawned, stretching as much as her overflowing arms would allow—"I'm bushed, and I've still got calc to do after this. I'm ready to call it a night too."

"You two are no fun," Maggie whined, but she turned and led the way to the checkout counter nonetheless. "I should probably make a list anyway. A few more layers wouldn't be too bad."

Hollis caught Aini's eye.

She almost mouthed *Thank you*. But in the moment, with the feeling of getting caught while fat by the store assistant still burning hot in her cheeks, and with Aini's clearly intentional kindness filling her chest with another kind of warmth entirely, Hollis wasn't sure she would be able to do so without tearing up.

Instead, she reached out and grabbed Aini's hand. Aini shifted, redistributing her items into one arm to accommodate her. Fingers entwined, they fell into place behind Maggie, still headed toward the front.

"Is it weird," Maggie called back to them, "to thrift shoes?"

This was one of those rare times when being a resourceful art kid, a resourceful fat kid, and a resourceful broke kid combined in a way that served Hollis Beckwith better than any party store could have.

By Friday night, she had cobbled together a costume that was very cool, all things considered. Most of the pieces she'd scavenged from her closet: a pair of repurposed leggings painted with fabric-medium-treated paint to look like they had greaves attached; an old T-shirt cut into a bandana for her to wear, scarf-like, at her neck, to which she had sewn embroidery-floss tassels in red and cerulean and bronze; a sash at her waist, repurposed from a costume piece she'd worn in an ill-considered play freshman year.

But without a doubt, the crowning achievement of her costume was Honoria's cobaltril breastplate. Through a bit of trial and error—and more than one YouTube tutorial—she had fashioned a pattern entirely out of cardboard. She constructed it with the help of internal duct tape and external hot glue to hold all the seaming in place. Using more paint than she ever used before on a single project, she even gave it a realistic, textured paint job.

The finished breastplate didn't shine like real metal, and its intricate scrolling was very clearly painted and not etched on—but at the end of the day, Hollis had created a piece of cardboard armor that would make Honoria Steadmore proud.

As she regarded it in the mirror, *she* felt proud. She looked good in her costume. Powerful. Strong. At first, these feelings were uncomfortable for Hollis. But, so much like her breastplate armor, after a minute or so they settled into place on her chest and shone back at her in her reflection.

Still, something was off—something she couldn't put her finger on until she consulted the reference sketches for her costume.

Honoria had bangs.

It was such a small difference, but it threw the whole look off. Honoria wore her bangs the way some people wore glasses: as a major feature of her face, yes, but also so emblematic of her look that they became part of her personality. A confident Honoria had bangs that were neat and straight, falling in a blunt line against her forehead. A harassed Honoria had bangs that were askew and mussed. Honoria at rest had bangs that were a little wild, curling in odd places as if because no one was looking, or ruffled out of place by Umber during the watch hours they shared late at night.

Right now Hollis just had hair that was a little too frizzy to be considered wavy and a frown on her face.

And also, she realized, a pair of hair-cutting scissors.

They were old, left over from the early 2000s, when her mom cut her own hair to save a few bucks. Hollis ran the back of her thumbnail gently over the blade. They were still sharp enough—at least at the points.

It was surprising how little thought went into it from there. With her fingers, Hollis sectioned off a large chunk of hair at the front and center of her head, then tied the rest back with an elastic. Brushing out the front with her fingers, she measured a line against the bottommost point of her eyebrows. Then, with all the hair held between her scissored fingers—

Well, she had thought it would be a chop. But it was much more like a labored sawing.

And still, somehow, she didn't realize what the result would look like until the hair had dropped from her fingers, curling in the bathroom sink, and she'd lowered both her hands back to her sides.

Hollis didn't look like Honoria. She looked like a kindergartner who had gotten ahold of the big girl scissors.

"Oh," said Hollis with a strangled laugh, and then she released a string of swear words so vile she was glad her mom wasn't there to overhear.

But *someone* was. Three bold, confident knocks sounded on the front door.

Under her breath, Hollis swore again.

As quietly as she could—which was hard in armor, even armor made of cardboard; she now understood firsthand why Honoria got disadvantage on Stealth rolls—she made her way from the bathroom to the front door. She peered out the peephole.

There, with freshly dyed hair in a shade of blue so deep it was almost navy, was Aini, looking exactly like the dapper bard Umber Dawnfast, from the tips of her fake pointed ears to the blue-shimmered tip of her angular nose. She wore the most adorable smile as she reached up and knocked again on the wood directly over Hollis's cheek.

"I know you're in there," she called. "Don't make me cast—what spells does Umber even have? Seeking Smoke? Does he have that one?"

He did; he got it last session, when they'd all leveled up to Level 7. He would probably never use it, though, because Aini never used her spells.

Still.

"Aini," called Hollis through the door. "I can't come, actually. Sorry."

Outside, Aini's brow furrowed. "What are you even talking about, Beckwho?"

"I can't come tonight," Hollis repeated. "Tell Gloria I'm sorry to miss the Harvest Festival."

Aini laughed. "You think I'm going to stand between our Secret Keeper and running a festival session for all of us? You're dead wrong. Come on, Hollis, let me in."

"I *can't*," Hollis said, shaking her head. Her bangs waggled unevenly on her forehead. Hollis felt like she should laugh, or maybe cry. "Aini, I did something really, really stupid."

A beat passed, quick, and Aini's voice changed on the other side of the door.

"Are you safe? Hollis, open the door *right now*."

"Oh, God," said Hollis. "No! I mean, *yes*. I'm safe. It's nothing like that, it's just . . ."

"Christ, Hollis! Open up, you're freaking me out."

Hollis clenched her teeth. Sucking a breath between them, then blowing it back out (her useless bangs ruffling with the movement), she steeled herself, then unlocked the dead bolt. And the door. And then—regretting it already—she pulled it open.

"Hi, Aini," said Hollis and her bangs.

Aini, winsome in her bright doublet and high black leather boots, stood very still. Then she said, "You really had me waiting on your doorstep because you cut yourself some bangs?"

"Not just bangs." Hollis covered her face with her hands. *"Really, really terrible bangs."*

"Nah," Aini said, "they're Honoria bangs. Or—they almost are. If you'll let me in, I can help you"—she almost said *fix*, Hollis could tell. But she caught herself—"Honoria them up a little."

"Really?"

"Yeah, of course. I do all this myself, you know." Aini ran her fingers through her hair. The blue looked lovely against her dark brown skin. And Hollis found it even prettier knowing that Aini had dyed it herself. If she could do all that on her own, maybe there was hope for Hollis's bangs after all. Something close to hope bloomed in her chest.

"Okay," said Hollis. "Get in here."

When they were back in the relative safety of the hallway bathroom, Hollis handed the scissors over to Aini, who snorted.

"You might as well be using *spoons*, Hollis. These scissors are dead all through the middle." She opened and closed them a few times for emphasis. "But you mostly got the shape, so let's just neaten up what you have."

Aini went to work carefully, showing Hollis how to use the tips of the scissors to cut vertically across the line. Her hair stayed blunt, the way it was in all of Hollis's drawings, but it didn't look as . . . well, horrible.

When she was done, Aini ran her fingers through Hollis's bangs, fluffing them and making Hollis's nose tickle pleasantly, then smoothed them back down into place. "There. How are those?"

They were still shocking. But putting the sheer difference of them aside, she could see now that they didn't look bad, exactly. In fact, the way Aini had styled them made them look almost cute. Hollis smiled gratefully at Aini's reflection in the mirror.

Aini grinned in response. "There's my girl," she said, reaching up to place her arm over Hollis's shoulder. It felt as comfortable there as it had around her waist. "Now, are you ready to meet up with the others?"

The group had decided to go to Eden Park before their session tonight to take photographs together in their character costumes.

"Yes," said Hollis. "I think so."

Aini's smile widened. "Good. You look super hot, by the way."

"Says the girl looking like the most dapper bard in all the Eight Realms," Hollis quipped back before she could stop herself. She blushed at her own words, but they were honest, so she left them hanging there in the space between them. Hollis shook her head at her own reflection, eyeing Aini's. Hollis was sure there was something different about the way Aini's smile fit on her lips—something she hadn't seen before. "You're just admiring your handiwork."

"Well, that too." As smooth as ever, Aini shrugged, but there was something different about this, too. "Seriously, though, the armor suits you. It shows off how much of a badass you are."

"Um, I don't think a badass would have done this." Hollis waved like *All this* at her freshly chopped bangs.

"Are you kidding me?" In the mirror, the image of Aini bumped her hip against the image of Hollis. "Only a badass would be brave enough to hack off her own bangs with blunt scissors before a photo shoot."

At this, Hollis turned toward Aini (bangs still moving like a foreign object on her forehead), causing her arm to slide off Hollis's shoulder. She looked down. In the small space of her bathroom, dressed up in Umber's clothes, Aini looked at once familiar and like a whole new person. She was half here, in the real world, and half elsewhere, in the impossible world of their story. Where anything could happen— where they could *make* anything happen, together. It was a thrilling thought, one that sent butterflies soaring through Hollis's rib cage.

She leaned in, just a little. The bathroom light glinted off the shiny blue highlight on Aini's nose. "Do you really mean that?" she asked softly.

"Of course I do, Hollis." Aini's voice came just as quiet, echoing off the dated taupe tile walls. She reached up, brushing her fingers through Hollis's bangs again. Hollis suspected—with a strange thrill in her belly—that this motion had little to do with styling. "I think you're amazing."

For a flash of a second, Hollis allowed herself to really hear those words: Aini Amin-Shaw thought she was amazing. And then, half a second later, they overwhelmed her. Hollis crossed her arms over her chest abruptly, shook her bangs out. She grinned, but it was a shy and awkward thing, punctuated by sudden, clumsy laughter that felt like rocks in her throat.

"Yeah, well," said Hollis. "I'm going to get in your car now before you cast Charming Words on me."

Aini swallowed, blinking hard. "Do I have that spell?"

"Useless bard," said Hollis, grabbing her tote bag and heading toward the door.

On Halloween proper, another knock came at the door. And this time, Hollis had not been expecting anyone. She had no Halloween plans other than watching a scary movie on the sofa with her mom and handing out candy to trick-or-treaters—and eating a good amount of candy themselves, a time-honored tradition. Hollis was already in her favorite old leggings and a well-loved Sabrina T-shirt in preparation.

But it was still too early for even the most industrious of candy-grabbers: the sun hadn't set yet, and six o'clock (the official start of trick-or-treat hours, as determined by the city of Covington) was still an hour away. Curious, Hollis answered the door.

Leaning up against the railing of her front porch, wearing a black-and-orange-striped shirt and a brilliant grin, was Aini. "Why don't you wear that shirt more often?" she asked. "It's so cool."

"Uh," said Hollis intelligently, caught off-guard. The girl hadn't so much as dropped her a Discord message. Not even a joke in the group chat. And yet somehow . . . here she was, on Hollis's porch. "Because Halloween?"

Aini smirked. "Sabrina is a boss bitch all year, Hollis."

A smile slipped onto Hollis's lips as smoothly as Aini's hands slipped through her dark, gem-toned curls. "I'm sorry, I didn't realize today was Sabrinacon."

"You didn't get your ticket? Weird, I sent it like three days ago."

Hollis raised an amused eyebrow. Pointedly. "It's nice to see you, too, Aini."

"Oh, yeah." Aini shifted where she stood. "Hey, you want to go get donuts?"

Hollis's immediate answer was yes. To both Aini and donuts. But Hollis had never hung out with Aini alone. No—that wasn't entirely true. They rode to S&S sessions together, just the two of them, and sometimes their late-night Discord chats were so intense it felt like they were alone together somewhere else. Still, something about the idea of actually *going somewhere* and *doing something* with just Aini, something entirely unrelated to Secrets & Sorcery, left Hollis with a wriggly feeling in her belly.

The answer she actually gave was "Right now?"

"I mean, after Sabrinacon." Aini shrugged. "Or we can just skip straight to the donuts. Up to you."

Leaning against the doorframe, Hollis considered Aini. She stood on Hollis's porch like she belonged there, grinning up at Hollis confidently. Hollis considered, too, the new feeling in the pit of her stomach. It was an awful lot like anxiety, but there was an unfamiliar sparkling quality to it that Hollis didn't recognize.

With Aini's expectant eyes watching her, Hollis decided to follow that feeling.

"Okay."

A sudden brightness flashed across Aini's face. "Okay, donuts? Or okay, Sabrinacon?"

"Okay, donuts." A small smile crept onto Hollis's lips. "Let me get changed."

Aini beamed at her, triumphant. "Keep Sabrina. It's Halloween!"

Shaking her head to herself, Hollis waved Aini inside to wait in the cramped living room with her mom while Hollis went back to her bedroom to change. Because it was Halloween (and maybe more than a little bit because Aini had asked her to), she kept her Sabrina shirt on, but added a bra underneath it and slipped into the gray jeans she'd worn yesterday. When she returned to the living room, tugging on a seasonally appropriate black cardigan, Aini and her mom paused mid-chat.

"Donut-getting approved?" she asked them both.

"Very," said her mom with a curious smile Hollis determinedly ignored.

"Let's go," said Aini.

One heated-seat car ride and a stop at the Donut Palace drive-through later, the girls clutched a full bag of donuts each as they walked through Eden Park. In silent agreement, they headed toward the same bridge where they'd taken photos together the day before, as Umber and Honoria. The lighting was the same—it was the golden hour, the sun just setting, when everything in the world looked gentle and glowing. When they sat, the light haloed out around Aini's hair, a cobalt blue flame framing her face.

"So," she said, once Hollis had plunked down on the ground beside her, their backs against the concrete bridge. "How is school going?"

"Wow," said Hollis, pulling a Halloween-colored sprinkle donut out of her sack. "You really came to pick me up on Halloween, on a Saturday, to ask me about school?"

Aini crinkled her nose in amusement. "Well, yeah. And because I think you're cute."

Hollis shook her head at Aini's flirty compliment—*no, no, no.* She could feel color rising in her cheeks anyway, as red as Sabrina's dress. "I don't know. It's school. I think I bombed a test I had this week."

"History?" Aini hummed sympathetically. "Iffy said you've been making good progress with tutoring."

Hollis shot her a sideways glance. "How do you know about tutoring with Iffy?"

Aini shrugged. "We were talking about you and she mentioned it."

Hollis wasn't sure whether she was embarrassed or flattered. She settled for trying to look unfazed either way, matching Aini's shrug.

"Other than grades, then," Aini prompted. "How are you feeling about it? Senior year and all."

It wasn't the first time someone had tried to talk to Hollis about senior year, but it *was* the first time anyone had phrased it like that.

How *was* she feeling? Chewing her donut, Hollis considered. She licked her sugary lips. "Can I tell you a secret?"

Aini's eyes shone. "Yes, please."

Hollis, with a looseness in her limbs that she wasn't accustomed to, leaned in conspiratorially. She whispered, "I kind of hate it."

"Hollis Buckwheat." Aini grabbed at her chest as if clutching pearls. "Say it ain't so."

Hollis laughed. "But you know what I mean, right? All that teacher crap. *'These are your golden years!'* I keep doing it all, all this stuff they say I'm supposed to be doing—the assemblies and the forms and the tests—and I just keep thinking, *God*, I really hope they're not."

"I mean, they don't have to be." Aini's curls tossed as she shrugged.

Hollis looked up at her. "Huh?"

"Maybe that was true for them—which is totally valid, honestly." Aini fished a second donut out of her bag. "But not everyone's going to have the experience they did. I just think maybe there's something different for people like me and you. Don't you?"

Yes. A thousand times yes.

Hollis swallowed a mouthful of donut and nodded. "Then what's next, for people like us?"

"Oh, we're an *us* now, that's cute." Aini bit into her donut with a flourish. "Come on, you know what's next—life! The whole big world out there."

Hollis's heart sank. She felt as far away from all of that as she did from a golden, idealized senior year.

She shook her head. "I'm just staying around here, Aini." Because her mom was a teacher, Hollis got a discount on tuition at Northern Kentucky University. Between that and loans, it was almost affordable.

"What?" Aini actually looked taken aback this time, turning to look at her full on. Hollis was suddenly very preoccupied with getting her second donut out of her bag, eyes squinting together as she focused on the task. "The fabulously talented and ultra-amazing artist Hollis Beckwith is staying in Northern Kentucky?"

Hollis couldn't help it; she snorted.

"You know, my cat huffs at me the same way when she knows I'm right," said Aini. "But seriously, why aren't you going to, like, SCAD or something?"

Savannah College of Art and Design was *the* place to go for art. And it was for that exact reason Hollis had never even thought about going. That, and it cost more than her mom's house, probably, and it was far away, and—

"That's for real artists," she said, and shrugged. "I mean, I'm good"—this, she had started to accept about herself; she'd worked hard to get her skills to where they were, and she decided it wasn't worth trying to downplay her work—"but I'm not SCAD good. I just draw fan art for our S&S game."

"Hollis, are you being serious right now?"

Hollis looked up. Aini, her fingers glistening with donut glaze, looked almost mad at her.

But she *was* being serious. "Uh. Yes, probably."

"I mean, not to downplay how cool our game is," Aini said, "but we don't have *fans*. So you're not a fan artist—you're just *an artist*. An artist illustrating our original, collaborative storytelling."

The corner of Hollis's lips turned up. "When you say it like that, it sounds real."

Aini threw her hands in the air in frustration. "It *is* real!"

"I don't know, Ai," Hollis said, exhaling a deflating sigh. "It's just geeky fantasy art."

Aini narrowed her eyes, but there was only mirth, not real anger, in them. "If you call Umber Dawnfast geeky one more time, Hollis, he will have to fight you."

"But you know what I mean!"

"I don't, actually." Aini reached out and touched Hollis's shoulder. "I'm serious as a heart attack right now, Hollis. You should go to art school. You owe it to yourself to go somewhere that will get you ready for the *actual* best days of your life."

Hollis looked up, her brown eyes meeting Aini's darker ones. She blinked once, then twice. Even with her cardigan on, she felt a bit exposed, as if Aini was seeing into a part of her that didn't often get seen.

She took a small, shuddering breath. "Do you really think I should?"

"I'd be a little mad if you didn't, actually."

Hollis had never seen Aini so earnest. Under her tender gaze, Hollis couldn't look away. "It's just so far away."

"There are closer art schools. I can help you look." She squeezed Hollis's shoulder. "I'd really like to, in fact."

With the way Aini looked at her then, Hollis no longer felt the need to question it. And she no longer wanted to. She could feel color rising in her cheeks again, warm against the October night.

"Okay, okay," she said, sounding like Gloria and feeling a thrill in her chest, like she'd just agreed to a secret side quest. "I wouldn't want to make you mad."

"You know, if that's the thing that gets you to apply, Hollis, I'm okay with it."

"Oh—I just had a thought, though." Hollis paused, then took a thoughtful bite of her donut, purposefully making Aini wait.

Aini raised her eyebrows. "What's up?"

"Do you think SCAD has a Sabrina fan club?"

"Oh my God."

Hollis's face split with a grin, which she tried and failed to suppress. Her tone went serious. "I don't think I can go all the way out there if it doesn't."

Aini's eyes sparkled. "She's got jokes, doesn't she."

The Eden Park Bridge flooded with the noise of Hollis's and Aini's laughter.

"And I'll need to make sure fall break aligns with Sabrinacon!"

16

WORTH FIGHTING FOR

WHEN MAGGIE UPLOADED the group's Halloween cosplay photos to the Discord later that week, Hollis's first thought was that she couldn't believe how good they were. For all the grief she had initially felt about Maggie's double life (glam-grunge social media influencer by day, closet nerd by night), she understood the draw now. The pictures Maggie had taken of them all looked professional, edited and retouched in a way that didn't change them physically but made everything—from the scenery to their costumes—look more vivid and real than it had even in person.

Her second thought was that she, Hollis, looked good. No, she looked *great*. For a very long time, Hollis avoided pictures because she never liked the way her fat body looked in them. She had finally gotten beyond that, and during the shoot, she'd really tried to let go. In these photos, she looked like a girl who was fat, yes, but also like a girl who was strong and confident and beautiful. Even her new bangs looked—as Aini had said—pretty badass.

But more than anything else, what struck Hollis was how happy she looked. There, dressed up as a character whose courage she borrowed every Friday and posing by the bridge in Eden Park, was a girl in her element. She stood among her friends—hovering over Fran with Iffy, as they pretended to heal the younger girl; sneaking around a tree with Maggie; recreating her first Steadfast drawing with Aini, looking over their shoulders at each other, hand in hand—not at the outskirts of the group, or even simply there, but an integral part to the way everyone came together. In every frame, Hollis beamed. Even in the serious group shots, her eyes had a certain sparkle she was sure had nothing to do with Maggie's clever editing.

But as she looked at them again, lying in her bed after school, Hollis felt not joy but guilt—deep, dark guilt that pushed down on her from all sides, trapping her inside her sheets.

She couldn't recall when exactly it had happened, but all the evidence showed it had: Hollis's Secrets & Sorcery game was no longer just a way for her to bond with Chris. Sure, she still shared what happened in-game with him and the rest of the boys, and yes, it was certainly fun to talk about (when Landon wasn't being horrible, at least), but it was no longer the thing that made her want to play the game.

Maybe she played for the girls who had become her friends, but that didn't feel quite right either. Hollis had a sneaking suspicion that who she was *really* playing this nerdy, amazing game for was herself, which only made the weight of guilt press down on her harder.

Somehow, amid all the pressure, Hollis moved. Her stomach churned. She rolled over to her bedside table and grabbed her phone. She hesitated for quite a while, jittery and uncomfortable for reasons she couldn't pin down, and then she opened a text message.

hey.

can you give me a ride to my game on friday?

There was a delay in which Hollis was sure she'd crumple, but then a text came back.

christopher: y tho

christopher: u have a ride

Hollis frowned.

actually i don't this week.

iffy's having car trouble and aini might not come.

This was a blatant lie. But it suddenly felt important to bring Chris back into her game—to share some of the happiness in her photographs with him. Surely a small lie wasn't so bad, if it was for the right reasons. Besides, what she wrote next was the truth.

it would mean a lot to me if you could take me.

There was another long pause.

christopher: but the boys and i play the same nite

christopher: u know how it is

Hollis sighed at her phone screen. Of course she knew how it was; she'd been dealing with Chris's Friday-night schedule for four years. Maybe it was stupid to ask. Clearly, she already knew the answer.

Hollis stared at the text until the screen went black. When she pushed the button to unlock her phone again, her lock screen lit up with the photo of Honoria and Umber holding hands. As it had every time since she'd set it as her background, an involuntary smile burned across Hollis's lips, her cheeks blushing bright pink. And though she couldn't be sure, she suspected her eyes were brighter, too: the same brightness that twinkled in them in the photograph as she looked over her cardboard-breastplate-wearing shoulder not quite at Aini.

Guilt surged through her again, burning acrid in her throat. She unlocked her phone.

please chris?

you don't have to stay.

and you could finally meet the girls.

The three dots appeared faster this time, and Chris gave his answer.

christopher: yeah fine

christopher: ill take u

On Friday, Hollis was late.

She wasn't one or two minutes late, like when Aini drove her. They weren't even five or ten minutes late, like she sometimes was when Iffy drove her on busy weeks. When Chris backed into a parking spot on the street outside of the Castañedas' apartment, she was a full twenty-three minutes late, which Hollis knew because she was counting.

"Thanks," she said, squirming to retrieve her tote bag from the back seat. "I'll see you later tonight?"

Chris cocked an eyebrow, confused. "Don't you want me to come in with you?"

"Oh." She had, but that was well over twenty-three minutes ago now. A wave of nausea swept through her body. "I just figured since—"

She almost said *we're so late*, but Chris was, as he reminded her when he showed up to her house at 5:53, doing her a favor by taking her at all, so she didn't want to rub it in.

"It's probably best if I just run in real quick," she settled on instead.

"Come on, Hol," Chris said, and turned off the car. "Let's go."

Before Hollis could protest, Chris was already out of the car. Anxiety whirled inside of her, stirring up her insides. The last thing she wanted to add to being this late to S&S was a fight with Chris. Hollis got out of the car too.

"They're probably waiting on me," she said as she dodged around Miss Virginia's knockout rosebush, pushed open the apartment door, and led Chris inside. She nodded toward the hallway that led to the dining room.

"As you approach the bog, you smell something . . . strange," Gloria's voice echoed from around the corner.

They had not waited for Hollis after all.

Now that she realized this, Hollis felt she should have known coming in. She remembered, somewhere in the back corner of her mind, that they had all agreed to a *wait fifteen minutes and then start* rule when it came to late arrivals. It was just that, until today, no one had ever triggered its use.

The anxiety in Hollis's belly spiraled, making her queasy again. She gulped as if she could swallow it down, waiting for a break in Gloria's narration to slip in, but—

"A boy?!" shrieked Fran.

As one, the other girls turned to where Hollis and Chris stood in the doorway.

"I'm so sorry I'm late," Hollis said in a rush.

"A *boy*," accused Fran again, her eyes narrowed at Chris in suspicion.

But Gloria only smiled kindly, her red lips bright in the overhead light. She said, "Ah, yes, Aini said you'd be getting another ride tonight, Hollis. I'm glad you could make it. Come, take your seat. And thanks for bringing her . . . ?"

It was only a beat later, when Hollis was halfway to her seat next to Aini, that she realized this was her cue for an introduction. It was then, too, that Hollis realized she'd never actually mentioned Chris to the girls by name. Her palms began to sweat.

"Oh!" she said, turning awkwardly and waving her hand toward the boy framed in the doorway. "This is Chris, he's—"

"I'm her boyfriend." There was an edge to Chris's voice that Hollis hadn't heard in the car. He crossed his arms over his chest and leaned against the doorframe, taking up space.

"It's good to meet you finally," Gloria said charitably. "Really, thank you for dropping Hollis off."

"I thought he'd be taller," Fran muttered, not quite under her breath, to Aini beside her. This pulled a smile across Aini's lips, but she said nothing.

The moment stretched out, quiet and uncomfortable, before Chris asked, "So aren't you going to introduce me to everyone?"

Hollis threw Chris a look over her shoulder, but he met her gaze with a glare that would have been more at home on Landon's face. One eyebrow crept up his forehead, making his words a dare as much as a question.

"Yeah, sure," said Hollis, turning back to the table. "You know Iffy from school, she plays our sorceress. And this is Gloria, our Secret Keeper, and her little sister, Fran, our barbarian. Next to her is Maggie, who—"

"Hey, Maggie," Chris interrupted. "The rogue, right?"

Maggie nodded, her face impassive.

"I've played a rogue before," said Chris. "They get super OP after Level 10, so you have that to look forward to."

"Uh, cool," Maggie said, then turned back to Fran, head dipping to whisper something in her ear. Fran looked at Chris, then nodded.

"And this, uh," Hollis started, then stopped. She didn't *want* to introduce Aini to Chris. Something about it felt unsafe. Aini was something special—a secret, like the first songs on the Steadfast playlist or the way Hollis felt when she held Aini's hand. She said the words as fast as she could, getting them over with. "This is Aini, the party's bard."

Chris took a step forward in a way that made Hollis hiss "*Chris!*"

under her breath—like this step was a dare of sorts, too. He reached the table, looming over Iffy's shoulder so she had to duck out of the way, and held out his hand for Aini to shake.

He said, "'Sup?"

Hollis wasn't sure what she had *expected* to happen when Chris finally met Aini. It was somehow a reality she had never considered. But she certainly hadn't expected him posturing like some protective sitcom dad. Hollis turned to Aini, trying to give her a reassuring look, but she herself was so unsure of what was happening that it probably looked more like she might vomit.

"Hey, Chris," said Aini, taking his hand and shaking it like that was something normal people did. "Good to meet you, man. You have an awesome girlfriend. I'm so glad she joined our group."

Whatever *Chris* had expected, it apparently wasn't that. He let Aini's hand drop, then stepped back into the doorway.

"So where are you guys at?" he asked, looking past Hollis to Gloria.

"In the bogs on the outskirts of the Werewood," Gloria supplied easily. "But if you'd like to know more about our game, perhaps you can ask later tonight. We've already started this session, and as a general rule, we like to check in with all the players before someone new comes to the table, even just to visit."

"I'm sorry," breathed Hollis. She couldn't be sure if this was to Gloria or to Chris or to the room at large.

"Actually, I can't get Hollis later," Chris said. "I have to get to my game now."

Hollis's stomach sank. She hadn't asked him to pick her up, too, but she'd assumed he would. It was what he did for her. Now she was not only late, she was also stuck on the wrong side of the river with no ride home.

"It's cool," Aini volunteered immediately. "I've got Hollis."

"Yeah," said Iffy, crossing her arms over her chest. "We'll get her home."

"Whatever," said Chris, glowering. "I'll see you later, Hollis."

And without so much as a wave, he turned and walked himself out, closing the door too hard behind him.

It was like the whole table, Hollis included, could finally exhale. For a moment, they were all quiet, and then Gloria asked, "Everyone okay?"

Around the table, the girls nodded or shrugged. When the Secret Keeper's brown eyes met Hollis's, she tried to make the look she returned say everything she couldn't: *I'm so sorry* and *I didn't mean for this to happen* and *Ugh*.

"How about we play some S&S now?" Gloria asked.

And so they did.

But Hollis couldn't focus, not really.

As Honoria trudged through the murky swamps of the Werewood bogs, all Hollis could think about was the mess she had just caused at the table. She had meant to accomplish something by introducing Chris to the girls, she was sure of that, but it certainly wasn't this. All that had come out of that uncomfortable interaction was a deep understanding that Chris and the girls didn't mix—or perhaps, more accurately, that Chris didn't mix with the girls.

If Chris couldn't play nice with the girls, how much longer would it be before he couldn't play nice with Hollis, either? Her mind drifted back to their fight over fried pickles, to Chris calling her *extra*, to how he had made her feel like too much. But when she sat at *this* table, she never had to worry about being anything other than exactly herself. The contrast pulled at her like feet being sucked into a boggy mire.

"What did you get?" Aini asked, nudging Hollis with her elbow.

"Hmmm?" Hollis blinked, pulled out of her thoughts and anxieties.

"We need to roll a Navigation check to make it through all this mess." Aini nudged Hollis's d20 in front of her.

"Oh." Hollis looked at Aini, who smiled back calmly. She was as gentle as ever, like an Emotional Navigation check rolled with advantage. Returning her smile, Hollis picked up her dice and rolled. "That's a 12."

On Monday after school, Hollis caught the crew up on her Friday session.

"We ended up finding this temple in the bog," she told them, as they all stood together near their parked cars in the student lot. "To some, like, weird old magic no one knew about."

Usually, this was where Chris would jump in and embellish the story, but just like Landon, Lacie, and Marius, this was the first time he was hearing it. After Friday night, she hadn't wanted to text and catch him up on the game session he'd made so difficult to start. And he hadn't bothered to text *her*, either, so the story was Hollis's alone to tell.

"This werebear was inside," she continued, "and it was hard to get in, but Tanwyn, our rogue—"

"That Maggie girl?" Chris turned to Landon and Marius. "She's so hot. Like, Instagram-baddie hot."

Marius grinned. "Is she single, though?"

Landon laughed, a nasally sound, and asked, "Is she even *straight*, though?"

The three boys looked at Hollis, who shrugged. Honestly, she didn't know Maggie's sexuality. It had never come up, so it had never been an issue.

"It's so selfish when hot girls aren't straight," Landon said. "Right, babe?" He dipped his head to give Lacie a quick kiss (with entirely too much tongue).

"Oh, *Lan*," said Lacie with a giggle.

"I'm just saying, I don't even get why that girl plays S&S," Chris said. "She's, like, way too sexy."

"Excuse me?" Hollis narrowed her eyes at Chris, a warning expression on her face. She couldn't believe the words coming out of his mouth. For one, what that implied about Hollis and the other girls didn't sit well with her. For another, what did that even mean, *Maggie was too sexy for S&S*?

But then her face fell slightly. That was exactly what she had thought about Maggie, too, in the beginning: that she was much too pretty to fit into such a nerdy space. Hearing it from Chris's mouth made her realize how absurd it was—and how absurd *she* had been when she first started playing. Maybe her reason for joining the group wasn't the only thing that had changed.

Hollis shook her head. "Maggie is actually smart as hell, and she knows the S&S handbook backward and forward, just like the rest of us." But Hollis didn't stop there. The rest of the words fell out like dice from a cupped hand. "And it doesn't even matter who she likes. No one picks that stuff; it just happens. So cool it, okay?"

The group fell silent. After a beat, Chris said, "Yeah, sure. So, the werebear?"

Hollis started her story again, but her heart wasn't in it. She just wanted to get it over with and go home. "We had to kill it, but underneath all that corruption, we knew it was just a person. Werebears are usually good-aligned, when they're not, you know, all messed up."

"Right?" Lacie gave Hollis a sympathetic look. "That reminds me of when we had to battle the werebear in the fighting pit in the Firedin."

Landon shot Lacie a look Hollis didn't miss. "She means when *we* did," he said.

Marius made a face and turned toward his truck surreptitiously, keys in hand.

Hollis looked at Chris, not Lacie, when she asked the other girl, "You play with the guys on Fridays?"

"Duh!" said Lacie, her face lighting up with excitement. "It's only the coolest game in town. I don't know why you didn't join them instead of your girl squad."

Landon put an arm around Lacie's shoulder, cutting her off. "Let's get you home, Lace," he said.

"I'll take care of this," said Chris to Landon as he turned to go, in what he must have thought was a soothing voice. Hollis scoffed.

"See you tomorrow!" said Lacie. To her credit, she was clearly oblivious.

Hollis waited until Lacie and Landon had pulled away, joining the queue of cars leaving the parking lot, before speaking again. "That's really interesting."

"Hollis, *please*," Chris said, his voice tight. "It's not what it seems like."

"Oh, that's good," said Hollis, "because what it seems like is that big, scary Landon budged on his immovable No-Girlfriend Rule to let his *own* girlfriend join the campaign."

Chris suddenly became preoccupied with selecting his car key from the ring of two on his key chain. He shrugged.

"Because that would be really shitty, wouldn't it," Hollis pressed. "If that's what happened?"

"Okay, yes. That's what happened," said Chris. "But it's really not what it sounds like."

Hollis just looked at him. "You keep saying that, but I'm not sure you understand what that phrase means."

"Fine, then." Chris avoided her gaze as he unlocked the car. "Then it's just not a big deal."

"Chris," said Hollis. "I . . ."

She trailed off, looking at him looking at his keys. Because of the No-Girlfriend Rule, she had spent almost a month looking for an open group that met in a public place so she would feel safe going on her own. Then the one she'd found exposed her to everything wrong with the game in one sitting, like some sort of cosmic joke. If fate hadn't found her in the vestibule waiting for Chris to come pick her up, if the sunset colors on Gloria's advertisement hadn't caught her attention, then she might never have played Secrets & Sorcery again. But because she had wanted to get—and stay—closer to Chris, Hollis had taken a second chance on the game with the girls. She had been brave, for him.

It *was* a big deal.

It just wasn't a big deal to *Chris*.

"You know, I'm really, really glad I found the girls to play with," she said, mostly to herself, after falling quiet for some time.

Chris groaned. "Come off it, Hollis," he said. "You're always talking about how great those bitches are."

"Excuse me?" Hollis held up her hand. "Did you just call my friends *bitches*?"

"No," Chris said, opening his car door aggressively. "I mean, yes, I did, technically, but what I meant was—you're always going on about them."

"Because you always give me so much shit about them!" Hollis shook her head. Her hands balled into fists at her sides, fingernails biting half-moons into her palms. "But you do realize, don't you, that I would literally have never started playing with them if it weren't for the No-Girlfriend Rule? Because it was such a nonnegotiable thing when I asked you if I could maybe join the group.

"I just wanted us to have something else in common, Chris. Something that wasn't *your* music or *your* video games or *your* friends. Something that was *ours*. And that was against the rules. But now you let that"—Hollis almost said *bitch* too, but she caught herself. No girl, not even Lacie, deserved to be called a bitch. This wasn't her fault—"*girl* join, like it's nothing."

"It wasn't *me!*" Chris threw up his hands. His two keys jangled against each other. "Landon really fought for her!"

Hollis shook her head in disbelief. "Oh, how nice for Lacie to have a boyfriend who really fights for her."

Scattering empty Monster cans and crumpled-up gym shorts, Hollis snatched her backpack and her tote bag from the back seat of the Sentra. Once she'd slung them sloppily over her shoulders, she slammed the car door shut.

Chris rolled his eyes and sighed. "Hollis—"

"Nope," she said. "Just nope."

"If you—"

"You can go now, Chris. I'm going to walk home."

"It's like a thousand blocks, and you're—"

"Fat, I know." She knew it wasn't something Chris would say— he had always been neutral about her body, never commenting on her fatness, as if it didn't exist—but with how he had been behaving lately, she wasn't sure anymore whether the boy she was arguing with was the boy she thought she knew. "You might not think I'm as *sexy* as Maggie or as *worth it* as Lacie, Chris, but I'm kind of a badass, and I'd rather walk a thousand fat-girl blocks by myself than ride in the car with you right now."

With that, Hollis stalked off, her backpack already too heavy on her shoulders. She waited to readjust it until she was a block away, so Chris wouldn't see.

Nine hundred and ninety-nine fat-girl blocks to go.

The streets of Covington stretched out ahead of her, narrow and mostly one-way and paved with uneven sidewalks studded with clumps of dying grass. The odd car still trickled out of the parking lot occasionally, and now and then a TANK bus hissed by, but once she turned off Madison and onto the side streets, Hollis was suddenly very alone.

She felt the weight of it on her, pressing down in strange places. And as the adrenaline started to fade from her body, it only got heavier. Nothing felt comfortable, from the pull of her backpack on her shoulders to the sinking feeling that she had just done something she couldn't undo.

Before, Hollis might have just wallowed in the discomfort, accepting it as the punishment for the bad thing her brain was telling her she had done. But there was a different voice in her head now, too. It sounded a bit like Gloria's, even and low and sweet, and a little like Iffy's, painted Southern around the vowels, but mostly it sounded like her own. It was small but getting louder with each step she took.

She hadn't done anything wrong. And what was more, she didn't need to feel *bad* for anything. She had support now. All she had to do was reach out.

Hollis pulled her phone out of her back pocket.

beckwhat 3:44 PM
i need your number

please.

Before Hollis's screen even faded to black, Aini Amin-Shaw replied with her number.

It was in poor form, but in that moment, Hollis didn't care. She pressed FaceTime without a second thought, without even asking first.

Aini answered on the second ring, her face framed by a seat belt on one side and a headrest on the other. "Hey."

"You're in your car," said Hollis. "Are you driving?"

"I pulled over. Sounded urgent."

"You're not wrong," said Hollis, and she laughed. It wasn't a pretty laugh. It was too long and harsh and a little unhinged.

She laid it on Aini, everything that had happened—from Lacie to Landon to the way Chris spat the word *bitches* at her and hardly bothered to backtrack. She told her about Maggie and the oil-slick way Chris said *sexy* and how she had told him off, skimming over the part about playing S&S for him because that felt so insignificant now. When she finally finished, about a dozen blocks later, she wiped the sweat off her forehead with the back of her free hand. It was chilly in Covington this time of year, but with all the walking and talking and heat of emotion in her chest, Hollis wasn't even a little bit cold.

"No," Aini said at last.

"Yes," Hollis said in reply.

"Hollis, that's just . . ." Aini trailed off, looking not into her camera but at Hollis's face on her screen, her gaze angled slightly downward.

Hollis exhaled a relieved sigh. It felt good, hearing the anger in Aini's voice. "I know."

"Do you want me to fight them?"

Hollis snorted a laugh.

"I'll do it," Aini threatened.

"I know you would," Hollis said. "That's why I'm FaceTiming you."

One corner of Aini's mouth curled into a thin smile, then uncurled again as she sighed. "So this feels pretty shitty, huh?"

"Calling you?" Calling Aini actually felt pretty good. Her outrage about the game was what Hollis had wanted from her boyfriend. Somehow it felt even more satisfying coming from Aini.

Aini rolled her eyes. "No, the stuff with those jerk boys."

"Oh." Hollis wasn't used to someone cutting to the heart of something so quickly—or at all. Chris usually threw up his hands long before they even got close. "Yeah. I feel like an idiot."

"I can come get you," Aini offered.

Hollis shook her head. "I'll be home by the time you get over the bridge."

"The offer still stands."

"I know." Hollis paused, her breath huffing out in a visible cloud.

It wasn't just Chris who didn't talk about his feelings; it was her, too. But her relationship with Aini was different from her relationship with Chris. Maybe with Aini, she could try something new.

Hollis let out a sigh. "I just. I feel kind of sad, too? No, *sad*'s not the right word. Let down? And a little embarrassed. Like, what is it that's right about Lacie-with-an-*I-E* that's not right with me?"

This thought had crept out from the back of her mind and stuck with Hollis as she walked. She and Chris had known each other longer than Chris and Landon. When it came to the other boys, she had been part of their group for as long as it had existed. What made *Lacie* worth fighting for, when Hollis clearly wasn't?

"Don't." Aini was stern again. "This has nothing to do with *any-thing* about you, Hollis. It doesn't even have anything to do with Lacie, really. It says everything in the world about those boys, though. And too bad for them, because they're missing out on a real badass at their table."

It was a very Aini thing to say. And it almost made Hollis smile.

"I don't actually *feel* like a badass," Hollis confessed. And she didn't, despite everything she'd spat at Chris, which she realized upon reflection was verifiably a badass thing to have done. But it still felt hollow. Hollis frowned at Aini's face on her screen. "I just feel pissed off."

"And sad. And embarrassed. And somehow still really strong and amazing and cute through it all."

Hollis's frown curled up at one corner. "Aini."

"I mean it. What else are you feeling?"

Hollis thought for a moment, huffing in silence. On the other side of the screen, Aini waited patiently, parked somewhere on the Ohio side of the river.

"I feel really . . . glad? Like if it hadn't been for No Girlfriends, I never would have played that horrible Games-A-Lot game, and if

I hadn't been *there*, I wouldn't have seen Gloria's flyer. And I would never have started playing with you . . . all. And you all are my favorite people right now." Hollis was quiet for a beat. The cold on her skin and the deep tiredness settling over her body made her bold. *"You're my favorite person right now. I can't imagine having not met you, Aini."*

Aini smiled. "It's cool, because I feel the same way, actually. I'd still punch your jerk boyfriend in the face for this, but I'm also really thankful he's a jerk, because his jerkiness helped me find you."

When Aini said it, it sounded more real. Hollis played the words back in her head just to hear them again. She wished she'd asked Aini to pick her up after all. The words they were sharing felt important, a sort of definition to their relationship that they hadn't had before.

In that moment, Hollis wanted to hold Aini's hand more than anything.

"Yeah," she said to the screen instead. "That's it exactly."

"I'm sorry your boyfriend is so crappy," said Aini.

"Me too," said Hollis. "Thanks, Aini."

In Umber's lilting accent, Aini added, "'It's a good thing I'm a much better boyfriend, isn't it?'"

Hollis smiled. "Thanks, Umber."

"Are you sure you don't want me to come get you? It's got to be freezing."

Hollis almost said yes, but she could see the stained fish-scale roof of her house from the street corner. And she already felt selfish with Aini's time.

She shook her head, bangs sweeping across her sweaty forehead. "I'm almost home now, actually. Thanks for keeping me company."

"Thanks for calling me. You should do it again sometime."

"All right," Hollis said. "I will."

"That's my girl. Talk soon?"

Hollis's heart swelled. "Talk soon. Bye."

Aini waved, and then the screen went black. For half a second, Hollis was left only with the image of her own face reflected back up at her—red-cheeked, a little snotty-nosed, and grinning.

In that moment, she really was thankful for the No-Girlfriend Rule.

17
A THING

IT WAS ALWAYS strange when one of them missed a session, and the following Friday, Aini was out for a wedding. Iffy and Hollis copiloted Umber during the session, which went much better than the time Aini and Hollis had done the same for Iffy. Hollis felt a pang of guilt at how closely Iffy read the particulars of Umber's spells, especially when all they ended up doing was stabbing things or throwing daggers at things or, once, singing an S&S-ified version of "WAP" in an attempt to persuade a diviner to perform a high-level scry they needed without requiring an open-ended favor at some undefined point in the future.

The attempt had failed, despite Iffy's accompanying dance moves.

"And I swear to God," Iffy said, "if she gives me any lip about the favor, I'll remind her that your goofy asses got us all *arrested* when you ran Nereida for me."

It was a fair point. Hollis nodded.

"I still wish Aini had been here, though," she said as Iffy drove her home. The seats of the Accord were not as warm as the ones in Aini's sedan, but Hollis was just as comfortable. The light and noise of the riverside blurred together outside the passenger window. "She would have cracked up at how bad our lyrics were."

Iffy grinned. "Don't worry. I already texted them to her. She says we're horrible and she loves us."

Hollis smiled, rolling her eyes. She liked the idea of being loved by Aini.

As if Iffy could hear her thinking it, she looked over at Hollis. "It's cool that Chris is cool about Aini. I didn't expect that from a pasty Midwestern white boy like him."

Hollis cocked her head to the side. "What do you mean?"

"I mean, you and Aini being so close," said Iffy. "It's real twenty-first century of him to not be sketch about it."

"I mean, he's pretty sketch about *all* of you." Hollis wouldn't usually have admitted this, but after Chris's behavior when he dropped her off last week, there was really no denying it. "He thinks hanging around with the S&S squad makes me, and I quote, 'extra.'"

Iffy raised an eyebrow. "But he's cool about Aini? That's wild."

The pit of Hollis's stomach twisted.

"What do you mean, cool about Aini?"

"Just the thing you two have going on," she said, and then rushed to add, "which I'm not judging! I support the hell out of you both, you know me."

"We don't have a thing going on," said Hollis, her smile fading altogether. "We're just friends, the same as me and you."

"Hmm." Iffy spared her a glance. "I don't think you and me are the same kind of friends. I love you, but I'm not *in love* with you."

Hollis snorted. "Aini Amin-Shaw is not in love with me."

"Okay, girl." Iffy shrugged. "Maybe I misread."

"Maybe," Hollis said. Hollis shifted in her seat, stomach suddenly roiling. "Can we talk about something else?"

"Yeah, sure," said Iffy. "What about the Diviner's favor? Do you think it'll be something tough?"

"I don't know," said Hollis. "It could be anything, really."

They went on to speculate about what the favor might be and when the Diviner would call it in, but Hollis's heart wasn't in it.

When she got home, she turned her phone off and didn't join the postgame group chat like she usually did. Instead, she lay in bed, her faded quilt pulled up to her chin.

She couldn't get Iffy's words out of her mind. *The thing you two have going on.* The more she thought about it, the more she realized she had been wrong in how she'd downplayed it.

Hollis's feelings for Aini were complicated. Undefined. And they were always more of both when the two of them were apart. Even now, staring up at the popcorn ceiling of her room, Hollis couldn't quite pin them down. Anytime she got close, Landon's voice crept into her head, waiting to call her out on whatever the answer was.

Maybe what she *should* have said to Iffy was, yes, she and Aini definitely had a thing going on.

But Chris couldn't be cool with it because he didn't know about it. *Hollis* didn't even know about it, not really. Not until Iffy pointed it out.

But now that she had, it was all Hollis could think about. About the closeness she felt with Aini. About how it was more than could be explained away by friendship. About how Aini had become a constant thought, the doodles in the margins of her brain, always there to make Hollis smile at a little remembered something from the Friday before or the Discord chat or a text message.

Hollis had never felt this way about Chris. Hollis had never felt this way about *anyone.* But she had also never played Secrets & Sorcery with anyone. She was convinced that had something to do with it. Bard or not, there was simply no way someone could sit at the same table as Umber Dawnfast every week and *not* feel this way about the girl who played him.

Hollis's stomach churned, flooding her with a familiar anxiety. But underneath it was something new—an excitement that made her a little breathless, made her want to ask Aini if she knew this feeling too.

Maybe it was a blessing in disguise, then, that Thanksgiving break was coming up. With both Aini and Maggie traveling, Gloria had decided to postpone their game. Iffy was going to come over to help Hollis fill out her Common Application (and figure out which of the schools on the list she and Aini had put together would be the best fit), but otherwise, the group was also on a break. It would give Hollis an extra week.

For what, she wasn't sure. Right now she wasn't sure of much.

With a sigh, Hollis tried to set the thought aside, flipping over onto her stomach. It took her an especially long time to fall asleep.

Hollis pressed her back to the Sentra's locked door.

Chris should have been out of school by now; it was a full eight minutes past noon. Exam days were half days, and so even if he took more than the usual amount of time to make it from his classroom to the parking lot, he was, generously, three minutes behind.

Hollis swore into the cold sunlight. Of all the days for him to run late.

Under normal circumstances, she might not have minded. In her back pocket, her phone buzzed—likely notifications from the server, which had been full of giddy chatter about the upcoming session all morning. But Hollis wasn't feeling giddy. Her energy was far more nervous, tapped out in an angry rhythm on the inside of her shoes.

She was pretty sure she had bombed her history exam, and she was one step away from melting down about it.

As soon as she put her pencil to the paper, every fact and date and historical figure she and Iffy had crammed into her head was replaced by gears full of goo, gummed up and slowing her down. Now it whirred back to life with exaggerated speed, her thoughts chasing each other in shaming circles: *Of course* she failed. How could she have expected anything else?

Again, her phone buzzed in her pocket, and this time Hollis

reached toward it. Maybe she could message Aini; she would know what to do. But even though her relationship with Aini was the same as ever when they were together, it still felt strange—at least on Hollis's end—when they were apart. Besides, Aini was friends with Iffy, and the thought of Iffy finding out how badly Hollis had messed up after all the hours she'd wasted on her wasn't something she was willing to face yet. Especially after they'd finally gotten her important college applications sent in together.

Her head craned toward the doors again. Maybe it was the way the barren trees framed them, making them look far away—or the fact that most other students had already fled campus, leaving Hollis largely alone—but waiting for those doors to open was excruciating.

"Finally," she huffed as Chris approached the other side of the car, keys already in hand.

"Good to see you, too, Hols." His mouth quirked up at the corner like he might have been about to say something else, but then he looked at her—really looked at her—and his expression softened. "Come on, let's go."

Hollis nodded. She tried to open the passenger door three times before the lock clicked open.

What might have happened if she was getting into the car with someone else—like her mother or Iffy or certainly Aini—was that she would have been asked what was wrong. What would happen then was that Hollis would have to think about it: all those swirling dates and the drops of sweat running down her back as she tried to recall them. But this was Chris, and so instead he cranked on some music just loud enough that her thoughts were dulled by the double bass and the buzz of his blown speakers. Hollis ran her hands over the stained multicolored upholstery of the passenger seat. It felt just as familiar and fuzzy as the music.

"You know how Mrs. Grimes said that if she caught Landon and

Lacie with PDA again, she'd give them detention for the rest of the year?" Chris backed out of his parking spot with a jerk.

She nodded back just as jerkily, fingers worrying the same familiar spot on the upholstery. Chris kept his eyes on the road as he pulled out of the lot, so she added out loud, "Yeah."

"Well." Chris still didn't look at her, but the edges of his lips curled up in a smile. He spoke loud enough that his words were distinct over the music. "She caught them again."

Hollis said, "Yeah?"

"Yeah." And as they pulled out onto the main road, Chris was off, diving into the story as he drove her home.

The trials and tribulations of Landon and Lacie weren't Hollis's ideal topic of conversation. But the crush of anxiety still clung to her chest, making her rib cage feel a size too small. Her breath was testing these limits, coming hot and fast in her lungs. At this point, she was desperate for any distraction.

The story, like the music, was dull and droning. It worked through her slowly. Her clenched fists relaxed first, then her crossed arms. The rest of her body followed suit until finally the ball of stress inside her unraveled and collapsed. A numbing hollowness flooded in, filling the spaces where all the tangled pieces of her had been twisted together.

Chris downshifted at a stoplight, story still going strong. His hand grazed Hollis's thigh, and she didn't have the impulse to catch it in her own, to press their palms tight together. For the length of the light, she allowed herself to consider: What if she never did? Now that she knew what it was like, that effortless pull between herself and someone else, a part of her *wanted* that. Her fingers twitched in the direction of the gearshift, where Chris's hand rested. Maybe, just maybe, their hands would fit together as effortlessly as hers and Aini's did. Maybe if she tried one more time.

Then Chris accelerated through the green light, and the moment was gone.

They just weren't like that, Chris and Hollis. But selfishly, here in the Sentra with him and his nu metal, Hollis wanted them to be. Here, with the windows up and the heat just slightly too high for her liking, she didn't have to think about how she was feeling or what she wanted. She didn't even have to listen to the story he was telling her, or to the lyrics rattling through the scratchy speakers. She just had to sit with Chris, who was enough to fill the hollow spaces inside her with no effort on her part.

Maybe they weren't good for each other. Maybe they never had been. Chris had never made her heart skip in her chest or her Spotify recalibrate its suggestions to love songs. When Hollis was with Chris, she didn't get to be epic, but she also didn't have to be extraordinary.

She didn't have to be anything at all.

She still couldn't remember when the Triangle Shirtwaist Factory fire had occurred (or even what a triangle shirtwaist was), but she could remember this: crying under the slide in sixth grade during recess. Her parents had had the divorce talk with her that morning, and then Chris had found her hiding spot and talked her ear off about yo-yos until she blustered herself out.

She remembered, too, the hard drive full of *Mystery Science Theater 3000* bootlegs he'd brought over in eighth grade after she sprained her ankle in gym and could hardly walk—and how by the end of those two weeks, she'd actually started to like those old B movies. She remembered the weekend he got his driver's license, which had just happened to coincide with the weekend Hollis's father remarried, and how casually Chris had suggested they road trip to Chicago—because they could and because it was the most rebellious place either of them could think of. It didn't matter that they'd given up halfway, in Indianapolis, because they had done what they really meant to do: get away.

And while Hollis had forgotten enough to probably fail US History, she didn't have to forget *their* history. She owed him—and at least part of herself—that.

"So what do you think Mrs. Grimes will do?" Chris finally asked, taking a corner faster than he should.

"Oh, I don't know," she said, because she didn't. "Probably exactly what Mrs. Grimes wants to do, as usual."

The comfortable crackle of bad music carried them along for a quiet moment as Chris parallel parked in front of Hollis's house. They sat together for a full minute, not saying anything.

After a while, Chris asked, "You going to be okay, Hol?"

Hollis wasn't doing great, but she also wasn't doing horribly. And that was okay enough.

"Yeah." She smiled across the space between them. She didn't feel the same tug she did with Aini—the one that made her itch to lean in closer—but she didn't mind. That tug always left her feeling a little dizzy, a little out of control. Here, she only felt comfort—and that was enough, too. "Thanks, Chris."

"Yeah," said Chris. "Sure."

Hollis gave a small nod. "See you in the morning."

And as she closed the door behind her, watching as Chris sped off down the one-way street, Hollis was sure as ever that she would do exactly that.

18

MERRY CRITMAS

EXAM GRADES CAME and went about how Hollis expected.

She'd aced her art exam—a still life of everything on her bedside table, her new orange dice scattered to roll an artful Natural 20. She'd done better on her algebra exam than she'd expected, somehow managing a B. And despite her meltdown, she'd even pulled out a C on her history exam. She'd texted Aini three confetti emojis as soon as the paper was handed back. Aini had sent back a brown high five and a Black wizard lady and two hearts. The only test she had really done poorly on was economics; she'd earned a D+.

"But the plus has to count for something," she'd tried to persuade her mom as they packed essentials from her classroom into her ancient RAV4 to take home over winter break. "It's basically a C minus!"

"Oh, yeah," said her mom, rolling her eyes. "Basically."

But, by some end-of-semester miracle (or maybe because her mom was so tired from grading all her own exam papers), there wasn't much more fight than that. Hollis tried not to worry that it was because her mom had finally given up on her college prospects—at least not for the next few weeks. Winter break stretched out before her, full of possibility.

Kicking it all off was the S&S Generic Winter Holiday Festival at the Castañedas' apartment on Friday. Gloria had planned a fun festival for the group, complete with in-character contests and games.

Then, thanks in large part to everyone's general excitement to be out of school for a few weeks (and an excess of caps-lock screeching from Fran), it had mushroomed into a full-on party in real life, too. Everyone was bringing snacks, and they had even drawn names for a gift exchange. They were supposed to bring a present not only for their person but also from *their* character to that person's.

Hollis had drawn Iffy, and by extension, Honoria had drawn Nereida.

On Friday, in the living room, Hollis wrapped her gifts for them both. Iffy's she wrapped in glittery green paper with a shiny blue bow, and Nereida's in a fabric scrap left over from Hollis's Halloween costume, because she thought fabric was the sort of thing Honoria would have access to for wrapping.

Her mom watched, drinking hot chocolate "with a little extra holiday cheer," which meant a shot of peppermint schnapps. "This is such a neat idea," she said over the top of her old Cincinnati Zoo holiday cup. "The gift exchange I might even steal for my students. It's a brilliant character study."

"Well, I'll tell Fran you said so," said Hollis, sitting back to admire her handiwork.

"Now, which one is Fran again? I don't recall if I've met her."

"Oh, you would recall." Hollis grinned up at her mom from the hardwood floor. "She talks in all caps. She's also twelve. Her ego might explode when I tell her you like her idea enough to steal it."

Her mom laughed. "I'm just saying! She's a smart cookie. They're all smart cookies, those girls."

"Yeah." Hollis beamed down at her gifts. "They're all really, really great."

"I'm glad you found them," mused Hollis's mom, her cheeks a little rosy. "You're like a different girl with them around. No, no, that's not right. You're my same Hollis girl. But you've really come into your own since you took up with this crowd."

"Mom," said Hollis, rolling her eyes.

The doorbell rang.

"Oh, saved by the bell," her mother said, then yelled, "Come in!"

Hollis winced. *"Oof.* I'd like to be able to hear again one day."

"I just want to say hi!" her mom said, raising her shoulders innocently.

The door pushed open and Aini, her hair a festive pine green, walked in.

"Aini!" Hollis's mom beamed. "Come in, sit, say hello."

"Hey, Ms. Merritt. Oh, *wow,* look at your tree!"

The Merritt-Beckwith Christmas tree was, in Hollis's opinion, what Christmas trees were supposed to look like. None of the ornaments matched. They had been accumulated over the years from school projects and zoo visits and particularly good pinecone hauls from back when Hollis was a kid. Aini stepped closer, examining them. From the look on her face, Aini clearly thought this was what a Christmas tree was supposed to look like too.

"Hold on." Aini lifted up a plastic ornament shaped like a star. "Is this Baby Beckwith?"

"Which one is it?" Hollis's mom squinted toward Aini.

Aini tilted the ornament toward her.

"Oh yes, that's my Hollis. That was her third Christmas. Her father's family threw this big Christmas extravaganza every year, and the showstopper was always her aunt Patricia's red velvet cake. Hollis couldn't wait until after dinner, so she snuck into the den and climbed up on the dessert table and threw this huge tantrum, and when we caught her—well, you see, that's the red all over *everything.*" Her mom chuckled fondly. "Patricia was furious, but it was the best time I ever had at one of those things."

"Dang, Hollis," said Aini, impressed. "You've always been a badass. Uh—sorry, Ms. Merritt."

"It's okay." Her mom waved the apology away. "She has, hasn't she?"

"Well, if you two are going to be gross, I'm going to go change," said Hollis, "before I die of humiliation."

Aini shot Hollis a wide grin. "Come on, Buckwheat, you're so cute."

"Her poop was red for *days* after that, Aini," said Hollis's mom.

Her face turning a similar shade, Hollis pushed up from the floor and headed back to her room.

Most of Hollis's clothes were spread out on her bed from earlier, when she'd tried (and failed) to pick out an outfit. Usually, she wasn't one to fret over clothes—but the Critmas Party, as it had been dubbed on the Discord, felt like a special occasion, and Hollis wanted to dress accordingly.

For the third time that afternoon, she considered her options: the same black jeans she usually wore, a navy floral dress that wouldn't stand up to the Ohio River Valley cold, or a pair of leggings that were better suited for sleeping than slaying dragons. None of them felt right. She turned back to her closet with a sigh, its hangers empty spare a few last, desperate items. Her hands brushed over too-small jeans and scratchy old sweaters until they fell on something slick: a silver skirt with just enough metallic thread to really shine. She'd gotten it on clearance on a whim the last time her favorite plus-size store ran a sale, but she had never been brave enough to wear it.

Hollis tugged the skirt off its hanger, snipped off the tags, and stepped into it. It moved like liquid metal on her body, smooth and cool against her skin. But what was she supposed to pair with a statement piece like this? Hollis was at a loss until she remembered a photo she'd seen on Gloria's Instagram. In it, Gloria wore a T-shirt that was tied at the center, exposing a small triangle of skin above the waistband of her (admittedly much plainer) skirt.

"Oh, what the hell," Hollis said out loud to herself, and pulled a navy V-neck over her head.

Watching herself in the full-length mirror by her closet, it took—without exaggeration—fourteen tries before she got the knot to look right, and even then, she wasn't sure it looked right on *her*. In her reflection, Hollis frowned at the pale triangle of flesh that peeked over the top of that shimmering silver.

She didn't trust it, and she thought it looked cute. At the same time.

"Well," she said, stepping back into the living room, where her mom was now pulling down photo ornaments to show to Aini as she snapped pictures. "I hope Mom didn't bore you to death."

"Oh, come on, we're just enjoying some Hollis history!" her mom said.

"Yeah," said Aini. "Can we really help it if we think you're neat? Plus, your mom is never boring."

"Now you're just being nice," said Hollis's mom, but the color in her cheeks darkened a shade more nonetheless.

"Okay," said Hollis, "but maybe you two can bond over my embarrassment some other time. I don't want to be late."

"Sure thing," said Aini. She handed back the soda-can angel ornament she had been holding. "A pleasure as always, Ms. Merritt."

Hollis's mom raised her mug in farewell. "Have fun, girls. Tell Fran I said her idea is adorable!"

"She's part of the Fran Fan Club now," Hollis explained on their way to the door.

"I think it's called the Fran Club," Aini corrected her mildly.

In the living room, Hollis's mom laughed hard.

"At least one of us appreciates a good pun," said Aini.

Hollis smirked. "Okay, Umber."

"Okay, Honoria." Aini grinned back at her. "Cute outfit, by the way. Very modern-day paladin. Now, let's get you to your party. I hope someone brought red velvet cake."

It was Hollis who had brought red velvet cake, actually. She sat with a fat slice of it on one side of her character sheet and a mug of Colombian hot chocolate on the other. At first, Hollis had been skeptical about the drink—she loved chocolate, and she loved cheese, but it seemed counterintuitive to combine them—but she'd tried it anyway and was so glad she had. She took a second mug when Gloria's mom, on a rare night off from the hospital, offered them around.

"Okay, okay," said Gloria, a mustache of hot chocolate outlining her lip, "I'd like everyone to make their second dance competition rolls, please. Just a Performance check. *No*, Mercy can't use Intimidation instead."

A round of dice clattered on the table.

Their characters had spent the first part of the evening shopping for fancy clothes to wear to the Solstice Ball. Then, with all of them dressed to the nines—Honoria in a deep blue gown, out of her breastplate for once—they'd partaken of the planned events. Umber and Tanwyn had absolutely cleaned up at a card game called Night Knock, which was similar to blackjack. Mercy Grace had drunk three grown men under the table in a mulled-wine-drinking contest. And now the party paired off—Tanwyn with Nereida, Umber with Honoria, and Mercy with a terribly nervous NPC called Renald—to dance the night away in a bid for the title of Solstice Royalty.

"All right," said Gloria, grabbing another sausage ball from the tin Iffy had brought. "What did everyone get?"

"Welllll," said Fran, "I got a big 2, minus 2 for my Dexterity, so . . . 0."

"Ouch," said Maggie. "I got a 14 total."

"I got a . . ." Aini paused for effect, then twirled her hands in Hollis's direction. "Natural 20."

"Nice!" Hollis returned the gesture and took Aini's hands in her own, clasping them gently—as if they, not Umber and Honoria, were the ones about to take the dance floor. "I got a 19!"

"I got an 8," said Iffy with a grimace. "Sorry, Tanwyn."

"You're forgiven," said Maggie, "so long as you pass me some of that vegan cheese ball."

"All right, so." Gloria leaned forward. "Let's start with Mercy."

On the far side of the grand hall, Mercy Grace was struggling.

She led—no, *led* was not forceful enough a word for what Mercy was doing—she *marched* poor, unsuspecting Renald around the parquet dance floor. First her pace was entirely too fast, her feet pounding loudly as couples dodged out of her way. Then it was much too slow, a few couples piling up in the space behind them. Then, as her drinks caught up with her, it was nothing at all; Mercy Grace slumped to the floor, becoming little more than a pile of shockingly bright purple taffeta, and was out like a light. It took four palace guards to carry her off the dance floor. They got no help from Renald, who stood to the side looking disturbed by the whole experience.

Nearby, Tanwyn and Nereida twirled together with surprising grace. Nereida, charming in an understated golden gown, was a little stiff in the faun's arms. Tanwyn, on the other hand, took to dancing naturally, clearly leading the pair. Her hooves, polished a glittering red to match her extravagant suit, clipped and clopped with the beat of the music.

Then there was Umber, his arms held lightly around Honoria's waist. It was as if some unseen hand of fate guided them across the floor, their moves flawless, their lines long and lovely. Umber led Honoria effortlessly in a series of dramatic, well-executed twirls, which drew oohs and aahs from the gathering crowd.

"Okay," said Gloria. "Tan and Nereida and Umber and Honoria are still in it. Let's do one final round of rolls to find the outcome of the dance competition."

Another chorus of dice. "17?" Maggie asked, like it was a question.

"Also 17," said Aini, looking nervously at Hollis.

"Ah, heck, math," said Hollis, squinting. "That's . . . also a 17."

"Cheaters," Fran huffed.

It all came down to Iffy. She shook her head, saying, "Go on and get down, Steadfast. I rolled a 4."

On the dance floor, in a place very far away from the Castañedas' oak-finish table, Tanwyn and Nereida gracefully spun to the side of the hall. Other couples' dances started to end too, and the music slowed to something sweet and tender.

Still at the center of floor, Honoria spun in Umber's arms.

"I didn't know you could do this." Her voice was low, like the cast of her eyelids as she looked down at him.

"I could say the same about you," he said, his palm fitted to the curve at the small of her back, "but I learned a long time ago you'd always be surprising me."

"I don't want this song to end," murmured Honoria, aware that the rest of the ballroom was watching them now.

"Yeah," said Umber softly. "Me either."

They exchanged a look, and it said everything they couldn't say to each other out loud: *I need this. I need you.*

Maybe they didn't have to say it. Maybe here—with Umber's arms around her, with his body pressed lightly to hers, with her cheek still warm from where his had rested as they twirled together—there was another way.

Under the twinkling lights, Honoria leaned down, close enough to see the light reflected in Umber's eyes. "Umber, I—" she started, but then the voice of their host, Lord Brighton, resonated through the hall, sounding so much like Gloria Castañeda's.

"My esteemed guests," he said, "it is my distinct honor to present to you the Solstice Royalty: Honoria Steadmore and Umber Dawnfast!"

Around the oak-finish table, the girls erupted in cheers—Hollis breathlessly and half a beat late. She looked over at Aini, who returned her smile with a beaming one of her own. The stained-glass light of the chandelier reflected in her eyes.

Hollis took a deep breath. On the exhale, she reached out for Aini's waiting palm.

Aini raised their clasped hands in victory.

"Okay, okay," said Gloria. "Who should we start with?"

The hour had grown late, so the girls had retired to the cozy living room with gifts and full bellies. Aini, sitting on the rug, leaned her head back on Hollis's knee where it dangled down from the cream-colored sofa.

"*You*, of course," Aini said, like it was obvious.

"Shouldn't we save the best for last?" asked Iffy.

"We will," said Fran. "I'll go last."

"You're so modest, Francesca," said Gloria.

"Thank you. And you, as the worst, should go first." Fran gave her sister a devilish grin.

Gloria raised an eyebrow, switching into big-sister mode as it rose up her forehead. "Watch it, Franny."

"But no, really, go first," said Fran in a rush, waving her hands impatiently. "I've been trying to keep this a secret from you for *weeks*, and if I wait any longer, I'm going to have to bite someone."

Iffy, who was seated closest to Fran, gave her a warning glance from the other end of the sofa.

There was a flurry of movement as they all shifted and scooted and shoved their gifts for the Secret Keeper across the hardwood in her direction.

"Oh no. This is way too much," Gloria protested weakly, looking more than a little overwhelmed. "And I didn't get anything for any of you."

"You tell epic stories with us every Friday," said Hollis. "That's more than enough. This is only a fraction of that, from all of us."

"Oh my *God*," said Fran, flopping over dramatically. "Please open the big heavy one before I die."

Gloria rolled her eyes but listened, unwrapping the gift as instructed. All the girls had pitched in for it, Fran included, and Iffy and Hollis had gone together to pick it up from Games-A-Lot earlier in the week.

"No," said Gloria, her eyes widening in disbelief as soon as she opened the topmost corner. "You did not."

But they had. Stacked together in an unsuccessful attempt to disguise their shape were two books: the collector's editions of the Secrets & Sorcery *Player Handbook* and *Secret Keeper's Depository*. Their gilded edges glittered in the light of the scented candles on the coffee table.

"Um, *yes we did*," said Fran, loud enough that it sounded like her caps lock was on in real life. "They're so pretty! *Look at all the shiny gold!*"

"We're out of character now, Mercy," teased Maggie.

"Girls," said Gloria. Her eyes twinkled with emotion, her hand raising to her heart. "This is too kind of you. I can't tell you how much I appreciate it."

"Open the rest, open the rest," demanded Fran, already making grabby hands at the books.

And so they went around in the circle. Gloria gained a few new sets of dice, a Secret Keeper enamel pin, and a desk-size painting of the whole party that Hollis had done herself.

"Well, that spoils yours, Ifs," Hollis said as Iffy started to unwrap hers: a bust portrait of Nereida in a repurposed thrift-store frame, which she had painted the same silver and cerulean of Nereida's guardswoman uniform.

"That doesn't make this any less amazing." Iffy shifted over on the sofa so she could hug Hollis around the shoulders. "And tell Honoria that Nereida says thanks for the healing potion, too." In her spare time, Hollis had constructed a prop healing potion in the art room using colored resin, glitter, and a bottle she'd *borrowed* (forever) from one of the science labs.

And she wasn't the only one whose in-character gifts were a hit. Mercy Grace, in a stroke of genius (maybe her mom was right about Fran after all), gave Umber a bottle of catgut to use for stringing his lute, which she claimed to have saved all this time from their first battle with the nimyr. (In reality, they were Pull 'n' Peel Twizzlers, pulled and peeled and put in a mason jar.) Nereida gifted Tanwyn some Powder of Darkness, a magical item that created short bursts of pitch-black when thrown. Maggie opened the gold-painted, palm-size wooden box, took out a pinch of its contents, and flicked black glitter into Fran's hair.

"That means it's Hollis's turn." Aini was trying very hard to play it cool and failing spectacularly. She handed two gifts up to Hollis: one marked *to H from A*, and another *to H from U*. Both were wrapped in plain brown paper, folded carefully and tied up with blue satin ribbon. "I don't think Umber's ego could handle it if you didn't open his first, Honoria."

And so Hollis did, tugging on the ribbon.

A stone fell into her palm, smooth and glittering and deep, dark blue. It was about the size of a nickel, only vaguely round, and it had been carefully knotted up in a velvet cord, which webbed around it like a net.

It was Umber in necklace form: small and sparkling and exactly right.

"*Aini,*" Hollis breathed, gaze softening as she looked over at Aini.

"Um, I didn't make that," she said, eyebrows raised as she tried and failed to suppress a grin. "Umber did."

Hollis smiled back. "Well, tell *Umber*, then, that Honoria says this is absolutely perfect."

"I'll let him know. Can I put it on for you?"

"Yes, please." Hollis pulled the length of her hair up off her neck, balling it in her first. Aini slid the necklace over her head, then adjusted it so it stayed centered on her chest. It got a little gobbled up by her boobs—like every necklace she ever wore—but Hollis didn't mind at all.

"It looks good on you," said Aini, looking at Hollis instead of the necklace.

"Can I order one, too, please?" Maggie leaned forward, admiring the stone. "I'll take a blue goldstone too."

"You'll have to ask Umber," said Aini. "*I* don't know how to make something like that."

"Will you *please* open your other present?" Fran cut in impatiently, bouncing where she sat.

The second present, from Actual Aini, was small and weighed about the same as the necklace had. Untying this ribbon revealed a palm-size blue velvet bag.

"What is this?" Hollis asked, blinking down at it.

"Open it!" Fran nearly shouted.

"Not so keen to go last now, are we?" Gloria teased her.

Hollis tugged open the little bag. Inside, something glittered darkly. She looked down at Aini, who looked back with an innocent, angelic expression, one eyebrow raised questioningly. Hollis shook out the contents into her open hand.

There, on her palm, was the most beautiful set of dice she had ever seen. They were cerulean blue, their insides specked with several types of iridescent glitter. The numbered faces were painted the exact same color Hollis used for cobaltril in her artwork.

"*Oooooh*," Fran said appreciatively as Hollis turned the dice, catching the overhead light. As the glitter flashed within, flecks of red and navy shone throughout.

These were *Honoria*, in dice form, light and cool in Hollis's palm.

"Aini," Hollis started. "These are . . ." But there wasn't a word for how perfect these dice were. It didn't matter; this must have shown on Hollis's face, because Aini said, "Thanks. I know my game-girlfriend pretty well. I'm glad you like them."

Bright warmth filled Hollis's chest, colored her cheeks.

"I *love* them," she corrected.

"Score, Ai," said Maggie, and she leaned over to give Aini a fist bump.

"Well," said Fran. "I'd better go now, since I'm the best and also the last and also *you all took FOREVER.*"

"Yes, *please*," said Aini. Her eyes lingered on Hollis a moment longer before she turned away to watch. "I'm dying to see what you think of Maggie's present."

Aini had already told Hollis it was a phone case with a plastic hammer attached. The hammer only extended off the top of the case a few inches, but in the hands of Fran, she was sure it could do some damage. Personally, Hollis was more interested to see what Gloria— and their mom—thought about the gift.

But instead of watching Fran, Hollis watched Aini. When she laughed at Fran's sugar-fueled exuberance, her green curls tumbled and bounced. And Hollis smiled.

Aini had gotten it all exactly, perfectly right. It was like she had known Hollis forever. For the first time, Hollis really knew what

Honoria felt like, having someone who got her the way Umber did: seen, understood, and as lucky as if she'd rolled a Natural 20.

"Oh, Jesus, Mary, and Joseph," said Gloria. "Why in the name of all things holy did you get the girl *a hammer*?"

Fran broke Hollis's train of thought with a sustained shriek of glee.

"Well, I mean, they have to dance together on the regular now," Aini said from the driver's seat.

They had been headcanoning the whole drive back to Hollis's house. Umber's necklace was now actual canon, they decided, because it was too good not to be. This made Aini smile in a way Hollis was sure had very little to do with actual canon and much more to do with the obvious success of her gift. Hollis had scoffed at her cockiness, but a matching smile spread across her lips as she looked out the window, where Aini couldn't see.

Now they were talking about dancing.

"Yeah, they kind of have to," said Hollis. "They're the reigning champions. They have a title to uphold, so they have to practice."

"Well, it would be more than that for Umber, I think," Aini said as she turned onto Hollis's street. "He would want to dance with Honoria the most on late-night watches, when everyone else is asleep. Especially after long, hard days. Just this private, little moment between them."

"I like that. Like when they come together, the rest of the world melts away. No worries, no strife. Just each other." This was not a stretch, not something Hollis had to role-play. Anytime she and Aini were together, she felt exactly like this: Easy, effortless. A little dizzy in a way she kind of liked.

"Yeah." Aini parked behind Hollis's mom's car. The tail end of her sedan hung out in traffic—or it would have if there had been any traffic at this hour. "That's exactly what I mean, actually."

"They're so perfect for each other, aren't they?"

Aini hummed. "They really are."

Hollis turned her head to face Aini, leaning her cheek against the soft leather of the seat. It felt good against her skin. She wondered idly if it felt anything like Umber's cheek on Honoria's as they twirled across the dance floor. "I get a little jealous of Honoria sometimes, you know."

"Oh yeah?" Aini asked, craning her neck to the side, too. "Why's that?"

"Just to have someone who understands her the way Umber does. Someone who's what she needs, when she needs it, even if she doesn't know it yet."

"Well, I get a little jealous of Umber sometimes," said Aini, "because he always has someone to guide him in the right direction, even if it's not what he expects."

Hollis nodded against the seat, the motion warming her cheek. "And I love the way their hands fit."

Aini's eyes were soft. "What do you mean?"

"I just imagine they fit together." Though she didn't mean for it to, Hollis's voice had gone quiet, barely a whisper against the "Maps" cover playing in the background. "When they hold hands, I mean."

To illustrate, Hollis reached over to where Aini's hand rested on the console and scooped it up in her own, like she had so many times before. Their fingers slotted together.

Aini's eyes dropped down to look at their hands. Hollis watched Aini watching them.

"Ah, yeah," Aini said, her voice low too. Hollis leaned in to hear her. "I can see how you might be jealous of something like that."

Hollis nodded, dipping her head the tiniest bit closer. Here, alone in the car with Aini just inches away, she imagined she felt much like Honoria had at the Solstice Ball. In this moment, she wasn't jealous of her S&S character. Honoria had Umber, but Hollis had Aini.

Then, with no thought other than perhaps it would be nice, Hollis leaned forward and pressed a kiss to Aini Amin-Shaw's lips.

Just like their palms, this, too, fit.

Somehow both an eternity and an instant passed before Hollis pulled back.

Aini blinked into the space between them. "I want to put something out there, Hollis. And I hope you'll hear me out. Can you try?"

Letting go of Aini's hand, Hollis's fingers floated to her chest. Beneath them, her heart fluttered impossibly fast. Swallowing, she nodded.

"I'm just going to say it. Just *say it*, Aini." She shook her head hard, just once, and then she looked up at Hollis.

"I like you," Aini said, slow and purposeful and clear. "I mean, I *really* like you. I think you're brilliant, Hollis Beckwith. You're sassy and hilarious and talented and also really beautiful. I *really, really* like you. Like, *think about you before I fall asleep* like you. *Write our names in a heart on my notebook* like you. *Grin whenever someone says your name* like you. I like you, Hollis! I like you, I like you, I like you.

"And I know you've—" Aini took a breath, then let it out slow. Her eyes darted away before finding Hollis's again. When she spoke, her hands worked in front of her, in the space where both their bodies had just been, like she was trying to pull the words from thin air. "See, I don't even know how to talk about it, because we *haven't* talked about it, but I know you have a boyfriend. And I haven't really thought about it, because it's been easier that way, but I don't even know if you like . . . girls. Lesbians. Me. *I'm* a lesbian!

"But you feel this, right, Hollis? You feel *us*?" Aini paused, blinking at Hollis hopefully, but after a beat of silence, she continued:

"I just wanted to say it out loud, because I can't *not* say it anymore. I like you, Hollis. A lot. A huge, embarrassing amount. And I know saying it out loud means a change, but I think that could be a really great thing for us."

Hollis had gone very still. Even her breath was still in her chest. The cold feeling of being caught flooded through her body, spreading like ice through her veins.

"*Aini.*"

Hollis couldn't look away from her face. Aini's eyes were wide, intense, vulnerable. The blue light of the dashboard reflected on her brown skin, highlighting the sharp angle of her eyebrows where they pulled together above her nose. Wildly, Hollis thought that in this light, Aini looked half fae herself.

That was it, she was sure. It had to be a trick of the light.

"I think . . ." Hollis stalled as soon as she started. Why was her voice shaking? She tried to swallow the tremor but realized it wasn't just in her voice; it was in all of her—her hands, her thighs, even her lips, which quivered as she pressed them together. She licked them involuntarily and tasted the wax and mint of Aini's ChapStick. A fresh wave of panic rose in her stomach. "I think maybe we're getting some of our feelings confused," she tried. "I think some of what you're feeling are actually Umber's feelings."

Aini recoiled as if the words physically hurt to hear, her face falling fast and hard. All the cold in Hollis's veins sunk hard to the pit of her stomach, seeing Aini look at her like that.

"I think we both know that's not true," said Aini.

"Think about it, though." Hollis had to look away. Dread surged through her, pushing harder through her veins with each fluttering blink. "We were just talking about them. When they were dancing, Honoria almost—" Hollis stopped, swallowed. "It makes sense we would get all mixed up."

A sharp intake of breath from the driver's seat. "That wasn't Umber's hand you were holding, Hollis."

"*Aini—*"

"Those weren't his lips you just kissed, either."

"Please, just—"

"They were mine. And it felt . . . good. It felt *good*, Hollis." Aini paused. "I don't know, am I just being stupid? Am I being desperate? Am I imagining this?" Something broke in her voice at the end, and Hollis looked up. Aini, who always had a joke and a smile for her, looked close to tears. Hollis had the fleeting thought that she might be breaking Aini's heart.

The truth was even worse: Aini wasn't imagining it.

Hollis realized this with sudden clarity. Kissing Aini was the first time kissing someone had felt correct. Even now, shaking with anxiety and breathing in the smell of her, Hollis wanted to do it again. The feeling made her want to run away, to dissolve into the seat and never be perceived again—but it also filled her with a joy so pure and blinding her vision blurred with tears.

There was nothing wrong with her. She *could* feel this. She *did*.

"Aini, no," said Hollis hoarsely. "You're not imagining it."

The effect of those words played across Aini's face, her mouth splitting into a grin so bright it was like a crack of lightning. "Beautiful, Buckwheat. You don't know how happy I am to hear that."

"I just don't think . . ." Everything was happening so fast and so slow at once. Hollis swallowed, dropping her gaze. "I don't think it can change anything."

A beat passed. Aini's voice came back colder. "What does that even mean?"

The cold tightened around Hollis's rib cage, spreading a frost of anxiety through her heart. She had been avoiding this from the moment Aini and her ukulele came into her life. No, that wasn't true—she had been avoiding this from the first picture she'd ever seen of Aini's easy grin and big brown eyes and effortless charisma.

Though she hadn't been sure then, she was sure now: Hollis Beckwith wanted to be a part of *everything* that was Aini Amin-Shaw.

"Hollis." Aini's voice reached her through the cold. "I can give you time, I know it's a lot—"

It *was* a lot, and it was all crashing in on her in the heated front seat of a luxury sedan she didn't know the make of. While this conversation seemed as natural for Aini as breathing, for Hollis it felt like she was breathing ice. More than anything in the world, she wanted to reach for Aini's hand. She wanted to press her lips against Aini's again, to keep from having to say the words.

She balled her fists in her lap.

"It's not, okay?" Hollis didn't mean to raise her voice, but she did, ratcheting up a whole octave. "I don't need time. *I don't.* I'm not— I have a boyfriend."

She still couldn't look at Aini. She didn't want to see the effect of her words.

"That's cool, Hollis." Aini's voice sounded far away, distant in a way it never had before. "I just had to put the truth out there. And now I know yours."

No, she didn't. *Hollis* didn't even know her truth. She laughed—a high, thready thing. It burned like bile in her throat.

This was wrong. Everything about this was *all wrong*.

"I have to go." Hollis grabbed her bag from the floor. "Thanks for the presents, and the ride, and— I just have to go."

"Fine." Aini's words were curt. "I'll talk to you soon?"

It had never been a question before.

"Yeah, sure," said Hollis, opening the door.

"I didn't mean—" Aini started, but whatever she didn't mean, Hollis would never know. She shut the door a little too hard and walked up the front path to her house. Her silver skirt swished against her thighs, no longer liquid metal but instead heavy as lead, dragging her down. When she got to her bedroom, she choked out a strangled sob, tugged back the sheets, and crawled inside still fully clothed.

19
WINTER BREAKDOWN

IN A WAY, Hollis was thankful the Secrets & Sorcery group was on hiatus for the duration of winter break. It made it easier to not think about any of them, which made it easier to not think about a certain one of them. She turned off the notifications for the Discord app on her phone. Except for Iffy—one of the two girls who had her phone number and who'd texted that morning to wish her a Merry Christmas—the girls left Hollis alone.

Or maybe *she* left *them* alone.

In another way, though, the break from their regular game was disorienting. S&S had become such a part of Hollis's routine that, in its absence, she floundered. Even her art felt like a poor substitute. All her usual subjects suddenly felt uncomfortable to draw. Especially a certain lute-playing one.

So instead of relaxing, Hollis sat on the sofa in the living room brooding. In the kitchen, dishes clinked in the sink as her mom washed up from their Christmas-morning feast (takeout from Waffle House that they put on the good china, a tradition dating back to the first year of the divorce, when her mom was too tired to cook and all their normal Christmas food felt wrong). On the coffee table in front of her was her small clutch of gifts: new metallic watercolors from her observant mother, who'd noted the blue and bronze becoming barely more than rims in their pans; a set of dice mailed in from her aunt Rita; her own collector's edition of the Secrets & Sorcery *Player Handbook* from her father (its card signed without *love*, and also by his new wife and her daughter). Chris had never been the gifting type, so from him there was only a text message to the group chat that said *happy xmas* and included a picture of his new gaming system. Hollis ignored it.

As she waited for her mom to finish cleaning up, Hollis was left at the mercy of her thoughts. Try as she might to quiet them, they swirled in her mind like the snow-heavy storm clouds outside the window. Hollis had felt a little shivery ever since that night in Aini's car. That night was a secret she carried around, holding it so tight to her chest that no one (not even her) could see. Anytime she relaxed even the slightest bit, she panicked, thinking of what her friends might say.

But who even *were* her friends anymore? With her silenced Discord app as good as deleted and her group chat with the boys quiet, Hollis was no longer sure how to answer that question. No matter who she pictured filling the blank, she wasn't sure they were the right people for her (except for maybe Iffy, whom she promised herself she'd text back later).

If Hollis was being honest, she wasn't even sure *she* was the right person for *herself*.

Hollis couldn't tell who she was anymore, or if she was a person she liked. She'd never really liked herself *before*—doing so had never seemed important, or even possible. She'd been far more concerned with blending into the background, making sure she kept her anxiety quiet enough to not become someone else's problem.

But in the last handful of months, something had shifted. The person Hollis was when she played Secrets & Sorcery was someone she liked being. Honoria had a part in that; it was much easier to feel like a badass when she could pretend she actually was one. But Gloria did, too, with her encouraging smiles and how she always made

Hollis feel worth including. So did Iffy, with all the time they'd spent together in study hall or the front seat of the Accord or one another's kitchens. And so did Aini, with her stupid brown eyes and her stupid big heart, making Hollis believe she was brave enough and beautiful enough to go and do something like kiss her. A trickle of rage braided together with sorrow and longing, tying Hollis's stomach in a knot.

"Almost done in here, Hollis," her mother called from the kitchen. "Can you bring me those coffee cups?"

"Sure," Hollis called back, although she had never felt farther from that word. She stood up from the couch.

Hollis had had big plans for New Year's Eve, originally.

What Hollis had been planning to do was invite Aini Amin-Shaw to the Festival of Lights at the Cincinnati Zoo and Botanical Gardens. With all that light and noise and color, it was exactly the right kind of fun for Aini, so it was the right kind of fun for Hollis, too. She had even gone so far as to start saving up her pocket change—leftover quarters from the lunch line or the Coke machine—so she could afford not only her own admittance, but to treat Aini to hers, too.

Hollis had considered going alone, but what had been exciting about the idea was going *with Aini*. The sparkle of all those lights wouldn't be as dazzling if they weren't reflected in Aini's eyes. But— contrary to the last thing she'd said in the car—Aini *hadn't* talked to Hollis later, and so Hollis hadn't talked to Aini either. For just a moment, Hollis allowed herself to feel that: not talking to Aini Amin-Shaw. It was an acute, pointed longing in her chest. Hollis missed her.

But very quickly she replaced that feeling with the thought she wore like armor around her chest: by talking about it, Aini had ruined them. Hollis was angry.

She was upset enough that she called Chris to ask what his plans for the night were, even though they'd barely talked since break started. Unsurprisingly, he would be ringing in the New Year playing S&S with the boys—or, more accurately, with the boys and Lacie.

"Well," she sighed into the receiver, "have fun."

"Are you sure you don't want to come out tonight, Hol?" On the other end of the line, Chris's voice was thin. "I talked to Landon. He'll let you roll a character as long as you fill a hole in the party. You'd have to figure out your own backstory, but as long as it doesn't change the party dynamic, it's fine."

There was a time when what Chris had just offered was everything Hollis wanted: a place at his table and in his life. But now she heard Gloria's voice in her head, telling her she didn't need to fill any holes in the party, and Iffy's voice telling her she was proud to be part of Honoria's backstory, and Aini's voice telling her change could be good.

"No," Hollis said. "That's fine. Tell everyone I said hi."

And so, at midnight on New Year's Eve, Hollis sat alone on her bed in her room.

She thought about making a resolution. Often she did, and just as often, she broke them. Sometimes they were about her weight, or about not caring about it, or about having a better relationship with her dad, or about finally doing well in school—wishing some kind of new Hollis into existence with the New Year.

But somehow over the course of a few months, she'd already *become* a new Hollis, without even meaning to. A Hollis who was a little brave and a little confident and actually pretty happy. A Hollis who did things for herself and wore clothes she liked and had friends who liked *her*. A Hollis who was beginning to question the company of her old friends and lean into the love of her new ones and fall for someone exciting and perfect and terrifying.

Hollis ran her fingers over the patchwork of her old quilt, the feeling of it against her skin much more comfortable than the thoughts circling in her head.

This—feeling this way about a girl—had seemed entirely new to her at first, but maybe that wasn't true. The whole reason Hollis had started drawing in the first place was because she'd seen a picture of Sailor Neptune from *Sailor Moon*. It was the first time she'd ever seen a girl that beautiful, and so Hollis—then a year younger than Fran, and her opposite in every way—had picked up a pencil to try to capture some of that beauty for herself. Plus, now that she thought about it, there *had* been something different in the way she felt about Courtney, her best friend in elementary school, in the way she hadn't wanted Courtney to be friends with anyone except for her. There had been something different, too, in the way she'd wept, stretched out face down on the living room floor and absolutely inconsolable, when Courtney had moved away before middle school.

Hollis knew there was a person she could ask all the questions she couldn't quite answer for herself. She picked up her phone. She considered texting Aini *Happy New Year*.

She didn't.

Aini didn't text *her*, either, even though Hollis waited for ten minutes before finally deciding that she wasn't going to.

Hollis turned off her phone and flopped down in bed, hoping this next year wouldn't end up worse than the last.

20

HOLLIS SKIPS A FRIDAY

hey. you don't have to come get me actually!! i'm too sick
to go to the game tonight.

Hollis's thumb had been hovering over send on and off for the last
several hours. Five thirty was rapidly approaching, and presumably
so was Iffy. It had been easier to text and ask for a ride yesterday,
when the first post-holiday game of Secrets & Sorcery wasn't just half
an hour away.

By the time 5:20 rolled around, Hollis still hadn't pressed send.
She sat, indecision pinning her to the sunken-in sofa in her living
room, her thumb too heavy to move. She hadn't pressed send by
5:32, either, which was when she heard Iffy's car horn in front of
her house.

She was out of time.

Hollis padded down the cold front path to the street, barefoot.
"Hey." She motioned for Iffy to roll down the window, then waited
as Iffy leaned over the passenger seat to crank it open. "I can't go
tonight. I'm sick."

Quickly, Iffy leaned away from the window. "Is it contagious?"

"What? Oh, no. Not physically sick, more, you know. Just . . ."

Anxious. Hollis was anxious. And not normal background,
always-anxious anxious. She was the kind of anxious that required

one of her big pills—the ones her psychiatrist said were for situational peaks in her anxiety—rather than the regular ones she took around this time every day. It pulled at the corners of her mind, sluggish and dulling.

"I get that," said Iffy. "Have you let Gloria know?"

"Uh. No."

"Do you feel like you can get on Discord and tell her?"

"Well." Hollis had been on a Discord vacation since *that* night. She shifted on her freezing feet. "Maybe also no."

"I'll tell her," said Iffy decisively. "Can I get your character sheet? I'll run Honoria for you."

"Good thinking." Hollis retreated inside and tugged her unused S&S notebook out of her tote bag. When she went back outside this time, she remembered to slip her shoes on.

"Thanks," she said, passing the notebook through the open window. "Really."

The smile Iffy gave her was both sympathetic and reassuring. "Of course, girl. Please take care of yourself. Do a face mask or whatever it is white girls do for self-care."

Hollis smiled. "Okay. Have fun. Tell . . . everyone I miss them."

Iffy heard the hesitation. There was something a little too knowing in how she said, "All right. I'll let everyone know."

Hollis headed inside again. Her mom was still on the sofa, watching end-of-season Christmas movies on the Hallmark channel. Sitting beside her seemed more appealing than sitting in her room alone, imagining Iffy showing up at Gloria and Fran's house without her, so Hollis plopped back down on the half-deflated cushions.

Her mom glanced over. "No S&S tonight?"

"No," Hollis said. "Or, well. Not for me."

"They're still playing?"

"Yeah." Hollis fiddled with the sleeve of her sweatshirt. It felt strange between her fingers. "It's kind of an important session. We're getting really close to the end."

"Well, why didn't you go, then?"

Hollis shrugged. "I don't really want to talk about it right now."

Her mom paused, looking over at Hollis the way she always did: with genuine interest, but without prying. After a few quiet breaths, she nodded. "Do you want to watch after-Christmas movies with me about it?"

That, she could do. Hollis nodded.

While her S&S party ventured toward their uncertain fate, Hollis sunk farther into the couch and the haze of her medicine, carried along by the story of a no-name Midwestern town with a Christmas cookie factory in danger of closing. She didn't feel much better for it, but she didn't feel worse, either. In fact, she didn't feel much of anything at all.

On Monday, Iffy returned Hollis's S&S notebook in the halls of Holmes High School. It bore two notable additions. The first were the colorful tabs Iffy had added as labels for the different sections (Honoria's character sheet, spells, equipment, loot, and notes). The second was a letter tucked into the front pocket.

Hollis recognized the looping, not-quite-neat script as the same from the flyer at Games-A-Lot. It was a note from Gloria, and it contained both a summary of what Hollis had missed and an outline of the important information they'd gained about the Vacuity. Following a tip, the party had headed into the frigid north, to a deadly region called the Highpeak Crests.

Reading this, Hollis couldn't help being upset that they'd decided something so big without her. If she'd been there, she would have asked them to reconsider, or at least to make sure they were properly prepared before they left.

But she *hadn't* been there, and so the Highpeak Crests it was. There was nothing she or Honoria could do about it now.

Maybe it wouldn't have made a difference. Though most of her knew it was irrational, her anxiety took hold of the thought and ran with it. Maybe, if the group could make such an important choice without her, Hollis wasn't as important to their game—or to them—as she thought.

She wanted to message Aini and ask if there was something she'd missed, anything Gloria's notes hadn't covered, that might slow down her racing mind. Instead, she glared at her phone and wished, for the thousandth time that day, that Aini hadn't made things so complicated.

21
COUNT TO TEN

WITHOUT HOLLIS EVEN having to ask, Iffy knew to come pick her up on Friday.

"You good?" she asked when Hollis plopped into her front seat.

"Yeah," Hollis said. "I think so."

If she was being honest, Hollis did not think she was good. In fact, she actively doubted it. But this arc of the campaign was coming to an end, and she couldn't afford to miss another game. If Honoria was going to lead the party into certain death, then Hollis was at least going to be the one leading Honoria.

But as it turned out, being resigned to their party's grim fate was the easy part of the night. As soon as she and Iffy arrived at the Castañedas' apartment, all Hollis could see was Aini. Aini, sitting in her car until Hollis and Iffy had gone inside. Aini, lingering on the porch and chatting with Maggie until 6:05 p.m. Aini, sitting on Hollis's right side, small and silent in a way Hollis had never seen her before.

Hollis's hand itched to reach out and grab Aini's, to smooth her thumb across the plane of her palm, to soothe her. She clenched it into a fist instead.

When Gloria finally started the game, it was almost a relief to dive into the dreaded Highpeak Crests.

It still went about as poorly as Hollis had expected.

"Uh . . . that's a 9," said Fran.

"Even with your Fortitude bonus?" asked Maggie.

"Yes," said Fran.

"But it's like, plus a million," said Iffy.

"*Yes,*" said Fran. She buried her head in her hands.

"Okay," said Gloria, grim enough to leave off her second *okay.* "Mercy, you're trying to hold up in all this freezing rain, but even your trollish fortitude is having trouble withstanding it. That's going to be—" Gloria paused and rolled a die behind her screen. "Damn it. 6 more Freezing damage."

"Damn it," echoed Fran. Gloria didn't correct her.

"How much Freezing damage is that total now?"

"Uh, 16?"

Gloria let out a slow breath. "All right, so. When you look down, you see your fingers have turned to ice. The way they almost seem to glow with blue light makes you think this is a magical effect. You also think that if it's not remedied soon, you might lose the tips of your fingers for good."

"*Damn it,*" Fran said again. Again, Gloria didn't correct her.

"It's fine," said Aini in her own voice and not Umber's affected British accent. "Honoria will heal you up, Merc."

"Honoria is trying to save her spells, actually," Hollis snipped, not looking to her right. "Because who even knows what we're about to walk into."

"Oh, you know," Fran quipped. "They're just fingers. Who needs them?"

"See, this is why Honoria wouldn't have done this yet," said Hollis. Everything felt rushed—moving too fast, leaving her behind.

"Well," said Iffy, not looking to *her* right—at Hollis—either. "Honoria wasn't herself last week. But she was doing her best, so let's give her some credit."

"No, you're right." The look on Iffy's face pulled Hollis back. She couldn't tell what was putting her on edge the most—Aini beside her (her hair dark neon orange again, the corners of her lips turned down), the Highpeak Crests, the fact that Mercy was going to lose her fingertips unless she expended a Level 4 spell to save them, or the tension mounting in Gloria's narrative.

She shook her head as if to clear it. "I'm going to . . ." Hollis mimed taking off a pair of gloves. She leaned across Aini (she smelled like flowers and things Hollis should forget) and offered an invisible pair of gloves to Fran. "'Here, Mercy. Take my Gloves of Warming. They should help.'"

"'Thank gods,'" said Fran for Mercy. "I put them on as quick as I can."

With Mercy's fingers saved for the time being, the party carried on, moving deeper into the frozen wasteland. "It's by no means an easy trek," Gloria said. "But Tanwyn's feet guide her true. She picks the most stable path through the treacherous, frozen crags, and you all follow. At last, you summit the first of the Crests' peaks."

"YES!" yelled Fran.

"*And.*" Gloria grinned.

"Shit," Maggie hissed.

"Below you is the most beautiful valley you've ever laid eyes upon."

"*What,*" said Hollis.

"No, we knew this," said Iffy. "We're looking—" But she was cut off by a sharp glare from Gloria.

"No more than a hundred yards before you is a verdant forest," Gloria continued into the silence that fell over the table. "Parts of it seem familiar to you, like they're native to the Southern realms. Other parts have grown familiar on your travels. You recognize the weeping oaks of the Werewood. You see the dazzling darkwyrm bushes of the Duskfain. Many of the trees look foreign to this world—strange, glowing things with trunks that vanish into puffs of clouds instead of leaves.'"

"'This,'" said Aini in Umber's voice, "'is breathtaking.'"

"'*This*,'" said Iffy, in Nereida's stoic tone, "'is what we're looking for. This is the Vacuity.'"

Hollis said nothing, but her palms began to sweat, the pace of her heart increasing.

Nothing this beautiful should exist in the Highpeak Crests.

"'Let's head on down, shall we?'" said Aini as Umber.

Everyone nodded, quiet with purpose and nervous anticipation.

"The air around you warms as you make your way into candy-colored grass," said Gloria, "which you realize shouldn't be growing under such a dense canopy of trees. But that's not the thing you see that's out of place.

"As you make your way farther still, you see the glittering green surface of a lake. Standing on its shore is a figure. As you get closer, you can tell that it's human. It's tallish, slender-bodied. Well dressed in shades of cerulean and bright green."

Hollis shook her head.

"I close my hand around the hilt of my hammer," said Fran.

"I'm going to ready a third-level Thunderbolt," said Iffy.

"As you draw closer still, you can make out finer features. The human has dark, curly hair, a high, long nose, and sharp cheekbones. He looks—"

Hollis clenched her hands, her fingernails biting half-moons into her damp palms.

"—familiar."

She hadn't seen this coming until this very moment.

But now it was *all* she could see. Her artist's mind filled in the gaps, turned up the colors: a man—still a boy, really—standing beside the sparkling water, sure of himself in the way only those who are born to unearned greatness seem to be.

"'I'm so very pleased to see you, Honoria,' says the man." Gloria locked eyes with Hollis.

Hollis laughed, high and short. The sound felt like it came from someone else's throat.

"'Hello, Wick,'" she said, her voice belonging to Honoria.

"NOOOO," shouted Fran.

"Really?" Iffy looked back and forth from Gloria to Hollis, her eyes wide.

Maggie just shook her head and dropped her pencil on the table.

Hollis swallowed. Her mouth was dry. Her palms were wet.

"'I thought you might have come sooner,' says Wick." Everything about Gloria changed when she inhabited his character. She held her body straighter, the tilt of her head equal parts daring and cocky. Her voice was smooth, but like oil instead of silk. Hollis swallowed uselessly.

"Yes, well," said Honoria, squaring her shoulders. "I'm here now. *We're* here now. We've come to take you home, Wick."

"Oh, Honoria. Don't be foolish. The Vacuity has chosen me, and I—" Wick smiled at her, toothy and sharp. "I have chosen you. Come." He gestured at the lake. "Drink of these waters. They are lovely but deadly; they remind me so of you.

"And that is the unfortunate piece, isn't it? But I promise it's quick, that part."

Honoria frowned, wary. "What part?"

"The dying part, of course," said Wick, waving a hand like this was nothing. "How else will you become one with me here in the throes of glorious undeath?"

In a flash, Hollis was no longer in Honoria's cobaltril breastplate. She wasn't even in her own striped T-shirt. She felt her consciousness drift somewhere outside herself, where it hovered and observed at a distance. Her lungs, so dry this whole time, were suddenly thirsty—for air, *oh God*, for air.

There was a brief instant where Hollis understood what was coming and told herself it was irrational—that nothing bad was actually happening to her, or even to Honoria. They would save the day—they always did—and Wick would be punished for running toward the Vacuity, for welcoming himself into its empty, beautiful arms.

But the thing about anxiety attacks was they never listened to reason.

The room blurred around her, all the cream colors and wood grains and stained-glass lighting morphing from a warm embrace into something sent to smother her. Her breath came in short, frantic bursts. She was cold but also hot, and her body swam with sweat in an attempt to control those contrary sensations. Her eyes burned, swimming with the feeling of fever. In her mind, her own voice screamed at her in a loop: *You're in danger, you're in danger, you're in danger.*

"Out, please," said a different voice, soft enough to break through all the screaming inside Hollis's head.

Hollis was distantly aware that people were moving, that chairs were dragging across hardwood floors, that a door was opening, sweeping in freezing air that made her rock where she sat. She was aware, too, that someone was moving closer, but she couldn't tell who it was until a blur of brown and orange entered her narrowed vision.

It was Aini—of course it was—her hands steady as they closed around Hollis's. Hollis wanted her first impulse to be to rip her hands away, but instead her fingers involuntarily closed harder against Aini's. Somehow, impossibly, her breath came faster.

"I'm going to get your medicine from your tote bag," Aini said. It wasn't a question, which was convenient, because Hollis couldn't answer. Her lungs were empty. And they wouldn't fill.

There was rummaging and then a swear. Then, both faster and slower than seemed possible, Aini used her own fingers to open Hollis's. Into her drenched, trembling palm, she placed a white pill.

Aini being so kind somehow made everything so much . . . *more*. Hollis registered dimly that, in her dire attempt to get air into her lungs, she was wheezing. This realization made said wheezing worse.

Into her other hand, Aini pressed a glass of water.

"Here we go, Hollis." Her voice was even, calm. It felt as out of place as the grass in the strange forest of the Highpeak Crests. "Let's take our medicine. It'll help."

Hollis listened. But she was too slow to swallow. The pill started to dissolve on her tongue, acrid the whole way down.

Aini sat next to her—close but not too close, so their knees were in line with each other but didn't touch. With a surge of wanting closeness that was immediately chased by a surge of guilt for wanting closeness, Hollis shifted back in her seat to create space. Aini didn't stop her. Instead she asked, "How long does it usually take for your medicine to help?"

Hollis shook her head; she didn't know, she didn't know, she didn't know. Her lungs were so thirsty they were on fire. She was burning.

"You know this, smart girl. Thirty minutes? Ten?"

"Ten," said Hollis between gasping breaths. She was light-headed. The logical part of her brain knew that this was because she was hyperventilating. But the crush of anxiety in her chest wouldn't let her lungs stop.

Ten minutes seemed like an impossibly long time.

"We can do ten minutes." Aini sounded so sure that Hollis almost questioned the voice in her head screaming the opposite. "What do you need, Hollis?"

She shook her head again. And then, on an exhale, "Breathe."

"Good. Good job. I can help with that." Aini shifted in front of

Hollis as much as the table would allow. "I'm going to count to ten. Try to match your breathing with my counting. One, inhale; two, exhale."

Hollis's breath raced on uselessly, much faster than Aini's measured, slow counting.

"Three, four."

But she tried. For Aini, she tried.

"Five, six."

Inhale. Exhale.

"Seven, eight."

Aini's voice was so soothing, high and sweet. Hollis registered how much she'd missed it, the thought sticking even through the burning cacophony in her brain.

But in realizing that she missed it, that she missed Aini—

"Nine, ten."

Hollis shook her head again, her lungs redoubling their pace, working overtime once more. She was desperate for air. She took three breaths in the space of one.

"It's okay," said Aini. "You're doing great. One, two."

Hollis tried again.

"Three, four."

And again.

After several more counts of ten, her lungs finally started to settle. It was slow, putting out that fire. It felt like sleep and looked like the peaked bone of Aini's kneecaps in her jeans. Hollis focused on them, her eyes locked on their shape beneath the denim, as if everything hinged on those kneecaps. "Seven, eight," said Aini—and this time, on the exhale, Hollis's breath stuttered then relaxed, like a wounded animal finally easing down for much-needed rest.

"Nine, ten," said Aini. "Good work. I'm proud of you. I'm *so* proud of you."

She stopped counting. Out loud, at least. Aini still breathed to the same beat, the whooshing sounds of her working lungs taking place of the numbers. Hollis tried to match her breaths to Aini's. Her light-headedness slowly subsided. In its wake, the fuzzy flood of medication soaked in.

She wasn't sure how much time passed before she said, "I would like to go home now."

"That's a good plan," said Aini between breaths.

Aini made a motion with her hand that Hollis saw only through the blur of periphery. The porch door creaked open, letting in a gust of frigid January air. Though Hollis could hear the footfalls of the other girls, no one spoke, like the cold had stolen their voices.

"Hollis would like to go home," said Aini. "Are we at a place where we can pause?"

"Yes, of course." This was Gloria, suddenly behind her. "I'll work it out. Don't even worry, Hollis."

Hollis's chest ached too much to react.

"Is she okay?" This was Fran, also close by.

"Yeah. She's a badass, like always." Quickly but calmly, Aini collected Hollis's things: her dice, her notebook, her good writing pencil. "She just needs to get home. Iffy, would you mind?"

"Not at all." Iffy was closest of all. She slung Hollis's tote bag over her shoulder. "Let's get you back on the right side of the river, girl."

Hollis nodded. Slowly, she stood. It was as if her body were moving through honey, or water. Whether this was from the medicine or from all that deep breathing, she couldn't be sure.

"Let me know when you get home safe, please," said Gloria. "Or, Iffy, if you could text us?"

"You got it."

"Thank you," said Aini, her voice raw and fervent. If Hollis weren't so tired, it might have made her cry. Instead, she just reached out for

Iffy. Lean, strong arms reached back, snaking around Hollis's waist, holding her up.

"Sorry," said Hollis. It was too small a word, but it was all she had right now.

"Don't be." Iffy steered the pair of them out the front door, which Maggie held open. "Let's get you home so you can rest."

But Hollis didn't make it that far. She hardly made it as far as Iffy's front seat. With her head slumped against the frosty window, Hollis let her eyes drift closed.

22

ABOUT HONOR

AFTER A WEEKEND spent collecting all the parts of her that her anxiety attack had rattled loose, Hollis felt like a whole person again. And she assumed the next school week would be as normal as any other. Things had mostly smoothed over with Chris since New Year's, the two of them sliding back into the same comfortable routine they always had. And after being helped by her on Friday, Hollis was pretty sure she was on good terms with Aini again, too—or at the very least, on neutral terms.

But the reality was different. Chris at school was not the same Chris he was when he and Hollis were alone, and she couldn't ignore how his eyes looked elsewhere whenever there was somewhere else to look. On the Discord server, with each playful group message she and Aini exchanged, Hollis also had the sneaking suspicion that they could never be neutral again—that they had never really been neutral in the first place.

There was a way to make all the pieces fit, she was sure of it, and when they did, the sick fluttering in her stomach would vanish like a nimyr into the Vacuity. But until then, she was stuck with the grating feeling that *everything*—especially Hollis herself—was wrong.

Something had to change. And so, on Thursday, when her mom went to shop at a theater-supply store in Cincinnati, Hollis caught a ride with her to the other side of the river.

Though she'd made the walk from the street to the Castañedas' front door countless times, this time felt different. Emptier. Hollis was so used to experiencing this sidewalk filled with the noise and laughter of friends having just played Secrets & Sorcery that to walk it alone now was disquieting. As she dodged around Miss Virginia's propped-up rosebush, she didn't have to double-dodge Iffy on one side or Aini on the other. She hardly even had to dodge the bush. Its blooms were long gone, its leaves curled and dying from the long Midwestern winter.

At least she was here to talk face-to-face. Gloria had been obliging when she had asked. It was impossible to read tone into the simple text of a Discord message, but Hollis was pretty sure she had been expecting this. That didn't make it any better.

With two knuckles, she knocked on the door. It sounded hollow on the other side, the house missing its usual pregame chatter.

It was Ms. Castañeda who answered. "Hollis," she said warmly. It was strange to see her out of her scrubs. This afternoon, she wore a pair of leggings, a cozy sweater, and a welcoming smile. "Come in."

They moved into the living room. Scattered around, as if by a tornado, was what looked like approximately a week's worth of math homework. At its epicenter, Fran sat cross-legged at the coffee table, wiggling as she focused. Hollis raised her hand to say hello, but then remembered that Fran had to finish all her schoolwork before they played S&S on Fridays and thought better of it.

"I'm, uh." Hollis dropped her voice to a stage whisper. "Here to see Gloria."

"Yes, she said you'd be by," said Ms. Castañeda, nodding at the hallway. "She's in her room. It's the door that doesn't have glitter all over it. Go on back."

"Thank you," Hollis said, and she went on back. With the same two knuckles, she knocked on Gloria's door.

"Come in," shouted a familiar voice from the other side. It

sounded so correct—the only thing about this visit that did—that Hollis thought she might cry.

Instead, she pushed open the door to Gloria's small bedroom, and was stuck at once by how perfectly it fit the Secret Keeper. It was the exact right blend of very cool and nerdy. Secrets & Sorcery posters from the most recent edition release were sticky-tacked up beside local band flyers. Flower garlands draped over the top of her window and the headboard of her bed, their buds the same deep red as the lipstick Gloria always wore. A University of Cincinnati pennant hung beside a Pride flag that Hollis didn't immediately recognize but whose colors she liked: magenta, yellow, and cyan.

Sitting at the center of it all on her black-and-white-striped comforter was Gloria.

"You can come all the way in," she said, a little amused. "You don't have to stay in the doorway."

"What?" said Hollis. "Oh, sorry." She came in, closing the door behind her. "Do you mind if I sit?"

"Sure, sure," said Gloria. "Anywhere you like."

After a moment of light panic (*The desk chair or the beanbag by the window or the bed corner?*), she settled on the corner of the bed closest to the door. "Your room is really cool," she said.

"Thanks," Gloria replied with a small proud smile. "But I really hope you didn't come just to talk about how cool my room is."

"Well, uh." Hollis sucked in a nervous breath. "No."

"Come on, then. Let's talk. Pillow?" Gloria reached behind her, then offered one forward.

"Yeah, okay," said Hollis, balling it up in her lap. Right away, her hands started worrying the pillow cover, working the corner seam between her fingers. "Here's the thing, Gloria. I need to quit the game."

Gloria laughed, a rich and rolling sound. It lasted for a breath too long, then cut off. She raised an eyebrow at Hollis. "Wait. You're not serious, are you?"

That was the thing—even now, Hollis wasn't sure if she was serious. She had felt like running away all day, like hiding somewhere no one could find her. She fluttered her knees where she sat. "I am. I'm sorry. I just can't keep playing right now."

For a moment, Gloria just stared at her. She wore her Secret Keeper expression: unreadable, assessing the situation. "Would you like to tell me why?"

The short answer was no, Hollis wouldn't. Talking to anyone about what she had done—and about what Aini had said—that night after the Critmas Party would make it all too real. Hollis was trying not to let herself even *think* about it, much less say it out loud. She only knew that in light of it all, it felt right to quit. Or maybe, more accurately, it felt wrong to keep playing—as if removing herself and Honoria from the Eight Realms (and Umber) was one less piece for her to have to make fit together.

But Gloria had spent months telling this story with Hollis, and so she could at least try to tell Gloria this.

"Well," Hollis started, "I was blindsided about Wick, obviously."

Gloria nodded, a little sympathetically. "Yes. I probably should have checked in with you more about it before the session. I'm sorry."

"Yeah, maybe." Hollis picked at the pillow cover. "I just feel so stupid. I didn't mean to ruin the game. I'm sorry about that."

"You're not stupid, Hollis, you just have an anxiety disorder," said Gloria. "And it takes more than a panic attack to ruin one of my games."

This was true. Gloria was a good storyteller. It *would* take much more than Hollis's anxiety to derail her campaign. Hollis only hoped it could withstand a party member leaving.

"Well, thanks. I think. I'm just." Her words came out in an

awkward staccato. She was just *what*? Frustrated, maybe. The feeling rose inside her like the color in her cheeks, the prickles in her eyes. For the first time, Hollis tried to talk about it. "I have some things to think about. Big things. And I'm afraid the big things going on in the Eight Realms are just going to make it harder."

"They might," said Gloria with a shrug. "I can give you that. Or they might make it easier."

Hollis stared at her blankly. "What do you mean?"

"One of the things I really love about this game," Gloria said, "is that it takes all the same problems we face in life—all the things about the world or ourselves that keep us up at night—and puts them in our hands. Here, it's safe to hold them for a while. Work them over, spend some time with them.

"And then there's this whole other layer of character—so it's not *your* hands, even, that are holding these big, scary things. So you get a little distance from them, maybe see them from another perspective. It adds a layer of safety to something that can be dangerous to look at directly for too long. A pinhole projector. Does that make sense?"

Hollis nodded. Being brave and bold always felt easier at the table, when she was playing Honoria—and when Aini was playing Umber. But she also heard Aini's voice in her head.

That wasn't Umber's hand you were holding, Hollis.

Gloria went on. "When we can look at things in a different way, sometimes the things that would usually frighten us seem a little less frightening. The game can give us a safe space, with safe people, to explore parts of ourselves we might not be comfortable with in the real world. Sometimes, it's easier to find your truth when you're just trying it on for size first, without the pressure of having to make a big, sweeping change."

I don't want one of those things to be you, Hollis, Chris's voice echoed in her mind.

I think that could be a really great thing for us, Aini's voice countered.

They were both silent for a minute, and then Gloria gently asked, "Have you talked about this decision with the other girls at all?"

Hollis shook her head. The idea of having to tell Aini—or Iffy, or even Fran or Maggie—that she was leaving the group made her stomach flop again. The feeling robbed her of her words.

"You're going through a lot right now, it sounds like." Gloria gracefully sidestepped the subject that was so obviously Aini-shaped. "So I think they would be understanding. Maybe more than we could guess, even. I can't speak for the other girls, but I can see the difference in Francesca since she started playing with us. She covered it with a lot of noise, but she was really struggling for a long time." Gloria paused for a moment, her eyes a little far away, before continuing: "But now, because she gets to be Mercy Grace once a week—someone who's loud and impulsive and creative and overwhelming and still ultimately loved very much by our group of ragtag adventurers—I can see some of that confidence bleeding into *her*. She's making friends at school again. And sure, it still takes her two hours to do her math homework some nights, but she always finishes before we play on Friday. I think our game isn't just a pinhole projector for you but for the others, too—one that's maybe big and troll-shaped sometimes."

Something stuck heavily in Hollis's throat, and she didn't dare move for fear of shaking it loose. But Gloria was right; Hollis had seen Fran at work in the living room just now. She felt a surge of pride for having had a small part in that.

But change *was* something that could happen to other people. Maggie, who'd seemed so poised and unapproachable in the beginning, had relaxed into her own skin and now had a much easier time being who she really was—and standing up for that person, too, even among the group. And Iffy, with moral support from the others, had sent in her Howard application with two weeks to spare. She wouldn't hear back for a few months, but she'd already asked Hollis and Aini to help her manage the stress of waiting with a weekly trip to Uncommon Grounds for some S&S-free hang time.

Her friends made change look easy, as effortless as putting their faith in the roll of a die. But Hollis still felt like this trust was a luxury she wasn't sure she could afford. She swallowed thickly.

Gloria went on. "Of course, you're free to leave the game whenever you like. But I hope you won't." She held Hollis's gaze, open and honest. "You're important to me, Hollis. And so is Honoria."

Hollis was quiet for some time, and Gloria made space for the silence. It wasn't uncomfortable; Gloria had seen her quiet before. But this time, Hollis was searching for her own words instead of Honoria's.

"I think I'll stay," she said at last, her voice suddenly husky, her eyes prickling. "I wouldn't want to let the group down. It's not what Honoria would do."

"I think it's also not what Hollis would do," said Gloria gently. "Don't give Honoria so much credit for things that are yours to own, hm?"

And for a moment, Hollis let herself feel this. She thought about the first time she spoke up at the table, and in the Discord server, and even in that original email when she was sure she was too late to join. She thought about dancing at Games-A-Lot, and her art as her friends' lock screens, and her painting of the party there on Gloria's desk. For a few deep, shaking breaths, she thought about cutting her bangs, and that tiny triangle of bare skin over her skirt, and being the one to reach her hand down to Aini at the sleepover.

Honoria had been there for all these moments in a way. But it had been *Hollis* who'd actually done all of those things. And that meant something, even if right now she felt completely unsure what Hollis—not Honoria—should do.

Gloria's voice broke through Hollis's thoughts. "Now, do you mind if I give you a hug?" she asked.

Hollis nodded. "Please do, actually." Both girls shimmied forward on the striped comforter until Gloria could wrap her arms around Hollis, the balled-up pillow pressed between their bellies. When they moved apart again a long moment later, Hollis's eyes (and Gloria's shoulder) were wet. "Thanks for talking, Gloria."

"I'm your Secret Keeper, Hollis," she said. "It's what I do."

Hollis tried to tell herself that what happened on Friday wasn't because of her.

What happened was this: Wick, seeing the party and not hearing an immediate agreement from Honoria, fled deeper into the Vacuity.

Why it happened was . . . probably because of Hollis, actually.

She should have felt a little guilty, but she didn't. Gloria had done her a kindness, one that made returning to the table feel less daunting. Not that any of the others *did* make it feel daunting; everyone, even Fran, was incredibly cool about what had happened last Friday. They didn't talk around it like Chris tended to do. They named it. "I'm sorry you got so anxious," said Fran. "Let me know if we need to take a break, okay?" said Gloria. Aini didn't say anything, but she'd brought Hollis an extra brownie. Hollis might have been imagining it, but she was fairly certain hers had more caramel swirls than the rest.

But Wick's retreat wasn't just a kindness to Hollis, either—it also handed a moment of respite to the ailing party. They spent the first half of the game collecting themselves and gathering herbs, which proved bizarrely simple in the Vacuity since it was filled with such a beautiful abundance of plants from across the Eight Realms. With a complicated series of rolls aided by Mercy and Tanwyn, Honoria and Nereida turned the herbs into a healing poultice. And after slathering the gloppy green stuff over the parts of their bodies that pained them most, the party made camp for the night in the mouth of a shallow cave on the banks of a river.

To Hollis, though, what happened in-game was less important than *how* it happened. Though they played at the table tonight, the casual do-over vibes of this session made it feel more like the night of the sleepover. Fran propped first one foot and then the other on the table, painting her toenails a shade of Mercy Grace–worthy green. Gloria protested at first but, tired from a long day with Miss Virginia, eventually gave in and allowed it. With her collection of minis finally painted (professionally, at a game store in Newport), Maggie staged scenes of the party and took a series of pictures illustrating their downtime. Even Aini seemed more relaxed, not as tense or quiet as the last time they sat around the table.

All of this helped Hollis settle, too. She drank deeply from her cup of water, leaning over to rest her head against Iffy's shoulder every now and then. Iffy rested her temple on Hollis's, leaning back, the weight of her pleasant and grounding.

Hollis had missed this more than she'd realized—just the girls being themselves, together. And now that she was here again, with the pressure of the game lightened and the pressure of the real world kept at bay for a night, Hollis couldn't remember why she'd ever thought leaving was the answer. She might not have been able to make the pieces inside her fit just right yet, but she *did* belong here— with Gloria and Fran, with Iffy and Maggie, and with Aini.

"And as we all drift off to sleep," Aini murmured, her fingers fitting to the neck of her ukulele. A twinkling melody floated around them, soft and soothing in the night. "I play us a Song of Slumber so our sleep is restful."

Gloria hummed appreciatively. "And *that*," she said, "is where we're going to end for the night."

"Oh *man*," said Fran. "No fight?"

"Francesca, it is almost eleven o'clock," said Gloria. "I have been subjected to your feet smell all night, and Miss Virginia's hospital smell all day. Your Secret Keeper is tired."

"And your sorceress has a volunteer shift with TransKentucky in the morning," said Iffy. "All the way down in Lexington."

Maggie gave a low whistle. "That's a *drive*."

"Yeah, so I should get out of here." Iffy stretched, then turned to Hollis on her right. "You ready to go, Hollis?"

Hollis, who had been quietly packing up her dice, pursed her lips.

"Actually," she said, "I'd like to talk to Aini about Steadfast a bit." Tentatively, she looked to her right, catching Aini's brown eyes with her own. "Do you think I could get a ride with you?"

"Yeah, sure." Aini said it casually, like it was no big deal. But she smiled like it was.

"Bless you, Aini," said Iffy, who smiled too. "I can get my tired bones to bed. I wish I had some of that poultice in real life."

And, by ones and by twos, the girls slowly filtered out from the table to where they needed to be: Iffy, out to the old Accord and back across the river; Maggie, to the Suburban and a hot date with her tarot cards; Fran, begrudgingly, to the living room, where she flipped on Netflix; and Aini and Hollis, after they helped Gloria clear the table and wash the dishes, out to Aini's sleek sedan.

"So," said Aini, shutting her door sharply and connecting her Spotify to start their playlist. "Lay this Steadfast stuff on me."

What Hollis wanted to say was that there was no Steadfast stuff, which was true. What she really wanted to do was apologize—to tell Aini that she missed her with a terrible fierceness and that now that Hollis had her back in her life, she didn't want to let go ever again.

Hollis opened her mouth to let out the messy storm of confused feelings raging quietly in her brain, but the words got stuck in her throat. She swallowed and tried something else instead.

"I was thinking about what might happen," she said, "after. If they survive all of this."

"You mean *when* they survive all of this," said Aini. "Give this little ragtag group of weirdos some credit. They'll make it."

Hollis wasn't so sure. Tonight had felt pretty final to Honoria: a last moment of remembering the things that mattered. The coming week of waiting to battle Wick would probably feel like an extended death march.

She shrugged. "Okay then, *when*. What do you think will happen? I mean, do you think that, when it's over, they could be happy somehow?"

Aini nodded immediately, as if she didn't even need to think about it. "Definitely. I know things haven't always gone right with them, but there will still be a *them* on the other side of this. For sure."

There was such certainty in her voice. It echoed with Umber's confidence—or maybe Aini's. Hollis couldn't tell anymore. Maybe she had never been able to tell at all. "But what if it all goes wrong? What if they don't work out?"

Aini cocked her head. "Do *you* think that will happen?" She seemed skeptical.

"I can't be sure," said Hollis. "It's a roll of the dice, isn't it?"

Aini shrugged. "Sort of."

"But, you know. I do think seeing the world has changed her. Honoria, I mean. And a large part of that's because of Umber."

"See? I think the same is true of Umber, with Honoria." Aini grinned at her. "They can't just come back from that. They're stuck together now."

"But . . ." Hollis trailed off. It was easier like this, to talk about Honoria. Through the pinhole projector, like Gloria had said. She looked down at her hands cupped in her lap, feeling strangely lonely with Aini so close and so far away at the same time. "Do you think they're doomed to be sad, then?"

"Maybe. But that sounds like too grim an ending for them, to me."

"To me too." Hollis's lips pressed together in a flat line.

"I still have higher hopes for them than that," said Aini. "And Umber is good to wait it out and see."

"Honoria might make him wait a long time." Even Hollis wasn't sure who she was talking about anymore. She spoke to the dash instead of Aini, to its familiar blue glow. "She seems so smart and put-together, but underneath that armor, I think she's just as confused as any of us, you know?"

There was a moment, quiet, in which Hollis wondered when the Steadfast playlist had stopped playing and if Aini was even following her tangled-up words. But then Aini's hand found Hollis's on the console. Their fingers didn't twine together, but her palm rested on top of Hollis's, warm and present.

"I know," she said. "So does Umber. And he'll be her friend anyway. Always."

"Always?"

"Always."

Hollis liked the sound of that.

23

THINGS THAT BREAK

BEING FRIENDS WITH Aini again didn't make things easier. It did make them nicer, though, especially now that Hollis could send her S&S bard memes in the middle of class again (something she'd discovered she really missed being able to do). It was nice to know she could keep doing so, always. That was the word they used: *always*.

Always was a *lot* of memes.

But reconciling with Aini didn't make Hollis's day-to-day life very different—at least at school. Things with the boys were still strange and strained. Part of this was the gulf that had opened up between her and Chris. She saw now that the first fissure had come from the No-Girlfriend Rule, long before Hollis had even realized it. And now it was easier to see the other cracks that webbed out from it: what and who Chris prioritized; the way he spoke and when he chose to; what he did and didn't want to change. Now Hollis could no longer ignore the same splintering within herself: the lengths to which she went to avoid Chris in the halls; the guilt that hung in the corners of her lips when she smiled at him; the way that her ability to disappear with him around now felt less like a comfort and more like something constricting she'd outgrown.

She couldn't avoid Chris on Friday mornings, though, because those were the days her mom left for school early to head up the school's Dead Playwrights Society (her version of a club inspired by some old movie). It was the social centerpiece of the theater kids' week. It was also the day Hollis always had to either ride to school with Chris or take the bus, and the latter was something to be avoided at all costs.

Like every Friday morning, Chris honked once and Hollis got into the car. They rode together in Sentra silence, which meant without talking but *with* Chris's nu metal playing over the speakers.

Everything that had once been comfortable now felt awkward. Like the rattle of the Sentra's muffler, all the puzzle pieces Hollis had been trying to make fit clattered around in her noisy brain. Maybe so much had shifted between them that they could never get the pieces to fit back together without something vital missing.

The song changed, and Hollis came to a realization.

Maybe that something vital was *her*.

As they neared the school, Chris finally spoke. "Lacie and Landon are pooling money for a river cruise after graduation. Do you think we should throw in?"

"Actually." Anxiety rushed through Hollis's body unannounced. It brought with it all the usual suspects: a racing heart, a sheen of sweat on the back of her neck, a desire to retreat into someplace comfortable and hidden away. But this time there was also something different: a kind of energy she hadn't felt in a long time—something a little wild and out of control—and a deep sense of surety that radiated out from somewhere in her chest.

Hollis tried, half-heartedly, to swallow the words down, but they burbled up regardless. She spat them out quickly. "I think we should break up."

Chris laughed. It was such a familiar sound that it made a part of Hollis ache. She didn't laugh back.

"Come on." He darted a quick look at her as he changed lanes and made a right turn. "Don't do me like that." When she didn't reply, his eyes darted over a few more times. "Are you serious?"

She hadn't meant to be serious. She hadn't actually meant to say anything at all. Hollis from the start of the year wouldn't have, and Hollis from a few months ago would have forced a laugh and taken the out. But the version of Hollis that sat in the front seat of the Sentra now was very different from either of those girls.

"I am," said this Hollis. "Serious, that is. I'm sorry."

Chris laughed again, but this time it was more of a scoff.

She thought he might yell, or ask why, or just generally do *something*. But that had never been what Chris did with Hollis. They never had the lowest lows—but they never had the highest highs, either. Chris didn't react, just kept driving, his slouched shoulders drooped the same way they always drooped.

"Is that okay," she asked, "with you?"

She waited four quiet minutes. Darke Complex played on the speakers, the bass line fuzzing them out. Out of habit, Hollis reached down the side of the bucket seat to the spot in the upholstery she'd worried thin, but as soon as her fingers skimmed the threadbare fibers, she realized her hands were solid and steady. She folded them in her lap instead.

"I just don't think it's been working for a while," she floated tentatively into the space between them.

"You mean because of your girlfriends." Chris didn't sound like himself. He sounded very far away and entirely too close at once. He downshifted at a stoplight.

A rush of guilt flooded Hollis's chest. She wanted to tell him no, that it had nothing to do with her girlfriends, but the word sent her chest fluttering awkwardly. Without question, finding her Secrets & Sorcery party had something to do with this. But coming from Chris, who spent so many lunch hours with Landon, the word *girlfriends* was loaded. Hollis was sure that if she denied it, it would make her a liar.

She shook her head and tried a safe shade of the truth: "We've always made better friends than boyfriend and girlfriend."

"God," said Chris. "This is bullshit."

"Chris," she protested. "That's not fair."

"No. What's not *fair*," he said, sounding angrier than he had at any point in the conversation so far, "is you choosing those girls over me."

In the front seat, Hollis shook her head. "I'm not choosing any-one, Chris." But that wasn't fair, either. She had tried—very hard—to choose Chris. Though it felt absurd now, she had met the girls in the first place *because* of him—because she wanted to be enough for him so badly that she'd tried to make herself into someone worthy of his Friday nights. What she'd found along the way was something much better: a game she loved playing, a group of girls who loved her, and a version of herself she liked both at and away from the oak-finish table.

But when Hollis tried to think of a way to explain this all to Chris, the words dissolved in her mouth. She should have had a plan going into this. It was unlike her not to invent whole conversations in her head before they happened. It was so much harder this way.

In some ways, though, it was so much easier.

"Things are changing," she said. Maybe *change* was a word she should have shied away from, but instead, she leaned in. "Everything's changing. *We're* changing. And I think that can be a really good thing. I think we can both find good things for ourselves and still stay the same friends we've been since sixth grade."

"I don't think I can stay your friend after this, Hollis," said Chris. They were both quiet a bit before he added, with some effort, "Not for a while."

Hollis nodded a little sadly. "That's fair. I know it's kind of a shock. It is for me, too."

He snorted a laugh, and they lapsed into quiet again.

"Yeah," Chris finally said. "Sure." A beat passed, and then: "Okay."

Hollis kept her eyes forward. She wished the music were more appropriate for the moment; the heavy guitar didn't match the mood. She wished, too, that Chris would fight for her, or at least protest in some way. Six years was a very long time. But he'd let her know a while ago that he didn't think she was worth fighting for—and now that she had friends who *knew* she was worth it, the difference was stark.

Hollis swallowed. "Okay what?" she asked.

"Okay, we can break up."

Hollis pressed her lips together.

"I *am* sorry," she said.

"It's whatever," Chris said, pulling into his usual parking spot beside Landon's Celica. "See you around, I guess."

"Okay," Hollis said, and—as if this was any other day—she got out of his car and closed the door behind her.

All day, Hollis felt a little bit like she had forgotten to put on a shoe, or like she'd put on two left ones. It was disorienting. She kept finding herself walking to the same places she had for the last four years and then remembering she couldn't anymore, because she was wearing the wrong metaphoric shoes.

She was already sad to lose Chris. She couldn't avoid that part, because they'd been so close for so long. But even that didn't feel entirely right. The Hollis who had been close to Chris didn't exist in the same way anymore. The Hollis who now walked the halls of Holmes High School was a different Hollis.

The lopsided feeling, and the disruption in her routine, was hardest at lunch. Her mom had a substitute for the second half of the day; she had a dentist appointment that had been on the books too long to cancel without fees and fines they couldn't afford. And so, even though Hollis had texted letting her know what had happened (*Oh, honey,* she'd responded immediately, *I am so sorry,* and then she'd sent the joy emoji instead of the crying emoji, which Hollis assumed was a Gen X mistake), she headed to the cafeteria instead of her mom's classroom, lunch box in hand. She was halfway to her old table, with Lacie and Landon and Marius and Chris, before she remembered that it wasn't her table anymore. Not for a while, at least. That was what Chris had said, wasn't it? Not for a while.

Quickly, she changed course, making an awkward beeline to an empty table at the edge of the crowded cafeteria. She'd only just sat down and taken out her ham and swiss when she heard a shout from a few tables over.

"BIIIITCH!" called the voice, letting the vowel stretch long. Hollis looked up; she had known who it was just from the *B*.

"Get your ass over here," said Iffy Elliston, gesturing down at her table.

With a small smile, Hollis did as she was told.

All but two of the chairs at Iffy's table were occupied. Hollis walked toward the side of the table where Iffy sat closely with a group of three others. She recognized one of them as Emily Tran, an Asian girl from her mom's various theater clubs.

"Girl, *please* don't tell me you were really going to sit on your own when I! Was right! *Here!*" said Iffy, still partially shouting. She slid a chair up beside her, then patted it.

"I'm sorry," said Hollis, sitting. "It's been a weird day."

"Why?" Iffy shimmied her chair over to give Hollis more elbow room as she unpacked the rest of her lunch. "Finally cut that old boyfriend loose?"

Hollis's stomach turned. Was she so radically different that Iffy could somehow just tell?

"Uh," she said. "Yeah, actually."

"I like whoever this is already," said the person on Iffy's other side. He was tall and blonde and so beefy he looked like he could hug someone in half if he wasn't careful.

Iffy was slow to reply, taking a moment to exchange a look with Hollis. Assessing. And then she said, "Well, welcome to the best table in the room. This—" She nudged the person beside her with her elbow. "Is—"

"Peter King," said the person who could hug someone in half, smiling broadly. "He/him or she/her pronouns and a big fan of dumping deadweight boyfriends."

"She just dumped her boyfriend, too," supplied Iffy, "so she's all about girl power."

"I'm Rian," said the person on Peter's other side. Rian was fat, too, with blue eyes behind oversize tortoiseshell glasses. "They/them. Do you like Twizzlers?"

"Red or black?" asked Hollis.

"Red," said Rian. "I'm not a grandparent."

"Then yeah, sure," said Hollis, and so they passed her three.

"I'm Emily," said Emily, her black curls bouncing as she leaned in toward Hollis. "She/her pronouns. Has anyone ever told you that you look a lot like Ms. Merritt?"

"Well, she's my mom," said Hollis. "So."

"Oh!" said Peter, lighting up. "You're *Hollis*!"

"Yes," she said, and then added, "I use she/her pronouns too."

"Oh, cool. You're in Iffy's Secrets & Sorcery game, right?" asked Rian. "She showed us some of the art you did while we were helping her out on a GSA project. It's so cool."

"Who do you play again?" asked Emily.

"The paladin," said Hollis, covering her mouth with her hand as she chewed a bite of sandwich.

"With the cool armor," said Emily, snapping her fingers. "Yeah, I remember now."

"Yes, we stan an armored queen at this table," said Peter.

"I keep telling him to join the Dead Playwrights Society," said Emily to Hollis. "He's clearly cut out for it."

Hollis smiled, and the banter carried on around her. It still felt strange, like she had lost her footing, but sitting at Iffy's table also felt like maybe she was finding a new pair of shoes.

For the first time in a very long time, Hollis Beckwith rode the bus home.

It wasn't as horrible as she remembered. In reality, it was mostly just a strange mix of uncomfortably cold and hot at the same time; the bus didn't have heat, but it did have a mass of teenage bodies crammed close together, smelling of cheap body spray and armpit. The stale air clung to Hollis the same way it did the faded plastic seats.

Hollis sat at the front alone: a small blessing. Hers was one of the last stops, and she gave the bus driver a smile as she stepped down onto her sidewalk.

The whole experience hadn't been so bad, really. She'd have happily taken this over Darke Complex, if she had known.

And so it felt out of place when Hollis started crying halfway up the walkway to her front door. For the life of her, she couldn't figure out why. The bus had been fine. The *day* had been fine. Maybe there had just been so much of it that now it overwhelmed her.

She fumbled for her house keys in her tote bag, but they eluded her. Her tears fell harder, faster. They picked up noise on the exhale: a soft sobbing, like even the sound was unsure why this was happening.

Her fingers finally found her keys. She unlocked the door sloppily, and it swung open to reveal a dark hallway. Her mom was still at her appointment, then.

Hollis was more alone than ever.

She crashed onto her bed, and everything crashed down on *her*. Finally, Hollis let herself cry. It wasn't pretty, and she couldn't seem to stop. But the longer her lungs heaved in her chest, the more it came back to her: she had broken up with Chris. She didn't regret doing it, but now that she was alone, she was absorbing the full weight of it. Even though she did still care about him, Chris wasn't who she needed anymore.

Who Hollis Beckwith needed now was herself.

A garbled laugh mixed in with her crying. Who even *was* Hollis Beckwith, anyway? And then, with this thought—in this moment—the truth hit her all at once, like it had been waiting for her to see it this whole time: *Hollis Beckwith was changing.*

This realization didn't feel as empowering as she'd made it sound to Chris earlier. Alone in her room, change felt lonely and uncomfortable, loud like the sound of Hollis's sobs in the silence of the empty house.

With all her defenses down, Hollis's thoughts took her back to the start of the year—to the start of the game—when Landon had called Iffy a weirdo. She hadn't told him off like she should have. She'd tried to tell herself this was because she didn't really know Iffy yet, or because Landon wasn't worth the energy, or because of her anxiety, but that wasn't the truth.

The truth was that Hollis had always suspected there was something weird about her, too, and she had been afraid that if she said too much, Landon would see it in her. Landon would *know*.

But what, really, was so weird about Iffy Elliston? What was weird about being—and loving—who you were loudly? Iffy was one of the most amazing people Hollis had ever met. No one—not anyone worth anything—could ever meet Iffy and not think they were better off for having done so.

And besides, what even was wrong with being weird? There were plenty of things about Hollis that already *were* weird, by the standards of someone like Landon. She was fat and she didn't hate herself for it. She had anxiety and she wasn't embarrassed about it. She was an artist who spent most of her time drawing powerful women in armor, and she didn't apologize for it. These were all things that Hollis *liked* about herself. And if she were to be honest with herself, *they weren't even that weird.* All the girls at her gaming table—the people who had become her best friends—had similar things that made them exactly who they were, and she loved them all just the same.

Maybe, just maybe, they could love *all* of what made Hollis *Hollis.* And maybe, just maybe, she could love it all, too.

Fat tears still fell down her cheeks. She couldn't quite think the words—the real ones that felt like they didn't belong to her yet—but she allowed herself to think about Aini. About *being* with Aini, really and truly and without the pinhole projector between them. She thought about holding her hand with their fingers laced together and about walking through Eden Park together that way and about how the sunshine might feel on her shoulders once they were free from the burden of what other people might think about them (about *her*). And for that moment, she could see it: a future like this, where she was exactly who she really was, nothing more and nothing less. In her imagination, Aini looked up at her over her shoulder, laughing and beaming, proud to stand beside her—and Hollis was proud too.

The tears fell harder. She wasn't crying from sadness, at least not mostly; she was crying now because of the beauty and because of the want. More than anything, Hollis wanted this. But there was still so much distance between the world she imagined and the one she inhabited, tangled in her own bedsheets at 4:47 on a Friday afternoon. She was so close to bridging them, and still so far away.

Down the hall, there was a shuffling and then a creak as the front door opened. A thud sounded, like a purse being dropped on a counter, and a novocaine-thick voice called, "Hols, honey? Are you home? All the lights are off."

Hollis drew a stuttering breath and wiped her cheeks with the back of her hand. She cleared her throat as quietly as she could.

"Yeah, Mom," she called back, pushing herself up and brushing herself off. "Sorry. I was about to start getting ready for S&S. I think we're almost at the endgame."

24

MORE PRECIOUS THAN GOLD

THEY FOUND HIM in a clearing, not even half a day's journey from the cave where they'd made camp for the night. It was the most beautiful meadow Honoria Steadmore had ever seen—but then it would be, wouldn't it? It was pieced together from all the most beautiful parts of the Eight Realms.

"There's no need for that, thief," said Wick, easily spotting Tanwyn sneaking through the tall grass. "I can smell the stink of goat in the air."

"Uh, that's racist," said Mercy Grace, or maybe just Fran.

"I mean, we knew he was a tool, but *damn*," said Maggie under her breath, and then she said in Tanwyn's affected lisp, "'Such fine words that fall from the mouth of the young man.'"

The rest of the party made themselves known then. Mercy stood from her close-by crouch. Umber melted into the clearing from the line of the trees that ringed the open space, with Honoria following close behind. Only Nereida stayed back, mostly hidden in the soft, flowing branches of a patch of cloudberry bushes. In the bright light of midday, the whole scene looked like a painting.

"I have no words for you, goat," said Wick dismissively. "I have no business with any but one of you." A cruel and devastatingly charming smile twisted across his lips. "Tell me, Honoria. Have you considered my offer?"

This was all happening very fast. Even though some strange shift in the fabric of fate had gifted her extra time, Honoria still didn't feel prepared to do this.

She took several bold steps forward anyway, positioning herself closer to Wick than the others. "We both know the answer to that, Wick," she replied, her voice sad but sure. "Where you're planning to go, I cannot—and will not—follow."

"A pity," said Wick, "though I suppose you are right. That is the answer I would expect from honorable Honoria."

He strode forward casually. Behind Honoria, the other party members braced: Mercy's hammer rising with a subtle shift of wind, Umber's fingers finding the hilt of his rapier, Nereida's hands shifting spell components in her hip-side pouch. Honoria didn't hear Tanwyn, but she never did; that was what made her so deadly.

"It appears, then, that we have come to an impasse," said Wick, still looming slowly forward. "I am sorry for what must happen next. I'll kill your friends first, which will allow you time to change your mind. I have always—"

"While he's monologuing," said Hollis, far away at the table in the Castañedas' dining room, "I'm going to cast Flaming Fist, Level 5, directly at him."

"Oh, *shit*," said Iffy beside her.

Gloria nodded, her face the blank slate of the Secret Keeper. "Please roll your attack, Honoria."

A stillness fell over the table as Hollis reached forward, hand hovering over her dice. She plucked a d20 from her small collection: one of her Honoria dice, her Critmas gift from Aini. In her palm, it felt right, as if it had been created for this very moment.

Six girls sucked in a collective breath as Hollis rolled the die.

"18!" She beamed. "23 total, with my mods."

The table erupted in cheers so loud it was as if they'd already claimed victory. Iffy clapped Hollis hard on the back. Hollis could tell by the look on her friend's face that she was thinking what Hollis was thinking: such a high opening roll was a good sign for this battle.

"That will hit," Gloria said, her Secret Keeper face slipping enough to reveal a smile at the corner of her lips.

Hollis rolled her diamond-shaped d8 five times for damage. "32 Fire damage," she said at last. "Uh, and he's pushed back ten feet."

Back in the Vacuity, tucked away in what should have been the frigid wastes of the Highpeak Crests, a flaming fist of arcane energy appeared in the space between Honoria Steadmore and Wick Culpepper. Wick had just enough time to curl his lips into a curious smile before it slammed into his chest, pushing him back through the meadow so hard his leather boots left streaks in the fine silt of the soil.

A moment of extraordinary silence followed, and then the most beautiful meadow in the Eight Realms exploded into action.

To Honoria's right, Mercy bellowed and stormed forward at top speed, her hammer swinging high above her head and arcing downward. Wick shifted out of the way at the last second—or rather, he was there, a hair's breadth away from the business end of Mercy's hammer, and then, in less than a blink of an eye, he was gone, appearing again on the other side of Umber. His hand reached out and caressed Umber's face with something close to tenderness. Where his fingers trailed, angry black streaks of decay blossomed.

"Umber!" cried Honoria.

The noise was lost in the sudden sound of sucking wind from the tree line behind her, where Nereida wove complicated, precise symbols in the air with her hands. Glowing runes solidified before her and circled in a vortex until she pushed her palms forward, and, like a storm, the wind surged toward Wick's back.

"Umber, *down!*" Nereida's voice boomed across the battlefield, but the bard didn't have time to follow through. As the wind tore into the fine silk of Wick's shirt, so, too, did it wash across Umber, chapping the opposite side of his cheek.

"It's all right," he called to Nereida, waltzing around Wick to put space between him and Honoria. As he danced, his fingers strummed the strings of his lute in a progression of pleasing chords, the sound alight with Umber's seldom-used bardic magic. He spoke directly to Wick. "Did you hear the one about the nobody, Wick? They say the only thing smaller than his brain is his—"

The end of the joke was cut off by a stream of raucous laughter. It exploded from Wick with a violence, the effect of Umber's spell doubling him over. He clawed at his sides as if to rip the sound from his lungs. As he did, Tanwyn stepped out from a clump of tall grass and sent a volley of copper daggers at him, streaking through the air bright as fireworks. Honoria ran into the fray too, her sword held high.

For the first half of the fight, it seemed like they had him, and handily. Honoria had never known Wick to be a magic user, and she could tell his newly gifted skills felt clumsy in his hands. He missed more shots than he made, and there were five of them bearing down on him from all angles. Honoria stood by Wick's side, striking at his weak points whenever he exposed them. Of course, he did the same, nearly fileting a piece of her arm off with a sickly bit of Death Magic that cut like daggers. But for each blow he dealt, she was sure they returned more.

She put it down to Umber. He was all over the battlefield, dancing in and out of the strangely colored grass of the meadow like it was his native terrain. Moved by the moment to use his magic at last, his blade flashing as furiously as his spells, he was everywhere at once, making sure everyone was covered.

But as they went on, Wick found his footing—and his confidence in his magic. Streaks of dark light the same sickly red as the lightning in the square of Fallon's Landing flew from his fingertips. For a frightening moment, Honoria was sure they were all a breath away from succumbing to the same fate as so many of the corrupted creatures she'd encountered on the journey here.

"Hold fast!" she called across the battlefield. "He may be strong, but we are many, and we have the power of the Just and Terrible Mistress on our side."

A shimmering light, as bright as Wick's was dark, flashed out of Honoria's cobaltril breastplate from the place just above her heart. It streaked across the meadow, finding the heart-centers of each of her party members, which glowed with the same light before it dissolved into their chests.

"And you all heal 15 hit points," said Hollis, from a round table far away. "*And* you have Advantage on any defense rolls against Necromantic magic for the next five rounds."

"Coming in clutch, paladin," said Aini in Umber's posh accent. Umber still held the space between Honoria and Wick—and in the few seconds it took Mercy to swing her battle hammer, connecting solidly with the man's shoulder, Umber chanced a look back at Honoria. He gave her a wink.

Honoria returned it—or started to. Her eye never quite winked closed. Instead, both her eyes went wide as the world seemed to slow its motion.

On Umber's other side, she could just make out the motion of Wick's hand. It was simple, really; he did nothing more than raise a finger at Umber's back. His mouth moved as he spoke a word Honoria couldn't hear over the din of battle, and then a ball of darklight appeared in front of Umber's chest.

"Umber," said Gloria. "I need you to make a Spell Defense roll."

"Is this Necromantic magic?" Aini asked.

"It is," said Gloria. "So roll with Advantage, because of Honoria's spell."

Good, thought Hollis. Light of Healing Protection, which she had just cast, was her highest-level spell. It was paying off now, even if it meant she only had one more Level 6 spell for the adventuring day.

In the tense silence of the Castañedas' dining room, Aini rolled two d20's. She let out a strange sound, half between a laugh and a sigh.

"That's a 12," she said.

"It's Advantage," said Fran, her voice tight. "You take the *higher* of the two numbers, not the lower."

"That *is* the higher of the two, Franny," Aini replied.

The quiet around the table deepened.

"So," said Gloria, after a breath. "The ball of darklight sinks into Umber's chest. You feel its energy sucking at your very life force, trying to draw it into the center of your body, into your heart, and stop it. You suffer"—on the other side of her screen, Gloria rolled more damage dice than Hollis liked—"28 damage."

"And it's . . . Necromantic damage," Aini repeated, her voice small and far away. Hollis's head snapped up instantly at the sound.

Gloria nodded.

A moment of perfect silence fell over the table. For how long, Hollis couldn't be sure. It was long enough for a strange calm to fall over Aini's face, for her lips to purse, for one corner—the left—to curl up in a tiny, excruciating smile.

"So I'm still smiling," she said, in Umber's effortless accent. "Even as the darklight enters my chest, I'm still smiling. My eyes are still open, and I keep them on you, Honoria." At the table, Aini kept her eyes on Hollis, who felt a hollowness growing behind her rib cage in about the same place the spell had hit Umber. "I catch one last breath, and my lungs fill, and I think of the way the air tastes like the grass in the courtyard of my mother's house, back home in the Duskfain. And I think of how she would have liked you, Honoria—for your bravery, and your goodness, and your honor. And I think of how beautiful your eyes are as they shine now, like the cobaltril on your chest. And I think of how I should have told you that more often. And then I don't think of anything at all." Aini put her pencil down on her character sheet. A tear splashed onto the page beside it. "Umber falls down, dead, in the grass of the meadow, his last smile frozen on his face."

"No," said Fran.

"He's just down," said Maggie frantically. "Honoria is close, he'll be fine."

"NO," said Fran, louder this time.

Iffy shook her head, her breath coming fast and hard, her nostrils flaring.

Aini looked like she wanted to say something, but she was crying now, noiselessly.

"I can't help him," Hollis said hoarsely. Her voice sounded like it was coming from far away—from the Eight Realms, from another life. She swallowed hard, trying to claim the sound as her own. "If you're reduced to 0 hit points by Necromantic magic, you're—"

"He's not dead!" yelled Fran. "He's not!"

"I'm sorry," Iffy started, "but—"

"No! Make him better!" cried Fran, but it rang so strong and clear from the twelve-year-old's throat that it was clearly also Mercy Grace yelling from the other side of the battlefield. "Do it! Do it now!"

They couldn't stop fighting. This was not over yet.

Honoria allowed herself half a moment, the space of three seconds, to look at Umber's face. How beautiful it was, even in death. Hot tears ran down her cheeks, mixing with salty sweat and blood. Then she stepped over his body, careful not to tread on the gold thread embroidery on his doublet, and shouted, "FOR UMBER!"

"For Umber!" cried Tanwyn, and she threw a bottle of Tanglefoot Treacle at Wick's feet in preparation for Mercy's attack. He didn't see it coming; now he stood glued to the ground, immobile.

"For Umber!" screamed Mercy, and she swung her hammer low, sweeping at Wick's knees. He faltered, falling at an unnatural angle.

"For Umber!" bellowed Nereida, and from the clear sky above, she called down a clap of thunder and a bolt of lightning. It solidified and held Wick immobile.

For his part, Wick tried to strike out at Mercy, but his fingers seemed disagreeable, made stiff by Nereida's spell. He wheeled around as best he could, useless hands grabbing at the ground to help him turn and face the approaching Honoria.

"It didn't have to be this way," she said, her voice soft and thick with tears. "I would have taken you home."

"I *am* home," he said, lifting his chin defiantly. "Your dead friend will keep me company. He'll rise soon. You have no magic powerful enough to stop him."

Honoria just looked at him, her gaze steady. "You don't know me anymore, Wick. My friends and I have found something more powerful than you'll ever be able to understand."

"And what is that, Honoria?" he challenged. "What could there be that is more powerful than unending undeath? I can still take you, you know. We can leave them behind. Merely say the word and—"

"And as he's talking," said Hollis, her eyes narrowed to slits just as Honoria's eyes were narrowed to slits. Both sets still brimmed with tears. "I drive my sword into his heart."

It happened quickly and without fanfare. Wick's body relaxed, slumped against the back of her hand where she had driven the sword in to its hilt. In death, he looked more like the Wick she had known in her youth. All the bitterness fell away from his features, all the cruelty leaving his open eyes.

She left him there, skewered to the ground. There were more pressing matters at hand.

All of them moved as one: Tanwyn coming out of the shadows, leaving her copper daggers where they landed; Mercy, leaving her bloodied hammer at Wick's side as she stepped around his body; Nereida, her fingertips still alive with storm energy, making her way to the center of the meadow at last.

Honoria got there first, kneeling beside him. Umber looked so like himself still that she had to hold her hand to his face, the back of her ungloved palm resting below his stilled nostrils, to believe that he wasn't among the living.

"Honoria," said Mercy, quiet rage and silent tears shaking her voice. "Make him better."

All eyes turned to her.

"I don't know that I can." For all the weight on them now, Honoria's shoulders still shook. "I can try to cast Recall the Fallen, but the magic's still new to me. I'm not sure I can make it work."

"We have to try," said Nereida. "He would do it for us."

"He would," agreed Tanwyn. "Even if it might fail."

"It's not going to fail," insisted Mercy. "He's going to be okay."

"All right," said Honoria. "But I'll need your help."

So they got to work, both in the game and at the table. Iffy scanned her notes for any mention of the spell's components, bargaining with Gloria for Advantage on rolls based on the information she'd written down. Maggie used her real-life witchy knowledge to leverage the lunar phase, arguing that as a follower of a water-based deity, Honoria's power should be stronger during the full moon. Fran focused hard, describing in detail how and where Mercy searched for the various herbs and flowers the magic required. All the while, Aini sat quiet and still, silent tears rolling down her cheeks.

As the party members came back together, rejoining Honoria at Umber's side (she couldn't leave him, not here with Wick), they helped her lay out the intricate design in flowers: a pair of waves crashing in on themselves, with Umber at their center. The symbol of the Just and Terrible Mistress.

"The spell also requires a sacrifice," Honoria said as the dusk started to fall, a thousand brilliant stars coming to life overhead. "And it must be more precious than gold. I think we should all offer something. It might make it easier to call him back to us, if all of us are calling out."

Though she'd anticipated some grumbling from the others—particularly Mercy Grace—there was none. In fact, it was Mercy who added her sacrifice to the arrangement first.

"He always said he liked this one," she said, removing a palm-size stone from her bag. It was clearly a diamond—and even uncut, it caught light from the flickering stars, throwing arched rainbows on Umber's still, smiling cheeks. "He can have it now."

Tanwyn stepped up next. Instead of offering an object, she leaned close to the body and whispered something in Umber's unhearing ears.

"The secret of my Shadow Step," she said. "Maybe it will help him step back out of the shadows."

"I promise," said Nereida, reaching out a hand and clasping Umber's stiff shoulder, "that when you come back, I'll learn every one of your ridiculous songs, and I'll sing them far and wide, wherever I may go." Coming from the serious sorceress, who had not once helped them sing for their supper, Honoria knew how much this meant.

And that left only her. What did she have to offer Umber that he didn't already have? A stone, a secret, a song. It was all he needed in life.

But it was *death* from which she was trying to call him back.

Shaking, Honoria reached back, untying the leather thongs. Her fingers ached and her nail beds were still stained with blood—some of it Umber's. With a metallic scraping, she removed her cobaltril breastplate, the great treasure of the Steadmore legacy.

For a moment, she thought to lay it across his chest, for it was certainly more precious than gold in its own right. But instead, she placed it at her side. What was left when she knelt beside him was this: only Honoria, stripped of her defenses and exposed to the world, her heart no longer locked away from him.

Leaning forward, she pressed a gentle kiss to his lips.

And then, whispering a few well-chosen words, her hand floated up and pressed against his heart. A new sob, something deep and raw, bubbled up from her throat when she felt how still it was beneath her fingers.

"Not today," she spoke against the cold skin of his forehead. "It's not time."

And she cast Recall the Fallen on Umber.

Back in the Castañedas' apartment, Gloria fitted Hollis with a peculiar stare. "What I'd like for you to do is to roll a d20 and add your Charisma modifier. Don't say the number out loud, just text it to me, please."

Hollis stuttered a tearful breath but nodded. It all came down to this, then. With her Honoria dice, she made the roll, did the math, and texted the Secret Keeper. She wasn't sure of the outcome even as she reached out a trembling hand toward Aini Amin-Shaw.

In the hallowed meadow of the Vacuity, pure light trickled from Honoria's fingers like water, pouring into the spot on Umber's chest where the darklight had vanished. The moment stretched out infinitely, just as the impossible thought of carrying on without him stretched out in Honoria's mind. Honoria wept openly, her tears wetting Umber's face beneath her.

And then she felt a beat beneath her fingers. It was solitary, but it was strong.

"Oh," Honoria gasped between sobs.

And then there was another, and then another, and then came the warmth. It spread out through Umber's body with each pounding beat of his heart. The light of Honoria's magic flowed through his veins, leaving glittering tracks beneath his skin as it went. It swelled to a brilliant glow—something so bright and fierce that the whole of Umber's form was illuminated—and then it condensed again, vanishing back into his chest.

"Did it work?" demanded Mercy, shifting where she sat.

With a sharp intake of breath, Umber's chest rose, his brilliant eyes blinking awake. He took only half a second to assess the situation, his eyes landing on Honoria, and then the frozen smile on his lips came back to life too. His cheeks shimmered in the falling darkness as he pushed up onto his elbows, coming closer to the paladin than they had ever been before.

"Honoria Steadmore," he said, "would you mind very much if I kissed you right now?"

Honoria was a mess of tears and snot, but she was much, much too happy to care.

"Please," she said. "Please do."

Umber placed a hand on Honoria's wet cheek, and then he kissed her hard—the way he had wanted to since the very start of their long journey.

"And that," said Gloria with a smile, "is where we will stop for the night."

The whole table launched themselves at Aini, burying her in a group hug. They stayed like that, together, until all their tears had dried.

25
THE BRIDGE AGAIN

THE MORNING AFTER Umber Dawnfast almost died, Hollis Beckwith woke up with an image in her mind—one that she knew wouldn't let her be until she got it out onto paper. Still, she tried to avoid it for a little while. She rolled over and flipped her pillow, closing her eyes stubbornly. It was still *very early* for a Saturday.

But the image wouldn't leave her alone. She could see it even on the back of her eyelids.

She got out of bed.

Though she should have gone down for breakfast—or at the very least for a glass of water—it was to her cluttered desk Hollis went instead. She pulled out her notebook.

Using her favorite 2B pencil, she worked quickly, moving as fast as her head could relay the information. Now and then she grabbed a colored pencil from the box in her top drawer, working in cotton-candy-colored grass and otherworldly pastel treetops. It was a pretty background, but Hollis wasn't drawing a background.

The image was of Umber with Honoria at his side.

What stuck with Hollis last night was the moment of Umber's death: how beautiful it was, how serene and tragic. But what had shaken her from slumber in the light of day was the moment just after he'd been brought back to life. It hadn't been something they'd spoken out loud, but she thought Aini would agree with the way Hollis drew it—the look of sudden, profound realization on both Umber and Honoria's faces. She roughed it in: the light in their eyes, the color in their cheeks.

But when she finished, the image wasn't quite right. It didn't match the feeling that had gotten her out of bed. Hollis erased all the work she'd just put in, until both Umber and Honoria were featureless.

Onto Umber's face, she worked a round-tipped nose and deep-set brown eyes beneath spirals of orange curls. Onto Honoria's went a pair of not blue but brown eyes, then full lips and a more pronounced double chin. As the sun rose, Hollis worked, until it wasn't Umber and Honoria suddenly realizing how overwhelmingly thankful they were for each other, but Aini and Hollis.

When she had worked the last light of understanding into her own eyes on the page, Hollis sat back. The feeling she'd been trying to capture was finally there.

She picked up her phone.

beckwhat 10:01 AM
hey.

i would like to go to the park.

would you like to go to the park?

Aini 10:02 AM
There's nothing I'd rather do on a Saturday.

I'll pick you up at noon?

beckwhat 10:02 AM
actually.

now would be good?

Aini 10:02 AM
I'll pick you up now.

The ride from Covington to Eden Park was both surprisingly quiet and surprisingly loud. Quiet in that the two girls didn't talk much. Loud in that they sang instead. Hollis had put the Steadfast playlist on the car's Bluetooth system as soon as she'd been able to connect to it. Since then, she had been belting out all their greatest hits. Aini didn't ask questions, just sang along in her sweet soprano. Hollis's alto was thin by comparison, but that didn't stop her.

The sheer volume of her own voice kept her nerve up. She belted out the lyrics to "Cut Your Bangs" as they made their way through Eden Park, until they got to the bridge where they'd taken pictures as Honoria and Umber on Halloween a few months ago. Those pictures were the first time Hollis had recognized the spark of happiness in her own eyes. That same brightness grew in her now, pushing out against her chest like it needed to be freed.

"Okay." Hollis's voice was remarkably even, if a little hoarse from all that singing. It surprised her. "I'm going to say some things, and I'd like if you could just listen, okay?"

Aini nodded wordlessly and hopped up with a little half jump onto the cold concrete bridge railing.

"So," said Hollis. And it was at that exact moment she realized she had no idea *how* to talk about any of this.

The Hollis she'd been before she started playing Secrets & Sorcery might not even have tried. But by now, she'd borrowed Honoria's voice enough that she had more practice talking about things she didn't fully understand.

Hollis had worn Honoria like armor for so long. It was time for *her* to be the brave one.

"Aini," she warned, "I'm going to have to talk *a lot*."

A smile ghosted at the corner of Aini's lips, like she might laugh. But she only nodded.

Hollis swallowed. Slowly, she said, "I . . . like you."

She had been so *afraid* to say it. But now, with those three words warming the space between them, Hollis had to laugh at herself. Speaking them out loud lifted all the weight off her chest. Suddenly her whole body felt lighter—her hands, her head, her heart.

"I like you," she repeated, the words warming her chest, "and I didn't think about that for a long time, because it's so easy to *not* think about it around you. God, that sounds mean. But it's not! It's just . . . when I'm with you, I don't have to think about doing the right thing, or finding the right words. Everything just feels *correct*. It's easy. We're easy. We just *are*."

Hollis pressed her lips together. This didn't feel quite right. She tried a different angle.

"When I was with Chris," she started, "I had to *think* about the couple-y things. I didn't really like any of that stuff. I mean—when we kissed, it was okay, but just. It was so much work. And then . . ."

Her next words faltered on her tongue. She hesitated to say them aloud—but they'd gone unspoken so long that she also didn't want to keep them quiet anymore.

"And then I kissed *you*, Aini, and it was so easy. It was the best thing I've ever done in my life," Hollis said. Her fingers traced the line of her bottom lip, remembering. "I guess that's why it felt like those moments were Umber moments? Because they felt so good and right and perfect that it was like they belonged in a story and not in the real world. It felt like—*duh*, this is the hand I'm supposed to be holding. These are the lips I'm supposed to be kissing." Even now, Hollis's body ached to be closer to Aini.

"So. Yeah. I like you, too," Hollis said, and then paused awkwardly. "So that's one part. Does that make sense?"

She looked over at Aini for the first time, holding her gaze. Aini was failing to suppress her smile, but she stayed silent, her curls bobbing brightly as she nodded. She was holding space. Letting Hollis talk it out, just like she had countless times on Discord, or on the phone, or in her car.

She really was the best, Aini Amin-Shaw.

"But the other piece kind of sucks, I think," said Hollis. "Because I don't know *how* to like you, Aini. Well, no, that's wrong. I think I actually do a kind of good job of it, unless I'm being a huge jerk, like in your car at Christmas—"

"Yeah," Aini cut in, an eyebrow raised. "You were kind of the worst."

"I know, I know." Hollis's hands floundered in the air. "I'm so sorry for that. I should have said all of this *then*, Aini. I think I knew, really, the important parts. It's just. I just—I don't know if . . ."

The words were sluggish on her tongue.

"I don't know if I'm gay?" She stopped herself, shook her head. She felt light, still. "Is that okay to say? A lesbian? Queer? See, I'm bad at this. I don't have the vocabulary. And I thought for a long time maybe there was something wrong with me, something *weird*, because I really didn't care about any of this stuff when it came to Chris, but suddenly it seems important. Like, I'd like to kiss you again. And hold your hand. And maybe be your girlfriend. But I don't know what that makes me at all, other than Not Straight, and that's . . . really fucking scary."

When she held Aini's hand—when they sat with their hips touching, when she was around Aini at all—Hollis couldn't be who she'd always thought she was: Hollis, probably straight, kind-of-crap girlfriend to a boy. Instead, with Aini, she was something much better. She was Hollis, probably in love, really happy with a girl. It was all the *rest*, all the things she felt she was supposed add on top of that, that seemed so big she couldn't get her head around it.

"Does that make sense?" she asked, her voice small.

This time, instead of nodding, Aini reached out, her lithe fingers searching for Hollis's thicker ones. Hollis reached out to meet her, their palms pressing tightly together as their fingers entwined.

"See, this?" With her free hand, Hollis waved at their joined hands. "I really, really like this part. It's all the rest that I'm scared of. But this part?" She squeezed Aini's hand with hers. "This part is so, *so* easy."

They were quiet for a moment. Aini's eyes were on her; Hollis could feel that as plainly as she could feel Aini's pulse against her palm. She couldn't meet her gaze, instead running her thumb over the side of Aini's hand. There was a scar there, a shade darker than her skin. Hollis wondered how she'd gotten it.

At long last, Hollis looked up.

"Uh, so," she said. "That's it. You can—you should talk now."

"Are you sure?" asked Aini, a small smile curling up the corner of her lip.

"Yes."

"Because you're really cute when you wave your hands around like that."

Hollis snorted a short laugh. "Yes, Aini, I'm sure."

"Okay, good, because I have two things to say," said Aini matter-of-factly. "One, this makes me the happiest girl in the Ohio River Valley—and also probably the world—and two, so what?"

Hollis had grinned at the first part, but her smile fell abruptly at the second. "I'm sorry?"

"I think the first part is pretty clear," Aini teased her lightly, her eyes sparkling. "I'm really glad you like me and want to kiss me and maybe be my girlfriend because I'd like all of those things, too."

Without her permission, the smile crept back into onto Hollis's face. Her heart swelled the same way it had in the car that night after the Critmas party, pounding hard.

"And as for the second part—yeah, so what? About the rest. I don't care."

Hollis blinked at Aini in confusion. "What?"

It didn't make sense. Aini was *so* out and *so* proud. It didn't seem fair for Hollis to like her when *she* wasn't even sure which letter in *LGBTQIA+* she might be.

Aini shrugged like it was easy.

"I don't care if you don't have words for how you identify right now," she said. "Or ever, really. You have time to figure that out—or not! It's the *you liking me* part I care about. The rest is just vocabulary."

That it could be so simple had never struck Hollis as a possibility.

"Really?" she asked, eyes still wide.

Aini squeezed her hand. "Really."

"I mean, but I should probably figure it out, eventually."

"If you want to."

"I think I do?"

"Then you do. And I can help. I know it's really hard to believe, but I wasn't always the badass lesbian superstar you see before you. I was once a confused, closeted lesbian weirdo."

"I mean." Hollis smirked. "You're still a weirdo."

"Oh, *wow*," said Aini, her eyebrows raising in mock offense. "I thought you said you liked me, Buckwheat."

"I do." Hollis's heart beat faster, a stark contrast to the sure, settled feeling spreading throughout her body. "So much. But I like weirdos, so." She shrugged.

Aini laughed, and the sound of it swelled out into the park. "If you like weirdos, then yes, I'm absolutely a weirdo."

Hollis laughed too, and it felt warm and bubbling inside of her. She took a step closer to Aini. It wasn't deliberate; her laughter was motion, and Hollis simply moved forward with it. But it felt good being closer to Aini.

The second step *was* deliberate.

"Aini Amin-Shaw," she said. "Would you mind very much if I kissed you right now?"

Aini smiled—and this close, with her eyes on her lips, Hollis could see there was the smallest gap between her front teeth. This close, the floral smell of her was overwhelming. Hollis desperately wanted to breathe it in. To taste it. To never forget it.

"Well," said Aini. She reached forward, placing her hand on Hollis's hip. Hollis's hand tightened around Aini's. "I *do* mind that you're stealing my lines." She smiled. "But if you kissed me? I wouldn't mind that at all."

"Okay," said Hollis, looking down. Not sure what to do with her hands, she mimicked Aini, reaching out and guiding her palm to the other girl's bony hip. "I'm going to do that now."

Hollis leaned closer, but didn't kiss her yet.

"Okay," breathed Aini.

Then Hollis kissed her, with intention this time. She smiled into it. Aini's lower lip felt fuller beneath hers; she tasted like rose tea and the right choice.

Hollis didn't want to pull away from her—didn't think she *could*. But Aini's hand was still in hers; she wasn't going anywhere. Slowly, Hollis eased away just a little. Her lips felt electric where they had touched Aini's.

"You don't know how long I've wanted to do that again," said Aini, eyes smoldering and so, so close.

"I do, actually," Hollis said, and she laughed.

"Fair." Aini cocked an eyebrow at her. "So. Do you want to keep doing that?"

"Right now?" asked Hollis innocently. "Sure."

Aini laughed. "I meant more in a keep-doing-it-for-a-while-as-girlfriends way," she said. "But yes. I'm fine with right now, too."

It felt impossible—like a story they were telling, like a picture she was drawing. But her hand was still on Aini's hip, which was real and sharp and warm beneath her palm.

"I like the idea of both," Hollis said, and then she kissed Aini again.

26
YOU AND ME AND THE VACUITY

WHEN HOLLIS BECKWITH sat at the oak-finish table in the Castañedas' dining room again the next Friday, she had been Aini Amin-Shaw's girlfriend for almost a whole week, which felt like a very long and a very short time at once. Long because a week was a long time for something so utterly new. Short because it also felt a little like Hollis had *always* been Aini's girlfriend and was only now calling herself such.

She hadn't told many people yet. She *had* told her mom, which went something like this:

"So I'm Aini Amin-Shaw's girlfriend," Hollis had said.

"Wonderful," Donna Merritt had replied. "Can you bring me the chips from the kitchen?"

"That's all?" For better or worse, Hollis had been expecting something more. She brought her mom the chips from the kitchen.

"Hollis," her mom had said. "The reasons I love you have exactly nothing to do with whose girlfriend you are. Now, try these. They're supposed to be Spicy Thai, but I think they're more Chinese Five-Spice."

And that had been that.

She had told Iffy, too, because she and Aini had talked about who she might like to tell at school, if anyone, and Iffy had been the only name on the short list right now. It felt a little treasonous, waiting to do so until Monday when there were so many jittery feelings and screeches and squeals to be had about it, but it also didn't feel like a conversation Iffy would appreciate happening over text. There would be no way for her to throw her arms around Hollis and squeeze her, which was what Hollis anticipated happening.

What actually happened was this:

"So I'm Aini Amin-Shaw's girlfriend," Hollis had whispered to Iffy as they walked into the cafeteria together.

Iffy had made a sound that could only be described as cackling, which made Hollis start in surprise. Then Iffy had stomped her feet several times on the freshly waxed hallway floor and clapped her hands together once.

"*Well,*" Iffy had said. "If it ain't about damned time." And then she threw her arms around Hollis and squeezed her. (Hollis had been right about that much, at least.) Into Hollis's ear, Iffy had said, "And thank you for actually telling me and not making me pretend like I didn't know. Aini told me Saturday night."

That traitor, Hollis had thought mildly, with a smile. Aini must have told Iffy shortly after she'd kissed Hollis goodbye—a thought that had made Hollis think about kissing Aini, which had made color rise in her cheeks. She hadn't been able to send it away, even as Iffy walked with her toward the table they now shared.

But this was the first time she had sat at the gaming table as Aini's girlfriend, and that felt significant. In the chaos of everyone coming in for their last session (probably; they'd pooled a fund to order pizza, which seemed very final), the pair of them somehow slipped in, hand in hand, without being noticed. Hollis chatted quietly with her girlfriend—a strange and exciting word to think in her head—as they both unpacked their character sheets and dice bags.

"We really need to work on your collection," Aini said to her, poking Hollis's two dice sets where they slumped in their velvet bag. (Hollis had finally returned the borrowed Christmas-green set to Chris earlier in the week. It hadn't felt right to keep them anymore, and they had never rolled well for her anyway.)

"Not everyone can be a dice monster like you, Aini," said Hollis as Aini plopped down a bag that contained at least seven full sets and various extra d6's.

But then Iffy spotted them and shouted from the kitchen, "And here's our girls now!"

There was a sharp, high-pitched keening like a squealing balloon. Fran appeared as if from nowhere and flung herself into the small space between Hollis's and Aini's chairs.

"Babies," she shouted—altogether too loud and directly into their faces—as they both scrambled to support her weight.

"Oh my God," said Hollis.

"I *tried* to tell her to be chill about it," laughed Aini, and she had—they had decided it was smartest to let the group know they were together beforehand, to avoid any awkwardness at the table. All the squealing and key-smashing on the Discord server was one thing. Having human–key smash Fran screeching in her ear in real life was another.

"Come on, Fran," said Maggie, trying to disentangle her from the pair of them. "We can't see how cute they are together if they can't, you know, breathe."

"I thought we said we weren't going to make a big deal about this, hm?" Gloria came in from the kitchen with a pizza box in one hand and a cupcake in another. She slid the pizza box toward Hollis and Aini.

"But," started Fran, but Gloria gave her a look that stopped any other words in their tracks. Fran, looking chastised, ate a cupcake and scowled at her big sister.

"That said," said Gloria. She looked back and forth from Hollis to Aini and smiled. *"Finally."*

"Right?" said Iffy.

"Um," said Hollis. Her cheeks were red, but the smile she wore was genuine. "I came here to play Secrets & Sorcery and eat pizza."

"And she's all out of pizza," quipped Aini. She opened the box Gloria had given them. "No, just kidding, here. Double cheese."

"My favorite," said Hollis, reaching for a slice.

Somehow the chaos settled, though excitement still hummed through them all. This was the last battle—or at least they were all pretty sure it was the last battle. Everyone was a little on edge with anticipation.

Still, as they got to the story (there was some kerfuffle about whether to press on or take a rest; after some argument, mostly from Mercy, they did the latter), there was a sense of lightness at the table. Happy to have Umber back—bruised and beaten but *here*, theirs—the party lit a campfire. Normally, Tanwyn would have discouraged this. But Wick was dead (which Honoria still felt conflicted about, her eyes avoiding the crumpled corpse on the other side of the meadow), and they would draw the attention of the Vacuity tomorrow anyway.

What, then, was the harm in a little levity for the evening?

Nereida used a clever spell to transmute some of the meadow's grasses and berries into sweet, sparkling wine and bread swirled with Technicolor. They ate until their bellies were full and drank until their heads were light. And for once, the rest of the party took turns singing songs so Umber could dance. He leaped and spun in the light of the flames, alive with motion as if—well, as if he'd lost his life and then had it given back.

When they went to sleep that night, Honoria did so with her hand in Umber's, and Hollis narrated her doing so with her hand in Aini's.

Even when dawn broke the next morning—more beautiful than dawn had ever broken anywhere else in the Eight Realms—the mood didn't break. The party laughed and chatted as they prepared for battle, until:

"Wait," said Honoria. "We should . . ."

She trailed off, waiting for Umber to help tighten the last strap of her cobaltril breastplate, and then she walked over to Wick's body.

Hollis had worried about what to do in this moment all week. Of the dozen or so scenarios she'd run in her head, none felt exactly right. And now, sitting at the table, she still couldn't figure out the right way to finish things with Wick. But maybe that was okay. The story hadn't been about him, not really. It had been about the party, and each of the friends' places in it. Their journey together had started when Honoria made a promise to the High Alderwoman; maybe it was fitting that she could make good on that promise now.

"We should—" Hollis breathed a sigh, slipping back into character. "We should take something back for his mother."

"You're right," said Umber, beside her. The rest of the party gathered around them, everyone looking down at the body of the boy they'd come all this way to save.

"Is there some, you know, crest or something he wears?" asked Mercy. "Some kind of distinctive brooch? Here, I'll look."

At the oak-finish table, Fran swore and said, "That's a Natural 1."

In the Vacuity, Mercy stooped, patted Wick's body once on the chest, and said, "Nope, there's nothing."

But because Honoria had known him, she knew this wasn't true. With much more skill, she reached into the coin purse Wick carried at his side and removed a small wooden carving of a finely dressed woman on a horse. She tucked the figure into her pocket, then brought her hand to Wick's face, her fingers gently closing his eyes.

Then she and her party left him there, in the most beautiful meadow she had ever seen, and went on to destroy the Vacuity.

But even as they drew closer to the cause of all the *wrongness*, as the beautiful world warped and dissolved into twisting dust around them, none of them could strike the feeling that this was not the worst thing they had or would face. It was as if the true conclusion of their journey—the hard part, the part for which they'd struggled so long together—had passed without any of them fully realizing it. Now, with it behind them, all that was left was the fun of saving the world together.

So that was what they did, and it went something like this:

The Vacuity was at once a man *and* a place, and so, when they found him, it was hard to discern where exactly to attack. His twisted path had rendered the man the Vacuity had once been into less of a person and more of an idea: something warped, personified, and given shape. He shifted darkly, trying to consume the whole world.

They pursued him, but the chase didn't take a straight path. The Vacuity was a fickle, self-loathing and self-loving thing, and he'd put many fail-safes in place to safeguard his life. Just when they thought they had him, he would retreat farther into the exquisite wood he'd built for himself, using it to heal just enough to keep running. The party gave chase each time, moving through the beautiful, splintering world together.

On his third retreat, the thing that was the Vacuity fell away, and underneath was just a man—twisted and tired and cruel, but still only a man. And it was in this form that they vanquished him.

It was fitting, thought Honoria, that it should be not a sword but a song that finished him. Fingers striking his lute, Umber sang, "I've read that *Vacuity* means *nothingness*, and, honey, I believe it, because you're a hot mess." The music turned to magic—to shining blue light and sound—as the words wove through the air. And then there was only silence.

Abruptly, the Vacuity imploded on himself, his entire mass collapsing into a tight, black ball of light. Before any of them had time to register what was happening, the light exploded outward with the sound of a thousand rushing wings.

Honoria's first impulse was to close her eyes against the overwhelming brightness of it. But no—someone needed to bear witness to this. To the way the expanse of forest stretched out before them all, filled with every impossible and beautiful thing. To the colors, pushed by the light to the very limits of the spectrum, how they blurred and danced together until tree wove into river wove into waving seas of grass. To the sheer volume of the profound silence—or perhaps to the all-encompassing quiet of unfathomable noise; she could not be sure which.

With one hand, Honoria reached up and found the place where her heart pounded and thrummed and *lived* defiantly in her chest. With the other, she reached out for Umber. If this was the end, at least it was a good one. They had done it.

The light and sound stretched out forever.

"And then," said Gloria Castañeda, who sat a world away at an oak-finish table in an apartment in Cincinnati, Ohio, "the noise falls off, and the light falls off. The first thing any of you register is . . . cold. *Freezing* cold, actually. When you open your eyes, you wonder if you've been struck blind. All you can see is white. But as your eyes start to adjust, you pick out the gray of rock; the muted brown of scrubby, leafless brush. The wind howls in your ears.

"As you look around, you realize you're in the same place you were all along—only the beauty that the Vacuity gathered to it has disappeared. You're standing on the highest point of the Highpeak Crest, and night is falling.

"And *that*," Gloria finished, "is where I'm going to end it for tonight."

"NO MA'AM YOU ARE NOT," said Fran (though perhaps *said* was too mild a word for how aggressively she was speaking).

"Seriously!" said Iffy, in agreement with the younger girl for once.

Maggie's eyebrows knitted together in confusion and concern. "But . . . what happened to all the landmarks the Vacuity gathered?"

"And," Aini added, clutching Hollis's hand tightly, "how the hell are we going to get out of here?"

"Yeah," said Hollis, her heart still pounding. Like the others, she turned to Gloria. "Where do we go from here?"

"That's the question, isn't it?" On the other side of the Secret Keeper's screen, Gloria took her time packing up notes and dice, grinning all the while. "I wanted to put it to a vote. I don't think this party's story is done, even though *this* story is. So. Do you all want to continue with this game?"

"YES!" Fran burst out, then added, hopefully, "Tonight?"

"Francesca, *no*," Gloria sighed, exasperated but fond. "Next Friday."

"Yes," said Hollis over the end of Gloria's reply, unable to hold back.

"You know I'm in," said Aini with a grin.

"Wouldn't miss it," said Maggie.

"If y'all think you can get rid of me now," said Iffy, "you're sorely mistaken."

"Oh! I still need my *loot*!" shouted Fran. Aini threw half a pizza crust at her head.

"Oh, Franny," teased Aini. "Don't you know the *real* treasure is the friends we made along the way?"

Fran munched her pizza crust and made a crumb-spraying deflating sound, but Hollis giggled. Aini was right about that.

Gloria beamed at them all. "Perfect," she said. "Then I'll start answering your questions next Friday."

"*Or* you could start now," said Aini with a casual shrug.

"No." Hollis knew she had a space at this table for as long as she wanted it. And she had a space outside the game, too, with the girls who'd become her friends both in *and* out of character. "I want to speculate wildly about what's next before she lays it on us."

"I have a few theories already," said Iffy.

And although the story had ended, the party had not, so Hollis had plenty of time to hear them.

Even though the girls had agreed to keep meeting up, they'd still been hesitant to leave each other, and so it was an hour later when Aini Amin-Shaw finally pulled up in front of Hollis Beckwith's house to drop her off.

"Do you really think it all just went back to where it came from?" Aini asked her. "All the beautiful things, I mean."

"I do," Hollis said. "And when we play next Friday, you'll see why."

"I can't wait. Well, Buckwheat, I'm afraid this is your stop."

Hollis unbuckled her seat belt, smirking. "You really know how to talk to a lady, don't you."

Aini turned to face her fully, eyes sparkling with mischief. "Would you rather I try some pickup lines?"

"No."

"Because I *am* a bard. I can—"

"*Aini Amin-Shaw.*"

Aini waggled her eyebrows suggestively. "Are you a parking ticket?"

"You're going to get one, parked like this—"

"Because you've got—"

"—*don't*—"

"—*fine* written all over you."

Hollis groaned. "I'm leaving." She opened the door.

"Don't go, I've got mo—"

Hollis leaned forward and pressed a kiss to Aini's lips, which did a much better job of stopping her pickup lines than Hollis's protests had. When she pulled back, she asked, "Donuts at Eden Park tomorrow?"

Aini grinned, the blue light of the dashboard illuminating the soft lines of her cheekbones. "The world couldn't keep me away from it. Or, you know, you."

Hollis grinned back. "Or, you know, you, either. Bye, Aini." But she didn't stand up yet.

A beat passed, and the girls watched each other over the space of the central console, wearing mirrored smiles. There was nothing else for it; Hollis leaned back in.

Florals and heady leather washed over her, trying their best to pull her back to Aini's lips. And if the night had been a different one, she might have let them do just that. But this night was extraordinary, and Aini Amin-Shaw was extraordinary. What was more, Hollis Beckwith was starting to suspect *she* might be extraordinary, too. She inhaled, holding the scent of the night in her lungs, then exhaled it through a grin.

"Actually," she said. "I want to get a jump start on my notes for next session, and if Honoria is going to keep writing her story with Umber, then I want to keep writing mine with you."

In the blue light of the dashboard, Aini didn't look like Umber anymore. She just looked like herself: Aini, who was half a breath away from either laughing at Hollis or kissing her.

"Well, Buckwheat," she said instead. "Who's the bard now?"

Hollis snorted, very un-bard-like. "Do you want to come hang out in my bedroom and talk S&S or not, Aini?"

In the front seat, Aini pushed the engine-off button. She was out of her seat before Hollis, and their doors slammed shut at the same time.

"So," she said, coming around the front of the car. "Where do we start?"

Hollis grinned as she took Aini's hand in her own, their fingers tangling together in the night.

ACKNOWLEDGMENTS

For me, writing this book was a solitary act—long hours alone at my desk with only coffee and good tunes to keep me company. But bringing this book into the world was a community effort, and it's now my great joy to say thank you to the absolutely amazing people who have come along on this adventure with me.

A warning: this is going to be sappy as heck. This is who I am. I am not at all sorry.

To my amazing rockstar of an agent, Becca Langton—I am so glad we found each other on the internet. Fifteen-year-old Christen thinks it's cool that you're based out of London. Thirtysomething Christen thinks it's cool that you have understood exactly where I want to go from day one and have gotten me there with style and grace. Let's keep going. Thank you, too, to everyone at Darley Anderson for supporting me like a big lit nerd family from across the ocean.

Feather Flores, my editor and a most beautiful soul, I will always be grateful for your gentle, passionate belief in me and my girls. I knew we were meant to be from the moment you made that playlist. To my team at Atheneum, especially Kaitlyn San Miguel, Jeannie Ng, Tatyana Rosalia, Kristie Choi, Clare McGlade, the entire sales and marketing team (particularly Tara Shanahan, Antonella Colon, Brendon MacDonald, Emily Ritter, Amy Lavigne, Emily Hutton, Victor

Iannone, and Michele O'Brien), and everyone who has helped shape *The No-Girlfriend Rule*, I cannot imagine a better home for this book or this author. Thank you for all your work.

I am thankful, too, to the other editors, translators, and fantastic publishing professionals who have worked to bring Hollis from Covington, Kentucky, to different territories and languages around the world.

Seeing a fat girl lovingly depicted on a cover has meant more to me than I could have ever guessed, and I owe a deep-seated thank you to Simini Blocker for rendering Hollis and Gloria (and everyone, but especially them) with such care, truth, and beauty. Also to my art director, Rebecca Syracuse, for a second chance, and for making my book absolutely stunning.

Thank you to everyone who has recommended, promoted, hand-sold, or told a friend (my favorite compliment) about this book. As the child of two teachers and a huge library nerd, I would also like to thank teachers and librarians, specifically; now more than ever, the work you do is important and often thankless, so here are some extras for you: thank you, thank you, thank you.

Jenny Lane, I am glad you slid into my Twitter DMs that one time, and that you introduced me to Mary Morris, and that we all together took the brave step from the internet to a group text. Our friendship challenges me to grow not only as a writer but as a person. I am so grateful to have had you both for every step of this journey and am thankful to be there for yours.

Jonny Garza Villa, my mentor, a true bard, and a brilliant friend, thank you for picking me. So much of the heart of this book manifested under your guidance. Thank you to Sami Ellis, Anita Kelly, and everyone at the Write Team Mentorship Program for existing as a space to foster community, honest conversation, and the next cohort of authors.

Double thanks to Jonny, and to Melissa See, Cara Liebowitz,

Michelle Mohrweis, and Jared Deptawa for the longest and most KidLit D&D sessions I have ever been part of. Petty may not *actually* be twenty-two, but y'all are actually amazing.

I've been incredibly lucky to be in the company of some amazing authors. Jenna Miller, one of the first Real Live Authors to reach out to me, thank you for making me feel like I could do this thing. Clare Edge, you are literally magical. I'll be crying to you about this in a voice note later. Linda Codega, my world-(in)famous friend, we'll write dancing one day soon, I swear. Thank you for telling me I could get out. To everyone at Cactusland, especially M. J. Rose, Michelle Kulwicki, and Emma Lindhagan, thank you for all the sprints and the screaming. To the family I found when I didn't make it into AMM that one time—Justine Pucella Winans and Taylor Tracy, Sydney Langford and Ann Zhao and Safa Ahmed (look at us!), all the Scribblers—if failure brought me y'all, let me fail again. To Beth Phelan and #DVPit, thank you for connecting me with Becca and changing my life with one lucky like. To Jenny L. Howe and everyone in Writing While Fat, we are doing good work and I am so proud to know you. To all the wonderful authors who gave blurbs or promo, I'm honored by your time spent and kind words. To every writer or agent or publishing professional who has read pages or tweaked queries or just said hi over the years, you have helped keep me going and I appreciate you.

Thank you to all my early readers, but especially Kaitlyn Altobelli and Amelia Thompson—you were the first readers to make me feel like an Author, capital A. I can't wait to see where you both grow in this world.

And now thank-yous for the folks who have held me up or together over the years—Vincent Young, for being patient and kind and who I need when I need someone steadfast; Caitlin Beach and Julie Sutton, Angela Kaesheimer and Lauren Brandstetter, Logan Rains and Sam Bloom and everyone at Kenton County Public Library, for helping me find myself and still liking me when I realized that person was kind of a weirdo; Alyssa Gully and Dana Crouch, for the craft hangs and for being my real life all-girl tabletop crew; Ronnie, Amy (especially Amy), Nova, Shan, Jamie, Courtney, Jenny, Juan, Rachel, and Yas, for teaching me how to write; my mom and dad and Abby and Clay, for always believing in my stories; every cat I have ever met, just because.

And finally—most importantly—thank you to *you*, who are reading this now. You are the reason I write. Existing in this world can be frightening, but you are doing it. Find your people. Be brave. Create your own story, one roll of the dice at a time. You are so, so worth it.

Until our next adventure,

C